"I think they want to ——————————
Eriksen, in a low voice. "They're playing Chicken."

Spock raised an eyebrow. "I fail to see the connection between this encounter and a species of Earth poultry."

"It's a *dare*," Kirk explained. "That, or a suicide run."

"So"—Sulu shot the captain a look—"do we blink, sir?"

Kirk shook his head. "Let's play this out. But fortify our forward shields, just in case."

"Intercept point in ten seconds," said Eriksen. "Nine. Eight. Seven."

Spock turned back to his viewer and trained the full capacity of the starship's sensors on the alien vessel as it came at them, and no one spoke as the navigator counted down the last few instants.

Kirk's hands tensed on the arms of his command chair, and the momentary doubt that he might have miscalculated flashed through his mind; then in the next second, the unknown suddenly veered off and shot away in a wide, looping turn.

"That was close," said Sulu. "Our shields were a few microns away from clashing."

Eriksen peered at his screen. "The target is coming about. They're moving to a parallel course."

STAR TREK®

THE ORIGINAL SERIES

THE LATTER FIRE

James Swallow

WITHDRAWN

Based upon *Star Trek*
created by Gene Roddenberry

POCKET BOOKS

New York   London   Toronto   Sydney   New Delhi

Pocket Books
An Imprint of Simon & Schuster, Inc.
1230 Avenue of the Americas
New York, NY 10020

This book is a work of fiction. Any references to historical events, real people, or real places are used fictitiously. Other names, characters, places, and events are products of the author's imagination, and any resemblance to actual events or places or persons, living or dead, is entirely coincidental.

First Pocket Books paperback edition March 2016

POCKET and colophon are registered trademarks of Simon & Schuster, Inc.

For information about special discounts for bulk purchases, please contact Simon & Schuster Special Sales at 1-866-506-1949 or business@simonandschuster.com.

The Simon & Schuster Speakers Bureau can bring authors to your live event. For more information or to book an event, contact the Simon & Schuster Speakers Bureau at 1-866-248-3049 or visit our website at www.simonspeakers.com.

Manufactured in the United States of America

10 9 8 7 6 5 4 3 2 1

ISBN 978-1-4767-8315-4
ISBN 978-1-4767-8319-2 (ebook)

This book is dedicated to the memory of Leonard Nimoy,
who passed away during its writing.

THE LATTER FIRE

One

He stood with the last few items of packing in his hands—a couple of off-duty shirts he had picked up at a market on Axanar, a paper book that had been a gift from his grandparents—and hesitated, his gaze ranging around the small cabin.

Aside from the kit bag lying on the bed, the compartment was bare of any touches that might have indicated the personality of the officer who had lived there for the past three years.

Pavel Chekov sighed; he was about to depart the *U.S.S. Enterprise* and leave no footprint behind. Given all that had happened to him during his tour, all the amazing things he had seen and done, it seemed anticlimactic to think that this was how a chapter of his life was going to end.

Chekov glanced around, peering into the corners of the room. He pretended he was looking for anything he might have forgotten, but he knew there was nothing. The truth was, he was more reluctant to leave than he wanted to admit. And despite the goodwill, well-wishing, and speeches that were offered last night in the officer's lounge, he couldn't escape the fear that he was making the wrong choice.

In many ways, his time on the *Enterprise* had been the making of him, leading him to where he was now. Chekov fingered the unfamiliar red uniform tunic he wore, indicative of his recent change of assignment from navigation to security.

A high-toned chime sounded at his door, and the young officer's face tensed in a frown. "Come in," he called, returning to the work of packing the bag as the door hissed open. "I will be ready in a moment—"

"Take your time, Ensign." His commanding officer entered, a wry smile playing on his lips.

Chekov immediately straightened to parade-ground attention, a reflexive reaction to the presence of Captain James T. Kirk that he had never quite been able to shake off. "Sir! Is there a problem?" Kirk didn't typically make it down to "junior officers country," the decks where section heads below the rank of lieutenant commander were billeted, and Chekov couldn't hide his surprise.

Kirk's smile widened. "I was heading down to the transporter room, Pavel. I thought I'd walk you out."

That wasn't strictly true, and both men knew it. The captain had come out of his way to stop by Chekov's quarters, and the gesture meant a lot to the ensign. He nodded and closed up the kit bag. "Thank you, sir."

Kirk wandered to the circular porthole in the

outer wall of the cabin. "Good view. I'm the captain, and even I don't get a view." Outside, hanging against a blanket of deep black and far distant stars, another Starfleet ship the mirror image of the *Enterprise* kept pace with them.

Chekov rocked on his heels and didn't say what he was thinking, that senior officers had staterooms in the more heavily protected parts of the ship, while the lower—some might uncharitably have said more expendable—ranks had cabins on the outer hull. Instead he indicated the other vessel. "I thought you would be on the bridge for the rendezvous with the *Arcadia*, sir."

"Captain Matsumoto is not the talkative type," said Kirk, with a shake of the head. "As you'll find out. An automated hail was all we got." He looked away from the port. "So, you'll be going straight back to Earth for your security training?"

Chekov nodded again. "Aye, Captain. An intensive course at Starfleet's Reed Annex in London. I am looking forward to the challenge."

"You'll make us proud," Kirk replied.

"I will do my best." He picked up his bag. "I should go."

Kirk took a breath. "I remember when I came to the end of my assignment on the *Republic*. Felt like . . . leaving home all over again." Then the captain stepped toward the door, and the two of them walked out. "But it's just a cabin. Just a ship. There will be others."

Chekov sighed. "I don't know, sir. The *Enterprise* . . . she is quite special."

"You won't get any disagreement from me," said Kirk, leading him to the turbolift. "But someday you'll have a command of your own. And then everything will seem different."

The ensign blinked. "You think I could be a . . . captain?"

Kirk shot him a mock-serious look. "Of *this* ship? That'll be the day." The turbolift hummed to a halt before them. "But in the meantime, there's always a place for you on my bridge, Pavel."

"I . . ." He was briefly at a loss for words as the lift doors opened. "Thank you!"

"This car arrived of its own accord," said Commander Spock, watching them from inside the lift. "No expression of gratitude is required."

"And of course I'm sure you'll greatly miss my first officer's wit," Kirk deadpanned.

Chekov gave a rueful smile. "I think I'll be back, Captain. You can count on that."

———

Kirk watched the ensign fade away into a haze of golden particles. He was going to miss the eager young Russian. Glancing across to the officer standing behind the controls, he waved at the transporter pad. "Were we ever that young, Scotty?"

The engineer gave the captain a sideways look.

"Age is just a number, sir," he offered, resetting the controls to synchronize with the *Arcadia*'s systems. "And youth is just a point of view."

"Spoken like a man with the wisdom of his years," Kirk replied with a grin.

"I find the human obsession with aging to be quite perplexing," noted Spock, standing close by with his hands folded behind his back. "The passage of time cannot be halted or reversed. What merit is there in opposing it?"

"Easy to say when your species has a life span that can reach over two hundred years." Kirk made a show of looking his first officer up and down. "You're in your forties, by Earth standards, is that right?"

"Correct, Captain."

"So by a Vulcan scale, that would make you . . . a teenager?"

Spock raised an eyebrow. "I have always been mature for my age."

"And then some." Kirk drew himself up. "Are we ready for our new arrivals?"

"Energizing." Scott deftly worked the control sliders on the console, and three columns of light appeared where Chekov had been standing.

The materialization effect phased out to reveal a trio of nonhumans on the pads. The first two were dressed in civilian attire. On the right was an austere and watchful Andorian male with a shorn scalp and pale azure skin, while to the left a willowy Rhaandarite woman in a flowing dress of earthy colors surveyed the transporter room with a cool, haughty air.

"Welcome aboard the *Enterprise*," began Kirk, showing the particular winning smile he maintained for every Federation ambassador, diplomat, or other non-Fleet representative. "Envoy Xuur, I presume?"

The woman nodded, and the light caught a jeweled band she wore across her wide, high-domed forehead. "Well met, Captain Kirk. I am Veygaan Xuur of the Federation Diplomatic Corps, and this is my aide ch'Sellor." She indicated the Andorian, who said nothing, his antenna drooping in silent greeting. "And you must be Commander Spock." Xuur stepped off the transporter pad, glancing between the other officers. "And Chief Engineer Scott?" Her voice had a musical quality that Kirk found quite charming.

"Greetings, Envoy," said Spock. "Forgive me, but I do not believe we have met."

"We have not," she said airily, the metallic flicker of her eyes darting back and forth. "But I make a point of researching the background of all the Starfleet crews I am tasked to work with."

"I wasn't aware the FDC kept records on us," Kirk noted. Starfleet's own briefing packet on Xuur had been thin at best, noting her successes as a first contact specialist but little else.

Xuur gave him an indulgent smile. "We do. In fact, Ambassador Robert Fox's reports on the *Enterprise* and her crew make some quite interesting reading."

"No doubt," Kirk allowed, schooling his expression to hide his dismay. A few years earlier, it had been Fox's obstinate manner that had led to the *Enterprise* being caught in a conflict between the planets Eminiar and Vendikar, and there was no love lost between Kirk and the ambassador.

The captain's attention moved briefly to the one person still standing on the transporter pad, a tall, gangly being in the mustard-yellow tunic and dark trousers of a Starfleet operations uniform. Thin-necked, with a lumpen head and deep-set eyes, Lieutenant Arex Na Eth's Triexian physiology meant that where most humanoid species possessed a bilateral symmetry of limbs, he had an additional third arm in the center of his chest and a third leg at the base of his spine. Kirk had met natives of Triex before, but never served alongside them, and he knew the reputation their species had as superlatively dexterous individuals. Many Triexians were notable surgeons or engineers, and there was even a particular concert pianist with a quadrant-wide following. Arex, however, was one of the finest navigation officers in the fleet and a former instructor at the Academy. When his application for shipboard duty had passed across the captain's desk in the wake of Chekov's planned departure, Kirk seized on it.

He gave the navigator a nod of greeting. "Mister Arex." Kirk felt the momentary impulse to offer a handshake, then halted, uncertain of what the protocol was for a being with three limbs.

Arex didn't seem to notice. "Reporting for duty, sir. I am honored to have the opportunity to join your crew." He spoke with a high, slightly nasal register.

Ch'Sellor discreetly handed a data padd to Xuur, who in turn offered it to Spock. "If I may direct us to the matter at hand, gentlemen," she said. "The documents contained on that device encompass the full scope of our mission."

"The opening of formal diplomatic ties between the United Federation of Planets and the people of the Syhaari Gathering," said Spock. "We have been fully briefed."

"By *Starfleet*," ch'Sellor spoke for the first time. His voice was dry and measured. "The Diplomatic Corps must address different requirements. We are about to embark upon a highly sensitive contact protocol, Commander Spock. The utmost care must be taken."

"I did not suggest otherwise," said the Vulcan.

"What my colleague means," Xuur added, "is that we wish to proceed with alacrity. Captain Kirk, if you could please call an immediate meeting with your senior staff, we can begin without delay."

"You wouldn't prefer to be shown to your quarters first?" said Kirk.

"I wish to start as I mean to go on," insisted the envoy. "I see little point in wasting time."

Kirk shot his first officer a loaded look, which Spock returned with typically impassive Vulcan calm.

"As you wish. The commander will escort you to the briefing room."

"We know the way." Xuur inclined her head and gave a graceful smile, pausing at the threshold of the corridor. "Captain . . . I am aware that your previous dealings with the FDC have not always run . . ." She paused, choosing her words with care. "*Smoothly*."

"That's for sure," muttered Scott, loud enough for Kirk to hear.

"I promise you that this mission will be different," continued the Rhaandarite, her gaze steady. "We are committed to bringing the offer of alliance to the Syhaari, with an efficient and untroubled diplomatic effort." Then her tone hardened. "All of which will come to pass as long as the crew of the *Enterprise* do their duties."

Whatever reply was forming on Kirk's lips was never spoken, as Xuur turned her back on him and set off down the corridor.

"I had heard that the Rhaandarite species were a simplistic race," noted Lieutenant Arex. "But on secondary consideration, the envoy seems like quite a willful person."

Kirk frowned and glanced at Spock. "Is it too late for me to go back to Earth with Chekov?"

———

Leonard McCoy didn't say much through the introduction of the envoy and her assistant, and the captain's précis of their new assignment. He and Lieutenant Nyota Uhura, who sat across the briefing room table from him, had been summoned from the middle of other duties without so much as a by-your-leave, and the doctor hadn't bothered to hide his irritation about it.

It wasn't that he didn't understand this mission was an important one, but he disliked the implicit suggestion that the work of a ship's chief medical officer was something that could just be stopped and started like the playback on a tri-screen. While the delegation to the Syhaari homeworld of Syhaar Prime was not laden with the same unknowns a true first contact would bring up, there were still a lot of things that could cause problems from a medical standpoint. McCoy had been working extra shifts with Nurse Chapel to run through all available data on the Syhaari and their native environment; the last thing anyone wanted was for someone in the *Enterprise*'s crew to have an unplanned-for reaction to unfamiliar bacteria or, worse, for a Federation representative to bring potentially hazardous offworld microbes into an alien ecosystem.

He scowled and took in the room. Uhura was attentive and focused, Spock had the same damned neutral aspect he always showed, and the envoy and her aide were listening intently to the captain's explanation of their planned course out across the unexplored fringes of the Beta Quadrant.

When the Andorian spoke up, it was from out of nowhere. "The Syhaari specifically asked for you and the *Enterprise* to convey us to them, Captain Kirk. Why is that?"

Jim gave a small shrug. "Simply put . . . they know us."

"They?" echoed the envoy. She smiled, and McCoy's dislike of the woman crystallized.

The expression wasn't genuine. It was like a learned thing that Xuur had been trained to emulate by rote. McCoy had little time for civil servants, it had to be said. In his experience, they tended to fill the air with words and get precious little done in the meantime.

Xuur went on before Kirk could reply. "Forgive me, Captain. I've read your mission report from the initial contact between the Federation and the Syhaari, but I would greatly prefer to hear the details directly from you. Would you indulge me?"

"Of course," said Kirk, shifting gears. "Uhura, can you bring up the file from that stardate?"

"Aye, sir." The communications officer's slender fingers tapped out a string of commands on her slate and the tri-screen in the middle of the table blinked to life. On the screen there was a sensor image of a Syhaari vessel, a sleek thing like an elongated dart with aerodynamic winglets that ended in stubby propulsor pods. It resembled the ancient, fanciful ideas of rocket ships that had once been part of the fiction of Earth's pre–Eugenics Wars age.

"Translated from the Syhaari tongue, they named this ship *The Explorer Beyond*," noted Spock. "A basic, if accurate, sobriquet."

"How many had perished before you found them?" The Andorian's question was flat and without emotion.

Kirk briefly caught McCoy's eye. "Six, out of a crew of fifty-four. Most of them killed by the radiation surge that had knocked the ship out of warp drive."

"The others died of complications due to delta radiation poisoning," McCoy snapped, remembering the familiar horror of the injuries written across the bodies of the aliens. "There was nothing we could do for them."

"But nevertheless, you intervened immediately?" Xuur aimed the question at Kirk. "Even though they were a completely undiscovered intelligent species?"

"Of course." Kirk didn't hesitate in his reply. "We had never made contact with these beings before, that's true. But they were in space, aboard a vessel equipped with their own version of a warp drive. A civilization capable of faster-than-light travel doesn't fall under the noninterference auspices of the Prime Directive."

"That is debatable," insisted ch'Sellor.

"But perhaps not relevant at this moment," Xuur intercepted easily. "Please continue, Captain."

Kirk leaned forward in his chair. "It was nearly two years ago. We came across the *Explorer* after Lieutenant Uhura had detected a series of low-band subspace radio emissions."

"They don't have long-range subspace comms as we do," added Uhura. "They were broadcasting a distress call. One that would never have reached their own people in time to save them."

Kirk nodded. "The ship was primitive by our standards, capable of reaching speeds just above warp factor one, but they couldn't sustain it. There was a serious malfunction in their power core and that led to the radiation surge. When we found them, they were adrift in deep space . . ." He paused. "They were, at best, a week away from total life-support failure. So we helped."

"They were lucky," said Xuur.

"Not all of them," McCoy muttered. "We quickly discovered that Syhaari physiology was compatible with a number of humanoid medicines. We adapted what anti-rad drugs we had and distributed them to Kaleo and her crew."

"Kaleo . . ." The Andorian used a panel in front of him to change the image on the view to one of the alien captain. "She was the Syhaari female in command of the mission."

Like the rest of her species, Kaleo was a muscular, rangy humanoid with long arms and a body covered with a downy coat of fur. Her kind were simian in aspect, with limbs that ended in dual-thumbed hands and feet, and round, animated faces not unlike some of the great apes of Earth. McCoy had immediately liked Kaleo on their first meeting, when she had demonstrated great concern over the lives of her crew before herself or her mission.

"She showed courage in the face of events that were clearly outside of her experience," continued Kirk. "For a *first* first contact, I'd say she did very well. Working together, our crews were able to bring the *Explorer*'s systems back on line and solve their surge problem."

Xuur studied the image on the screen. "The Syhaari went on their way, and several months later Starfleet received a subspace message from Captain Kaleo's people, extending an offer to the Federation to formally visit their planet and open diplomatic ties." She looked up. "Despite the unpleasant circumstances of the initial meeting, this represents the very thing the United Federation of Planets was created for. The prospect of alliance with a new life and new civilizations. We are about to take part in a momentous event."

"I am certain I speak for the entire crew," said Spock, "when I say that the gravity of the situation is not lost on us."

"Indeed, Mister Spock?" Xuur glanced at the Vulcan. McCoy didn't like how she seemed to make every statement some kind of challenge. "We are all citizens of the Federation, and for us a meeting with an alien sentient—even of a form we might have never before encountered—is not unusual. One might even say it is commonplace. But for the Syhaari, the meeting that lies ahead of us will radically alter the structure of their society *forever*. This will be something for the history books."

That point, McCoy had to give her. From what they had learned of Kaleo's people, while they were innovative and curious about the galaxy at large, the Syhaari had been largely isolated for much of their existence and knew little of what was going on beyond their local stellar neighborhood. *There's a lot we've got to tell them,* he thought. *And not all of it good.*

As if he intuited the doctor's thoughts, the Andorian spoke again. "Klingon probes have been detected at the far edges of this sector. There is no doubt that should the Empire become aware of the existence of the Syhaari Gathering, they too will send a vessel to investigate."

"And so once more, I underline the need for promptness in this endeavor," said the envoy. "These beings are taking their first steps onto the galactic stage. Each of our races has experienced that and emerged the better for it. We owe the Syhaari the opportunity to do the same."

"Starfleet agrees," said Kirk. "I'm glad we're all on the same page."

McCoy shifted in his chair, sensing that the meeting was coming to an end; but he was wrong.

Ch'Sellor fixed the captain with a steady glare. "I do not believe we are, Captain Kirk. You spoke before of Starfleet's General Order One, the Prime Directive. The legal framework that prevents the Federation from interfering with the development of a less mature culture. And yet this ship's records show that the application of that mandate has often been severely tested during your command."

The doctor watched the expression harden on the face of his captain and friend. "It's not easy to deal in absolutes when you're on the edge of the unknown."

Xuur blinked once, and she began to recite data like a library terminal. "Stardate 3156.2, the incident with the self-aware artificial intelligence known as Landru on planet Beta III. Stardate 3497.2, the Capellan mission. Stardate 3715.3, the encounter with the so-called Feeders of Vaal on Gamma Trianguli VI. Stardate—"

"That's a very accurate recollection," Kirk broke in. "And I stand by every choice I made in those situations, and all the rest."

"There are many within the FDC who felt that Captain Matsumoto and the *Arcadia* would have been the better choice for this delegation," said ch'Sellor.

It was Uhura who said what McCoy was thinking. "Kaleo asked for Captain Kirk and the *Enterprise* because her people respect us. Because they trust the choices he made."

Xuur gave an indulgent smile. "It appears your crew hold you in the same esteem as the Syhaari, Captain."

Kirk met her gaze. "I've always believed that whatever opinion anyone has of me, or my ship . . . is one that has been *earned*, Envoy."

"Just so," she allowed. "Nevertheless, my colleague raises a valid point. While the Gathering may not be a pre-warp culture, their level of technological and societal development is without doubt less advanced than ours."

McCoy couldn't stay silent any longer and gave a grunt of disapproval. "With all due respect, madam, that's a matter of perspective. You don't just measure a culture's worth on the scale of how many gadgets they can make!"

"True enough, Doctor McCoy," said Xuur. "But you *can* measure how well they might fare against a galactic power with less-than-altruistic intentions. And that imbalance could lead to some ill-considered choices." She looked back at Kirk. "Captain, a moment ago you spoke about the difficulty in dealing with absolutes in relation to General Order One. I am making the same assertion. The application of the Prime Directive does not simply switch off once a civilization has discovered warp drive. I'm sure, given your experience, that you understand things are more complex than that."

"I do."

Xuur smiled again and stood up, signaling that she was done. "Then we are, as you said, all on the same page."

———

There had only been a brief moment in the *Arcadia*'s transporter room when Arex and Chekov had crossed paths, but nevertheless it had delighted the Triexian to see his former student again and speak with him. Inwardly, Arex was a little saddened by the fact that Pavel—whom he considered to be an above-average navigator for a human—had chosen to switch disciplines to a different operations specialty, but he respected his young friend's choice and wished him the best. Waiting in his data queue was a brief welcome letter from the Russian that he would enjoy at his leisure, but no sooner had the lieutenant deposited his meager luggage in his new quarters than he was drawn away by the need to see the bridge of the *Enterprise*. He had never served on a ship of heavy cruiser tonnage before, having previously been assigned to scouts and destroyers, and Arex was eager to get started.

After a moment of indecision, he elected to ride the turbolift to the bridge and report for duty, even though technically he had already done that.

The doors hissed open and he stepped out, taking it all in. Even while the ship was in a relatively neutral mode, the bridge was active. Sentients were at each station, busy with their tasks, and ahead on the main viewer, the elongated streaks of distorted starlight surrounded the *Enterprise* as she powered through space on course for the Syhaari system.

Arex almost lost himself in the display before someone coughed gently, and his attention was drawn back to the dark-haired human male sitting in the command chair. "Can I help you, Lieutenant?"

"Navigator Arex reporting," he replied. "Would I be correct in assuming you are Lieutenant Hikaru Sulu?"

Sulu grinned. "Arex! I'm glad to meet you. Pavel speaks very highly of you. When do you start?"

"Tomorrow," Arex admitted.

"Captain Kirk is still below, meeting with the envoy," Sulu went on. "Is there something I can help you with?"

At the navigation console, another human officer looked up and gave him an easy smile. "I'm betting the new guy is here to check out his office, am I right?" The lieutenant patted the astrogator panel in front of him.

"Mister Arex, this is Lieutenant Eriksen," said Sulu, by way of introduction. "And currently keeping my seat warm over there is Lieutenant Leslie."

"Lieutenant," offered Leslie, keeping his attention on his readouts.

Sulu pointed out the rest of the bridge crew—a human female named Haines at the science console, a Caitian called M'Ress at communications, and Zyla, a Cygnian in engineering crimson.

Arex bobbed his head in greetings to them. "Mister Eriksen is correct. I am eager to begin my assignment."

"I could generously allow him to work the rest of my shift," said Eriksen with a smile. "Consider it a welcome-aboard gift."

Arex was actually enthused by that idea, but the look on Sulu's face shut him down. "Commander Spock wouldn't approve, Ron. You know that."

Eriksen and Leslie shared a chuckle. "Can't say I didn't try. Okay, how about this? Arex came all the way up here, least I can do is let him try out the chair." The human slipped out of his seat, and Arex had to stop himself from leaping into it.

"Go ahead," said Sulu. "We'll call it a *familiarization exercise*."

Arex's three hands dropped into place on the panel, and he instantly felt a thrill. He had once heard a harpist from his homeworld talk about the anticipation she felt in the moment before beginning to play, and now Arex felt something similar. But his instrument was a powerful starship, his strings the course plots and navigation controls.

"Baseline settings are probably a little different from what you're used to," said Eriksen good-naturedly. "But the layout is the same."

Arex nodded. "I've operated a simulator . . . it does not compare to the real thing, however."

"No argument there," said Leslie. "Once you get a hand—in your case, a *few* hands—on a *Constitution*-class starship, everything else feels like a tug."

"How fast have you taken her?" Arex asked, wondering at the power humming silently beneath his fingertips.

Sulu and Eriksen exchanged looks. "That's a story in itself. I'll tell it to you when we're off-duty."

Arex nodded absently, as his attention was absorbed by the course monitor. "These figures . . ." He hesitated. It would be rude to amend another officer's settings, but the instructor in him couldn't stay silent. "I wonder if I might offer a suggestion?"

Leslie chuckled. "He's barely on board, and already he's questioning your navs, Ron."

"I don't meant to be impolite . . ."

Eriksen eyed him. "But?"

Arex took that as tacit approval and tapped in a quick correction on the deviation plotter. "This adjustment would shave a few minutes off our ETA. You see? The binary star system you bypassed here doesn't require so large a margin of avoidance."

Eriksen peered at the panel. "Yeah, new guy is right," he said, after a moment. "Guess I factored in the higher ratio."

"I would not have marked you down for it, Lieutenant."

Sulu laughed. "Once an instructor, always an instructor."

"Hey," Eriksen countered, "navigation is as much art as it is science, right? Cut me some slack, Sulu." He looked away. "So, Arex, what do you know about this sector, apart from gravity gradients?"

"I took the opportunity to study this zone on the way to the rendezvous," he explained, hoping once more to show his worth to his new crewmates. "The Syhaari Gathering is on the spinward edge of an area of largely unexplored space, sector designation 544-K. The zone is rife with nebulae remnants, gas clouds, and proto-stellar nurseries. Highly active, in a spatial sense, but considered unlikely to contain developed life-forms."

"Which is why the Syhaari were such a surprise," offered M'Ress, purring the words. "No one thought there would be sentients out here."

"Life always finds a way," said Sulu.

"The Syhaar home system is englobed within a particularly dense Oort cloud," Arex went on. "That may also have much to do with why they were able to evolve into a warp-age culture without attracting the attention of any of our survey probes."

"Ever taken a ship through something like that?" said Leslie.

Arex shook his head. "That would be challenging."

At his side, Eriksen grinned again. "This is the *Starship Enterprise*, Lieutenant. Challenging is what we do."

Then, without warning, the prism-shaped alert

light in the center of the console began to blink red. The relaxed, friendly manner of the *Enterprise*'s bridge crew immediately melted away and each of them turned wary. Arex sensed Eriksen's hand on his shoulder, and he swiftly scrambled out of the navigator's station and let the other lieutenant return to his post. Stepping back, his hands came together and clasped one another. Arex felt suddenly out of place, in the way, as the easy atmosphere of the bridge was replaced with a ready tension.

"Report," Sulu ordered.

"Unknown sensor contact, intermittent but gaining definition," replied Leslie. "Port quadrant, twenty degrees below the line."

"Confirmed," called Ensign Haines. "I'm reading it too. It's a ship. Unidentified configuration."

"It's approaching us on an intercept course," added Eriksen. "Velocity is warp factor three point one, holding constant."

There was a moment of silence as Sulu assimilated what the other officers were telling him. "M'Ress, any communications from it?"

The Caitian shook her head. "Negative, Lieutenant."

"There shouldn't be anything out here but us," Leslie insisted. "Syhaari ships don't have the range to make this distance from their homeworld. And every other system for light-years around is uninhabited." He took a breath. "If it's a hostile vessel—"

"We don't know that yet." Sulu stamped down on the lieutenant's speculation before it could take hold. "Let's not borrow any trouble before we actually have it. Mister Eriksen, how long until we're in visual range of the unknown?"

"At current rate of closure, two minutes."

Arex drifted to the rail that ringed the lower level of the bridge, close to the science station. He saw the same data that Haines was now reading, the sensor feeds trying to form a cogent view of the alien vessel.

"Power output for the target is high," said the ensign. "Lieutenant Sulu, I'm having difficulty getting through the energy bleed. Their deflectors are up, but I can't tell if they're running with weapons hot."

"If they mean to attack . . ." The words slipped out of Arex's mouth before he realized it.

Sulu gave a grave nod. "We can't take the risk. Leslie, raise shields and go to yellow alert. M'Ress, inform Captain Kirk we may have a situation here."

Eriksen glanced back at the Triexian and smiled without humor. "Told ya."

Two

Kirk listened carefully to Lieutenant Sulu's report without speaking, assimilating the data and running though possible scenarios as the helmsman brought him up to speed.

"Curious," noted Spock as Ensign Haines handed off the science station to the first officer. "The initial scans of the unknown craft indicate a vessel exhibiting a much higher power curve than its mass and speed would suggest."

"It's running hot," said Arex.

The captain noted the new navigator's presence on the bridge, but didn't comment on it. Instead he took his place in the command chair as Sulu relieved Leslie at the helm. "It's not Starfleet. It doesn't match any known civilian designs. What about . . ." Kirk stopped himself before he said the word *Klingons*. "What about aggressor ships?"

"Analysis inconclusive, Captain."

"Theorize, Spock."

The Vulcan paused, marshalling his thoughts. "It is possible that this craft belongs to a race we are familiar with, but if so it would be a radical departure from known design philosophies."

"I have a visual," said Eriksen.

Kirk leaned forward. "Let's see it, mister."

The main viewer displayed a heat-distorted blob that lacked definition, suggesting something that was curved like a manta ray, with an X-shaped silhouette the imager couldn't quite keep hold of.

"Possibly a quadrilateral warp envelope," Spock noted. "That might explain the power profile."

"Unknown is entering weapons range," reported Sulu.

"Still no contact, Captain," added M'Ress. "Shall I attempt to hail them?"

"Do it," Kirk ordered, but his gut told him they would get no reply. A moment later the Caitian confirmed it.

"They're slick . . ." At the engineering panel, Ensign Zyla let out a low whistle of approval. "For a warp three ship, I mean . . ."

"Feed your data down to Mister Scott," said Kirk. "I want his input on this. Sulu, alter our heading, put some room between us and our new friend."

"Aye, Captain." Sulu worked his panel, and Kirk heard the corresponding shift in the pitch of the *Enterprise*'s engines as the vessel veered away. Within a few seconds, the alien craft had altered course and returned to its intercept heading. "They don't seem to be interested in that, sir."

M'Ress cleared her throat. "Sir, I have Envoy Xuur on the intraship. She is asking for an explanation about the change in alert status."

"She'll have to wait," said Kirk, his eyes locked on the indistinct alien vessel.

"I think they want to see who is going to blink first," said Eriksen, in a low voice. "They're playing *Chicken*."

Spock raised an eyebrow. "I fail to see the connection between this encounter and a species of Earth poultry."

"It's a *dare*," Kirk explained. "That, or a suicide run."

"So"—Sulu shot the captain a look—"do we blink, sir?"

Kirk shook his head. "Let's play this out. But fortify our forward shields, just in case."

"Intercept point in ten seconds," said Eriksen. "Nine. Eight. Seven."

Spock turned back to his viewer and trained the full capacity of the starship's sensors on the alien vessel as it came at them, and no one spoke as the navigator counted down the last few instants.

Kirk's hands tensed on the arms of his command chair, and the momentary doubt that he might have miscalculated flashed through his mind; then in the next second, the unknown suddenly veered off and shot away in a wide, looping turn.

"That was close," said Sulu. "Our shields were a few microns away from clashing."

Eriksen peered at his screen. "The target is coming about. They're moving to a parallel course."

Kirk's lips thinned. "Enough games. What are we dealing with here, Spock?"

"New sensor data coming in, sir," said the Vulcan. "That . . . uncomfortably close pass enabled me to capture a great deal of information. Some elements of the unknown ship's inner structure have striking similarities to that of a vessel we have encountered before. *The Explorer Beyond*."

"Kaleo's ship?" Kirk looked back to the main screen. "How is that possible? The Syhaari craft we saw was barely able to maintain warp speed velocity . . ."

"Looks like they've had some upgrades," said Eriksen.

"In two years?" Sulu shook his head. "It took humans decades to develop a warp three engine."

Eriksen shrugged. "I guess they're quick studies."

A chime sounded from M'Ress's panel. "Incoming signal, Captain. They're hailing us . . . finally."

Kirk drew himself up, straightening his mustard-yellow tunic. "Open a channel, Lieutenant."

Somehow he knew who it was going to be the moment before the image changed from the starscape outside to the interior of the alien ship. A familiar simian face, round and smooth, with dark, laughing eyes that flashed with spirit. Kaleo of the Syhaari looked back at him, and she made a gruff chugging noise that Kirk recalled as her people's equivalent of laughter. *"Our friends aboard* Enterprise," she began. *"Greetings."*

He allowed himself to relax—but only a little. "Captain Kaleo. It's good to see you again. But tell me, was there something wrong with your communications system?"

Kaleo laughed again. *"Forgiveness is hoped for, Captain Kirk. I could not resist the opportunity to display my new command to you. Do you approve?"*

"It's an impressive craft," Kirk allowed. "And a surprising one."

"I say those words to myself each day. I christened it The Friendship Discovered, *in echo of our first meeting. It is an auspicious name."*

"It seems your people have been busy," said Spock.

"Commander Spock of Vulcan, it is agreeable to speak with you once more." Kaleo's buoyant manner seemed to falter for a moment before she answered the question. *"Yes, you are correct. We have made some rapid advances in our knowledge of space travel. I admit, I look forward to showing them to you. With the permission of the Gathering's Learned Assembly, we decided to come out to meet* Enterprise *and guide you to Syhaar Prime personally."*

Kirk accepted this with a nod. "We welcome the company, Kaleo. Thank you. I'd only ask that next time, you let us know your intentions first."

Kaleo's eyes glittered with amusement. *"Ah, Kirk. What joy would there be in that?"* If she was human, he imagined she would have winked at him.

The screen switched back to the exterior view as

the signal cut, and Kirk glanced at his first officer. "What do you make of that?"

Spock considered the question. "From what we know of the Syhaari culture, the act of physical display is an important one in the assertion of social status. It likely stems from a more primitive impulse connected to expressions of territoriality, dominance, submission, or mating ritual . . ."

"She wanted to impress us."

The first officer nodded. "Consider that in our first encounter, the Syhaari were very much in the inferior position. They no doubt wished to redress that balance to some degree."

"They may be worried we don't see them as equals, sir," offered M'Ress.

Kirk smiled slightly, thinking back to what Envoy Xuur had said in the briefing room. "You could be right, Lieutenant. The Federation stands on the principle of treating everyone as a peer, but sometimes we forget that others don't think that way."

"Nevertheless," Spock went on, "this particular display was inherently risky. A different captain might have reacted poorly, perhaps even perceived the *Friendship*'s approach as an attack."

"Good thing we didn't blink, then," Kirk replied.

Arex blew out a breath. "I do hope this sort of thing does not occur on a regular basis."

"No, Mister Arex," Kirk told him. "Usually, our days are much more exciting than this."

Before the Triexian could offer a reply, another chime sounded from M'Ress's panel. "Data signal from Kaleo's ship, sir. Detailed course projections and heading data for the approach to the Syhaar home system."

Kirk nodded. "Pass that across to helm and navigation. Anything else?"

"Yes, Captain. There's a formal invitation here for you and a party of associates to come aboard *The Friendship Discovered* for a tour."

"It seems that Captain Kaleo's desire to impress us with her new vessel has not been sated," said Spock.

"And neither has my curiosity," Kirk countered. "Are you aware of any spacefaring culture that made the leap from breaking the light barrier to a fully functional warp three drive system in so short a time?"

"I admit I am not. Vulcans spent many years developing faster-than-light travel to such a degree. But admittedly, we are of a far more cautious character than the Syhaari appear to be."

Kirk looked up. "Ensign Zyla, inform Mister Scott I want him to run an analysis of the *Friendship*'s warp-drive profile. Discreetly, of course. If they've made such advances in so short a time, I'm sure Starfleet will want to know how they did it."

"You think they've found a shortcut, sir?" said the Cygnian.

"You never know, Ensign," said Kirk as he stood up. "Despite what our chief engineer might profess about being the expert on warp engines, these people may have something new to teach us."

He caught Spock's eye as he walked toward the turbolift. Something in his first officer's manner told the captain that the Vulcan was considering a different possibility.

———

The familiar sensation of the transporter effect faded with a last, lingering tingle over his flesh, and Spock took his first breath of air aboard the alien ship. In an instant of sense-memory recall and analysis, the Vulcan picked out a riot of odors that were undetectable by his companions. Neither Captain Kirk, Doctor McCoy, nor the envoy from Rhaandar had the olfactory capacity that Spock possessed, and so they could not detect the myriad traces of the Syhaari embedded in the arched, curving walls and the grassy carpet of the floor.

Spock remembered boarding *The Explorer Beyond* for the first time, his boots crunching on the blackened and dead plants throughout the stricken ship. Here, things were much different. The oxygen-producing grasses were a genetically modified strain of a plant native to Syhaar Prime, ingeniously bred to not only remove carbon dioxide from the ship's environment but also to provide an ever-present reminder of the crew's place of origin. Like much of the Syhaari's approach to technology, it was a merging of many disciplines.

"Remarkable," said Xuur, a smile splitting her pale face. "Integrated biotechnology." She glanced around the atrium-like space they had materialized inside. "Where are we?"

"The mid-decks," offered the captain. "Kaleo's people lay their vessels out differently from most starfaring species. Instead of layered horizontal decks parallel to the axis of movement, theirs are stacked in a column from stern to bow."

"Like the floors of a tower? Oh, I see."

"I surmise it is a holdover from when their early spacecraft used the force of thrust as a means of simulating gravity on board," Spock added.

"And yet they now possess many of the technologies that we take for granted," Xuur went on. "Thank you for allowing me to see this firsthand, Captain Kirk."

Spock wondered about Xuur's statement. Kirk had *allowed* precisely nothing. In point of fact, the envoy had appeared almost the moment they had stepped off the bridge and insisted on accompanying them, politely but firmly demanding to know the full details of the "game" that Kaleo had played with the *Enterprise* and the conversation that followed. She had initially objected to McCoy's presence, in what Spock considered to be a rather disingenuous manner, citing the lack of a need for a doctor aboard the Syhaari ship and the veiled insult such a presence might suggest. While Spock had his own reservations about what McCoy could add to the landing party, he deferred to the captain's wishes, and Xuur soon found herself pressed to do the same.

"Here they are," said the doctor with a nod.

Kaleo and two other Syhaari ambled across the grass toward them. The alien captain was just as Spock remembered her, tall and gangly on first sight, but with a whipcord strength that seemed common to all her species. Her long arms trailed below her knees, and much of her furred body was concealed beneath a formfitting shipsuit with cutoff sleeves and shorts. The outfit was festooned with pockets and clasps to which were attached various items of equipment. Rank and status were designated by a lengthy plait of hair interwoven with metal wire, carved bone icons, and small pieces of jewelry. Spock's studies were incomplete in this area, but he had learned enough to know that the items entwined in any given Syhaari's plait designated such things as place of birth, parentage, clan affiliation, primary skill set, and more.

Kaleo gave a low grunt that was immediately rendered into Federation Standard by a universal translator module she wore on her belt. It had been a parting gift after first contact with her people. "Happiness fills me to see you again, James Kirk, Leonard McCoy, Spock."

"And under much better circumstances," agreed the captain, accepting a brief embrace from the *Friendship*'s commander. He gestured to the envoy.

"Allow me to present Veygaan Xuur, an emissary of the United Federation of Planets."

Xuur described an elegant curtsey. "Greetings to you, Captain Kaleo."

"Welcome aboard my ship," she replied. "Kirk, you recall my first mate, Zond?" The Syhaari captain waved toward the largest of the group, a big male whose flesh was coal black, but with fur age-streaked by gray. Zond gave a noncommittal snort in reply.

"These are the humans and the Vulcan, but what species is that one?" said the smaller of Kaleo's companions, a female whose fur had a burnt-orange hue. She pointed at the envoy.

"Manners," Kaleo admonished, then chuckled. "Hoyga here is one of our engineering specialists. She lacks delicacy."

"No offense is taken," Xuur said smoothly. "I am from a planet called Rhaandar, one of many member worlds of the Federation."

"What is that device you wear?" Hoyga pointed at the silver band ringing Xuur's head.

"It is merely a decorative object," said the envoy, flashing a brief, practiced smile. "A token worn by Rhaandarites of my gender while in the company of other beings."

"Oh." Hoyga did not seem satisfied with the reply, and Spock thought she was about to say more, but then Zond parted his large hands.

"Shall we proceed?" he asked.

"Of course!" Kaleo bounced gently on the balls of her broad, bare feet. Like all Syhaari, she went without any form of boots or shoes. Spock had surmised that the touch of flesh against the grassy deck was somehow comforting to them, but also part of the manner in which they maintained an intuitive connection to their vessels. He made a mental note to ask Lieutenant Commander Scott if he had an opinion on such behavior.

In the middle of the atrium, a wide, glassy tube grew out of the deck and rose away into the ceiling. Nestled inside it was a floating oval capsule—the Syhaari equivalent of a turbolift, Spock guessed. Zond pointed a wand-like device at the capsule's door, and it opened with an answering tone, low and organic like the sound of wood knocking on wood. Hoyga entered without ceremony, and the rest of the group followed the sullen alien engineer.

Once inside, Zond manipulated the control wand again, and the elevator car began to descend. "These travel channels run the length of the *Friendship*," said the first mate.

Kirk was nodding as the lift moved through a darkened between-deck section and then out into light again. The next area was similar to the atrium, an open-plan compartment with low walls dividing it into what might have been living quarters or recreation areas. "You must have a far larger crew here than you did aboard the *Explorer*."

"Many more," agreed Kaleo. "This is one of our largest classes of starcraft, home to some two hundred of my people." She pointed with a long arm. "Look there. Our mess hall."

Envoy Xuur craned her neck to look, studying the large, communal dining space. "Your crew mix freely? Or are there particular social strata aboard the ship?"

Kaleo shook her head. "Feeding is an important practice for all Syhaari, emissary. We regard the daily taking of food and drink as a special event, to be enjoyed and participated in by the group. In the past, before we developed the technology to leave our world, feast gatherings between tribal clusters were vital to our society. It was there that trade took place, ideas were exchanged, and so on. We maintain the traditions, even out here in the void."

"We saw your . . . botanical space up above," said McCoy. "Is that where you get your food?"

Zond made an airy gesture with his hands. "The fresh is always the best," he admitted, "but since the famines, all Syhaari have learned to live with fabricated meals. Our food synthesis machines are among the most advanced technologies our people have created." He paused. "The threat of starvation was a powerful motivator."

"Can you speak more of these famines?" asked Xuur. "And also, these tribal clusters you mentioned? It was my understanding that Syhaar Prime is governed by a single body. Is that incorrect?"

"Now we are so," Kaleo explained. "Before we sought unity to improve our lot, the clusters would compete against one another, sometimes forming temporary alliances. But the famines changed that . . ." She took a solemn breath. "There was a terrible blight that swept our world decades ago. Old divisions were put aside in order for us to survive as a species. We called it the Greater Gathering, and since that time, we have drawn together to forge a united government. A chorus of representatives from every cluster." The alien captain's lips pursed. "Not always a *fully* united one, if I speak with honesty. Overt conflict may be long forgotten, but there are always disagreements . . ." She paused, and Spock had the sense that Kaleo was uncomfortable with her admission. "You must think us very provincial."

"Not even a little." Doctor McCoy smiled. "You ought to come sit in on a session at the Federation Council. You'll see the same thing there, beings from dozens of different worlds, all arguing until they're blue in the face. Or purple, or green, or whatever, for that matter. A more disunited United Federation you won't see . . . but it's all part of the democratic process."

"It is only a difference of scale," Spock added. "Your government representatives speak for tribes, ours for worlds."

Zond made the deep-throated laughing sound. "You say that so casually, Vulcan. Until we met your ship, we did not even know there *were* other worlds and other beings."

"You never suspected such a possibility?" asked Kirk.

Kaleo showed something like a smile as the lift passed through the next deck and into the dark again. "Some of us did. And for the most part, we were thought of as romantics. Or fools."

"No one is making light of it now," muttered Hoyga, almost to herself.

The next sections of the ship were great industrial spaces filled with machinery and tall, heavy structures that seemed at first sight to be cast out of steel. Bright, orange-red light flickered through gaps in the towerlike constructs and Spock shifted his perception slightly, allowing him to place what he was seeing into a more familiar context. "This is your engineering compartment," he said.

"Correct, Mister Spock." Kaleo pointed out four great conduits emerging from a large central module, explaining how each of them extended out past the walls of the *Friendship*'s fuselage, through its wing-like superstructures to the active warp drive nacelles beyond. The Syhaari craft's power systems had a thick-set, overengineered look to them that made the Vulcan wonder about their energy efficiency. Certainly, aboard the *Enterprise* he had been able to observe the power flux signature generated by the alien vessel's systems.

"That's a warp core down there?" asked McCoy. "Doesn't look like one of Scotty's machines."

"Safety is our primary concern," Hoyga said firmly. "As a healer, you should see the merit of that."

"A logical design philosophy," offered Spock. "Given your previous negative experiences with warp drive systems. Your design favors heavy layers of inert shielding around your matter-antimatter collider. While it increases the mass of this vessel, it will protect the crew from any potential delta radiation leakage."

Mentioning the lethal energy brought an uneasy silence into the lift car as they continued their descent. McCoy shot Spock a disparaging look, doubtless attempting to admonish him for reminding the Syhaari of the accident aboard *The Explorer Beyond*.

"It's impressive," said Kirk, breaking the change in mood. "Can we get a closer look?"

Hoyga opened her mouth to protest, but Kaleo was already using her control wand to bring the elevator to a halt. "Of course! Follow me."

The glass hatch rolled open, and the two captains exited together, moving down a suspended walkway over the thrumming heart of the alien starship. Flickering light the color of naked flames spilled out from narrow observation grilles in the radiation armor, but there was little to give any clue to the actual configuration of the Syhaari drive system.

Spock regretted that he had not brought a tricorder with him, but Envoy Xuur had insisted that to do so might be seen as intrusive. As such, he was left only with his senses and a keen eye for observation to determine what he could about the Syhaari's rapid advances in shipbuilding.

Ahead of him, Captain Kirk was doing the same. "Remarkable," he said. "You know, it took my species a long time to build starships that could travel faster than warp three." Kirk nodded toward his first officer. "And that was with the help of Mister Spock's people into the bargain."

"They didn't help *that* much," said McCoy, in a low voice.

"We have been fortunate . . ." Kaleo frowned. "Our . . . scientists made a number of breakthroughs that we were quick to exploit."

"Is that so?" Envoy Xuur crossed to where the two captains were standing. "And you were part of that?"

Kaleo inclined her head in a dismissive gesture. "Not I, emissary. My skills are with the sailing of ships and the knowledge of stars and planets." She gestured at the great bulk of the warp engine. "This device is almost magic to me! I trust Zond and Hoyga to make it sing for us."

Xuur peered down, over the catwalk rail, to where members of the *Friendship*'s crew were hard at work. "Those power channels . . . they bear a marked resemblance to similar mechanisms on board the *Enterprise*."

"You think so?" McCoy eyed the envoy. "I didn't know you'd been down to main engineering on our ship."

"I have not," Xuur replied smoothly. "I do read quite widely, however."

Spock cleared his throat. "Warp engine design typically follows a basic structure, no matter where it originates, Envoy. It is not unusual that there would be some gross structural similarities."

"But you were an inspiration for us," Zond broke in, unaware that he was undercutting Spock's statement. "Your *Enterprise* showed us what was possible. That's why we've been working so hard to get back out here."

"Indeed?" Xuur gave Kirk a level look that the captain didn't seem to be aware of.

Spock studied the thick brass casing around the warp core and decided to see how far the innate Syhaari desire to impress would go. "If it is not an imposition, I would be fascinated to observe the workings of the *Friendship*'s power core at close hand." He glanced at Zond. "Would it be possible for me to access the interior of the shielded compartment, if only for a short period?"

"That could be—" The Syhaari first mate was never allowed to complete his sentence.

"Not permitted," Hoyga insisted, raising her voice for the first time. "Safety of this vessel is of paramount concern. Accessing the secured inner compartment of the space drive while we are under way would be a violation of our control protocols. As a senior engineer, I cannot allow it. Please understand, it is for the safety of all of us."

"Your . . . concern is admirable," said Kirk. "And of course, we wouldn't want to do anything to disrupt the operations of your vessel." He glanced at Kaleo. "Perhaps my first officer's curiosity could be sated in a different way? Would you be willing to allow him a look at your technical schematics?"

Kaleo gave Hoyga a glance that Spock could not read. "I believe so. See to it, engineer."

The other Syhaari female did not seem pleased with the compromise. "As you wish, Captain. But I will need to clear it with the Learned Assembly first."

"Thank you," said Kirk. "Kaleo, you've been most welcoming to us. I'm excited to see your world and learn more about your civilization."

The alien captain bared her teeth in something approximating a grin. "I would say the same to you, Kirk." She patted him on the shoulder. "There are many among my kind who await your arrival with great expectation."

"No pressure . . ." McCoy muttered, under his breath.

"We will do our best not to disappoint them," insisted Xuur.

———————

They returned to the *Enterprise*, both ships moving to warp velocity as soon as Kirk relayed the order to the bridge, but the captain had only taken a few steps from the intercom panel before he sensed the frosty change in the envoy's mood. With a nod he dismissed Spock and turned to find Xuur glaring at him.

The diplomat's arms were folded across her chest, and the pleasant manner she had displayed up until now was absent. "I think an explanation is in order, Kirk," she snapped.

"How's that?" said McCoy. "I thought that went just fine."

"Bones." Kirk waved him to silence. "Can you give me a moment?" He nodded toward the engineering officer at the transporter controls. "You too, Ensign."

McCoy scowled, but he obeyed, following the other crewman out into the corridor. The door hissed shut, and then Kirk and Xuur were alone.

"You have something on your mind, Envoy?"

Xuur cocked her head, the jeweled band around her temples catching the light. "I'm starting to wonder if Ambassador Fox's warnings about you were on the mark, Captain. He said you played fast and loose with the regulations, and after our tour of Kaleo's ship I have to ask myself if you did that all those months ago, during your first contact with the Syhaari."

"Let me guess, this is about what Zond said. The power channels." Kirk matched her pose, folding his arms. He could already predict where the conversation was going, and the inference was troubling.

"I will ask you this just once," Xuur said firmly. "Is it possible that you, or someone in your crew, provided critical design information or technology to the

Syhaari on your initial encounter?" Before he could even draw breath to answer, she continued on. "I'm giving you the opportunity to be honest with me. Your logs of the first contact were brief at best. If something was omitted . . ." Xuur let the sentence hang.

"The answer is no," Kirk shot back. "I'm not in the business of handing out advanced technology to alien beings we know little or nothing about."

She seized on his words, and belatedly he realized he had given her the very opening she wanted. "Isn't that *exactly* what you did on Capella and Neural? Granted, those were just bows and muskets, but advanced inventions all the same to the native population!"

Kirk tamped down his growing annoyance. "If you insist on using my past record as a stick to beat me with, at least have the good grace to take into account my successes as well as my failures. I told your aide, I stand by the choices I made in the past, because of the circumstances that led them to take place. But those things did not happen here with the Syhaari. You heard Spock—a few basic similarities between engine design elements does not mean my crew handed Kaleo's people a copy of the *Starfleet Technical Manual* and a box of parts!"

"I have to be certain," Xuur countered. "We are in uncharted territory here in relationship to the Prime Directive. The contact with the Syhaari is a rare confluence of events: a meeting with an early-stage warp-capable species that has evolved without us becoming aware of it. They are an outlier . . . and if their advancement was artificially stimulated by contact with the Federation, it would be a most serious issue."

Kirk gave a sigh. "You're looking to stop something that has already happened. You said it yourself, we're going to change everything for Kaleo and her kind. We already *have*. We changed their worldview by meeting them in space, by opening their minds to the reality of other intelligent life in the universe." He walked away a few steps. "If that inspired them to pour their intellect into creating a better warp engine, then the damage is done and I don't regret it one bit! But I promise you, what those people have built was not the fruit of some sort of misguided boon from me or my officers. We kept them off our vessel during our first contact, only one or two of the most badly injured were kept in sickbay. Kaleo and Zond were shown some of the ship . . . but that's all." He took a breath, fixing her with his gaze. "I won't stand for baseless accusations being thrown around concerning the integrity of my crew, is that clear?"

Slowly, the intractable expression on Xuur's pale face softened, returning to the pleasant aspect she had worn on their first meeting. "Forgive me, Captain Kirk. Sometimes I can press a point too far. It is a failing of mine I do my best to keep in check. But you must understand, your record." She stopped and reframed her words, bowing her head slightly. "I had to be certain. I had to hear it from you."

Kirk considered her for a moment. When the emissary allowed her carefully constructed diplomatic façade to drop, she was a very striking woman, and he had to admit, he was interested in knowing the *real* Veygaan Xuur. "I have an offer for you," he began. "Let's try this again, from the top. I'll put aside all my preconceptions about the FDC and any snap judgments I may have formed on the nature of envoys. In return, you do the same for me. Forget Ambassador Fox's secondhand opinions and make your own."

"He really does not like you," she said with a slight smile.

"The feeling is mutual."

Xuur's head bobbed. "Fair enough. But don't think that I won't take you to task if I find something I don't like."

She walked away, but Kirk found himself frowning. *We just cleared the air,* he said to himself. *So why do I feel like the tension is still there?*

"Mister Spock!"

The Vulcan turned as the *Enterprise*'s chief engineer came jogging up to him, his manner suggesting that he was troubled by something. Spock said nothing and waited for the human to explain; he found that in most circumstances an emotional being would be driven to share their immediate concerns with their fellows as quickly as possible.

"Do you have a moment, sir?" Scott held a tricorder in his hand. "There's something I'd like to get your opinion on."

There was a maintenance alcove a short distance away, and the first officer led the other man to it, so they could speak without being interrupted. Scott brought up a set of scanner readings on the tricorder's screen and handed it to Spock. "This would appear to be sensor traces from the *Enterprise*'s secondary scan array," Spock noted. "Low-bandwidth, passive wavelengths."

"Aye, sir, just like the captain ordered. A discreet sweep of the alien ship, but at low power. Don't want to seem like we're invading their privacy." Scott paused as the scan unfolded before Spock's eyes. "By and large, nothing anomalous detected."

"Until the sweep passed over the engine core." Spock correctly predicted what the other officer would say, and the display proved him right. Large sections of *The Friendship Discovered*, mostly concentrated around the drive core and the four warp nacelles, read as inert and empty—a clear impossibility, given that Spock had seen several of those systems with his own eyes.

"There's more shielding in there than I've ever seen," Scott went on. "If I didn't know better, I'd say they were sealed so tight, even their own crew wouldn't be able to get a peek inside."

"The Syhaari are overly concerned about the

propagation of lethal exotic radiation throughout their craft," said Spock. "Not unusual, given their negative experiences in the past. But even with that in consideration, the density of shielding present here is far greater than it needs to be."

"It's overkill, that's what it is," Scott added with a brisk nod. "The only way we could get a look in there was if we put our sensors into full-power active mode, and that would light up the *Friendship*'s threat board like a Christmas tree!"

"Not to mention the discourtesy such an act would show toward the Syhaari and Captain Kaleo."

"If they did the same to us, I'd think it the height of rudeness, aye." He tapped the screen. "Which begs the question, sir, if they're so proud of building a warp three engine in a couple of years, what are they hiding?"

Spock had no answer that he was willing to voice. "Continue all passive scan operations, Mister Scott. Once we reach Syhaar Prime, we may find a more direct route to answers for the questions this data raises."

"How's that?" said Scott.

"We will ask politely."

———

The door to the quarters given over to the diplomatic party slid open, and Envoy Xuur entered, her shoulders sagging as it closed behind her again.

The Andorian ch'Sellor looked up from a desk

nearby, tapping the keys of a portable unit they had brought on board with the rest of their luggage. "Do you believe him?"

Xuur gathered a cup of tea from a food slot and found a chair to settle into. "*He* believes himself," she replied. "Captain James T. Kirk is certainly as self-assured as I have been led to believe." The envoy sipped her drink, then delicately removed the ritual headband she wore. Hidden on the inner surface of the band's large jeweled centerpiece, a mesh of micro-electronics glittered with captured light.

Ch'Sellor flicked a look at the monitor. "That is what the sensor says. According to all standard human bio-signature ratings, Kirk spoke truthfully. Heartbeat rate, pupil dilation, skin temperature, all within positive ranges. But the unit is not infallible."

"That's why we are here," she retorted. "To make a judgment. And for now, I agree with the unit." Xuur gestured with the headband. She went on, changing the subject. "You were able to observe and record everything that took place while I was on board the *Friendship*?"

"Yes." He tapped another key, bringing up a play-back captured from the optical modules secreted in the headband's ornamentation. "I have already begun calibrating our bio-signatures for a Syhaari baseline. When the program is complete, we should be able to use it to read their body language and anticipate their emotional states as easily as those of any other species."

"What is that device you wear?" A voice piped up from the monitor screen, and Xuur recognized engineer Hoyga's earlier question.

"This one is quite perceptive," ch'Sellor noted. "She might have guessed the ornament was more than you said it was, given time. Envoy, if the aliens become aware that we are covertly monitoring them, they may react poorly."

"That won't happen," Xuur insisted. "We are entering the unknown here, my friend, and we need an edge." She sipped at her tea again and gazed out at the stars streaking past the viewport on the far wall. "The Syhaari contact is too important to risk any mishaps. And the act of diplomacy is too sensitive to be left to guesswork."

Three

In the immeasurable distances of deep space, the domain of the Syhaari would seem at first to be a great ellipse of cloud and dust—if one were capable of standing off at a range to observe such a phenomenon.

Like many star systems throughout the galaxy, the sun known as Sya was orbited by a handful of planets in orbits that were, by cosmic standards, close at hand. Beyond those, at a distance of thousands of astronomical units, an unusually dense cloud of icy planetesimals and proto-comet materials existed within a thick fog of dust. The wispy shell of gas and particles, trapped forever in strange equilibrium between the gravity of the isolated star system and the slow pull of the interstellar medium, surrounded the Syhaari worlds in a permeable globe that allowed in only the strongest light from nearby suns. For much of their existence, the simianoids who grew to sentience on their birthworld believed they lived in a barren, sparse universe, where other stars were few and far between. Only when they hurled their first crude space probes beyond the outer planets did they venture through the membrane surrounding them and see the true magnificence of the universe beyond.

The dense cloud—which ancient Syhaari astronomers had named the *Great Veil*—had not only kept them from seeing what lay past it, but it had also allowed their species to evolve in relative safety. The star Sya had formed on the fringes of a vast zone of nebulae, where new suns were being born, an area of great turmoil. The Veil, formed from the remnants of stillborn superplanets that had never fully cohered, became the very thing that protected the nascent civilization from the sea of radiation that surrounded it. And now, millions of years on, the place the Syhaari called home sat like a great, dusty pearl on a blanket of riotous color, bounded by incredible fires of creation.

Two vessels, one a sleek, winged dart and the other a sculpture of disc and rods, fell toward the outer edges of the Veil at speeds beyond the velocity of light.

———

Sometimes the viewscreen just didn't seem big enough, Hikaru Sulu reflected. The small window on the universe that sat before him across the bridge was too enclosed to gather in the sheer scope of what lay around the *Enterprise*. Not for the first time, the helmsman entertained the fanciful idea of what it would be like to work under a glass dome, if the walls and bulkheads all about him could suddenly be rendered transparent.

It would be something powerful to see, he told himself. Even the comparatively keyhole-sized view they were getting of the protostar nursery was awe-inspiring—and perhaps that was for the best. Sulu could imagine himself mesmerized by the sight if the whole horizon were open to him, at once humbled and exhilarated by what it represented.

"It is quite an impressive display," offered Arex at the navigator's station.

Sulu was so engrossed in the view that at first he didn't realize the lieutenant was talking to him. He smiled. "And then some, Arex." With effort, he drew his gaze away. "How's our heading?"

"Within optimal parameters," piped the Triexian. "I estimate we will pass through the outer edge of the cloud shell in five minutes. Interception with Syhaar Prime will be approximately thirty-one minutes after that."

Sulu accepted the report with a nod and peered into the hood of the sensor scope that extended out of his own control panel. A display there showed a basic tactical plot of what awaited them.

Inside that oval gas cloud was a small K-type orange star and a system of five planets. Farthest out was Hokaar, a Class-C ball of geoinactive stone and ice; it was overshadowed by its nearest neighbor, a massive double-ringed ultragiant called Yedeen that itself had a small population of shepherd moons and captured asteroids. Much farther in were two worlds in the habitable zone, the Class-M Syhaari Prime and the rocky Class-L planet Gadmuur. Lastly, closest to the star Sya was a heat-cracked sphere of rock that resembled Mercury in Earth's solar system, a Class-B world called Neliin.

The system did not present a difficult plot for an experienced helmsman to fly, even though his opposite number on *The Friendship Discovered* had sent Sulu a complex data packet showing the intricate web of mandated spacelanes the Syhaari used inside their own domain. For the purposes of the *Enterprise*'s formal arrival, however, they had been given clearance to bypass all of that and take the direct path to Syhaar Prime. Sulu recomputed his standard orbit chart for the alien planet once again, even though he knew it was solid. It wouldn't do to pull into position over this world and then have to adjust headings like some fresh-off-the-shuttle cadet. This was official business, and everything the *Enterprise* crew did, down to the smallest detail, would be documented forever in the annals of Syhaari history. It was important to make the best possible showing.

"Helm." Sulu turned in his chair as he heard Mister Spock call out to him. "Cross-check your sensor readings with my station."

"Aye, sir." His fingers tapped the glowing keys before him, and Sulu brought up the data Spock was referring to. Becoming more distinct as they closed in on the cloud shell, the *Enterprise*'s long-range sensors were picking up hazy ghost images of other vessels moving on the far side of the Veil. For a moment, Sulu wondered if the ships were more escort craft, out there to accompany them to the inner worlds, but their flight paths suggested otherwise. The Syhaari ships were moving in what could only be standard geometric sweep patterns.

He frowned and looked back at the science officer. "I'm seeing the same thing as you, Commander. Multiple spacecraft in motion."

"On screen, Mister Sulu." Spock gave the order, and the helmsman shifted his data to the big display. "Four vessels within our current sensor range," Spock went on, looking to Captain Kirk. "Engine power curves and radiant output are a match to the Syhaari warp one vessel we encountered many months ago. These craft are of the same class and tonnage as *The Explorer Beyond*."

"Except they don't appear to be doing any exploring," Kirk noted, taking in the information.

"That's a border patrol, Captain," said Sulu. "Quadrant by quadrant. I'll bet there are ships we can't read yet on the far side of the system flying the exact same pattern."

"Are they interested in us?"

"It would seem not." Spock shook his head. "I read no deviation from their courses."

Kirk tapped a finger on his chin. "Picket ships. That implies a state of military readiness . . . for what?"

"Maybe they don't trust us," offered Lieutenant Uhura.

"If I may, Captain," said Arex. "They could be showing the flag. Attempting to impress us once again."

"Possible," agreed Spock.

Sulu felt a moment of doubt pass through him. Arex's suggestion didn't ring true. The helmsman's experience suggested something else. He knew an alert formation when he saw it. "Or perhaps . . . they're expecting trouble."

The statement hung in the air, and for long seconds, no one answered it. Then a gentle trilling tone sounded from communications, and Uhura pressed a finger to the receiver module in her ear. "Captain, we're being hailed by the *Friendship*. Zond reports that a signal has been relayed from the Learned Assembly on their home planet. We are clear to pass through the Veil and continue at warp three to Syhaar Prime." She paused. "They welcome us warmly as new friends."

"Respond with our gratitude, Lieutenant," Kirk told her. "Helm, maintain present speed and heading. Shields at the ready as we cross the gas cloud; we don't know what effect it might have on the ship."

"Aye, sir," Sulu responded, entering the command. "Steady as she goes." The viewscreen switched back to exterior sensor input, and the majestic starscape was now replaced by a glittering, misty wall of gray fog as the *Enterprise* approached the Veil.

"Friends." Arex said the word quietly, so only Sulu heard him. "With all those ships out there, I speculate how warmly the Syhaari would greet those they considered otherwise."

Sulu said nothing, carefully guiding the starship into the depthless haze.

———

The last stage of the journey passed swiftly, although Captain Kirk felt oddly unsettled by the strange sky they encountered once they were inside the gas and dust shell surrounding the Sya system. Instead of the deep, inky black of the interstellar void he had come to consider the working backdrop for his career, the familiar was replaced by a peculiar, cloudy gray the shade of ancient slate. He wondered what it had to have been like for the first Syhaari to see what lay past the Great Veil. His species had evolved on a world where the stars had always been there, their meaning and origins peeled back layer by layer as humankind's knowledge grew. But to Kaleo's people, what a shock it must have been to learn that the pocket of space in which they lived, behind the Veil, was a grain of sand against the scale of the true universe. It was a testament to their character that the Syhaari hadn't simply fled back to the safety of their worlds and hidden there forevermore.

Sulu placed them in a pitch-perfect orbit over Syhaar Prime, on a transit that would quickly circle the planet, a course that was deliberately designed to carry *Enterprise* over the major population centers of the green- and amber-hued world. The choice was deliberate, so that anyone down below with a powerful telescope would be able to look up and see the Federation starship with their own eyes, flying in formation with the Syhaari's most advanced space vessel. A simple but powerful statement.

Adjourning to the transporter room, Kirk saw Uhura fiddling with her tricorder before they beamed down and noted that the communications officer was switching between digital data channels being broadcast from the surface. "These are Syhaari news feeds," she told him, noting her captain's attention. "From what I can tell, the mood of the local population appears to be somewhere between *fascinated* and *guarded*."

"Any negative interest?" asked McCoy, checking the portable medical kit attached to his uniform.

Kirk frowned, but Uhura responded anyway. "Some demonstrations in a few outlying locations."

"That is to be expected." Envoy Xuur brushed a speck of lint from the sheer silver dress she wore. "Not everyone welcomes alien contact. Not at first."

Kirk's gaze flicked from Xuur to ch'Sellor at her side. "If you feel we need a security escort . . ."

Xuur shook her head firmly. "Captain, you, your doctor, science officer, and linguist are sufficient for our initial appearance here. Let's not make this look like the scouting party for an invasion."

He said nothing and turned away. "Mister Scott? You're in command. You may energize when ready."

"Aye, Captain." Scotty stepped behind the transporter controls and worked the sliders. "On your way . . ."

There was that sudden, peculiar state-change transition—and then Kirk was standing on another new world. He and the landing party were the first alien beings to breathe Syhaari air, the first to feel the pull of this planet's gravity. As Kirk's eyes adjusted to the bright orange sunshine, he was reminded again of what the emissary had said a day or so before. *For us, this is another day at the office. For them, a life-changing moment.* Kirk promised himself that he would not take a single second of this for granted.

The air was crisp and sweet, and it tasted of blossom. Looking around, his first thought was that they hadn't materialized in a city after all, but instead in some kind of nature preserve. But looking again, Kirk saw that what he had initially thought to be low hills were actually artificial structures, domed complexes covered with carefully manicured lawns and other plant life, some with roofs that were open to the sky. Rising up all around them were wide, sprawling trees that were half Terran banyans, half Izarian cedars, each festooned with thick vines that drooped to the ground or entwined above in a random web. Amid the trees, there were bone-white stone minarets holding up lines for trains of bubble-canopy cable cars. The more Kirk looked, the more he picked out clusters of large organic-looking bulbs, something midway between a giant bird's nest and a woven hut.

Up above the landing party, a flock of patient drones floated on spinning impellors, artificial insect-forms pointing recording gear at the new arrivals from space. Kirk lifted a hand in a wave and gave a close-mouthed smile, careful not to show any teeth for fear that might be seen as aggressive.

"Just remember to look nonthreatening, Spock," said McCoy. "We don't want these good people getting the wrong idea about us."

"I am confident in my ability to remain passive, Doctor," replied the Vulcan. "I wonder if you could say the same?"

"Look sharp," Kirk admonished as a group of Syhaari approached, climbing the low rise of the grassy hillock where the landing party had materialized. Among them were Kaleo and the engineer Hoyga, as well as several others of their species who wore odd gowns made of scarf-like strips of cloth. Their outfits seemed to have a ceremonial cut to them, and the captain guessed correctly that these beings were the Syhaari equivalents of Xuur and ch'Sellor.

"Welcome to our planet," said the tallest of them, an elderly being with silver fur and deep-set eyes. "Gatag is my name. I am a functionary of the Learned

Assembly, and it is my honor of honors to speak with you this day."

Kirk opened his mouth to reply, but Envoy Xuur swiftly beat him to the punch. "That honor is shared equally by us, sir. On behalf of the United Federation of Planets, we thank you for your hospitality." The diplomat made quick introductions, and Gatag bowed slightly to each of the landing party in turn—pausing only in amazement at the sight of the blue-skinned Andorian—before ending with his gaze on Kirk.

"You are the captain of the *Enterprise*," said Gatag. "Our brave sister Kaleo speaks highly of you, Kirk from Earth."

"She's very generous," Kirk deflected. "Like your explorers, I am just a fellow traveler."

"Nevertheless, you saved the lives of our precious kindred," Gatag insisted. "A debt is owed."

"Consider it paid, sir," he replied, "with your offer of friendship. I hope today will mark the beginning of a long association between the Syhaari Gathering and the Federation."

That seemed to please the old functionary, and he gave a low grunt of approval. "Come, then. The Assembly awaits you."

"A moment . . ." Hoyga stepped forward and gestured sharply to a subordinate carrying a large cube-shaped device with a scanning dish on one face. The other Syhaari moved down the line of the landing party, tracking each of them briefly with the unit.

"A sensor tool, Captain," suggested Spock. "A less-advanced version of our own tricorders."

"It is required," Hoyga added. "For safety."

"Of course," Kirk allowed, sharing a look with McCoy. The captain knew his chief medical officer had already made sure the *Enterprise* crew carried no pathogens hazardous to the Syhaari biosphere, but it didn't hurt to allow the locals to make their own confirmation of that too.

When the scan was complete, Hoyga's cheerless expression did not change. "Clear," she said.

Gatag beckoned them toward a waiting cable-line with long fingers. "Come, this way."

―――――

They boarded a glassy capsule as wide as a shuttlecraft and twice as long, and with a clatter of ceramic cog-wheels, the transport was gathered up from the grass by spools of cable, rocking gently as it found its way onto one of the many elevated byways crisscrossing the Syhaari cityscape. Only the deck of the capsule was opaque; the rest of the large pod was made of a clear, flexible plastic that deformed slightly when Kirk pressed it with a finger, before springing back into shape.

The cable car picked up speed and moved over points to a higher route atop the tallest towers, and the captain had to admit that the view was breathtaking. The strange hybrid of metropolis and natural space flowed away in all directions toward the horizon, blending seamlessly into the landscape. He saw a river gorge far below, with buildings cut right into the sheer living rock on either side of the flowing water. Rainbows formed across the span in soft clouds of spray. Other towers, thinner than the cable-car supports, expanded out into spinning windmills with helical, ribbon-shaped sails. Others were crested with what looked like solar panels. He saw little that seemed to be heavy industry to mar the sight.

"The Syhaari exhibit a fascinating architectural balance with nature," noted Spock, examining the same view. "Very likely an outgrowth of their status as a civilization late to the impulse to explore space."

"Harmony is our watchword," said Gatag. "This planet birthed us, her sister-worlds gave us resources. We owe it to them to treat their bounty with respect."

"A laudable attitude," said McCoy. "Something it took my people a long time to learn."

"Are there many cities like this on Syhaar Prime?" asked Uhura, looking up at the rangy, apelike humanoid.

"Many?" Gatag's old face creased in confusion as he processed her question. "Ah, you misunderstand, human. Our conurbation is a single entity that spans the entire planet, a great number of districts connected node to node by the skyways and rivers. Some zones are more sparsely populated by others, but we consider it all to be of one body."

"A city bigger than continents . . ." McCoy wondered aloud. "But still in harmony with the natural world? That's an achievement."

"You may see more of it, if you wish to, Doctor," Kaleo offered. She glanced at Kirk. "Perhaps I could show you the zone where I grew up, Captain?"

"I'd like that," said Kirk. The carriage trembled as it switched to another aerial track and began to descend. As it passed behind a broad, mirror-surfaced dome, he caught sight of a huge landing field off in the distance. Great curved gantries of shimmering white extended up into the sky, several of them occupied by the elongated shapes of Syhaari spacecraft. "Your starport?" he asked, turning back to Kaleo.

She bobbed her head in an approximation of a nod. "Central control for our expeditionary fleet. Beneath it are the yards where the next generation of our ships are already taking shape—"

"That zone is under closed protocols," Hoyga said, speaking over her commanding officer, earning a look of censure that the engineer didn't seem to notice. "For safety reasons."

Kirk sensed there was more to be said, but before he could press the point, Envoy Xuur was at his side. "There is so much here to take in," said the diplomat, smiling politely. "Your world is admirable."

Gatag thanked her again as the capsule slowed. Ahead of them, a fluted obelisk rose up—an ornate skyscraper covered in intricate carvings and strange webs of vine that lay like vertical gardens along its flanks. "The Gathering is governed from here," Gatag explained. "And within, the Assembly welcomes our visitors in the manner of our ancestors, with a feast of communion!"

Xuur glanced at Kirk and spoke quietly, without breaking her placid smile. "I hope you and your officers brought an appetite."

———

There were a dozen more greetings and welcomes and sundry other how-do-you-dos, to the point that McCoy was starting to get dizzy with it. In the space of a few minutes, as the landing party was walked through the great hall of Assembly, he had to have said hello to at least a dozen senior Syhaari officials from all aspects of their administration. He was finding it hard to keep track of who was who, of what each unusual combination of colored scarf and ornamental hair braid meant. McCoy elected to remain close to Spock, knowing that the Vulcan's keen memory would retain every last element of that information. If he blanked on a face or name, he would rely on Spock to supply it for him.

They were seated at a long, S-shaped table, on low stools that were not really designed for the less elastic bodies of non-Syhaari, but everyone made do. Gatag announced proudly that the foodstuffs presented before them had all been prepared in accordance with data provided by the Federation Diplomatic Corps on humanoid biochemistry, so it was all perfectly palatable for the *Enterprise* crew. McCoy had to admit the bowls of succulents, leafy salads, and cooked meats looked and smelled quite appetizing, as did the great urns of steaming teas lining the middle of the table—but caution nagged at him. He wanted to pull up his tricorder and scan the feast, *just to be certain*, but the steady, cold glare aimed at him from ch'Sellor's eyes told the doctor that would be a *faux pas* of the highest order. The Syhaari had made a big deal about not poisoning anyone, and it would be rude to openly challenge that.

He started carefully, with some warm breads and what looked like olives. Then a kind of fish and a slice of heavy, rich meat. It was surprisingly good, and with his usual diet of shipboard meals coming from the *Enterprise*'s adequate-if-basic food slots, McCoy found it increasingly tempting to indulge himself.

The locals didn't stand on ceremony, so it seemed. They ate and talked, moved from chair to chair along the table. After the stiff formality of all the meet-and-greets, the more relaxed nature of the actual feast was refreshing. McCoy found himself warming to the Syhaari. He sipped at a green tisane brew and listened to Gatag speaking around mouthfuls of fruit.

"The act of sharing food," he was telling Uhura, "is a scared tenet of our culture. In the ancient past, when game was scarce and our people were made up of disparate tribes, the resource of food was the main reason for conflict between them. But it also became the bond by which tribes could unite. It became forbidden to seek conflict of any kind on a feast day, and an unbreakable rule that one should share their meal with others if so asked. Those simple ideals still have great resonance in our culture to this day, even after we developed the technology to synthesize foods from base chemical components."

Xuur paused, examining a piece of doughy bread. "This is fabricated? The quality is very good!"

"When yours is a society where food has traditionally been in short supply, you focus your technology on such areas," Kaleo offered. "We put our energies into feeding our hungry long before we turned our eyes to space."

Spock paused, studying the items among the salad he was eating with a wary eye. "These vegetables are also replicated items?"

"Some of them," said Gatag, and he was clearly pleased to have impressed his alien visitors.

"I know some technicians at Starfleet Materiel Command who will want to talk to you about your advances," McCoy said, with a smile. "To paraphrase a famous leader from our planet, a crew marches on its stomach."

At his side, Kirk punctuated his point with a bite from a piece of spiced meat that had been placed in front of him. "This is quite flavorful. Can I ask what it is?"

Gatag gestured at the captain. "Ah, as you are the leader of our honored guests, you are served a special dish that we call the *ruokaan*, given as a gesture of fealty."

From the corner of his eye, McCoy saw Uhura freeze with an eating utensil halfway to her mouth. Delicately, she put it down and turned to Gatag. "Pardon me, sir, I've studied your language. That word, *ruokaan* . . . am I correct in thinking it translates as—"

"*Visitor's flesh*," Gatag said agreeably. "Yes. It is your flesh." He pointed at Kirk.

"What?" All of a sudden, McCoy's appetite died, and what he had already eaten lay like lead in his gut.

"I don't understand," said Kirk. "You said this meat was artificial, but then you're saying it is . . . from a human?"

"No, Captain, it is from *you*." Gatag gestured at the air. "In the deep past, when our warlords met, they would each cut a length of skin from their bodies and ritually cook it for their rivals to eat. It symbolized the sharing of food and of one's self. We have evolved beyond these barbaric practices now, but with our synthesizer devices we can duplicate the meat of any creature. Even of each other."

"The scan they took of us," said Spock. "That would reveal enough genetic data for the basis of a biosynthetic model."

"Then we're also . . . eating some of you?" ch'Sellor asked. "In this food?"

"All of us," replied Gatag. "It is the sharing."

"Remarkable." Spock glanced at McCoy, seemingly oblivious to the look of shock on the doctor's face. "A wholly synthetic meat substitute, virtually identical to the real item down to a molecular level. But without any of the ethical quandaries raised by the farming of live creatures. Fascinating . . ." The Vulcan continued to eat his plate of leafy greens.

"It raises a hell of a lot of other things!" McCoy pushed his plate away and swallowed a deep draft of the tea to wash away the taste in his mouth. "Can I get one of those salads instead?"

———

For a long moment, Kirk paused; then he finished his slice of the cooked meat. It wouldn't do to look squeamish, he reasoned. "Tangy," Kirk remarked, washing it down with some water.

Rather than complicate the issue with a discussion of what might or might not be taboo when it came to eating habits, Envoy Xuur deftly changed tack. "Those starships we saw on the way here . . . it seems your people are equipping themselves for a dedicated progression into interstellar space."

Kirk caught a warning look between Kaleo and Hoyga, as if the engineer was silently warning her commander not to rise to the bait. Kaleo deliberately looked away. *Something going on there,* he thought to himself, and made a mental note to talk to Spock about it when they were back on the *Enterprise*.

"We are in the process of an accelerated development program, yes," Kaleo was saying. "We are training many new crews. But our intent is not to range too far from home, at least for the immediate future."

He got the sense she was offering an opening, and so he took it. "Those patrol ships we saw as we passed through the Veil . . . forgive me, but they don't seem designed for long-range exploration."

It was telling that Kaleo didn't correct his deliberate description of the vessels in a military context. "No," she admitted. "Our newer craft are designed to fulfill a number of other functions with a lesser focus on exploration. Search and rescue. Planetary survey. And . . . defensive operations."

Combat vessels? The unspoken emphasis was right there. Kirk couldn't be a hundred percent certain, but what he had been able to intuit of Syhaari body language told him that Kaleo was uncomfortable with the idea of warships.

"The new direction for the fleet is the brainchild of one of our greatest commanders," said Gatag, apparently missing the subtext. "Tormid. He is responsible for the revision in our starcraft deployment and many of the great leaps forward in our technology!" The old ambassador clasped his hands together, and showed a toothy grin to Kaleo. "Your former colleague is now our rising star!"

"Tormid and I were the first two captains chosen to take explorer ships out beyond the Veil," Kaleo explained. "When we returned home . . ." She paused. "Well. I think Tormid is equally adept with the business of politics as he is with command of a ship. It's a skill I lack."

"My old friend is too modest!" said a voice, and all eyes turned to a new arrival, a Syhaari male dressed in a uniform similar to Kaleo's, but with much bolder colors. He had dark orange fur and sharp, searching eyes that made him look like he was sizing up potential appetizers.

"Tormid," said Kaleo tightly. "Of course you're here."

A number of the Syhaari elders left their seats to greet the other commander, with grunts of amusement and backslapping, but he quickly disengaged and made straight for the *Enterprise* party. Tormid moved from person to person, making gestures of greeting to everyone in turn. "My great apologies for my lateness, offworlders, but I was delayed by important matters in the shipyards. Welcome to you, welcome to our domain! Ever since Kaleo brought back news of the grand Federation and your mighty *Enterprise*, I have wanted to meet you—" He stopped suddenly as they came face-to-face. "*You*! You are Kirk from Earth, the Rescuer!" He put a heavy hand on the captain's shoulder. "Thank you. On behalf of all Syhaari, and myself, you have our deepest gratitude for your act of selfless kindness." He looked toward Kaleo, whose expression had become rigid and brittle. "She and her crew would have died out there in the void if not for you. You took pity on them."

"I wouldn't put it like that," Kirk managed. "We did what anyone of good conscience would have. We helped our fellow sentients in a time of need."

Without waiting for an invitation, Tormid interposed himself between Kirk and Spock and poured a cup of tea. "Yes. Of course."

Kaleo stood up and gave a shallow bow. "If you'll excuse me . . . I must check in with Zond . . ." She walked away without looking back, trailing frosty air in her wake as she spoke quietly into a wrist communicator.

Envoy Xuur introduced herself, earning a cursory nod from Tormid in return. "I wasn't aware that the Syhaari Gathering sent out multiple exploration missions."

"We did," he said, barely giving the diplomat any of his attention. "*The Explorer Beyond* and *The Searcher Unbound*. Such bold endeavors, to be certain. But each of us met with ill fate." He hesitated, drumming his long fingers on the table and looking toward Hoyga. "Strange, is it not? That in a crucible of failure and disaster, amid the death of our crewmates, a greater cause was served. Despite our losses, we brought back prizes."

Gatag mirrored Tormid's gesture. "So true. Kaleo returned to us with news of your Federation and of potential friendships, while Tormid—"

"I came back with insight," he broke in. "Hard-won, I hasten to add, is that not so?" Again, Tormid looked to Hoyga, who gave a sullen nod of agreement.

"Your vessel, the *Searcher*," began Spock, "it also suffered a malfunction?"

"A design flaw," Tormid said bitterly. "Almost killed us all. The one responsible for it has since been given other less-critical duties. Yes, offworlder, you are correct. Hoyga here was my engineer at the time, and only she and I lived to see Syhaar Prime again. Together, we managed to repair our craft and limp back to the Veil."

"A heroic saga," intoned Gatag. "Worthy of our ancestors."

Tormid looked away. "We did what we had to do. And although I mourn my lost comrades each day, I comfort myself with the fact that their sacrifice has helped our people reach new heights."

Kirk nodded. "My world's early forays into space travel were often tempered by the loss of brave explorers."

"You understand! Remarkable!" Tormid patted him on the shoulder. "Strange to hear that from an alien, that we have shared common experiences." He went on, barely pausing. "Even though your comrades perished, you learned from them. So too did I. On our journey back, I was forced to improvise with what was to hand . . . and in that, I gained unique insights into space-warping. I took risks. They proved fruitful."

"So you're the one behind the leaps forward in Syhaari science?" asked McCoy.

"I am only a being with many ideas," he deflected. "I consider it my duty to bring them to my people."

"You have made rapid advancement in faster-than-light drive technology," Spock noted, then gestured to his plate. "And it appears your people are skilled in the design of replication systems."

"This is so," Gatag agreed. "But we have yet to perfect the science of your impressive matter-transit machines or your speaking tools." He tapped the universal translator unit on the table before them.

Kirk studied the alien commander and decided to see if he could press him to reveal more. If the Syhaari were culturally attuned to shows of prowess, he might be able to draw more out of Tormid than Xuur would get in days of polite discussion. "Your people built a warp-capable starship, then a few years later you've broken through the warp three speed barrier . . . was that just a matter of blind luck?"

A moment of annoyance flashed in Tormid's dark eyes. "I do not believe in such things. Grave need led me to that knowledge. If I had done any different, Hoyga and I would have been dead and the fate of the *Searcher* never known." He leaned in, and the anger faded, replaced by a steady certainty. "Warp factor three is only the beginning, Captain Kirk. I am already leading the design of a drive system capable of achieving factor five velocity, or even higher."

"An impressive progression," said Spock. "Perhaps the Assembly would consider an exchange of information at some juncture? Certainly, I believe our engineers would be interested to learn more about your design process."

"The Federation Diplomatic Corps would have to oversee it, of course," ch'Sellor was quick to add.

"And we might be able to offer some assistance," Kirk added, even as Xuur shot him a warning look. "Caution you about potential hazards your scientists may not yet be aware of."

Tormid reeled back, and his tone and manner shifted. "You believe so? Captain, I am afraid that you may think of us as primitives compared to your star-spanning empire!"

"We're not an empire," Uhura corrected gently. "The Federation is a democratic coalition of free states."

The alien commander didn't acknowledge her words, instead keeping his eyes on Kirk. "With all gratitude to the offer, we do not need your help. Not again. What happened to Kaleo was unfortunate, but it is not the nature of our kind to require rescue. We can look after ourselves. We have the means."

"You are referring to your patrol ships?" Spock dropped the question into the conversation, and Kirk let it happen—he was willing to risk it if only to see how Tormid would react.

"Those are an expression of our new effectiveness in space," said Gatag.

"A precaution," Tormid added, his guard rising.

"Captain Tormid, I was talking about avenues of friendship." Kirk took a breath, framing his next words carefully. "I spoke about my own people's first ventures into space . . . those brought us to the attention of Mister Spock's race, the Vulcans. They had more experience of warp travel than we did, and together we entered into an alliance. That relationship was the bedrock for the thriving Federation that exists today."

"Generous," Tormid said, after a moment. "But we have an axiom here, Kirk. *Do not fill your plate at a stranger's house.* And as much as you have done, and even with your kind words, you are still aliens to us. And the alien can be a dangerous thing."

"The United Federation of Planets respects the independence of every world we deal with," Xuur said, a firmness beneath her ever-present smile. "If the Syhaari Gathering opens formal relationships with us, that will not change."

"Let us say that is so," Tormid allowed. "But there are others beyond the Veil who would not do the same, yes? Your Federation is not the only power in the universe. I would guess that not everyone out in the greater galaxy may be as welcoming to us as you seem to be. Is that not so?" He shot Spock a challenging look.

The Vulcan gave a reluctant nod. "Regrettably, I must concur. However—"

Whatever Spock was going to say next, it was cut short by the insistent alert tone of Kirk's communicator. The captain removed the device from his belt and stepped away from the table, frowning. "Kirk here," he began, "this better be important."

"*Captain, your exact words, were: 'Don't contact me unless it's something big.'*" Scotty's tone told him immediately that this wasn't a trivial matter. "*So it is. An object approximately five thousand kilometers in diameter, moving through the outer edge of the dust cloud surrounding this system.*"

That brought him up short. The engineer was describing something larger than the Earth's moon. "Artificial or natural?"

"*Unknown, sir. Mister Sulu's got full sensors on it, but the readings are inconsistent. Whatever this anomaly is, we picked it up on long-range sensors a few moments ago, and you can bet the locals will be seeing it as well, any second now.*"

As Scott spoke, Kirk glanced across the room and saw Kaleo talking into her wrist communicator, her expression agitated. "I think they already know, Scotty. Put the ship on yellow alert, stand by on the transporters to beam us back." A long few seconds passed and there was only silence. "Mister Scott? Do you hear me?"

"*Aye, sir,*" came a hollow reply, a moment later. "*Captain, some new information . . . Lieutenant M'Ress is intercepting the slow subspace transmissions from the Syhaari ships out on the perimeter. They're under attack.*"

An instant later, a lowing tone sounded through the hall, and Kirk knew that the same news had reached Kaleo's people.

Four

A wall on the far side of the Assembly hall dropped away into the floor, revealing a large oval screen behind it. Spock saw the Syhaari elders leave the dining table in a rush, some knocking over glasses of steaming tea in their haste, other snarling into handheld communicators in their gruff native language.

"What is wrong?" said Xuur, rising to her feet after Gatag, Tormid, and Hoyga.

The older Syhaari ambassador gave a grave shake of his furred head. "I do not wish to alarm you unduly, but that sound you hear is a planetary alert. It sounds only in the most extreme of circumstances."

"Are we in danger?" said ch'Sellor, looking up as Captain Kirk strode back to the table.

Kirk hesitated, and Spock knew immediately that the message from the *Enterprise* was part of whatever was happening.

Tormid glowered at streams of text that were filling the screen from bottom to top, then he growled at Gatag. "The offworlders should vacate the hall,

Ambassador." His earlier manner toward the landing party—by turns challenging and unctuous—was gone, replaced by a dismissive attitude. "They should return to their ship and leave this to us."

"If there is a direct danger to the *Enterprise*," Spock began, "we will be compelled to act on it."

"You are *visitors*," Tormid insisted, putting heavy emphasis on the word. "We insist." Belatedly, Gatag gave a rough nod of agreement.

"I'm not sure that's the best idea." Kirk folded his arms over his chest. "One of my officers just informed me of the presence of an intruder object entering your star system. You need to tell us what, if anything, you know of it."

The screen was now switching between various low-gain still images of the object Kirk referred to. Spock parsed each one for information as it flicked by: a large planetoid of indeterminate origin, much of its surface detail lost in the shadows of the gas cloud mantle. One image showed what appeared to be a Syhaari patrol ship in the foreground, and the science officer attempted a rudimentary estimate of the planetoid's size. "Curious. Were your observers unaware of the proximity of this object?"

Tormid ignored him and spoke quietly into Hoyga's ear. Nearby, the look of shock on the faces of the other Syhaari elders was mirrored in Gatag's aspect. The ambassador's lips trembled. "What . . . is it?"

"A rogue planet?" suggested McCoy.

Kirk was frowning. "Ambassador, those signals you're receiving . . . they are time-dilated, correct?"

"Yes," Tormid snapped.

"No long-range subspace radio," Uhura noted.

Tormid turned on Kirk. "This is clearly some kind of extreme event. We had no warning of it. We know as little about it as you do!"

Kaleo strode over to them, gesturing with her communicator band. "Voice transmissions are being received." She fell silent for a moment as the Assembly members released a collective gasp of fear.

Spock looked up again to see a troubling image on the screen. Most of the view was blotted out by a flash of light that appeared to be caught in the act of consuming the patrol ship he saw earlier.

"Let us hear them," Gatag said weakly.

Hidden speakers in the ceiling over their heads hissed into life and suddenly the air was filled with a mix of overlapping, panicked Syhaari voices. The universal translator struggled to make sense of the chaotic refrain, but Spock managed to pick out snatches of speech here and there. What he heard was troubling; a handful of picket ships were caught in the gravity shadow of the alien object, and the crews were reporting attacks being directed at them from some unknown source.

Whatever threat force they were facing, the Syhaari ships were no match for it. The members of the landing party and the Assembly alike held their breath as they listened to the patrol crews dying millions of kilometers distant.

"We have to do something," McCoy muttered.

"It is already too late, Doctor," Spock told him. "What we are hearing took place several minutes ago. I am afraid the crews of those ships have already perished."

"I've heard enough," Kirk stepped up to the alien scientist. "Tormid! Let us help your people. My ship can—"

"This is not a matter for offworlders!" said Tormid, turning to jab a long finger at Kaleo. "Get to the landing fields, take a flight of our ships out there! I authorize you to deputize a quad of warp three star-rangers! Go now!"

But as he spoke, the voices issuing out over the communications channel began to cut out, one by one. A deathly quiet fell over the Assembly hall as the screen became a wall of blank static.

"This is no time for foolish pride!" barked Kaleo. "How long will it take me to get to the port, get the ships active and into the void? If there is still anyone out there, we won't make it in time!" She didn't wait for Tormid to reply and pushed past him toward Kirk. "How fast can your *Enterprise* get to the edge of the Veil?"

"At high warp? Two minutes. But we have to go right *now*."

Tormid opened his mouth to say something, but Kaleo spoke over him. "Then we go!"

Spock's captain flicked open his communicator. "Kirk to *Enterprise*. Scotty, I need you to go to warp as soon as we're aboard. Set an intercept course with that thing out there."

"Understood, sir. Transporter's ready."

"Ch'Sellor and I will remain here," Xuur said quickly.

Kirk nodded and beckoned Spock, Kaleo, and the others to him. "Five to beam up. Energize!"

"What the hell are we getting into now?" said McCoy as the shimmering glow of the transport effect enveloped them.

———

"Transporter room to bridge, we've got them." Lieutenant Kyle's crisp English accent issued out of the panel under Scott's right hand, and he tapped the intercom button in return.

"Acknowledged." He looked up. "Mister Sulu? Don't spare the horses."

"Course laid in," replied the helmsman, "accelerating to warp speed." On the main viewer, the curve of Syhaar Prime's green-blue surface suddenly leapt away, and the distant haze of the dust cloud shell shimmered with distorted light.

Arex read off a report from his panel. "Estimated time to contact point: one hundred and thirty-three seconds."

The chief engineer nodded, his eyes still on the

screen. Out in deep space, the view would have been a curtain of darkness lined with warp-elongated stars, but here inside the gas-dust sheath around the Sya system, the display seemed oddly inert, with little to give a sense of forward momentum. He looked away.

"Put all decks on red alert," ordered Scott, throwing a glance over his shoulder to M'Ress. "Warn sickbay to prepare for wounded, just in case we come across any survivors."

"Aye, sir," said the Caitian, her paws patting the console in front of her. "Doctor McCoy has just reported in down there." M'Ress's slender tail flicked in agitation; she was monitoring the Syhaari communications channels at the same time, and Scott could tell by the draw of her lips that what she was hearing was not good. "For what it's worth . . ."

"Weapons status, sir?" Sulu asked, pulling Scott's attention back. "We don't know what we're going up against here . . ."

Scott nodded grimly. "Let's not take a chance. Spin up the phasers, put photon torpedoes in the tubes. Better to have them and not need them, then . . . well, you know how it goes."

As the order left his lips, the turbolift doors behind the command chair hissed open, and the captain bolted onto the bridge with the rest of the landing party following a step behind. Scott stepped smartly out of Kirk's seat and took up a place alongside it.

"Report," said the captain.

"Less than a minute to intercept, sir."

Spock exchanged a few words with Haines before taking her place at the science station. He hesitated, peering at the junior officer's readings, his eyebrow rising. "Ensign, you are quite certain these figures are correct?"

"Yes, Commander," she said, with a wary nod. "But I can't explain them either. It's gone, sir. The object . . . it just fell off the scopes."

"What is she saying?" Kaleo stood close to Kirk's chair, her eyes darting around the bridge. "That . . . *thing* we saw on the screen? How could it just disappear?"

"Spock?" Kirk shot him a questioning look.

"I require more data, Captain, before I can provide a cogent theory."

Scott crossed to the engineering console, where Ensign Zyla was standing his post. "Sir," said the Cygnian. "I'm reading a rise in subspace radiation as we approach the target. Decay particles in the delta, berthold, and cochrane bands."

"Confirmed," said Spock, picking out the junior officer's words from across the bridge with that pin-sharp Vulcan hearing of his. "We may be seeing the aftereffect of a warp core breach or a localized spatial rift."

"Danger to us?" said the captain.

"Negligible," Spock replied. "As long as we maintain our shields."

"Intercept point in ten seconds," Arex reported. "Reducing to impulse power in five. Four. Three. Two. *One*."

The blurry skyscape flickered and shifted as the *Enterprise* dropped out of warp speed a few thousand kilometers short of the Veil's diffuse inner surface. It was hard to measure where the matter of the cloud truly began, the thick haze constantly in motion under the gravitational force of the star and planets it enveloped.

But what was clear was the storm of debris that appeared off the bow of the starship, spread out in a slick of shattered fuselages and broken engine nacelles. Pennants of spilled electroplasma trailed from holed warp drives, and sparkling fields of flash-frozen atmosphere caught the weak light of a distant sun. Everywhere Scott looked he saw burnt twists of wreckage, and it made his gut knot. These were not his ships, and they had not been crewed by his people, but a man could not be a spacer for as long as Montgomery Scott had without sharing the common horror that any starship crew would feel at such a sight. From the corner of his eye, he saw Kaleo stiffen, saw her heavy jaw drop open in shock. *Poor lassie*, he thought. *No doubt she'll know the names of every unlucky soul on those boats.*

"Scanners to full power," Kirk ordered, his tone muted by the same sight. "What's out there?"

"The . . . aggressor . . ." Spock began, grasping for the right words, "does not appear to be present."

Uhura shook her head, exchanging a wary look with M'Ress. "How can something as big as a moon hide itself?"

"Perhaps it retreated into the dust cloud?" offered the Caitian.

"Possible," Spock conceded. "But difficult to determine due to the radiation in the area affecting our sensor acuity. We could deploy a probe."

Kirk shook his head. "Hold on that for the moment. Mister Sulu, focus all scanners on the wreckage. Full-spectrum analysis. Look for any life signs, no matter how weak."

"Help him with that," Scott told Zyla. "Channel some auxiliary power into the sensor dish." He turned toward the two captains. "It might boost the sensitivity, at least at close range."

"Good thinking, engineer," Kirk replied, and he took a moment to talk to Kaleo. "Is there anything you can tell us that might be important?"

"I can only echo Tormid . . ." The Syhaari woman's eyes glittered. "I know nothing about this!"

"I didn't mean that. Your ships, Kaleo. Do they carry lifeboats, escape pods?"

She swallowed, clearly regretting her outburst. "Of course . . . the explorers do have a kind of storm-shelter module amidships. But those were omitted from the craft refitted for patrol operations."

Spock bent over his viewer hood, reading off the results of the sensor scans. "Detecting mass equivalent to four explorer-type ships. Metallic debris. Polymers. Organic . . . matter." He paused, avoiding saying the word *bodies* in Kaleo's presence. "No mayday beacons evident. Whatever caused this was swift and deadly."

"How could that happen?" said Haines quietly.

"An intense energy bombardment, Ensign," Spock said gravely. "They may have simply been overwhelmed."

Kirk accepted this with a nod. "What about specific kinds of weapons fire? Any traces of that?"

"Inconclusive, Captain. If this was an attack, it was by a means unfamiliar to us, and the Syhaari ships were unable to initiate any retaliatory action."

"Sir." Sulu peered at his panel, a look of confusion growing on his face. "I think . . . I may have something. Off the starboard quarter, five degrees over the bow. A nonmetallic object, low mass, low velocity." He glanced up. "Captain, I think it might be . . . someone."

"I have the trace now," Spock offered. "A single biological form adrift in space. Syhaari physiology. Life signs failing."

"Scotty!" Kirk called out to him. "Get down to the transporter room, we're bringing that survivor aboard."

"I want to be there!" said Kaleo, and Kirk gave her a nod.

As Scott dashed for the turbolift, the Syhaari captain came in after him, vaulting over the bridge handrail. "Don't worry, we'll save them," said the engineer.

"Only one . . ." Kaleo said, almost to herself. "Out of dozens . . ."

———————

McCoy entered transporter room one at a run, a heavy medical kit swinging off his shoulder. "What have we got?" he demanded, eyes flicking to Scott and Kyle at the control panel.

"One survivor," Scott told him. "I hope." He shot a look at the lieutenant. "Cross-circuit to phase B and boost the matter gain!" Kyle nodded silently and obeyed the order.

A figure was already forming on the beaming pad, warped by the shimmering glow of the matter-transport flux. He was no technician, but McCoy could tell by the strangled sound of the device that the transporter was having difficulty assembling its target back into a coherent form. The doctor's lip curled. It might be a common part of life aboard a starship, but Leonard McCoy had never, ever been comfortable with transit through a device that tore a man into his component atoms and then shot them through the void to be reconstituted someplace else. If he had his way, no one would ever travel on anything other than shuttles.

Kaleo was standing nearby, wringing her furred hands and staring at the transporter as if she could will it to work correctly just through force of hope. McCoy felt a pang of concern. If this poor fool didn't come through in one piece, if the transporter malfunctioned, then the last thing he wanted was for Kaleo to have to witness the result. McCoy had seen what could happen when beaming went wrong, and it was a horror he wouldn't wish on anyone.

But then she met his gaze, and he knew that she wouldn't take kindly to any insistence that she wait outside. McCoy saw a flash of determination in those eyes and remembered where he had seen the same thing before. *Jim Kirk*, he mused. *Maybe the obstinate streak is a captain thing.*

"Ambient radiation is interfering with the rematerialization process," Kyle said with a frown. "Sir, I'm not sure we can hold on to the target much longer . . ."

"Oh no, laddie," Scott retorted. "We've come too far now to let him go." He shot a look at McCoy. "Doctor, are you ready?"

"Just reel him in, Scotty. I'll take care of the rest."

"Here we go." The engineer's hands danced over the panel. "Stabilizing flux. Energizing."

The transporter's atonal song shifted again, and the figure on the pad gained definition. For one ghastly moment, McCoy thought the survivor's body had bloated into something horrific, but then he realized it was actually an environment suit made of tanned, leatherlike material. The suited figure on the pad staggered as it became solid, and when the beaming cycle terminated, it dropped to its knees with a heavy crash.

Kaleo bolted forward, her long arms reaching out to clasp the vapor-fogged dome helmet covering the survivor's head. McCoy's tricorder bleated a warning about radiation traces and cellular damage, but Kaleo wasn't about to wait for him to give her the all-clear.

She wrenched off the helmet and tossed it away. A hot stink of stale air and something like cooked meat wafted free, making McCoy grimace. He saw a male Syhaari's face, pale with shock and sickness, marked with lesions and patches of wilted fur. Immediately, the doctor loaded a hypospray with shots of tri-ox compound and hyronalin to compensate for the effects of oxygen deprivation and radiation damage.

Kaleo held the survivor's head in her hands, studying his face. "Duchad . . . you're alive!"

"You know this person?"

"We trained together . . ." She leaned in close as the other Syhaari blinked and gasped like a landed fish. "Duchad! Do you know who I am?"

"Kaleo . . ." He wheezed. "How . . . are you here? Never thought . . . I would survive."

"The Federation helped us," she told him, releasing her grip to let McCoy place the head of the hypo against Duchad's throat.

"Easy, friend," McCoy told him. "You're safe now." The drug injector hissed, and Duchad twitched as the ampoule discharged. The doctor had been careful to make sure the medicine was configured for Syhaari biology, but until he got Kaleo's compatriot down to sickbay there was no way to know how badly injured he was.

"We are *not* safe!" he hissed, grabbing Kaleo's arm in a viselike grip. "Tell them to flee, tell the humans that they must leave before it comes back! Warn . . . warn the homeworld."

For a moment, Kaleo's personal concern was set aside, and McCoy heard a captain's manner beneath her next words. "Duchad, what happened out here? You must tell us."

The doctor's tricorder chimed insistently, and McCoy saw Duchad's biosigns spiking. He was close to losing consciousness, his body reacting to the shock of being plucked from deep space. "Kaleo—"

She waved away his warning. "Answer me," she insisted.

Duchad's eyes lost focus, and he was caught in a moment of terrible recall. "Rose from the dust, as a predator comes from the ocean deeps. Lashed out at us with chains of fire. It was a monstrous thing, Captain. And I swear on my tribe, it was *alive*. So vast. It should not . . . not have been able to move so fast. Could not see it, before it was too late . . ." He coughed and shook. "Warn them!" Duchad's eyes fluttered closed, and he sank into unconsciousness.

"I have to get him to our sickbay," McCoy demanded. "Kaleo, he could die here!"

His words got through to her, and the Syhaari gave a bleak nod. "Of course, Doctor. I will help you carry him." For her size, Kaleo was surprisingly strong, and she gathered up Duchad in her arms. "Lead the way."

"What was he talking about?" said Kyle as McCoy made for the door.

"Hopefully, we'll find out later rather than sooner," said Scotty.

But they had barely entered sickbay when the alert sirens started to sound, and McCoy realized that the engineer's estimate had been a vain hope.

"Curious," said Spock, unable to keep the fascination from his tone. "The object's mass shadow appears to be in some kind of flux state. As if it is able to deliberately destabilize its own elemental structure . . ."

"Back us off, Sulu," ordered the captain. "Keep a safe distance."

"What distance would constitute *safe*, sir?" asked Lieutenant Arex as the object emerged before them.

"The Delta Quadrant?" growled M'Ress, her suggestion only partly made in jest.

"Let's get a good look at it," Kirk ordered. "Standard magnification in viewer."

Suddenly the full scope of the object was revealed on the bridge's main screen, silencing them all.

A huge, pockmarked orb of dark umber rock, veined with dull rivers of what might be crystal, loomed ponderously over the *Enterprise*. Spock was reminded of a great sea creature seen through a clouded ocean as the vast planetoid slowly emerged from the wall of gray dust that surrounded the Sya system.

Crackles of bright lightning rippled over the surface of a thin, rudimentary atmospheric envelope around the object, flashing sharply where trailing streamers of matter from the gaseous dust cloud grazed its magnetic field. It was sheathed in a coruscating glitter of greens and blues, whips of excited molecules forming brief auroras that snaked back and forth along the lines of its poles. In terms of sheer mass, the object dwarfed the *Enterprise*, easily as large as many inhabited moons or asteroid colonies throughout the galaxy. Spock attempted to calculate the dimensions of the orb in his mind, but the way it moved and turned, almost as if it were under its own power, threw him off his estimates. This was something new and strange, but as with much that the science officer had encountered on his travels, something that might be dealt with.

The object pushed itself through the inner edges of the Veil, and for an instant, the play of light and energy haloing the planetoid seemed to suggest the presence of great tentacles of corposant, like the limbs of a cephalopod, folding and unfolding.

Spock heard Kirk mutter something low, under his breath—a fragment of half-remembered poetry the sight had brought to the captain's mind. "'Until the latter fire shall heat the deep; then once by man and angels to be seen . . .'"

"Alfred, Lord Tennyson," he recalled, his perfect memory pulling the name from his studies of Earth's ancient classical works. " 'The Kraken.' "

Kirk shook off the moment of introspection and pointed at the screen. "Analysis, Spock?"

"Doctor McCoy's suggestion that the object may be a rogue planet of some kind seems at first to be the most logical suggestion . . ." He paused, considering his next words. "But it exhibits behavior unlike any rogues I am aware of."

"A world thrown off from its own star system . . ." said Ensign Zyla. "I've heard of such things but never seen one before." He paused. "But wouldn't we have detected it on our approach from deep space?"

"An excellent question," Spock agreed. "I have already begun a search through our computer records to seek out that data. However, I believe we are dealing with something other than a planetoid that has been cast away from another sun to simply drift into this system."

Sulu was nodding in agreement. "A rogue wouldn't fade in and out on sensors. It wouldn't be able to disappear and reappear into dust clouds and subspace backscatter . . ."

"Surely you do not think it is some kind of *vessel*?" Arex's heavy brow furrowed. "Not possible! It exhibits no propulsive power. No identifiable form of instrumentality, no obvious defensive or offensive systems."

"Lieutenant," said Kirk, "if there's one thing you'll quickly learn being part of this crew, it's that the definition of what is possible is a lot broader than you might think." He turned in his chair toward the comm station where Uhura and M'Ress were studying the displays. "Are we getting anything?"

The human and the Caitian exchanged a look. "A lot of noise on many frequencies, Captain," began Uhura. "Nothing that resembles an ordered structure of transmission, like data or language . . . but we'll need to conduct a deeper analysis to be sure. "

"It all sounds like interference," M'Ress added. "Unusual, yes, but just what you would hear if you pointed the sensors at any geologically active space body."

"Is it possible that whatever attacked the Syhaari ranger ships is on the surface of that . . . *leviathan*?" Kirk gestured at the planetoid.

"Sensors are having difficulty returning a clean reading through the planetoid's atmosphere," said Sulu. "It's laced with highly charged particles and exotic radiation."

"We need to take a closer look, but I'm damned if I'll put this ship on top of that thing." The captain looked back at Spock. "I think it's time we launched that probe you suggested earlier."

"I concur," said the science officer. He had already taken the liberty of preparing such a unit and tapped out a command on his panel that released the small impulse-powered drone. "Probe is away."

Similar in mass to a standard photon torpedo casing, the probe was compact and swift, deploying a fan of passive and active scanning arrays as it dove into the rogue's gravity well. Immediately, new blocks of data were transmitted back to the *Enterprise*, adding more to the puzzle of the intruder object.

Spock nodded to himself. "Captain, one potential explanation occurs to me. It could be that the Syhaari ships were caught in an energy discharge from the . . . the leviathan's atmosphere. That might account for the 'attack' they suffered."

"You're suggesting it was a natural phenomenon?" said Kirk.

"It is a possibility I am considering, Captain." A spike in the sensor feedback broke the Vulcan's chain of thought. He glanced at his panel as Ensign Haines gave a shocked gasp.

"Energy build up!" she reported. "Directly in the path of the probe!"

Spock glimpsed a surge in ambient power levels in the area nearest the drone, and then a heartbeat later that power was suddenly transmuted into a violent discharge of energy. A blazing line of electrostatic force briefly connected the *Enterprise*'s probe with the turbulent atmosphere of the planetoid, acting like a fork of lightning in reverse—and the remote craft was instantly destroyed.

The science officer's eyebrow rose as the screens relaying data from the probe went dead. "I believe my initial hypothesis may have been premature."

Lieutenant Sulu studied his console with amazement. "Captain, the power of that energy strike . . . a discharge one-tenth of the output would have been enough to wreck the probe! It wasn't just destroyed . . . it was annihilated."

"Overkill," muttered Zyla, the Cygnian's pale face flushing pink.

"A reflexive defense reaction," Spock mused aloud. "Almost an autonomic response to a perceived intrusion."

"Commander, you're talking about that thing like it's an animal," said M'Ress.

"Indeed." The Vulcan gave a nod, exploring the thought.

"Fall back, but slowly," Kirk ordered. "Mister Arex, what's our shield status?"

"Operating at one hundred percent, sir," said the Triexian.

A warning tone swiftly brought Spock's attention back to his viewer, and he peered into the hooded scope. "Reading another surge of energy . . . now registering multiple sources of emission, converging on a single site."

"There!" Arex's center arm rose to point at the viewscreen.

A series of glowing streamers raced around the

curvature of the planetoid's surface from all points, coming together at a locus directly in line with the *Enterprise*. Visually, they resembled the same ghostly bands of aurora-like energy that ringed the object, each with a flashing nimbus of corrupted atmospheric particles surrounding it. The streams came together in a collision of forces that wove to form a ragged sphere of deadly potentiality.

"Forget slowly," Kirk amended, seeing the danger along with the rest of his crew. "Impulse power, full reverse, now!"

The object receded, but even with the sublight engines pushing them away, the starship's escape speed was too sluggish for comfort. Somewhere in the heart of that churning energy, a point of criticality was passed, and Spock called out another warning as the surge became a jagged spear of actinic lightning. It reached for the Starfleet ship like a grasping claw, the lethal electroplasma shock lashing up out of the turbulent atmosphere and through the vacuum.

Enterprise was in the pivot of a hard turn as Arex and Sulu tried to put the ship about and throw distance between them and the planetoid, but even in tandem the two officers were not fast enough to prevent the vessel taking a massive hit from the attack.

Spock grabbed the edge of his console with one hand, his other shooting out to snag Ensign Haines before the shock of the impact tossed the junior officer off her feet. He felt the bridge's gravity invert for one sickening moment as the ship's inertial compensators struggled to maintain some degree of stability.

The starship groaned as the twin forces of sheer kinetic power and overwhelming electrical energies slammed into the hull and raked down the length of the vessel. Breakers blew out in a chatter of explosive blasts, barking chugs of noise that sounded like old chemical-ballistic firearms. For one grim moment, the entire bridge was plunged into pitch darkness, a blackness so deep that not even Spock's superior Vulcan eyesight could pierce it. Then the lights flickered back to standby status, and he caught the scent of burned polymers and acrid smoke.

Ensign Haines gave Spock a grateful nod, and then to her credit, his subordinate went straight to the damage control station, bringing the console to active status.

"Report!" called the captain. In the deep crimson glow of the ship's emergency lighting, Kirk's face seemed pale and drawn.

"Still collating crew status," said Uhura.

Sulu was wrestling with his controls. "Course erratic. We've been knocked into a tumble . . . stabilizing."

"Shields are . . ." Arex faltered in the middle of his reply, and Spock heard the Triexian draw a tight breath. "Captain, our shields are *gone*."

"With *one* hit?" Ensign Zyla seemed unable to believe the evidence of his own sensors. "That thing blew down our deflectors with a single strike? What kind of monster are we facing?" The young man's voice was wavering close to the edge of panic, and Kirk gave him a hard look.

"To your post, mister," he said firmly. "Do your duty!"

Zyla blinked, and nodded weakly. "A-aye, sir . . ."

Kirk's attention returned to the navigator. "Arex, can you get the deflectors back?"

"Working on it," came the reply. "Captain, I do not have to tell you—"

"Another hit like that and we're done for," Kirk finished the lieutenant's sentence. "Sulu, get us the hell away from that object."

Spock studied the *Enterprise*'s damage-distorted power curves and knew what the helmsman would say next. "Warp engines are not responding to command inputs, sir."

"Heavy damage to both main propulsion units," reported Haines. "That hit fractured the primary intercoolers and caused major malfunctions in the flux chiller arrays . . ." She looked to Zyla, who gave another nod to confirm the ensign's statement.

"Object is turning," said Sulu. "Yes, confirmed. The planetoid is altering its course."

"It's coming after us," M'Ress said quietly.

"We'll discuss how that's actually possible when we get out of this," Kirk said. "Deflectors. Engines. Everything else is secondary." He glanced at Spock. "Options?"

Kirk's initial order—to vacate the immediate area as swiftly as was possible—was still the most ideal choice, and Spock reiterated that. But whatever was guiding the actions of the planetoid had another outcome in mind. For a third time, the strange ambient energy fluctuations in the object's upper atmosphere grew visible as they accumulated potential. This time, the science officer knew what to watch for in the traces from the sensors, but he feared the information might come too late to save the ship. Part of the Vulcan's mind closed itself off from the others, rapidly calculating the odds of survival for the four hundred plus souls making up *Enterprise*'s crew, should the order to abandon ship be given. The estimate was a sobering one; Spock's crewmates would most likely suffer the same fate as the pilot Duchad's less fortunate colleagues.

"Energy configuration is different this time," Spock noted. "Distributed, not collimated. Multiple points of discharge. Building to release in the next twenty seconds."

Kirk's hands tightened into fists. "Sound strategy. First it threw everything it had at us. When that didn't destroy us like it did with the probe, it changed the attack pattern."

"A scattershot approach?" offered Sulu.

"And I have an idea of how to deflect it." Kirk climbed out of the command chair. "A firebreak." He placed a hand on Sulu's shoulder. "Torpedo status?"

"Two birds in the tubes, Captain . . ." Spock never quite understood the human desire to name unlike devices after animal forms, but he refrained from commenting. "Weapons control appears to be active. Sir, I can fire those shots but after that, nothing. The loading system is nonoperational."

"Mister Sulu, we save those photons right now and we may not live to regret it." Kirk gave Spock a look, and the Vulcan returned a nod. The captain's plan, while crude, had the clear merit of being the most expedient. "Set warheads for timed fusing, full-force detonation, and put them between us and the object."

"Aye, sir." Sulu set to work, tapping out the settings.

"Time to next discharge?" Kirk turned back to his science officer.

"Imminent," Spock reported. "Captain, I must remind you that we are still without full warp drive capability."

"Foremost in my mind, Spock," Kirk replied.

"Here it comes!" shouted Zyla, eyes wide and fearful. "Look!"

On the screen, it appeared briefly that the planetoid had grown a forest of towering, shivering white trees, their branches reaching into the dark to blanket the space around the *Enterprise* with a mesh of electroplasma the starship would be unable to avoid.

Kirk gave the order. "Fire when ready, Sulu!"

The helmsman nodded once, and the twin thuds of the heavy antimatter warheads launching rumbled through the deck plates. Spock saw two white blobs streak away from beneath the starship's primary hull and, a moment later, blossom into a storm of fire.

Out in the vacuum, the staged detonation of the torpedoes threw up a wall of expanding energy that met the oncoming blasts from the planetoid in a collision of incredible forces. The captain's "firebreak" lit up the sky, reflecting off the inner surface of the Veil, brightly enough that observers on Syhaar Prime would see it through their telescopes several minutes hence.

Spock hoped that they would not soon after witness a second, brighter flash as the *Enterprise* went to a bleak fate.

"This ship has a charmed life," Kirk said, as if he were intuiting the Vulcan's thoughts. "And I'm about to prove that once again." He stabbed a button on the arm of his chair. "Scotty! I've played my aces up here. Tell me you can give me some speed."

The stress tonality in the chief engineer's reply was severe, Spock noted, but as ever Mister Scott proved himself up to the challenge. *"Aye, I can give you what you want, sir. But not for long. A short burst of acceleration, warp one and little better. Anything more than that, and we're wreckage."*

"I'll take it," said Kirk, switching to intraship address. "All hands, this is the captain. Look sharp and hold your stations. That is all." The order was a simple one, yet it seemed to have an immediate effect.

Curious, Spock thought, *how just a few words can stimulate the courage of others.* He kept his own logical evaluation of the situation to himself. In the next few moments, they would be alive and clear of the intruder's reach, or they would fail to escape and then nothing said or done would be of consequence.

"We're ready," Sulu announced.

Spock saw the telltale readings showing another buildup of power occurring in the mantle of the planetoid, but said nothing. He looked up as the helmsman turned the ship away, aiming it toward the core worlds of the Sya system.

"Go," said Kirk.

With a wounded, shuddering moan of tortured tritanium, the *Enterprise* threw itself beyond the speed of light—and fled.

Five

Kirk swallowed a mouthful of strong coffee and leaned forward in his chair as his first officer continued his report.

"Our present heading places us here," Spock was saying, indicating a tactical display on the briefing room's viewscreen. The image put a blinking dot of light close to the orbit of Hokaar, the barren outermost world of the Sya system. "The . . . leviathan appears to have reversed course and passed back into the Veil." A second dot illuminated in the band of fuzzy gray that denoted the dense dust cloud.

"How does a planetoid reverse course?" demanded McCoy, shaking his head. "I may have just barely passed my astrogeology elective at the Academy, but even I know that rocks the size of a moon don't wander back and forth like lost dogs!"

"Nothing about that object is by the book, Doctor," said Sulu, scowling. "I've never seen anything like it."

"That is not, in the strictest sense, correct," Spock went on. "This ship and this crew have encountered phenomena of similar scope in the past."

"Rogue planets?" said Kirk. "Once or twice, that's true. But this is unprecedented."

"Simply put, I do not believe an errant planetoid is what we are dealing with," Spock replied. He flicked a switch built into the surface of the briefing room's table. There was a media slot nearby, and he exchanged the data card plugged into it for another. The screen display became a complex series of sensor images, one overlaying the other. Each built a ghostly model of the leviathan, piece by piece. "I believe this object is a form of alien life."

"That's a bit of a reach for you, Spock," said McCoy with a snort. "Wild theories aren't exactly your strong suit!"

"Bones." Kirk silenced the doctor with a wave of his hand. "Let him talk."

Spock paused, and his captain knew that spoke volumes. McCoy was right, the Vulcan was not given to speculation, but the sparse data the *Enterprise*'s scanners had been able to fish from the sea of subspace interference did not lend itself to a definitive explanation. Kirk knew that on some level, that frustrated his taciturn first officer. "We have little to go on," Spock continued. "But given the behavior we have witnessed, I suggest that the object is a hitherto unknown variety of cosmozoan entity. A spaceborne creature of great mass and power."

"*A living planet*?" McCoy couldn't hide his surprise. "You're serious?"

Spock eyed him. "Have you ever known me to be otherwise, Doctor?"

"Of course . . ." Sulu nodded to himself, thinking it through. "Yes, I understand now. The commander is referring to life-forms like that gigantic amoeba we encountered in the Gamma 7A system."

"Correct," said Spock. "But distinct from that creature, this one appears to be based on a silicon chemistry. We all recall the Horta of Janus VI. I believe the leviathan is simply an expression of the same biotype, but writ larger."

"Much, much larger!" McCoy noted, his eyes widening as he processed the incredible notion. "Good grief . . . I take it back, Spock. Suddenly this doesn't seem like so wild an idea after all."

"And if we accept your hypothesis, we suddenly have a boatload of new questions," Kirk broke in, pinching the bridge of his nose in frustration. "For starters, is it native to this system? Why did it attack us and the Syhaari with such violence? And will it do so again?"

"From the fragmentary scans our sensors were able to capture, I can offer an answer to the first query," Spock replied. "The composition of the leviathan is dissimilar to any of the other planets in the Sya system. Therefore, I would suggest its origins lie elsewhere."

"That tallies with the information we have from our approach to the star system, sir," added Sulu. "On

Mister Spock's orders, I sifted all the nav records in our memory banks from the moment we made contact with the *Friendship Discovered* to the point we entered orbit of Syhaar Prime. If there had been an object of such mass and dimension as that rogue planet drifting around out there, *Enterprise* would have picked it up on our scopes. The mass displacement alone would have tripped the sensors."

"So it can either cloak itself somehow or move at great speed." McCoy shook his head. "Neither option is a good one. What the hell are we dealing with here?"

Spock went on, letting the doctor's question hang. "As for the reasons behind the object's attacks, I have only supposition at this time. It might be an instinctive territorial reaction, as it was with the Horta, or a feeding impulse as with the Gamma 7A creature. I will need to examine the data we have in greater detail in order to build up a more coherent picture, and that will take time." He hesitated. "There is one other factor of note. During our near-fatal encounter with it, Lieutenant Uhura reported the presence of unusual patterns of spatial distortion in close proximity to the object. With your permission, Captain, I would like her to assist me in my ongoing analysis."

"Granted," said Kirk, with a brisk nod. "Use whatever shipboard assets you require, Spock. This leviathan is a clear threat, and we need to understand it better."

"Do you . . ." Sulu halted, then began again. "I

mean, is it possible that it might be sentient, like the Horta?"

"We cannot rule that out at this stage," Spock noted. "But until it emerges from the dust cloud once again, we have no way to observe its actions to determine one way or another."

"How does that Tennyson poem go?" Kirk drew up the words. " 'Below the thunders of the upper deep, far, far beneath in the abysmal sea, his ancient, dreamless, uninvaded sleep . . .' "

Spock nodded. "But it appears, Captain, that someone or something has awakened it."

"We weren't ready for it, and we damn near lost the ship," Kirk went on, his jaw hardening. "If we cross paths with the leviathan again, we need to be prepared. I want solutions for any future encounter. Best- and worst-case scenarios."

"A combat response?" asked Sulu.

"That's as good a place as any to start."

"Is that realistic, Jim?" McCoy gave him a questioning glance. "If we don't know what it is, can we really advocate—"

"Killing it?" Kirk returned a hard-eyed look. "I don't need to tell you how many casualties that thing has inflicted on our ship and to the Syhaari."

The doctor nodded warily. "True. I have a dozen crewmen in sickbay with various injuries suffered during the attack. Not to mention Kaleo's friend Duchad. But we can't just respond in kind."

"You know me better than that," Kirk replied. "But I need to have that option, Bones, even if I don't use it." Before McCoy could say more, he changed tack. "Tell me about our survivor. Is he going to pull through?"

"It was touch and go for a while," McCoy admitted, "but M'Benga and I managed to haul Duchad back from the brink. It helped having Kaleo on board. They have compatible blood types. She saved his life."

"Can I talk to him?"

"Not yet. He's still unconscious, and I don't want to mess around with the normal Syhaari healing process. It could be a couple of days."

"With the damage to the warp engines, it'll take us at least that long to get back to the inner planets," noted Sulu.

Kirk drew himself up. "I'll talk to Scotty and see if I can't get him to work one of his miracles for us." He nodded to the other men, signaling that the meeting was over. "Dismissed."

Sulu and Spock stood up and departed, but Kirk noticed McCoy's obvious hesitation. "You have something else you want to say?"

"Plenty," McCoy said with feeling. "Just when I think I've seen it all, we run smack-dab into something else that's not in any of the files. But that's not what's bothering me."

Kirk eyed him. "Spit it out, Bones."

"There's no doubt in my mind that Captain Kaleo is as honest as the day is long," he began. "I could tell when she was talking to Chapel. This is all as much a shock to her as it was to us."

"*But* . . . ?"

"But those others we met . . . Gatag, Tormid, Hoyga . . . call it a gut feeling if you want, but I don't trust them."

Kirk didn't want to admit that he shared some of that sense too. "I'll admit Tormid comes off like a blowhard . . . but there's a long road between that and, what? Some connection to what happened out here?"

"I'm not making accusations, Jim, I'm just saying . . ." McCoy turned and walked away. "Don't take anything at face value. Not until we get a better handle on all this."

———

Scott stood there in the center of main engineering and listened to Captain Kirk's précis of Mister Spock's initial analysis, halting his commander now and then to bark out orders to his subordinates as they raced back and forth around them.

The odor of smoke still hung in the air where the environmental system had broken down, and on the upper gantry of the systems bay, a black smear of soot showed where a short-circuited auxiliary console had gone up like a bomb. Lieutenant Masood had taken the brunt of the blast and even now was clinging to life in a medical support capsule under Nurse Chapel's expert care. Scott did his best to keep an open mind as Kirk talked to him about *living planetoids* and half-cooked theories from the first officer, all the time thinking of the wringer his team, his engines, and his vessel had been put through.

"Sometimes, sir," he said, after Kirk finished, "I think this ship is a magnet for everything strange the universe has to throw at us."

"I don't disagree, Scotty," the captain said wearily. "Some of the logs I've submitted back to the records office at Starfleet Command, they message me back asking if it's a joke or if my crew have been . . ." He tilted his wrist, miming a cup-and-drinking action. "But this is deadly serious."

Scott nodded, thinking again about Masood. "That it is. The ship took a hard cross, there's no mistaking that. My people are shoring up structural damage on every deck from the keel to the bridge. We've got most of the main systems running at seventy percent capacity, but the engines . . ." He trailed off, sighing. "Well, sir. I could give you chapter and verse on the technical details, but the long and the short of it is, we're hobbled. At best, we can make a cruising speed of warp one point seven, maybe warp two with a following wind. Anything faster than that, and we risk a catastrophic overload." He gave a humorless chuckle. "For now, we're reduced to riding in the slow lane along with the Syhaari rangers and explorers."

"How long until you can get us back to fully operational status?"

"Three days, I reckon. That's if we don't take any more damage." He threw a glance at the warp core, pulsing flame-orange beyond the safety grid at the back of the compartment. "And then we'll need some dock time at a starbase to top and tail her."

"We can't leave yet," Kirk told him. "Not until we understand what we ran afoul of out here. If there's a threat to the Syhaari, it could be a threat to the Federation as well. For their sake and ours, we need to know."

"Captain, if we go up against that big beastie again, if that's what it really is, we may not come off best. Can we not call for some help, sir? Another Starfleet ship, maybe?" He paused, considering his own question. "The *Altair* is on patrol out here, is it not?"

Kirk nodded. "Not close enough to help us, though. I know *Altair*'s captain and chief medical officer, Adams and Ostrow. But they're clear across the sector, Scotty. More than a week away, even at high warp. Like it or not, we're on our own here. So do what you can, and keep me apprised."

Before the captain turned to walk away, Scotty cleared his throat. "Sir? Before you go, there's something else."

"Go on." Kirk frowned as Scott stepped closer.

The engineer's voice took on a conspiratorial pitch. "I didn't think it was worth raising the issue beforehand, but with the way things are progressing, I think you should have all the information."

"You're talking about the sensor scans of the Syhaari ships?"

He sighed. "I know that Envoy Xuur would probably tear us off a strip for doing it, but I made sure it was nothing invasive." Scott couldn't stop himself from sounding defensive.

Kirk studied him. "So. You found something unusual."

"*Confusing* is the word I'd use," the engineer admitted. "I checked the records of the scans we had of Kaleo's vessel from the first time we met her people, and they more or less match up to the configurations of the slower patrol ships we saw at the edge of the Veil, the ones the beastie took apart. Power distribution curves, energy output, warp signature, all within a similar range."

Kirk anticipated where he was going. "But the new ship, the warp three ship . . . that was different?"

"To put it mildly." Scott jerked a thumb at the *Enterprise*'s drive system. "I mean, a warp engine is like a wheel, Captain. Strip away everything, and the basic structure of the device is the same, no matter where it was made." The laws of physics made the theory and design of warp drives relatively constant, and almost every spacefaring civilization that had mastered faster-than-light travel had discovered the same basic truths about the technology. "With a few exceptions, any starship engineer worth their salt could find the similarities," he explained. "But in the differences, aye, that's where the interesting bit is."

"What are you getting at, Scotty?"

"The warp one and warp three ships flown by the Syhaari use two very different engine matrix designs. I mean *totally* different. I can't imagine how someone starting from the same theoretical model could have come up with two approaches so far apart. I'm wondering what they've got under the bonnet over there, sir."

"The scientist, Tormid . . ." said Kirk. "He told us that he'd had some kind of eureka moment on his trip back to Syhaar Prime. A 'unique insight' is how he described it, I think."

"I'm not saying it's impossible, Captain," Scott replied. "But in all the years of having my head stuck inside warp drives, I've never known the like. Space/Warp theory isn't the kind of thing you advance overnight. It takes generations, sometimes centuries, to perfect."

Kirk gave a slow nod. "I know where you're going with this, Scotty, and you can forget it. There's no way the Syhaari would let you crawl around in one of their engine rooms, and if we light up one of their ships with an active sensor sweep, you can bet we'd have a diplomatic incident on our hands as quick as Xuur can shout foul."

"I'm just calling it as I see it, sir." Scott opened his hands. "I could be barking up the wrong tree. Perhaps I'm seeing something that isn't there and this Tormid fella is the genius they say he is."

"Tormid certainly thinks so," Kirk offered. "And I'll admit, I'm nursing some reservations of my own. But for now, this is of secondary importance to our current situation. I need you to concentrate on getting the *Enterprise* back up and running."

"Understood," said Scott. "And . . . what about monitoring the alien ships?"

"I didn't say anything about stopping that." Kirk smiled thinly. "Keep an eye on them, but be discreet about it." He stepped away, then halted, turning back briefly to face the engineer. "And if you come across anything else you happen to think is *confusing* or *interesting*, you tell me straightaway."

"Aye, sir," Scott promised. "That I will."

———

Spock looked up as the doors to the sensor lab opened, and Lieutenant Uhura entered. She gave him a smile, which of course he did not return, and the Vulcan launched directly into his briefing.

"For the duration of this detail, you are transferred from your duty as senior communications officer and will report directly to me."

Uhura accepted this with a nod. "M'Ress can handle my station on the bridge. But what's so important that it needs a hundred percent of my attention, sir?"

"Observe." Spock crossed the compartment to a tall, narrow screen, stepping around a data stack filled with processor modules. The sensor lab was something of an afterthought in the *Enterprise*'s design, squeezed into what had once been a mechanical space for fabricator units, now repurposed after a minor refit at Starbase 6. It was cramped, and in Spock's opinion, not ideal for its intended function, but the alternative would have been to reconfigure a larger lab on one of the upper decks—and that would have taken time the captain did not want to waste.

Spock activated the screen, bringing up panels of data from the sensors and, in particular, the anomalous spatial distortions Uhura had discovered.

"Ah," she said, nodding again. "I've been thinking about these too, sir. The patterns don't fit easily into the category of random noise or manufactured signal. Frankly, I'm not sure what I trapped there."

"We will endeavor to find out," Spock replied. "Your expertise in the field of subspace dynamics will be key to understanding these patterns of energy."

"I'll do my best." Uhura stepped past him to get a closer look at the screen, and Spock automatically drew back. She gave him an odd look. "Pardon me,

Commander. I didn't mean to invade your personal space." The lieutenant glanced at the walls. "It's a little snug in here, isn't it?"

"I would prefer a less-confined area in which to work."

She smiled briefly, and Spock caught a glimpse of some very human amusement in her eyes, there and then gone. "Don't worry, sir, I'm no stranger to tight quarters. For a few years my parents and I shared a house in Nairobi with my uncle and his family. His very *large* family."

"Vulcan family units prefer solitude and tranquility," he noted.

"So do I, Mister Spock. And I probably appreciate it more than you do." Uhura studied the display, returning to the issue at hand. "The patterns . . . you believe they're connected to the leviathan's behavior?"

Spock studied her. "I see that the captain's colloquial term for the object has already become embedded among the crew." He nodded. "To answer your question, yes. At this stage, we have only theoretical models to work from, but the regularity of these impulses cannot be ignored."

"If it is a living being . . ." Uhura said the words and trailed off, considering the enormity of the concept. "Just the thought of that is staggering in and of itself . . . but if the leviathan is more than just a rogue planetoid, could the spatial distortions be part of its physiology? The beating of its heart, even?"

There was something in the human woman's voice that gave Spock a moment's pause. *An instant of wonderment*, he thought. Even though Lieutenant Uhura had been on the bridge when the object had attacked the *Enterprise*, and even though she had seen the terrible destruction it had apparently wrought upon the Syhaari patrol ships, she had not judged the lifeform—if it was one—for its actions. Even with half his nature drawn from a human mother, Spock could still be surprised by the human ability to show compassion and empathy to something so alien to their experience.

"If we are able," Spock told her, "we will find the answer to that question and to many others, Lieutenant."

She smiled again. "Then let's get started, Commander."

———

The captain entered sickbay and found Nurse Chapel preparing a series of hypospray doses for distribution among her patients. "Sir," she said, straightening to attention, but Kirk waved that away, letting her return to her work.

"Where's Doctor McCoy?"

"In the operating room with Doctor M'Benga. Ron . . . I mean, Lieutenant Erikson . . . He suffered a seizure, a delayed effect from his injuries. They're working on him now, trying to stabilize him."

Kirk frowned. "What are his chances, Christine?"

Chapel's expression became a merging of professional kindness and sad honesty. "Not good, Captain. But if anyone can help him, they can."

Kirk looked past the nurse and into one of the recovery rooms across the corridor from the main intensive care unit. "What about your Syhaari patient?"

She brightened a little. "They're a robust people, sir. Thanks to a blood transfusion, we managed to keep Duchad with us. He's still out, though."

"It's all right," he told her. "It's Kaleo I wanted to speak with." Kirk dismissed the nurse with a nod and crossed to the occupied recovery room. The door was open, and inside the little cabin lit with a dim night-cycle glow, he saw the tall Syhaari female sitting awkwardly in a human-scale chair. Her attention was wholly on Duchad, lying on a biobed beneath a monitor that quietly chimed the tones of his heart.

Still, she must have sensed his approach. "Kirk," began Kaleo, without looking up. "How is your ship?"

She spoke quietly, and he found himself doing the same. "Still here. Just barely, though."

"You saw it, then?" Kaleo didn't look up. "This predator that Duchad spoke of?"

"Damn near tore us apart," he admitted, and with as much detachment as he could muster, Kirk gave her the high points of their encounter with the leviathan.

Kaleo kept silent through the explanation, and when he was done, she hung her head. "I was always afraid that something like this might happen," she said. "Some of us, we Syhaari, are given to moments of morbid introspection." The captain gave a bitter chug of dry amusement. "It is more a thing for melancholy poets and the like, but I occasionally succumb. I think the worst, that there is some cosmic equilibrium upset out here. We met you, Kirk. Strangers, but good people. And I know there are those in the galaxy who would do us harm. In my darker moments, I kept waiting for the balance to be righted. For the good to be counterbalanced with the bad." She sighed. "And so it has."

"You're not to blame for this," Kirk told her, but a part of him was wondering, *Is she?*

Kaleo looked him in the eyes for the first time since he had entered the room, and even over the gulf of species between them, he could see true sorrow there. "Will you grant me access to your subspace communications, Captain? I must report what you have told me to the members of the Learned Assembly."

"I'll see to it. Lieutenant M'Ress can assist you. My first officer has already prepared a data packet containing all the information we were able to glean about the object."

She gave a broad-shouldered shrug. "I regret you and your people were exposed to this danger, Captain Kirk."

"I offered to help, remember?" he replied. "Things might have gone very differently if your star-rangers had come out here instead." That seemed to strike a chord with her, and Kaleo's gaze went back to her comatose comrade.

Against his better judgment, Kirk made a decision to try and use the opportunity to gain some insight into his opposite number. Part of him disliked the idea of pressing Kaleo in a moment when she was clearly troubled, but a colder aspect warned him that there were already too many unknowns circling around them.

"You said you trained with Duchad. Was he another commander, like you and Tormid?"

"Yes, but of a lower grade." Kaleo absently touched the woven thread in her hair, along which were strung the tiny charm-like beads denoting her rank and status. Kirk saw a distinctive sapphire orb there that Tormid had also displayed. "He was disappointed that the Learned Assembly did not choose him to captain one of the ships sent beyond the Great Veil."

Kirk saw an opening and took it. "You think he would have made a better choice than Tormid?"

"Tormid's command was given to him as much for political capital as it was for his experience. He is an accomplished pilot and scientist, that is not in doubt. But I cannot help but wonder if someone like Duchad would have brought back more of *The Searcher Unbound*'s crew alive." She paused, her wide face creasing in a frown. "Dismiss my words. I speak out of turn."

He took the other seat across from the biobed. "You're free to say what you want to me, Kaleo. We both know what it's like to face death out here." He motioned at the walls, but his gesture took in the void of space beyond. "To have other lives balancing on each order we give."

"It is a great weight, yes?" she agreed. "Sometimes, it lifts off your neck long enough for you to raise your head and be the first to see something incredible . . . but it soon settles once more."

"Would you give it up?"

"Never." Kaleo showed her teeth in a brief grin. "Would *you*?"

"Not in a million years."

"I wonder if Tormid would say the same." Kaleo came forward as Duchad gasped and turned slightly on the bed. She used a damp cloth to moisten his dry lips, and the injured man settled back into silence. "He was swift to surrender his ship for a vessel more suited to his temperament . . . the Assembly. I always expected him to end up there, but perhaps not quite as quickly as it occurred. Tormid and I . . ." She halted, framing her words. "I suppose you could say we were rivals, of a sort. In the early years of the explorer missions to the outer planets, our ships vied for the Assembly's favor. I used that rivalry to challenge Zond and my crew to travel farther and learn more . . . but for the joy of it, Kirk. You understand? For our species, not because we wished to be storied."

"Glory is fleeting," he agreed. "But knowledge . . . that lasts forever."

"And now Tormid is rich with both. His discoveries have made him the most widely known face on all the Syhaari worlds, and the works of those who allowed him to venture into space have been all but eclipsed, forgotten. My people can be very entranced by the glimmer of the new, Captain. We are sometimes too swift to overlook the long road taken to find it."

There was a question Kirk had been considering for some time, and he put it to her. "Why did your people wait so long to leave your homeworld? In almost every sentient species the Federation has encountered, there were always some reaching for the stars long before they even had the means."

Kaleo spread her long-fingered hands. "What stars, Kirk? You've seen our skies, the shroud that the Veil put between us and the rest of the universe. Stand anywhere on Syhaar Prime's nightside, and you will observe a blanket of shadows that does not beckon. It is not stirring to the soul to look up, do you see? I can only imagine what it must have been like for you, on your Earth, to stare at the heavens and see into the infinite."

"You didn't think there was more out there?" He struggled to grasp the mindset that Kaleo hinted at, and for a moment Kirk remembered lying on his back in an Iowa cornfield in the depths of night. Just a boy, but his heart already captured by the thought of worlds and stars beyond his own. He felt a pang of sorrow for the Syhaari for never having known that.

"The Veil kept us safe, but it also hid much from us. Our nonoptical telescopes saw only faint traces beyond it, things that hinted at great danger. Our civilization had grown up believing we were the only sentients in existence. Some thought that what lay outside the Veil were the ashes of a dead universe and that we alone had been preserved by a higher power. Others thought it was a punishment for our sins, that we were locked away for the misdeeds of our progenitors. I knew the only way to know for sure was to go and take a look."

"I can't imagine what it must have been like for you," Kirk admitted. "Being there on the bridge of your ship. Passing through the Veil and seeing the universe for the very first time."

"It was my honor," she told him, her voice thick with emotion. "And I want to make sure the meaning of that moment is never lost. It goes beyond politics and temporal issues. You understand." Kaleo pointed at him. "You have seen things of such scope, Kirk. You have stood where I stood that day."

"In a way," he agreed.

And then she pointed at Duchad. "Your kind have been doing this for centuries. Tell me, is this the price of it? Brothers and sisters sacrificed for knowledge? Agents of the unknown, motivated by alien impulses, threatening our lives? Were we naïve to think that we could reach out from our home to touch those distant stars and not be burned by them?"

"I would be lying to you if I didn't say there's a cost to every new frontier we cross." Kirk's lip curled in a sympathetic half smile. "A few years ago, my crew and I found ourselves facing a dilemma of similar dimensions. A chance to gain great knowledge through contact with an incredibly advanced alien species. The dangers were equally great." He met her gaze. "I'll tell you now what I told my people then, what I still consider to be true. *Risk is our business*, Kaleo. That's why we're out here. And I believe you feel the same way."

"For one so hairless, you are very perceptive," said the other captain. "And yes, *I* am ready to take that risk. But I will not put my people and my homeworld in harm's way. Some will say this leviathan has come because we dared to go where no Syhaari has gone before. I have to know if they are right."

At length, Kirk gave a solemn nod. "We'll help you." He got up. "I'll have M'Ress pipe a subspace channel down here, you can speak to your people from this room."

As he approached the door, Kaleo took his hand to halt him. "Why are you doing this, Kirk? You owe us nothing. You could simply put us off your ship and be on your way, out of any potential danger."

"If our circumstances were reversed, is that what you would do?"

"No."

"Then you already know the reason why."

Six

The turbolift deposited Leonard McCoy on the bridge and he stepped out, advancing on the captain, finding Kirk in the middle of a conversation with Sulu and the Syhaari woman, Kaleo. "What's this about?" he demanded before anyone else could speak. He had been in the *Enterprise*'s operating theater for hours, struggling to make sure that Ron Erikson would live to see another day, and fatigue was fraying his temper.

Kirk saw right through that in an instant. "Bones, when did you sleep last?"

"That's your question?" he retorted. "I can never tell what time of day it is on these damn ships." The fact was McCoy had been about to take a shift in his quarters, crash out, and let himself rest, but the captain's summons to the bridge trumped that. He folded his arms across his blue duty tunic and eyed his friend and commander. "Never mind that. What's so important you've got me running up here?"

"Forgive me, Doctor," said Kaleo. "I asked Captain Kirk to bring you in. I wanted you present to address any medical questions." She sighed, and McCoy felt a little churlish as he saw the mirror of his own fatigue in her. This was the first time he had seen Kaleo away from Duchad's side since the man had been brought aboard, and if she had slept or eaten in all that time, he hadn't noticed her doing so.

"Questions from who?"

"We're about to find out," said Kirk.

At the communications console, Lieutenant M'Ress plucked the comm unit from her arched ear and spoke up. "Incoming signal. I've patched in our subspace arrays to boost the power and reduce lag time, sir."

Kirk nodded toward the main viewer. "On-screen," he said, by way of answer.

The display wavered, a picture of the gray void of Syhaari space re-forming into something McCoy recognized as the Great Hall, where they had sat down to the unusual feast. It had been less than a day ago, but it felt like months had passed since then.

Tormid entered the range of the imager at the other end of the transmission, and he gave them a stern glare. "*Captain Kirk. Where is your vessel now?*"

McCoy shot his commanding officer a look. Tormid clearly wasn't one to waste time on the niceties, but then, James T. Kirk could play the same tune when he needed to.

"We are inside the orbital track of the gas giant Yedeen, on a return course to Syhaar Prime. We estimate—"

Tormid didn't let him finish. *"You will alter your heading,"* he said firmly. *"Bring your ship about and make for Sya III, the planet we call Gadmuur. I will meet you there."*

McCoy recalled what he could about the third planet from the initial mission briefing. Gadmuur had once been a lot like Mars in the Sol system, but where humankind had set to work terraforming the red planet to make its environment habitable, the Syhaari had turned their Mars equivalent into a manufacturing colony. For all intents and purposes, it was a factory world to which the majority of Syhaar Prime's heavy industry had been outsourced.

"Why?" said Kaleo. "The Assembly—"

"They agree with me," Tormid broke in again, and McCoy scowled at the being's seeming inability to let anyone end a sentence. *"In light of the visuals you sent us from the outer system and the report that accompanied it, I put it to the elders that our best response is one of strength and speed. Your people require your presence, Kaleo. And you, Captain Kirk . . . we must have every fraction of data you have on the monstrosity."*

Kaleo glanced at Kirk and McCoy. "Gadmuur is home to our primary orbital shipyards and supply stations," she explained. "It is the main base for our space fleet."

"I have instigated a mass recall of all our vessels," Tormid went on. *"The authority for this was granted to me in the wake of the attack. Even as we speak, every*

ranger and explorer is converging on the docks to take on weapons and supplies. As of this day, our civilization is on a war footing."

Kirk took this in, but didn't press the point right away. "Tormid, where are Envoys Xuur and ch'Sellor? I'd like to speak with them, if I may."

"They are currently being transferred to my command ship by shuttlecraft, and they will be repatriated to your care when we rendezvous at Gadmuur." He paused, anticipating Kirk's next request. *"Given the seriousness of this situation, extraneous use of communications will not be permitted outside of signals sanctioned by the Learned Assembly."*

In other words, thought McCoy, *no, we can't talk to them.*

The captain sat back in his chair. "Sir, let me be direct. What are your intentions at this time?"

"I will not address details of operational deployments on an open channel. But the only sensible response is the obvious one, Kirk. Retaliation in kind, with the full force of our military."

McCoy's lip curled. "With all due respect," he began, meaning none of that, "your military have already taken a heavy hit out here. You might want to think twice about repeating that on a larger scale."

"My chief medical officer is correct," Kirk added. "We rescued just one single survivor from your people's first encounter with the leviathan. And we barely escaped destruction ourselves."

"*Yes, Captain Duchad . . .*" Tormid seemed to ignore the comment about the *Enterprise*'s near-fatal engagement with the intruder. "*He lives, then?*"

"He does," McCoy confirmed. "The man was lucky."

"*The Assembly will require Duchad for a thorough debriefing,*" Tormid went on. "*You also, Kaleo.*"

"I can't guarantee Duchad will be well enough for anything," insisted the doctor.

"*Your responsibility for him ends when you arrive in orbit around Gadmuur,*" Tormid said tersely. "*Duchad will follow his orders. As will Captain Kaleo.*"

"As the Gathering calls," she replied, tight-lipped. "But I must question."

Tormid glowered down at her from the screen. "*As you always do. Speak, then. It is a right you have earned.*"

"Your reasoning is flawed, Tormid. You are reacting without full balance of the facts. We have to consider all aspects of this situation before we commit our entire fleet!"

"*What is it you think we have been doing since you sent us your terrifying message? You inform us of an alien invasion, a threat of such scope that the Syhaari have never before encountered. And now you seek to counsel for restraint?*" He eyed Kirk and McCoy. "*What have these offworlders said to you?*"

"Nothing," she insisted. "My concerns are my own! I simply do not wish to see us rush into danger."

"The Assembly does not agree," replied the other Syhaari, and McCoy wondered how much of that was being driven by Tormid's force of personality. *"Our brothers and sisters are ash and bones, and we cannot let their deaths lead to more of the same."*

"I know what they are!" Kaleo growled, her temper rising. "I saw the ruins of our ships, Tormid, with my own eyes!"

"Then you know we must strike back as forcefully as possible!" Tormid matched her tone.

McCoy could sense that Kirk was biting his tongue, reluctant to get in the middle of what was a Syhaari issue. But with his ill mood, the doctor didn't feel the need for any such reserve and made it clear. "You do understand, sir, that the object of your fury is more than just some random astronomical occurrence? We are very likely talking about a unique life-form here, a living being with the same right to exist as the rest of us! It may have hurt your people just as it did ours, but we can't destroy it until we know what it truly is!"

"Kirk, your officer speaks out of turn," said Tormid, ignoring McCoy. *"And he offers only suppositions and vague possibilities. I am dealing in facts. And this 'leviathan,' as you dub it, is a clear threat. That fact is not in question. The matter of its nature, alive or not, self-aware or not, is pure conjecture!"*

The captain's eyes narrowed. He wasn't about to be lectured on the bridge of his own vessel. "However forthright Doctor McCoy may be," he replied, "his statement stands. The Federation cannot condone the kind of unilateral action you're proposing."

"Fortunate, then, that we are not in your Federation," Tormid replied. *"Go to Gadmuur, and make haste. If you do not arrive before the fleet deploys against the intruder, we shall not wait for you."* The signal cut with a crackle of static, and the image faded.

———

Uhura watched as the computer-generated image on the screen seemed to come apart, layer by layer. The rendition of the alien sphere transformed into a series of exploded elements, each drawing away from the others, until the display was some great three-dimensional jigsaw puzzle. She extended a slender finger and pointed into the heart of the image.

"Mister Spock, am I right in thinking that these veins of mineral are crystalline in nature?"

"Correct," said the first officer, standing close by at one of the lab's input consoles. "A type four isotope of dilithium, to be precise."

"It couldn't be anything other than that," she said to herself. "The dispersal pattern of these veins is remarkable. It's so even. I don't have to be a geologist to know that's not how these things usually occur." Uhura traced lines of the crystal around the circumference of the opened sphere. "And the latent energy detected by the sensors? It's collected in these subsurface structures?"

"A great amount, but not all," Spock noted, and he highlighted several large vault-like caverns. "The deeper layers of the object exhibit many of these underground chambers, each filled with a chemical sea of electroactive elements. I believe they may function as a kind of colossal liquid battery."

"So, it can channel raw natural energy into these dilithium concentrations at will?" Uhura's eyes widened at the thought, and she followed it to its conclusion. "That means, if it is capable of doing that with any degree of control . . ."

"The leviathan may possess a naturally occurring variety of warp drive." Spock seemed to lose himself in the possibility. "Fascinating."

"That would account for why we didn't detect it on our approach," said Uhura. "It wasn't in range of our sensors at the time. It warped here on its own!"

"Very possible, Lieutenant. It may have been dismissed as an inert planetoid on the extreme edge of scanner range."

She took a step back, folding her arms. "All right. We have a working theory as to how it got here. Now we need to build an understanding of why it reacted as it did."

"And there, the question becomes problematic," Spock admitted. "Extrapolating our theoretical model from the closest extant example of a silicon-based life-form in our data banks—"

"The Horta?"

He nodded. "There are a number of key physio-logical similarities, but our estimations of a behavioral structure are incomplete. According to my conjecture, this creature should be highly unlikely to behave in an adversarial and intrusive manner."

Uhura frowned. "But the Horta was capable of violence, sir. It attacked mine workers in the tunnels of Janus VI."

"Agreed, but only in the most extreme situation, when it believed its nest and its eggs were under threat. We have seen nothing to indicate the Syhaari or the presence of the *Enterprise* pose a similar threat to the leviathan. On both occasions, it attacked without apparent provocation. In addition, it appears to have come to this star system specifically to do so."

"It came looking for a fight?"

Spock raised an eyebrow. "An overly colloquial, if accurate, analysis, Lieutenant. And therein lies the issue. While the leviathan is dangerous in one sense, simply because it possesses great mass, I find it hard to characterize it as a predatory organism. I would hy-pothesize that such a life-form would exist more like the extinct whales of your planet. It seems more suited to a life cycle of cruising peacefully through the outer reaches of nebulae, most likely sifting interstellar dust for sustenance."

"And we are close to that protostar nursery, relatively speaking," Uhura noted. "If that's where it originated, why did it cross open space to get here?

Not to feed? It would have more than enough to eat at home."

The Vulcan highlighted a different section of the alien orb, a fuzzy rendering of what could be determined of the leviathan's core. "The composite structure of the being, the lattice of crystal and rocklike materials. It has a much greater degree of flexibility than a normal planetoid's crust. A strong gravity well would exert a powerful deleterious effect on its physiology."

"You mean . . . cause it pain?"

"Indeed. In fact, I would posit that close proximity to a planet or a main-sequence star would distress the leviathan greatly. It is evolved for life in extrasolar space. All the more reason why this close approach to the Sya system is highly unusual."

They both fell silent for a long moment before Uhura spoke again, dismay in her tone. "Mister Spock, the deeper we look into this, the less answers we have and the more questions we find."

"It would seem so." He examined a data slate. "There is clearly more to this conundrum than we know. But until we can gather additional data on the object, we can only continue to speculate on the leviathan's motivations."

Uhura nodded, frowning at her own lack of results. She went back to the console she had been using to analyze the spatial-distortion patterns, this time displaying them in a different context, hoping to find something in them she had missed the first time around. "If it is like the Horta," she ventured, "do you think we could communicate with it?"

Spock paused. "In that instance, I was able to make direct mental contact with the mind of another being." He shook his head. "At the end of my most recent duty shift, I entered a meditative state in my quarters and attempted to reach out with a telepathic probe. I sensed no such centralized intellect in the leviathan. It is likely a creature of pure, animal instinct."

"Maybe this one is a true rogue, then," said Uhura. "A man-eater." The Vulcan gave her a questioning look, and she went on. "When I was a child, my uncle would always get into trouble with my aunt for telling us scary stories about the lions of Kenya. He'd spin tales about the rogues that would split off from the pride and come chasing after humans instead of wildebeest or zebra, even if it meant risking death at the hands of hunters."

"A cogent parallel, Lieutenant," Spock agreed. "Such aberrant actions in animals occur because of starvation, old age, or infection. We may be observing something similar here."

"Well, I just hope . . ." Uhura's words faded on her lips. Suddenly, all she could see, all she could think about, was the pattern moving on the screen in front of her. She couldn't explain it; somehow, the act of replaying the data anew had triggered a flash of insight. She saw something there she hadn't seen the first time around, and quickly Uhura ran the simulation again to make sure it wasn't a mistake.

"Lieutenant?" Spock noticed her change of manner. "Is something wrong?"

The thought, still half-formed, spilled out of her. "The spatial distortions. What if we have been looking at them all wrong? You and I, we approached the data thinking this was some kind of random side effect of the leviathan's internal energy matrix, a waste product of its life cycle. Like an exhaled breath or surplus body heat. What if it isn't that at all?"

"You are suggesting the distortions are *not* a random consequence? I am intrigued. Go on." Spock watched her expectantly.

Uhura migrated the display on her tri-screen to the viewscreen. She assembled a matrix of patterns, one building on the next, and slowly but surely, something resembling a coherent signal began to emerge. Buried in the middle of the data was a regular pattern that appeared to repeat itself at a steady interval. "I was wrong before, I don't think we've caught the sound of some alien heartbeat here. Sir, I think these patterns may be deliberately generated." Her breath caught in her throat. "Mister Spock, this could even be a message being broadcast from the leviathan itself!"

The Vulcan eyed the screen coldly. "This may also be an artifact of the sensor relays. Ghost echoes rebounding off the Veil. Perhaps even trace signals from the wreckage of the Syhaari patrol ships. I would urge caution."

Uhura matched his gaze. "With all due respect, Commander, if this thing is still out there, and still hunting, do we have that luxury?"

When the *Enterprise* finally limped into a wide orbit around the third planet of the Sya system, her crew was greeted with a sky full of silver darts and long, skeletal-frame orbital platforms. Above the craggy, rust-red world, vessels of every tonnage were resting at anchor in mustering zones or chained out in long lines as they took turns docking at supply stations and work yards. Glitters of bright laser light flashed here and there where many of the craft were receiving last-minute refits, as weapons pods were welded to hardpoints.

Beneath the lone Starfleet ship, Gadmuur's orbital space resembled a quiver of arrows ranged together in anticipation of bloody battle. The stark import of that image lodged in James Kirk's thoughts as he materialized in the command atrium of the primary star dock. Kirk had seen preparations for war in other places and at other times, and he knew that only death could follow them.

At his side, Kaleo tensed as she took in the room. Everywhere they looked, Syhaari were moving back and forth with grave focus, each crew member doubtless engaged in some element of the military operation to come. The tension of the moment, silent and invisible, was palpable.

"Look sharp," said the captain from the side of his mouth, gaining a nod in return from Lieutenant Sulu. Along with his subordinate officer and the Syhaari captain, the rest of Kirk's landing party comprised three security personnel, each of whom visibly wore a type-2 phaser on their hips and a hawkish cast to their faces. *If the Assembly see that as an insult,* he told himself, *then let them.* The captain of the *Enterprise* deemed the situation too fluid to take more risks than he needed to.

"Sir," said Sulu, with a nod of the head. "Here they are."

Kirk turned to see Tormid approaching, with Envoy Xuur and her Andorian aide close behind. Other Syhaari supernumeraries walked with them, but he concentrated his attention on the alien commander. Tormid seemed to be carrying himself differently from the last time they had met: then, the scientist-explorer had moved with a kind of lazy confidence; now, he was stiff and formal.

Kirk's thoughts returned to his conversation with Scotty in engineering, to the other man's doubts and concerns, and in that instant the captain decided on a course of action. He fixed Tormid with a hard eye. "You understand what you're doing?"

The Syhaari hesitated, for the moment wrong-footed by Kirk's flat, challenging statement, his lack of preamble.

He didn't allow Tormid the time to frame a reply. "I've spent my entire career face-to-face with unknowns like that object out there. I'm telling you now, you send your ships into battle with it without stopping to measure your steps, and they will not come back. More lives will be lost."

Tormid found something he could grasp, and his heavy lips curled in a thick sneer. "Again you underestimate us, offworlder. You denigrate our skill, our knowledge, now our courage?" He gave an angry snort of derision.

Kirk glanced at Kaleo. "I know Syhaar courage very well. I don't doubt your people have it. But what you need now is *restraint*. You're reacting, sir, with instinct instead of intellect."

"What Captain Kirk means to say," Xuur broke in, with a painted, unmoving smile, "is that the Federation's concern is not just for its own citizens, but for all others. No one wants more casualties."

"Your concerns are noted," Tormid grated, glaring at the envoy. "Once again. But the choice has been made." He gestured to Kirk. "Your people are returned to you. I bid you to do the same with mine."

Xuur and ch'Sellor crossed toward the landing party, but the captain noted that they never fully joined the *Enterprise* group, instead electing to stand between Kirk and Tormid. Was the ambassador trying to show a deliberate neutrality in the situation, or was it that she wanted to keep the two of them from breaking into a full-fledged argument?

"Captain," said Xuur in a low voice that didn't travel. "I see you came prepared." Her gaze raked across Sulu and the security detail. "I'm disappointed."

"For all we knew, you might have been kidnapped," Kirk said, equally quiet so only she could hear his reply. "And frankly, I'm starting to think the polite approach isn't getting much traction."

Kaleo took a wary step away from the group, holding up a small container as she went. "This is the data from the humans," said the other captain, cracking open the lid. Inside, there were two glassy cubes studded with interface sockets, each filled with the fluid memory media used by Syhaari technology. M'Ress and Raines had worked together to pull all the sensor information from the *Enterprise*'s memory banks across to the alien format; but for all his earlier insistence on having it, Tormid barely gave the cubes a second look, instead directing Hoyga to relieve Kaleo of them.

"Where is Duchad?" demanded the Syhaari engineer. "He should be here."

"I asked Captain Kirk's crew to use their matter-transit device to send him directly to the hospital complex," Kaleo replied. "He was in no condition to be interrogated."

Tormid turned his annoyance on her. "That was not your decision to make."

She cocked her head. "And yet I did."

Kirk realized that Kaleo was of the same mind as him, pushing at Tormid to make him justify himself. Now that he was looking the alien commander in the eye once more, the wrong note that had been ringing ever since their first meeting sounded loudly in Kirk's mind. Over whatever gulf of species there was between them, there was one intuitive conclusion that Kirk could not dismiss. *He's hiding something. Why else would Tormid push so hard for a military response?*

"Very well," Tormid was saying. "Then I would suggest—with respect—that the *Starship Enterprise* and all Federation citizens depart Syhaari space until such times as we have dealt with our current problem."

"For reasons of safety," Hoyga added.

"We've been hearing that a lot," muttered Sulu.

Tormid continued, giving Xuur a bland nod. "We may choose to reestablish diplomatic contact at that time."

"I must speculate, is that for the best?" Xuur replied, the question devoid of weight. Kirk wondered how much of her reluctance to leave was based on the same concerns he had and how much was the Rhaandarite's desire to keep her assignment from turning into a failure.

"Whatever decision you make," Kirk went on, "it's a mistake to send us away. We came to help the Syhaari people, and we can still do that."

Tormid eyed him. "Is that so? I confess, Kirk, with all your much-vaunted advancement over our civilization, many of the Learned Assembly wished to petition you to destroy that monster for us. But you proved unwilling and unable. So unless you are willing to turn over that ship of yours to my command, or failing that, share with us the secrets of your weapons technology, there is little you can do for us now. Stand aside!"

Kirk went for the question that was pressing at his thoughts. "Why do you want us gone so badly, Tormid? Are you afraid we'll happen on something you'd rather we didn't?"

For the briefest of instants, Tormid's expression was one of shock and dismay. He covered it quickly, but no so fast that Kirk could miss it. From the corner of his eye, he saw Xuur react to the moment as well. *She saw it too. I hit a raw nerve there.*

But in the next moment, the envoy was turning on him. "I think you've said enough, Captain Kirk."

"I don't agree."

She leaned in, her voice dropping again. "Tormid is being groomed by the Learned Assembly for high office," insisted the envoy. "I won't allow you to jeopardize the diplomatic groundwork I've laid here by browbeating him. Let me do my job, Kirk!"

"Let *me* do *mine*," he snapped back. "Before we all regret it."

Xuur's eyes flashed. "You—"

A grating alarm tone sounded once across the command atrium, drawing everyone's attention to a cluster of video screens on the far wall. Kirk caught a quick exchange of gruff Syhaari speech that was too fast for his universal translator to parse.

"Your ship is hailing us," explained Kaleo. "They say it is a matter of urgency."

The fact that Scotty was contacting them in this way, rather than directly over a communicator, did not bode well. Tormid barked out an order, and the screen cluster shifted from dozens of scrolling information feeds to a visual of the *Enterprise*'s bridge. Scott rose out of the command chair to address them, and Kirk felt an odd sense of dislocation, for once being the person on the other side of such an exchange.

"*Captain, d'ye hear us there?*"

Tormid glared at Kirk and made a brisk "hurry-up" motion with his long fingers.

"We're here, Scotty. Go ahead."

"*It's back, sir,*" said the engineer gravely. "*Sensors just registered a large warp-effect deceleration inside the system. Now we know what to look for, it was easy enough to find. Mister Spock's on his way up to the bridge now, but he didn't want me to wait before warning you.*"

A ripple of fear washed over every Syhaari in the atrium, and it was only Kaleo who broke their silence. "What is the intruder's location, Mister Scott?"

"*It's on an intercept course with the fifth planet, the ice world.*"

"Hokaar," said ch'Sellor. "Is it . . . inhabited?"

"There is a small outpost on the surface," said Tormid, grim-faced. "And a wing of our fastest rangers in orbit."

Kirk's blood chilled. "You sent more ships out there? After what happened to the patrol vessels, you sent *more*?"

"What other option was there?" said Tormid, daring him to disagree.

Kaleo reached out and touched the other commander's arm. "Tormid, tell me you sent them to evacuate the Hokaar complex . . ."

He shook her off. "They were dispatched as a defense force. Their crews know what is expected of them."

"*Captain,*" said a familiar voice, and Kirk looked up at the screen once again to see that his first officer had arrived on the bridge. "*I took the liberty of deploying more sensor probes along our route as we returned to Gadmuur. I have telemetry incoming from the unit closest to the planet Hokaar.*"

"Show us," said Kaleo.

Kirk gave a reluctant nod. "Do as she asks, Spock."

New images captured by the *Enterprise*'s probes filled the Syhaari monitors, grainy with distance but still stark enough to be horribly clear. For a moment, it seemed like a strange lunar eclipse was taking place, as the great shadowed mass of the intruder object passed between the probe craft and the blue-white disc of icy Hokaar. In those brief seconds, Kirk caught sight of what looked like glowing rivers of lava on the leviathan's dark side; they shimmered with an angry, livid firelight.

"Any contact from the rangers out there?" said Sulu, his eyes wide with shock.

Hoyga had dashed to one of the control consoles nearby, and Kirk saw her make a negative gesture toward Tormid.

There was something unreal about watching the silent play of the probe's images, relayed via subspace through the *Enterprise*'s antennae to the command station. The angle of the visuals made it difficult to judge exact distances or relative scale—but when great whips of crimson lightning coiled off the surface of the craggy alien orb, Kirk knew they had to be as big as mountains.

"*Subspace radiation discharges detected,*" Spock reported. "*Magnitude seven and increasing.*"

"Impossible," breathed ch'Sellor. Kirk hadn't figured the Andorian to be knowledgeable about anything other than diplomatic issues, but the shift in the color of his face to pale blue showed he knew enough to understand the import of the Vulcan's words.

Tiny sparks of light flickered and went out as the arcs of red fire lashed the surface of Hokaar, and Kirk felt sick inside as he realized they had just witnessed the destruction of the ranger ships. Hating to give the order, he told Spock to magnify the image. The ice planet leapt closer, now only partly concealed by the motion of the leviathan around it.

"What is it doing?" gasped Hoyga.

"Killing," said Kaleo, in an empty, dead voice. "It's killing the planet."

Once she had said the words, there was no other way Kirk could think of the unfolding events. He felt his hands tightening into fists with all the unspent emotion inside him, the anger and resentment at being forced to stand here and watch, robbed of any opportunity to lend aid. *But even if we had been there, what could we have done?* The question echoed in his mind. *Torn some luckless souls from that doomed outpost, then fled? Or would we have perished too?*

As the leviathan spat torrents of lightning toward the icy world, the captain could not take his eyes from the screen cluster. Even at this distance, he could see great canyons opening across the vast plains of nitrogen snow, yawning fissures wide enough to swallow cities, gases and fluids from far below surging up into mile-high plumes. Hokaar cracked open—and slowly it began to break apart.

Huge plates of ice detached from the surface and crumbled, and the thin atmospheric envelope of Hokaar came apart under the continuing bombardment. Matter streamed off the ruined globe, blown out by gravitational stresses as it entered its death throes. But there was no final, catastrophic detonation; instead, the ice world became a mess of jagged fragments. Great, serrated planetesimals collided and tumbled around one another, still captured by their own weak gravity. A halo of gas and dust shimmered in the distant light of the Sya sun, a shroud about the corpse of a world.

"So much power . . ." breathed Sulu. "It'd take twenty starships firing full phasers to come close to that."

"Why?" said Xuur, her face frozen with shock. "Why did it attack again?"

"We don't know," Kirk admitted, watching as the leviathan's lightning blasts slowed and finally stopped. As if it realized its target was now a ruin, the intruder object turned away from its close orbit around Hokaar and began to arc away from it.

"Curious." Despite the dreadful sight they had just witnessed, Spock's scientific interest was undimmed. *"It appears that the leviathan is preparing to leave its target behind. It is not remaining to feed on the . . . the residue."*

"It is a cruel beast, then," Tormid said, nodding to himself as if some great truth had been confirmed. "A predator loosed upon us from some dark place beyond the Veil. I have always said the alien is a danger to us. It gives me no pleasure to be proven right."

On the screens, the leviathan seemed to shimmer, and then it was suddenly looming large in the probe's scanner window. Before the *Enterprise* crew could react, the display was washed out by a brilliant discharge of crimson, and then there was nothing.

"*The probe has been destroyed,*" reported Scotty. "*Object leaving orbital path of fifth planet and accelerating.*"

"Back to its hiding place," Tormid grated.

"No," said Hoyga, the long fur along the sides of her round face wilting. "According to the data from our orbital telescopes, the target is on a heading that will take it past the orbit of the gas giant Yedeen and then deeper into the system." She swallowed audibly. "Tormid, it is on course toward the inner planets."

"It's coming after our homeworld," said Kaleo.

Seven

Leonard McCoy watched the replay of the images from the *Enterprise*'s remote sensor probe in silence, his eyes never leaving the briefing room's tri-screen. When the playback finally terminated, he found that he had been holding his breath, and he gave a long, low sigh. "This just keeps getting worse."

"The doctor is, regrettably, quite correct," said Spock, sitting across the table from him. At his side, Lieutenant Uhura sat with a hand pressed to her face, as if she were trying to hold in her shock and sorrow.

"Do we have an ETA on the leviathan?" Kirk asked the question that was on all their minds, keeping his tone steady, keeping them focused on the job at hand.

"If it maintains its current speed and heading, the object will cross the orbit of Gadmuur in approximately four hours." Spock nodded toward a tactical plot on the tri-screen monitor in the middle of the briefing table.

"The Syhaari are already assembling a battle flotilla in orbit," said Envoy Xuur. She had insisted on taking part in the meeting, and there had been no reason to deny her. The events of the past few hours seemed to have changed something in the Rhaandarite woman's behavior, and McCoy felt like he was now seeing the person behind the calm, smiling mask. If that was a good or a bad thing, he couldn't tell. "This will not end well," she added.

McCoy looked back at the last images on the main monitor. "I don't understand. Why didn't it feed? I mean, the creature expended a colossal amount of energy on cracking Hokaar like an egg . . . and then it turned away. An animal would never do that. It's not . . ." He threw Spock a look. "It isn't *logical* behavior."

"In other circumstances I would concur, Doctor McCoy," said the Vulcan. "However, in the light of new information gleaned by myself and Lieutenant Uhura, it appears we may have been mistaken about the leviathan's motivation."

"We're ascribing intelligence to it now, then?" Xuur frowned. "It is a sad fact that only a sentient being can commit murder and then walk away."

"Yes," said Uhura, "and no." She sighed. "The situation is more complicated than we first thought."

"It usually is," said McCoy with a scowl.

The lieutenant looked to Spock and he gave her a nod, encouraging her to continue. Uhura took a breath and launched into their theory. "This life-form *is* what we believed it to be. A gigantic cosmozoan with a silicon-based biochemistry. Using Doctor Mc-Coy's records from his scans of the Horta species, we found dozens of points of correlation that show a similar evolutionary path, but nothing to indicate the same level of cognitive development. By all modes by which we measure sentience, it reads negative. Which is why we were confused when I discovered *this*." She inserted a data card into a slot on the table, and the tri-screen lit up with new data.

A steady, repeating series of tones issued out of a hidden speaker, and there was an unmistakably artificial cadence to them. Xuur cocked her head to listen. "This is coming from the creature?"

Uhura shook her head. "Not exactly. At first we thought the leviathan was generating the signal itself, but deeper analysis indicates the message is coming from a location close to the surface of the object."

"There's someone *on* that thing?" McCoy's eyes widened. "How the hell are they still alive?"

"Not *on* it," Uhura corrected. "But probably aboard some kind of craft within the leviathan's atmospheric envelope. We can't locate the source directly because of the spatial distortions clouding our sensors."

Kirk leaned across the table. "More to the point," the captain said firmly, "what's this about a *message*?"

"To reiterate, it is not the leviathan that is attempting to communicate with us," Spock explained. "But these unknown entities in synchrony with it. Lieutenant Uhura's intuitive leap has allowed us to isolate a discreet subspace signal in the highest ranges of the sigma band."

"It's far outside the capabilities of Syhaari technology to pick it up," added the communications officer. "Even for our more advanced systems, it's a stretch."

"Why didn't you speak of this when we were on board the star dock?" demanded Xuur. "Did you know then?" She glared at the captain. "Did you, Kirk?"

"This is the first I've heard of it." Kirk eyed his first officer. "Mister Spock, the envoy's question is a valid one."

"The decision was mine. I ordered Lieutenant Uhura to say nothing until we could gather to discuss this," said the Vulcan. "Given the circumstances, I felt it best to keep this information under our control until we can determine how best to reveal it. As we are all well aware, the situation with the Syhaari is already a delicate one."

McCoy gave a humorless chuckle. "Spit it out, Spock. Because you damn well have everyone's attention."

Uhura produced a second data card and placed it in the reader slot. "Once we isolated the signal, I put it through every linguacode matrix and translator algorithm we had in the database. The sample wasn't much to go on, but I believe we have a solid conversion of the message . . ." She trailed off as she flicked another switch, and the speakers groaned out a series of throbbing, atonal pulses that made McCoy think of the strangled croaks of swamp frogs from his childhood. "This is the filtered feed," Uhura went on. "A single phrase, repeated over and over again."

Spock addressed a panel on the table before him. "Computer."

"*Working,*" responded a metallic female voice.

"Analyze and render input signal using translation matrix Uhura-one-four."

There was a brief chatter of computation, and then the voice spoke again. "*Analysis forms three distinct notional nodes. First group: collective unit. Second group: official statement. Third and final group: armed conflict.*"

"I don't like where this is going," McCoy muttered.

"*Closest translation rendering . . .*" said the computer. "*We. Declare. War.*"

Xuur shook her head, as if she couldn't believe what she was hearing. "A formal announcement of hostilities? From whom? For what reason?"

"I see now why you kept this quiet, Commander," said Kirk. "Tormid has his people on a hair-trigger already. If they heard that . . ." He paused. "Something has been off since the very moment we arrived in this system. If there's a war brewing here, and the Syhaari are involved in it, then we need to know the full truth."

"That assumes this is an act of retaliation," noted Spock.

Uhura shook her head. "I think that's implicit in the use of terms, sir. From what I can determine, the structure of the alien language would be different if they were proclaiming an invasion."

Xuur rose slowly from her chair and took a few paces. Her gaze turned inward as she tried to process the new information. "This changes everything," she whispered.

Again, McCoy stared at the frozen image of the leviathan on the screen, thinking it through. "I think I get it now. It makes a sick kind of sense."

"What do you see, Bones?" said Kirk.

He pointed at the screen. "When we realized that thing was a living creature, we thought we were dealing with some kind of random event. An . . . *animal attack*, if you want to call it that, just on a huge scale. But it's not that at all." McCoy glanced at the first officer. "Spock, Uhura said earlier your analysis of the leviathan raised parallels with the Janus Horta . . ."

"Also your Terran whales and the cloud-sifters of Procyon," agreed Spock.

"The point is," McCoy went on, "all of them are typically docile animals, even when they're at megafauna scale."

"Correct, Doctor. Common to all those species is a nonpredatory behavior pattern, a pattern that is disrupted here."

"By force!" he retorted. "Don't you see? Whatever ships or craft are riding in the atmosphere of the leviathan, they're not just like fleas on a dog! They must be *herding* it! Using it as a weapon!"

Kirk nodded gravely. "It's a sound tactic. In Earth's ancient past, preindustrial armies would use beaters to drive wild elephants into enemy villages to trample everything before them. What you're suggesting is just the same thing on a far larger scale."

"Barbaric is what it is," McCoy replied, sickened by his realization.

The room fell silent. No one could refute the doctor's words.

Finally, Kirk spoke. "All right. We don't have a lot of time to act on this. Spock, pass orders to Mister Sulu to take us out to the Syhaari flotilla."

"What do we tell them when we get there, Jim?" said McCoy.

The captain looked away. "We tell them everything. And hope they'll be just as open with us."

———————

His people dismissed, Kirk lingered a moment in the briefing room to collect his thoughts; but not everyone had left.

"Captain," began Xuur, "I would speak candidly with you."

He gave a wan smile. "I thought I already made that clear, Envoy. You can tell me whatever is on your mind."

She eyed the door, making certain they were alone. "James," she said, using his given name for the first time since they had met. "Don't misunderstand me when I say this, but that message Lieutenant Uhura discovered. It may actually be a positive development."

"You see an escalation from an interplanetary disaster to a declaration of open warfare as a good thing? Since when has the Federation Diplomatic Corps been taking lessons from the Klingon Empire?"

"You're not a diplomat," she retorted, showing a little heat. "So perhaps the nuance escapes you." Xuur took a step toward him. "Tell me, if you meant to do me serious harm, would you hit me, or would you tell me you are *going* to hit me?"

He saw where she was taking the discussion. "You're talking about the difference between the act of violence and the threat of it."

"Exactly!" She nodded briskly. "In many ways, diplomacy is the art of delaying the act of violence until it becomes a redundant choice." Xuur waved at the screen and the image of the planetoid. "If the beings directing your leviathan are making threats, then they are *talking*."

"They're doing more than just making threats," Kirk corrected. "They're *making good* on them. Or did you miss what happened to Hokaar and the patrol ships?"

Xuur dismissed the question with a shake of her head. "The point is, they are communicating. And if we can talk to them directly—"

"There's still a chance we might be able to stop this."

She clasped her hands together. "Now you see, James."

"I do, Veygaan," he replied. "More than you realize." He let the sentence hang, but they both knew what had been left unsaid. *We both know how ambitious she is. And what better way for a young envoy to make her mark than by stopping a war?*

Her practiced, placid gaze hardened. "This will not be easy," she warned. "The Syhaari are not members of the Federation, they're not a protectorate or even an associated nation state. We have only the most basic agreement in place with the Gathering. Any involvement by agents of the FDC or Starfleet with what is technically a local issue is strictly prohibited."

"That's right. Unless of course a formal request for assistance is made by a member of the Learned Assembly." Kirk's lips thinned. "But from what I've seen, our friend Tormid and his supporters seem to think they're fully capable of dealing with the leviathan. You heard him before. He wants us gone. That won't alter."

"There's a big difference between declaring war on a rogue animal, and doing so with another alien species. Tormid may change his mind when he hears what your officers have to say."

He shook his head. "I thought you were good at reading people. You've seen how the Syhaari culture works. Status is everything to them. Tormid won't back down in the face of this new data . . . If anything, he'll be more convinced he's right to take up arms."

"Correct," she said, and suddenly Kirk had the sense he was being maneuvered into something. "So it will fall to you and me to find another way."

———

The Light of Strength could only be considered a warship, and it was with something like disappointment that Kirk studied its interiors. The other Syhaari spacecraft he had encountered were elegant and poised in their structures, refined in a way that reminded him of the racing yachts he had crewed as a youth or the fast and agile trainers he flew in the Academy. Not so the *Light*; it was a brutal collision of hulls and wings, something bolted together in haste with the pure intent of acting as a weapon. Every hundred meters along the central passage, the captain saw laser gunnery pods that had been hurriedly welded to the fuselage or clusters of deadly nuclear-tipped rockets.

"Tormid's work," said Kaleo, by way of explanation. She had met him on the command deck when Kirk had beamed aboard with Xuur, worry lining her usually smooth features.

This time, the envoy had insisted that no other *Enterprise* crew members come with them, and the captain had reluctantly agreed. Even so, it had taken some argument from Kaleo to make it happen, and Tormid had openly snubbed them by refusing to meet their arrival.

"He's on the launch tier with Gatag," Kaleo went on. "Giving the ranger pilots a briefing. A *speech*," she corrected.

In his hand, Kirk held a tricorder loaded with Uhura's data. Before leaving the *Enterprise* under Spock's command, the captain had ordered the communications officer to render the ominous message from the leviathan into a simulation of the Syhaari native language, so that Tormid and the others could hear it without any obfuscation. Now he met Kaleo's questioning gaze and felt a different kind of regret building in him. "I'm sorry," he said, the words escaping from his lips, "for what's going to happen."

Kaleo gave him a wary look. "Kirk, what do you mean?"

"Tell her," said Xuur. "Her support could be of use to us."

He took a breath, momentarily angry at the diplomat, even as he knew she was right. "Uhura found something," he began.

———

Kaleo did not speak again until after they had presented themselves to Tormid, and then her words were clipped and severe. "You need to hear this," she told him.

Tormid glared at her with open hostility, clearly irritated at her interruption. They had found him in *The Light of Strength*'s wide docking bay, where a flight of armed ranger ships were gathered like waiting raptors. More visible weapons pods hung from their stubby winglets, and loose knots of space-suited Syhaari crew waited impatiently at the foot of each craft's boarding ramp. Tormid had been in the process of going from crew to crew with Gatag by his side, giving each of them the same stirring homily on fortitude and dedication.

Now he stood in cold, stony silence as Envoy Xuur repeated what Spock and Uhura had said in the briefing room. Kirk watched him for any kind of reaction, for some sort of indicator of shock or surprise. There was none, only a gradual hardening of the scientist-explorer's flinty gaze. It was only when Xuur asked Kirk to run the playback through the tricorder that he showed any emotion—and it was anger.

Tormid turned to Gatag, whose flesh had paled at the alien utterance of the word *war*. "You are a witness to this, learned elder. You have heard all the off-worlders have said to me."

Gatag nodded woodenly. "This is most troubling. If the object is a tool of invaders." He swallowed hard. "Wh-what if there are more on their way?"

"All the more reason to strike now," Tormid replied. "Nothing has changed. Our enemies have revealed themselves. A grave error on their part."

"You cannot go through with military action," Kirk insisted, looking to Gatag for some kind of support and finding nothing. "Let me be blunt. Your weapons are simply not powerful enough to make a dent in that creature's hide. There has to be another way."

Tormid made a spitting sound, and Kirk saw the crews of the rangers react. At his side, Xuur tensed, reading the same spread of antagonism through the assembled Syhaari.

"There is a blood cost to be paid, human!" snapped Tormid. "The old ways speak of this, of the conduct of warriors and the need for strength!" He reached out with a long arm and prodded Kirk in the chest. "Those who strike without cause are not to be given passage! They do not deserve our restraint! They must answer!"

"He quotes words from one of our ancient texts," said Kaleo sadly. "From the ages before plenty." She advanced on Tormid. "Those edicts were written in a different time! We are facing a new threat now! One we cannot defeat!"

"So *they* say!" Tormid shouted, waving his hand at Kirk and Xuur. "The great *Starship Enterprise* was humbled by this monster, so of course it follows that the primitives of Syhaar would stand no chance against it!" He spat again. "I tire of this disparagement. There is not a soul here who would not fight for the future of their species! And we will!"

Kirk's temper broke. "Then you'll be killed. That is, if you have the courage to lead from the front instead of sending your rangers in first."

"Captain!" Xuur tried to silence him, but the words had already been spoken.

"You doubt my will?" Tormid's reply was low and dangerous. He advanced, and Kirk tensed, well aware that the simianoid's rangy arms and lengthy fingers concealed great strength. If he struck, Kirk would be hard-pressed to fight the muscular Syhaari. "You call me coward?"

"I doubt you," Kirk replied, holding his ground. "I question your inflexibility. Gatag told me the Syhaari were an evolved people who grew beyond tribal warfare and self-destructive acts, just as my species did. But now you're rushing headlong into a conflict that could lead to the death of thousands, even millions! Why?" He mirrored Tormid's earlier action and prodded him in the chest. "What are you afraid of?"

And there it was again, that momentary flash of doubt that made Kirk certain Tormid had something to hide.

"Let us try to make contact with these entities," Xuur insisted. "Let us attempt to open a line of communication. We may be able to reason with them—"

"You will *try*? You will *attempt*?" Tormid barked the words back at her. "You throw around vague possibilities and expect us to accept them? These are *our* worlds at stake, alien! Our brothers and sisters who are dead!" He brought up his hands and made clawing gestures, as if making ready to attack. "I will confess a truth now! I knew your Federation's involvement in our affairs was a mistake, but I allowed my interest in your advanced technology to silence those concerns.

Kaleo wanted you to come here, it was her voice that carried the vote in the Assembly!"

"These people are our allies," Kaleo told him. "They helped us!"

"Helped *you*!" Tormid retorted harshly. "Because of your mistakes, you made us beholden to them!" He shook his head. "You brought us this debt!"

"There is no obligation here," Kirk insisted. "Kaleo, none of you owe us for what we did. We didn't come here to collect from you. We came as friends. As—"

"Do not say *equals*, Kirk!" Tormid glared at him. "You think little of us. That has been clear from the start." The Syhaari puffed out his chest, and when he spoke again, he was performing so that everyone within earshot would hear his words. "The presence of the Federation was foisted on us. It is unwanted, it is a distraction at best. At worst . . ." He turned a cold glower on Kirk and Xuur. "It may be the reason behind these attacks on our worlds and our ships."

"You think we would do such a thing?" Xuur was appalled by the accusation. "What possible gain could there be?"

Kirk met Tormid's gaze and held it. *Does he really believe we somehow caused this attack,* thought the captain, *or is he just playing to the crowd, trying to turn them against us?* More than ever, Kirk was certain that Tormid knew something he was keeping from everyone else, but if the captain said as much now, it would trip off a reaction that would only end badly for all of them. At length, he took a breath and spoke again. "You've made your position clear, sir. Now let me do the same. It is my mission and that of my ship to serve the cause of peace, and we will. Even if that means going in harm's way, right to the very face of that leviathan out there."

Tormid snorted. "Your *Enterprise* barely escaped whole last time. Approach the creature again, and it will obliterate you."

"Maybe. Or maybe we'll find a way to reason with whoever sent that message—"

"I forbid it!" Tormid spoke over him.

"You have no right," Xuur countered.

"*Stop!*" The shout came from Kaleo. "All of you, stop!" She stepped forward, directly toward Gatag. The elder had watched the argument build in silence, but now he found all eyes on him and the other explorer captain. "I petition the Learned Assembly," she said. "I will join Captain Kirk in his effort, as a representative of the Syhaari Gathering. And together, we will put ourselves in the line of fire between these alien invaders and our homeworld, before any more damage can be done! We must take the risk!"

"At the very least," Kirk offered, "we'll buy you some time to prepare your defenses and evacuate your people."

"So confident of yourself," Tormid rumbled, and Kirk was uncertain if the words referred to him or to Kaleo. "Why should I—"

"It is agreed," said Gatag suddenly, silencing Tormid, much to the other commander's surprise. "On the authority of the Assembly, I grant approval of this."

Tormid was silent for a long moment; then he turned and leaned close to Kaleo, muttering something into her ear. The Syhaari stalked away, and Gatag followed after him.

Kaleo's expression was troubled. "What did he say to you?" said Kirk.

She glanced at him. "He told me that if I wished for death to take me, I should have allowed myself to perish when *The Explorer Beyond* was lost."

"No one else is going to die. Not if we can do anything about it." Kirk pulled his communicator from its belt clip and flipped it open. "*Enterprise.* Three to beam up."

———

McCoy turned the corner and found Spock approaching along the corridor. The first officer threw him a cursory nod. "Doctor."

"Are you getting as tired of this as I am?" he asked, falling in step with the Vulcan.

"I am well rested," Spock replied.

"You know what I mean. So far this mission has been nothing but meetings, and every time Jim calls me in to one, the situation is worse than it was last time."

Spock glanced at him as they walked, moving

deeper into the *Enterprise*'s senior officers' deck. "Would you prefer that the captain *not* seek your counsel at such junctures?"

McCoy grimaced. "Oh, I'm sure you'd like that, Spock. You don't get rid of me that easily." He shook his head. "The logical position doesn't always carry the day, you know. Sometimes you need an illogical, emotional, *human* perspective on a crisis!"

"Perhaps so. You are certainly one of the most emotional beings aboard this ship," Spock noted as they approached the door to the captain's cabin.

"That's a real talent you've got there, Spock," said the doctor, after a moment.

"I have many talents," he replied. "Can you be more specific?"

McCoy reached for the door chime. "The ability to say something in a way that I can't tell if you're complimenting me or insulting me." He tapped the button and a tone sounded inside the room.

"I will attempt to be clearer about such matters in the future," said Spock.

"Come," called Kirk, and the door hissed open.

The captain sat at the desk in the day-room half of his cabin, in the process of loading data discs into the memory carousel of a tricorder. He beckoned them in. "Take a seat," he told them.

Spock, as ever, elected to stand ramrod straight, with his hands folded behind his back. McCoy took the offered chair, though, dropping into it to give Kirk a measuring look. "I take it the Syhaari didn't react well to the new information?"

"Tormid did not," said the captain. "I don't know, Bones. I wanted to believe he was all empty bluster and bravado, but now I'm not so sure. This is past the point of reason, and still he wouldn't step back from military action."

"We know he has not been completely open with us," Spock offered. "Mister Scott's scans of the warp drive systems and the uncertainties they raised have yet to be resolved."

"How do starship engines connect to an alien invasion?" said McCoy.

"That's an interesting question." Kirk paused, frowning. "But not our primary one at this moment." He drew himself up. "I asked you both here because I'm giving you new standing orders. Spock, you'll take command of the *Enterprise*. Bones, I know you'll give him your full support."

"Wait." McCoy held up a hand. "Jim, what are you saying?"

"The captain intends to join the diplomatic mission," said Spock.

"In what galaxy is that a good idea?" said McCoy. "Last I heard, that sortie was for volunteers only."

"It is," Kirk replied. "And I'm volunteering to take part. Kaleo will be with me, acting as a representative of the Syhaari Gathering, Mister Arex has offered his services as pilot . . ."

"Lieutenant Uhura has also made a very cogent argument for her assignment to the mission," added Spock. "I could find no reason to disagree with her."

"So there we have it," concluded Kirk. "Scotty's preparing the shuttlecraft *Icarus* for departure as we speak."

"You're going out there *in a shuttle*?" McCoy's eyes widened. "Why don't you all put on life-support belts and go for a spacewalk? It'd be just about as safe!"

"Bones." Kirk gave him a wry smile. "The decision's been made. I'm leading the mission. Kaleo is risking her life, and I can't let her go it alone."

"Is this some kind of *Captains Courageous* thing?" All McCoy could think about was his commander and friend putting his head in the mouth of a lion—a giant beast that had already bitten down a few times already.

"It's what needs to be done," Kirk went on. "We came here to show the Syhaari we can be allies, partners for the future. I can't delegate that now. I won't."

"I know you won't," said McCoy. "But it's my job to remind you."

Spock took a breath. "Jim. The doctor makes a fair point. You are putting yourself in danger. Let me take your place on the *Icarus*."

"You have your orders, Commander," Kirk said firmly.

"Aye, aye, sir," Spock replied, at length.

But even though he could see Kirk wasn't about to budge, McCoy couldn't let it go just yet. "All right. Let's suppose for a second that living planetoid out there actually lets you get close to it, without ripping open the shuttle like a food packet. And let's assume you manage to make some kind of contact with whatever alien entities are spouting off threats of war and tormenting that thing into violence. What are you going to say to them? 'Would you mind awfully backing off a little?'"

"Something like that, yes."

McCoy leaned in. "What happens if they say no?"

When Kirk replied, his tone was grave. "Then I imagine I won't get to hear you say 'I told you so.'" He rose slowly from his chair, and McCoy found himself doing the same. "If we can't stop the leviathan in its tracks through diplomatic means, then we are out of options. And I will not stand by, treaty or no treaty, and allow Gadmuur and Syhaar Prime to go the same way as Hokaar. Kaleo's people may not be members of the Federation, but they're not to be ignored either." He tapped the top of the monitor on his desk. "I've recorded a log containing my orders to you and my intentions for the mission. If, at some future point, someone wants to drag in the Prime Directive and say we violated the spirit of it, I'll take all responsibility for that personally. But right now, we move forward. We protect these people, even if Tormid doesn't want us to."

Spock hadn't moved all time they had been in the cabin, but now he did, turning to glance at McCoy and then Kirk. "Captain. If the *Icarus* mission is not a success, *Enterprise* and the sum of the Syhaari fleet does not have enough firepower to stop the leviathan."

"I know." Kirk laid a hand on Spock's shoulder, and a chill ran through McCoy as he realized what would have to be done. "You are ordered to halt the advance of the planetoid creature and the invaders at any cost, Commander. Even if that means sacrificing the *Enterprise* to do so."

Eight

Kirk watched as the *Icarus*—technically, the *Icarus II*, as it was the second *Enterprise* shuttle to bear that name—rotated lazily on a turntable to present its sloped prow to the clamshell doors at the end of the hangar deck. He glanced up at the control pod on the high wall of the bay, and threw the sketch of a salute to the red-shirted engineering officer up there. In return, lights flashed and the distinctive sound of the prelaunch alert echoed around him.

At his side, Lieutenant Uhura gathered up the equipment pack she had brought with her, and Kaleo shifted uncomfortably as she eyed the small auxiliary vessel.

"The size of it," began the Syhaari. "It is little larger than one of our cargo crawlers. Yet you say this shuttlecraft is capable of warp factor speeds?"

"For short periods," he clarified as the shuttle's door slid open. "They're good workhorses. Rugged and adaptable. And most importantly for this mission, *unarmed*."

"You believe the leviathan, or its alien masters,

will ignore a craft that carries no weapons," Kaleo noted. "What are you basing that on, Kirk? Other than hope?"

"This entire mission is based on that, Captain," said Uhura, offering her own opinion. "Hope for a peaceful resolution."

"I want to share your certainty," Kaleo told her. "But after seeing Duchad and his ships, then what happened at Hokaar . . ." She trailed off.

"You have doubts," Kirk said quietly as Uhura set off across the deck to the *Icarus*. "So do I. But we have to put them aside for now."

"I know," she said wearily. "But you are the only person I can confess this to, James Kirk. To say it before my peers would see me diminished in their eyes." Kaleo snorted disdainfully. "Tormid would never let me forget such an utterance, if he heard it. He already thinks of me as weak."

"Asking for help is not a sign of weakness," Kirk replied. "It takes strength to admit one's limitations. And to trust a stranger." He cocked his head toward the shuttle. "Shall we? I'm sure Mister Arex is eager to get going."

"I will admit one more thing before we depart," she said as they walked across the hangar. "That first time *The Explorer Beyond* exited the far side of the Great Veil, I was not afraid. I was elated. But I am afraid now."

"You fear that you'll fail," Kirk replied, his gaze

turning inward. "You fear you will let your people down."

She gave another deep chuckle and eyed him. "Since when does your species read minds, Kirk?"

"I'm not reading your thoughts, Kaleo. I *share* them. Those fears . . . they're a captain's lot. Comes with the job."

"But we would never tell our crews that, would we?"

Kirk shook his head. "That's the other part of the job." He paused to let her board first, and she gave him a nod of agreement.

He had one foot on the lip of the hatch when the hiss of a door opening made him hesitate and glance over his shoulder. A familiar female figure with a high forehead came running across the landing bay, and she was no longer dressed in her diaphanous silver gown.

"Stand aside," said Envoy Xuur, breathing hard.

Kirk surveyed her new outfit; it was the kind of nondescript, standard-issue jumpsuit that many noncommissioned crew aboard *Enterprise* wore as a matter of course. Strangely out of place, Xuur still wore her metallic headband, and the willowy young woman was able to give the clothing a kind of grace. "If I didn't know better, Envoy, I'd say you were slumming it."

"I'm coming with you," she told him firmly. "I've authorized ch'Sellor to assume my duties aboard the *Enterprise* in my absence."

"And if I refuse?" Kirk stood in the hatchway, barring her from climbing inside the *Icarus*. "Will I get my name on another disparaging report back at FDC headquarters?"

She held her ground. "I said it before, Captain. *You're not a diplomat.* You need me on this mission."

He wanted to argue otherwise, but the fact was, the Rhaandarite woman was correct. They were about to venture into unknown territory, and Kirk could use all the help he could get. "All right," he said, after a moment. "But from now on, you follow my orders to the letter. Clear?"

Xuur nodded. "Of course."

He stepped aside. "Welcome to the landing party."

"Shuttlecraft *Icarus* is now ready for takeoff," called Arex from the cockpit area. "Secure the hatch, please."

Kirk tapped the control that sealed the door behind him. "Secured. Signal dock control to open up, Lieutenant." He made his way forward and took the copilot's station. "Let's get to work."

———

With a low hum of impulse drives, the shuttlecraft lifted off the deck and drifted away, picking up speed as it passed through the hangar deck's clamshell doors. The *Icarus* made a wide, flaring turn that sent it racing past its mothership and away on a parabolic course that rose over the plane of the ecliptic. In short order, the auxiliary craft put distance between itself, the *Enterprise*, and the constellation of Syhaari vessels orbiting nearby Gadmuur.

At full power, the sled-like shuttle moved like a loosed arrow, straight and true toward the outer reaches of the star system.

After a few hours of flight, the emptiness of interplanetary space gave way to a hulking, ponderous mass that loomed large against the gray backdrop of the inner Veil. Armored in its corposant-flecked atmospheric shroud, the leviathan gradually filled the horizon before the *Icarus* until it blotted it out completely. Chains of slow lightning snaked along above the planctoid's pockmarked, craggy surface, discharging into nothing.

Somewhere down there, hidden in the shadows cast by the gargantuan cosmozoan, cold eyes turned to fix on the *Icarus* and consider its fate. As insignificant as it was, insect-small to the vast body of the leviathan, it was still a potential danger.

And so, goaded onward by those who watched and waited, the slow, instinctive understanding of the great being began to turn toward violent action.

"Sensors are lighting up," called Uhura from the seat behind him.

Kirk didn't look around; instead he reached for the spherical globe on a retracting arm over the control console and pulled it toward him. A repeater display gave him more information. "I see it, Lieutenant. Energy building in the lower atmosphere," he announced. "Mister Arex, how long until we reach our programmed intercept point?"

"Two minutes, twenty seconds," reported the Triexian, his three hands simultaneously working the flight controls and the astrogator panel.

"It seems they deem us a threat after all," muttered Kaleo.

"They're not hurling lightning bolts at us yet," said Xuur.

"Let's not give them the time," Kirk added. "Uhura? I hope you're ready to work that translation protocol of yours in reverse."

The communications officer leaned over the systems console before her, her dark brow furrowed with concentration. "As ready as I'll ever be, sir. At this range, there's no way they won't be able to hear us." She place the silver comm receiver in her ear and called up the program.

Kirk laid a hand on Arex's nearest arm. "Reduce speed to dead slow, Lieutenant. We need to fly like we're harmless."

"Complying," said the navigator, his large head bobbing on his thin neck. "I will attempt to project a nonthreatening aspect."

Kirk looked back at Uhura and gave her a nod.

She took a breath and tapped an activation stud.

"Protocol running. Basic linguacode messages are now being broadcast on the deep sigma band using the translator matrix." Kirk heard a peculiar sound, like the noise of bubbles popping but slowed down a hundred times.

"Are they responding?" said Kaleo, stretching up in her seat to peer out of the shuttle's forward port.

"You could say that," said the captain, frowning. Flashes of yellow fire gathered across the curvature of the leviathan's surface, following the same pre-discharge pattern he had seen before the *Enterprise* was attacked.

"Anything?" Xuur watched Lieutenant Uhura work her console.

The communications officer shook her head without looking up.

"Sir, shall I raise the shields?" Arex's hand hovered over the control pad, and Kirk considered it for a moment before shaking his head. They had to show no signs of aggression, even in a passive sense. The truth was, the *Icarus*'s shields would do little to slow down the brutal power of the energy discharges. Even a glancing hit would mean the end for them all.

"We wait," said Kaleo in a low voice, repeating exactly what Kirk was thinking.

"Translation is still transmitting," reported Uhura, keeping her voice level. "No response on any channel."

Kirk pushed the monitor globe aside and narrowed his eyes as he peered through the port. Out there in the leviathan's atmosphere, it was like looking down on the mother of all thunderstorms, a churn of lethal power seconds away from criticality.

His hands gripped the armrests of the copilot's chair. *It's not going to happen*, said a voice in his thoughts. *I gambled wrong.* He turned to Arex, about to give the order to evade and go for broke.

"Contact!" called Uhura. "I'm getting a return ping on the hailing frequency!"

At the same moment, Arex pointed with his central arm. "The lightning!"

The killing discharge came, just as Kirk had feared it would—but rather than bathing *Icarus* in its punishing fires, the crackling rope of energy lashed out at nothing and dissipated into the void. The shuttle shivered in the wake of the blast, systems flickering as the ghost of an electromagnetic after-aura washed over it.

"Was that a warning shot?" said Xuur.

"They never gave us one of those last time," said the captain. "I'll consider that a step forward."

Uhura frowned, pressing her receiver to her ear. "Sir, the universal translator is patched into the new program I wrote. We're getting the first clear message from . . . from whoever they are."

"On audio," he ordered.

There was a teeth-gritting skirl of feedback, and then suddenly Kirk heard the breathy, bubble-popping sound again. In mutated into something with a dry, croaking quality that formed into recognizable words. *"Your embassy is unwanted,"* they began. *"Breg'Hel have zero interest in parley with cloud-dwellers. Go on your way and prepare for ending. War comes. Ending follows."*

"Breg'Hel?" Xuur repeated the alien word. "The translator couldn't parse that term. It must be their name, perhaps their species or some other term of address."

"They must be referring to my people when they say 'cloud-dwellers,'" said Kaleo. "They're talking about the Great Veil."

"Uhura," said Kirk, turning to face her. "Transmit this: We come to seek peace. We are a gathering of many from beyond the realm of the . . . the cloud-dwellers. On their behalf, we wish to speak with you before the conflict progresses any further. May we do so?"

The lieutenant sent the reply, and Kirk found Xuur watching him. "Not a bad opening statement," she offered grudgingly.

"I can be as soft-spoken as anyone," he replied. "When the situation calls for it."

"They're replying," said Uhura. "No delay this time."

Kirk held his breath and listened. *"Peace is broken,"* said the alien voice. *"But the Breg'Hel did not shatter it. There is interest. Questions. You will answer them."*

"If we can—" began the captain, but Uhura waved him to silence.

"Communications channel has been closed, sir. They said their piece and then cut us off."

"I am not the only one who saw a threat in that statement, yes?" said Kaleo.

Kirk was about to reply, but the alert light in the middle of the shuttle's command console blinked crimson, a warning tone sounding with it. He pulled up the monitor, and what was displayed there made his jaw set. "Arex, do you see this? Sensors are picking up three objects moving away from the leviathan's dark side. Ships of some sort."

"Confirmed, sir," replied the navigator. "Design and configuration unknown, but certain elements are similar to Tholian crystal-grown technology."

"As we suspected, they were on the surface of that living planetoid all along," said Xuur. "Remarkable."

"They're on an intercept course," said Kirk. "Engines to the ready, mister. If things get unpleasant, we may have to light out of here in a hurry."

"Aye, sir." Arex brought power to the *Icarus*'s flight systems and eased it into a gentle turn.

"I see them!" said Kaleo. She stood up, hanging from support rails overhead, looking out into the darkness. "There!"

Kirk followed her line of sight and found the trio of Breg'Hel craft. Despite all being of similar mass and basic arrangement, none of the three vessels

were alike. Shards of cut glass, each glowing with an
inner amber fire, were grasped in fists of dark metallic material. They seemed to roll across space as they
moved, sliding back and forth on flashes of energetic
discharge. Each was easily as big as a Starfleet *Archer-*
class starship.

"Try hailing those craft directly," Kirk ordered.
"Repeat our earlier messages."

"Yes, sir," said Uhura.

"Captain!" Arex stabbed at his controls with long
fingers. "Yes, I'm certain of it . . . for a moment I
thought the lead craft was making a passive scan, but
it's anything but!"

Disappointment filled Kirk. "They're targeting us."

"It may not be an actual prelude to attack," Xuur
said quickly. "We don't know anything about these beings; it could be a ritual show of force or—"

"Or they could be about to blow us out of space,"
Kaleo broke in.

"Back us off," Kirk ordered. "Raise the shields. Engines at one-third power."

Icarus began to move, turning to keep the smallest possible aspect pointed toward the Breg'Hel ships,
as Arex worked to maintain a minimum separation
between the craft. But the invaders were not playing
along; one ship surged forward while its two cohorts
moved to flanking positions, angling to cut off the
shuttle's potential avenues of escape.

"They're signaling again!" said Uhura.

"*There is interest,*" repeated the alien voice. "*There are questions. You will answer them.*"

And then the nearest Breg'Hel vessel opened fire.

Spock jerked forward in the captain's chair before he was fully aware of his own reaction. The motion came from somewhere buried in his subconscious, far down below layers of dense Vulcan control, an echo of a very human thing that faded even as it happened.

"Damn it, no!" Standing at his side, Doctor McCoy's reaction came from exactly the same place—but as might have been expected, it was much closer to the surface and far more emotionally charged.

On the bridge's main viewscreen, a long-range display of the shuttlecraft *Icarus* and its encounter with the leviathan became the shocking view of the auxiliary craft suffering a brutal attack. The imagery was grainy and lacking in fine detail, transmitted from another of the free-floating sensor probes Spock had previously deployed. But it was clear enough for the bridge crew to see the *Icarus* taking hits from the alien interceptors. The brief, brilliant threads of particle beams connected the shuttle and the asymmetrical alien vessel for an instant, and a tiny flash of firelight blew out from the belly of the *Icarus*. Spock saw a distinctive tubular section of tritanium spinning away from the damaged shuttle and knew immediately that the attackers—these Breg'Hel—had used pinpoint fire to blast apart one of the *Icarus*'s engine nacelles.

"Curious," he said aloud. "They clearly mean to take the captain's party intact."

McCoy rounded on him. "Blowing great pieces off them isn't *intact*, Spock! They'll be losing power and atmosphere! We've got to get out there, now!"

"We are far beyond transporter range, and the captain's orders were quite clear." Spock said the words aloud, but it was a dead, mechanical recitation. Outwardly, the first officer showed not even the smallest flicker of reaction, but inwardly he was being pulled in two directions. Not just for his friend James Kirk and his long-serving crewmate Nyota Uhura, not just for Arex and Xuur and Kaleo—whose lives carried equal weight even if they were not familiar to him—but because it was his training and his moral impetus to rescue the *Icarus*.

But that would fly in the face of Kirk's orders and against the oath he had sworn on joining Starfleet. Going after the shuttle would be a supremely illogical reaction. Silencing the warring impulses in his mind, Spock took a breath and looked past McCoy to the main viewer. "Status of *Icarus*, Mister Sulu?"

The helmsman swallowed hard. "Damaged but still functional, sir. Engines have shut down. Still reading crew life signs. The ship that fired on *Icarus* has closed to point-blank range."

From Spock's usual station at the primary sciences console, Ensign Haines reported the readings she saw through the sensor viewer. "They appear to be deploying a restraining field around the *Icarus*." She looked up. "They're taking it in tow."

"They want prisoners," mused Lieutenant Leslie. The young officer had stepped in to handle navigation duties. "That's a new wrinkle. They didn't do that with the Syhaari ships."

"That we are aware of," Spock corrected.

"The ships are retreating with the shuttle," said Sulu. "Moving back toward the leviathan."

"We're going to lose our sensor traces in the radiation backwash from the object," added Haines, but Spock had already anticipated that eventuality. "We won't be able to follow them across the dark side."

The view from the probe's sensors was reduced to dots of light moving against grayness, then nothing. Spock glanced at Haines. "Ensign, program our nearest probe to leave its current station and make a stealthy approach toward the planetoid. Keep it in low-power mode and inform me when it is within ten thousand kilometers of the object."

"Aye, sir," she replied, her expression tightening. "Commander, that will take almost three hours, with the probe traveling on thrusters only."

"I am aware," he noted, turning away. "The journey will be approximately two hours, three minutes in duration."

McCoy grimaced. "And meanwhile, Jim and whoever managed to survive being shot at will be at the mercy of these . . ."

"Breg'Hel." Spock supplied the name. He, and everyone else on the bridge, had been listening in on the *Icarus*'s communications. They heard every word that passed between the shuttle and the aliens. "Starfleet has no record of any species, galactic political power, or association identified as such."

"Confirming that," offered Lieutenant M'Ress at the communications console.

"We know enough to know they're damned hostile," McCoy snapped. "I knew this was a bad call from the start! We should have gone for the gunboat diplomacy approach."

"Need I remind you, Doctor, that the *Enterprise* did not fare well in its first encounter with the leviathan? We have no assurance that would differ on a second approach."

"So we sit here and do nothing?"

If he were to be completely and fully honest with himself, that option did not sit well with the Vulcan, but unlike his human colleague, Spock was able to distance himself from whatever emotive content clouded the issue and concentrate on the most logical course of action. "I am considering every possibility. And once again, I remind you. We have our orders."

He saw McCoy draw a breath, making ready to continue his invective—even though Spock had made his position clear—but the doctor never got the chance to harry him further.

Instead, M'Ress called out, her usually purring tone curt and clipped. "Commander. We are being hailed by a Syhaari ship. *The Light of Strength*."

"Tormid," Spock guessed, and M'Ress nodded. "Open the channel, Lieutenant."

The viewscreen switched from the sensor probes' telemetry to a grainy view of the *Light*'s command deck. Tormid came forward until he almost filled the image pickup, glaring out at them as if he were some great predator beast peering in at prey animals out of his reach. *"You see what your foolishness has brought upon you, offworlders?"* He turned away briefly and made a spitting noise. *"Your Captain Kirk killed himself, and dear Kaleo too, as surely as if he had put a laser pistol to her head."*

"We maintained a life-sign lock on the *Icarus* until it was withdrawn," Spock told him. "Despite the attack, no one aboard was killed."

"They are dead now," Tormid stated coldly. *"These creatures know nothing else but murder, clearly."*

Spock raised an eyebrow. Like the *Enterprise*, *The Light of Strength* had also been looped into the communications feed from the *Icarus*. Tormid, Gatag, and the Syhaari elders had heard exactly what Spock had heard—the statement about *questions* that made him believe that Kirk and the shuttle party would be kept alive, if only until those queries were put to them. It seemed apparent that Tormid interpreted that message in a very different way. "I do not agree," said Spock.

"*Then you deny the evidence of your own eyes, Commander. There will be no diplomatic solution here.*" Tormid sneered through the words, as if the thought of them sickened him. "*Kirk's folly in this only cements my intentions. Gatag and the Learned Assembly see things as I see them. These creatures, these Breg'Hel . . . they want a war? We will grant it.*" He drew back from the imager, his manner changing. "*Now a new choice lies before you. You may leave our space and go home to your Federation with your failure. Or come with us, and join in the defense of our worlds. I would think you might want an opportunity to avenge your friends.*"

"The need for revenge is an illogical and unproductive emotional state," Spock said plainly. "It solves nothing, changes nothing. It is not the mission of the *Enterprise* to be party to an escalation of violence."

"*I have never known one so bloodless. So calculating.*" Tormid made the spitting noise again. "*Then you may leave at your earliest convenience.*" The Syhaari gestured to one of his crew, turning away.

"We're not going to stay?" Lieutenant Leslie's shocked whisper wasn't quiet enough for Spock to miss.

The Vulcan answered both of them with his next words, and Tormid stopped to listen. "You misunderstand. As of now, I am in command of this ship, and my duty has not changed. The *Enterprise* will accompany the Syhaari flotilla, and we will render assistance as required. But only toward the goal of resolving this dispute as peacefully as possible."

Tormid's expression froze for a moment, and then he let out a yelping series of guttural snorts. He was laughing. *"Follow if you wish,"* he grunted, *"and if we happen on your dead we will give them back to you. But in the meantime, stay out of our way."* The screen flashed to gray static as he cut the channel.

Spock looked away to find every eye upon him, awaiting his next order. He settled on McCoy, whose grim scowl had not shifted a single iota. "Doctor, make sickbay ready for multiple casualties. I would also advise you to prepare a cargo bay as additional ward space, in the event it is needed. If a battle takes place, we may need to provide medical aid."

A dozen emotions warred across McCoy's face in the space of a few seconds, and Spock looked on impassively, letting his fellow officer come to the inevitable conclusion in his own time. At length, the human nodded. "All right, Spock. You're in command. I'll get it done." Then McCoy leaned in, dropping his voice to a whisper. "But when the shooting starts—and with a man like Tormid with his finger on the trigger, it *will* start—you're going to have to decide how many more lives you're willing to lose."

"I do not consider the captain and the *Icarus* crew to be lost." Spock said the words without being aware of them. The answer came from nowhere, but now that it had been voiced, he felt certain of it.

McCoy saw that conviction in his eyes. "I hope you're right."

———

They had no choice but to evacuate the shuttlecraft after it had been towed into the cave-like landing bay of the largest Breg'Hel ship. Smoke spilling from damaged duotronic circuits was filling the *Icarus*'s cabin, and Kirk waited until the last possible moment before activating the emergency release on the main hatch. He shoved Uhura and Xuur out first, then let Arex support Kaleo as the Syhaari captain half walked, half stumbled. She had burns on her right leg where an exploding power console had caught her with the edge of its discharge. Coughing hard, Kirk managed to salvage an equipment pack from the *Icarus*'s gear bay and staggered out after them. There was a pair of type-2 phasers in a side pocket of the pack, and he groped for them, his eyes still streaming from the smoke.

If blasting us is the Breg'Hel's take on diplomacy, he thought, *I'll feel better carrying a weapon from here on.*

"Gods, what a mess," wheezed Kaleo, looking back at the stricken shuttle. *Icarus* was nose-down, painted with streaks of carbon scorching. Desultory flashes of sparks popped and fizzed along the stubby pylons where an engine nacelle had previously been attached. "An ill fate for a brave . . . a brave craft . . ."

Kirk nodded, casting around. His first impression of the alien landing bay resembling a cavern was not far wrong. As much as he could tell, the decks and walls of the ship looked as if they were cut out of a synthetic rock material, perhaps something similar to the thermoconcrete the Federation used for quick-build colony outposts. The entrance the *Icarus* had passed through was shut now, sealed by a copper-colored iris hatch. He tried to take stock of the dimly lit environment aboard the alien craft; the gravity was lower than Earth-standard, putting an unexpected bounce in his gait. The air was heavy and humid, oxygen rich with a peculiarly loamy odor—and then there was the heat. It was almost tropical, and he felt sweat beading his brow.

Kirk's fingers found the grip of one of the phasers, and he drew it just as Uhura managed a warning shout. "We have company!"

Another smaller hatch on the far wall dilated to allow a troop of reptilian beings to come scrambling into the chamber. They moved with great speed, clambering over one another, some of them adhering to the curved walls as they advanced on the *Icarus* party. The aliens made the same bubble-popping speech sounds Kirk had heard earlier, but now there was an additional layer of verbiage, a series of rapid chirps that were almost birdlike in tone.

Instinctively, Kirk and his people drew together into a cluster as the aliens surrounded them.

"The Breg'Hel, I presume," said Xuur, almost to herself.

At first, Kirk had thought the creatures walked only on all four of their limbs, but as they came upon their prisoners, several of them reared up onto their hind legs, their forelimbs flexing or reaching for tools that dangled from the metallic waistcoats they wore. Rising to a height of around three meters—with another meter of thick tail flicking behind them— the Breg'Hel were an odd mix of skinny form with athletic bodies. They were covered in an epidermis of tiny, sharply defined scales. Coloration was not uniform across the species—Kirk saw some that were bright green, others sky blue, some with patterns of black spots, others with white stripes. All of them had a common marking, a set of red rings around their forearms, but it wasn't clear if that was naturally occurring pigmentation or something akin to an identity mark.

He immediately thought of a Terran gecko as the closest animal parallel to the Breg'Hel physiology. They shared the same kind of spade-like heads, wide mouths, and large, slit-irised eyes. For the most part, the aliens went near-naked, with little more than a series of support belts or surcoats to act as anchor points of the equipment they carried.

Some of them pointed dish-shaped devices in their direction, and Kirk hesitated, uncertain if they were weapons or scanners. He kept his phaser aimed down and away.

"If they wanted us dead," said Xuur, anticipating

his thoughts, "they would have not stopped firing at the shuttle."

Above them, lean Breg'Hel clung to the rough ceiling and used extending batons to point at the shuttle crew, as if they were trying to herd them away from the *Icarus*. Arex let Kaleo find her feet and faltered, as if he didn't want to leave the shuttle to the mercy of the aliens.

"Easy, Lieutenant," Kirk told him. "Don't give them an excuse."

A canary-yellow Breg'Hel with white spots and black circles about its face came forward through the line of guards, and something about its body language, its swagger, told Kirk that this creature was used to being obeyed. It gestured at him, chirp-speaking in short, clipped bursts of noise.

Uhura still had a universal translator to hand, and she tapped a control on the side of the unit. A moment later, the alien language was rendered into the same synthetic voice they had heard out in space. "You are taken. There will be no resistance."

"We are not here for violence," Xuur began, and she laid a hand on Kirk's gun arm. "We are here to talk." She gestured toward the shuttle. "There was no need to attack us."

"It was done to prevent escape," chirped the Breg'Hel.

Kirk's lips thinned. It had been touch and go, but Arex and he had put the *Icarus* down in one piece. If the aliens had wanted to hobble them, they had failed. As damaged as it was, the shuttle was still space-worthy. The Class-F's were tough little crafts, and Kirk was certain that, in a pinch, he could get the wounded bird back into space. If their erstwhile captors thought otherwise, then he was happy to let them remain mistaken.

"Is this how you treat all emissaries of peace?" Kirk snarled, his tolerance for deferential behavior slipping away.

"We have never met peace in the words of aliens," said the Breg'Hel, its glistening black eyes taking him in. "Who is in command among you?"

"I am." Kirk drew himself up, ready for the worst. "I am Captain James T. Kirk, of the Federation Starship Enterprise."

"You address Zud'Hoa, secure-master of this starcraft. By my deed and word, you are to be held in our holding zone until we wish to question you." The alien pointed a thick, fleshy finger at Kirk's phaser. "That is a weapon. Surrender it and all others, or there will be aggression."

"Captain . . ." Xuur gave him an imploring look. Reluctantly, Kirk tossed the pistol to the deck, then did the same with the other phaser in the pack. Outnumbered as they were, any fight would have been a short one.

The alien guards made no move to take the translator, Uhura's tricorder, or the team's communicators.

That led Kirk to wonder what the Breg'Hel had determined of them from their own scans.

Xuur collected herself and made a slight bow. "Honored Zud'Hoa, I am Veygaan Xuur. I speak for the Federation. I respectfully ask that we might begin a conversation between our two nations in the spirit of peace and open exchange."

"There will be conversation," replied Zud'Hoa, making a slow motion with its head, "when we decide it is best. Until then, you will wait." The guards came forward and shoved Kirk and the others forward with their batons. Then, very deliberately, the Breg'Hel officer approached Kaleo and peered at her face. "Another one. Unusual that you came to us willingly. More will be learned." It stepped back. "Take them away."

"What did that mean, sir?" said Arex as they were force-marched out of the landing bay and down a narrow, tubular corridor.

"I don't know," admitted Kirk as he watched Kaleo for any kind of reaction. *Another one.* He turned Zud'Hoa's words over in his thoughts. *That's something you'd say if you had met a Syhaari before, but Kaleo told me her people had never encountered any other beings apart from us.*

Then suddenly the Breg'Hel guards made them halt before another iris hatch, calling out in their atonal birdsong voices to activate a sound-sensitive lock. The hatch whispered open, and they were shoved into a shadowy compartment, partly lit by fat buds of bioluminescent plants that grew out of the walls.

There was already someone else in the holding chamber. A hunched figure in the corner, dimly drawn as Kirk's eyes adjusted to the gloom. He immediately recognized a familiar scent—the musky perfume that he had always associated with Kaleo—and his question was answered.

The prisoner looked up, and Kirk saw a wide, round simian face, lined with age and exertion. Dark eyes widened as they found Kaleo's shocked expression.

"Rumen?" Kaleo could barely speak the name. "Is it you? But they said . . . Hoyga told me she saw you perish!"

"Not . . . so," said the other prisoner, his words rough and half formed, as if he had almost forgotten how to use them. "Not so, sister."

Nine

"Report, Lieutenant," said the captain.

Uhura sighed and offered him the tricorder. "No ventilation shafts, no access panels," she replied, gesturing at the rough-hewn walls around them. "I'm no geologist, but at a guess our air is coming through the rock itself."

"It's porous?" asked Arex, then corrected himself. "It must be. How else would these light-plants be able to grow through it? But that means we might be able to weaken the walls . . ."

"You're suggesting we *tunnel* our way out?" Envoy Xuur sat cross-legged on the floor, picking at one of the glowing buds, and spoke without looking up. "I neglected to bring a spoon."

Uhura frowned. She could never tell if the Rhaandarite was being sarcastic or not, as the diplomat's tone never seemed to shift off the same middling register. "The only way in or out is through that hatch," she went on, concluding her report. "I'm sorry, sir."

Kirk gave her a brief smile. "Don't worry. We've been in worse places. We'll get out of this one too."

She believed him; she believed the captain would do all he could to get them back to the *Enterprise* in one piece. She just hoped it would be enough.

Uhura anticipated the next question he would have for her. "As for getting the word out . . ." The lieutenant drew her communicator and flipped it open. The usual clicking tone of activation was replaced by a dull buzz, showing that the device was unable to detect a subspace carrier wave. "There's a large percentage of boridium in the material this ship is made of. It's blocking any outgoing comm signal." She hesitated.

Kirk saw her pause. "But?"

"But I might be able to create a boosted signal strong enough to punch through the interference. I'd need every communicator we have, to daisy-chain them."

The captain considered her proposal for a moment. "Hold that thought, Lieutenant. But be ready."

Uhura nodded, and her gaze slipped past Kirk to where Kaleo and the other prisoner were sitting in one of the holding chamber's shadowed corners. Like everyone else, Uhura was just as surprised to see a Syhaari captive being held by the lizard-like Breg'Hel. At first, she had thought that Rumen might have been one of the crew aboard the ranger patrol ships that first fell victim to the leviathan, or some luckless survivor from the Hokaar outpost. But that didn't seem to be borne out by the look of the Syhaari male—his uniform, a shipsuit much like Kaleo's, was ragged and well worn. He reminded Uhura of some unfortunate left beached on a desolate island after a shipwreck. He was unkempt and hollow eyed, his fur overgrown and matted.

"Anything else?" Kirk prompted.

She looked away. "Just that." Uhura pointed at the far wall, where part of the stone had been filled in by a roughly rhomboid-shaped piece of crystalline glass. Many of the glow-plants grew over it like ivy, hiding it from anyone who didn't take a second look. "It resembles quartz, and there's a low electrical charge running through it. At a guess, I'd say it was some kind of monitoring device."

"Screen." The other prisoner said the word in a gruff, low voice.

Kirk and Uhura turned toward him. "Say again?" said the captain.

Kaleo reached out to stop Rumen from getting up, but he slipped out of her grasp and rose unsteadily to his bare feet. "A screen. For displaying images. It is my punishment."

Kirk shook his head. "I don't understand."

"At a regular interval, they show me my crime." As Rumen spoke, his words seemed to age him. "That is what they call it. Images captured of the deaths. Over and over again."

"What deaths?" said Arex. "You mean the ships that were attacked?"

Rumen shot the Triexian a horrified look. "What ships?" He turned on Kaleo, his panic rising. "What does the alien mean, *what ships*?"

Kaleo sighed. "Much has happened in recent spans. There have been grave losses."

The older Syhaari fell back against the wall. "I would have known them."

"Yes," said Kaleo sadly. "You knew them all." She looked toward Uhura and the others. "Rumen is one of my oldest friends, a pioneer of our starflight program. He was my instructor during my training. But he was declared dead cycles ago, after the . . ." She faltered, losing her momentum.

"I was the pilot of *The Searcher Unbound*," said Rumen, his gaze turning inward.

"Tormid's vessel," said Xuur quietly. "The other explorer ship."

"The Assembly chose me," he went on, laboring over each word. "To be at the helm. They believed I would temper Tormid's more impulsive tendencies. I failed."

Kirk gave Kaleo a level look. "We were told that the *Searcher*'s crew were killed during a catastrophic malfunction. Tormid and Hoyga were the only ones who made it back alive."

"*All. Lies.*" Rumen spat out the bitter reply. His large fingers gathered into heavy fists, and Uhura felt a surge of unspent rage coming off the Syhaari like heat from a fire. She had noted places here and there along the walls of the holding area that looked like points of blunt-force impact; now she suddenly understood how they had gotten there. Rumen straightened and turned back to glare at them. "There *was* an accident, yes. Several of the *Searcher*'s crew perished when a plasmatic coil overloaded. But three of us survived. Hoyga, Tormid, and I."

Kaleo came to her old friend's side, placing a hand on his arm, trying to calm him. "I know it will hurt you, Rumen. But you must tell us everything that happened."

Uhura listened as the other Syhaari fumbled with his explanation, faltering and falling over the painful memories as he slowly tried to reconstruct them. He talked haltingly about leaving the Great Veil for the first time and setting off into the unknown. The pilot spoke of how the *Searcher*'s engines had unexpectedly gone into a dangerous overload that threatened to cause a matter-antimatter explosion. Deploying their emergency solar sails, the crew attempted to shut down the drives without success—but rather than be obliterated, the explorer had been picked up by an unseen energy stream that carried them across interstellar space at speeds far greater than the *Searcher* was capable of. By the time the stream had dissipated, they were adrift close to the protostar nursery several light-years distant from the Sya system. They were *lost*.

"You are describing the effect of a tachyon eddy," offered Arex. "The solar sails were caught in a kind of spatial current that caused the ship to travel such a great distance."

Rumen gave a wan nod. "Where we found ourselves . . . that was the domain of this kind." He gestured at the walls. "The ones that call themselves Breg'Hel."

"You encountered them there?" Xuur cocked her head, listening intently. "They attacked you?"

"That was not their intention." Rumen's hands relaxed as emotion thickened his reply. "No. They were curious, I think. Cautious. But they did not bring violence. Not until later. At the time, we were not sure what they wanted. But I think I know now."

Uhura exchanged a wary glance with her captain, and she knew that he was asking the same questions she was. *If this is true, Tormid has known of the existence of the Breg'Hel since the very beginning. But instead he feigned ignorance. Why?*

"A small ship came to us," Rumen went on. "A scout, I believe. It was so fast, so agile. It was easy for us to be impressed . . . and afraid. They boarded the *Searcher*, and when Tormid saw what they were . . . alien life so totally unlike us . . . he panicked." Rumen blinked slowly. "He insisted they were hostile. We didn't know. There was no way we could communicate with them."

"*He* attacked *them*," said Kaleo, in a dead voice. "I am right, yes?" Rumen gave a wooden nod, and she let out a sighing breath.

" 'The alien is a danger to us,' " said Kirk. "I heard Tormid say those exact words. I didn't realize how seriously he meant them."

"I think they might have come to rescue us. Instead, Tormid let his fear take charge. He killed them, Kaleo. First those who boarded the *Searcher*, then the ones remaining on their scoutship." Rumen closed his eyes. "I can recall the savage look on his face. How he shouted me down when I tried to stop him. And then it was done, it was too late. He ended them, and I did not do enough to prevent it."

"That's your crime," said Xuur.

"It is," Rumen agreed, "but it is not the sum of what was done." He advanced to the glassy screen and banged on it with the flats of his big hands. "Show them!" he shouted at the air. "Do it! You force me to watch every day, why hide it now?"

Someone had to have been listening, because at once Uhura saw a milky glow shimmer through the quartzlike pane and abruptly there were fractured images being displayed upon it. Each was washed out, framed by a strange fish-eye aspect, but the collage of moving pictures clearly showed the same kind of interior spaces that she had walked through inside the Breg'Hel starship.

Xuur made a choking noise and looked away, her pale skin even more ashen than usual. Uhura wished she could do the same, but found it impossible to avert her gaze. She watched as a figure—or was it dif-

ferent figures?—in a Syhaari environment suit moved
through what had to be the corridors of the scoutship
Rumen had described. Some of the images showed the
same sequence of events from a different angle, some
looped in an endless cycle. In every one, the invader
in the bubble-helmeted suit used a handheld laser
weapon to commit murder, over and over again.

"Tormid told me we were compelled," said Rumen.
"That once it had been done, there was no turning
back. None of them could be left to speak of our existence. Hoyga, she was as sickened as I, but his logic . . .
his force of will silenced her."

Then the images changed. Time had passed. Some
of the visual displays remained static, empty, the bodies of the dead lying motionless where they had fallen.
Uhura saw the suited figure again, this time in only
one image. He was in a part of the Breg'Hel ship filled
with active devices, screens and panels and modules
dedicated to functions she could only guess at. As
she watched, time seemed to jump forward in fits and
starts.

"What is he doing?" said Arex.

"Taking salvage." The sudden understanding hit
Uhura hard. "Pulling their systems. He's ransacking
the ship."

Then time jumped again, and the views of the ship
showed no movement for long seconds. "Tormid came
back aboard the *Searcher* with a hoard of stolen technology," Rumen explained. "Everything he could carve

out of that death ship. He used what he could adapt to fix the damage to our vessel."

"He always was innovative, in a callous way," Kaleo said bitterly.

"So now we know where those 'insights' of his came from," said Kirk, in a low, cold voice. "Tormid plundered the Breg'Hel craft." He shook his head.

Xuur nodded to herself. "All of a sudden, their belligerence seems understandable."

"Their warp engines are quite clever," Rumen noted. "The basic design and configuration was clear to us . . . and Tormid was always a quick study."

"How could you let him do it?" Kaleo's question was not an accusation, but a sorrowful thing.

Rumen released a solemn sound that was somewhere between an animal cry and a gasping sob. He reached up and pulled at the fasteners on his shipsuit, peeling open the ragged material. "Fear stopped me at first. He was my commander. I was duty-bound to obey him. But then I realized what road he was taking us down. So, I challenged him to answer for what he had done." Rumen bared a section of his chest, and there was a patch of ugly, burned skin where his fur did not grow. Uhura had seen such injuries before, the mark of laser-fire wounds. "He shot me and left me for dead aboard the scoutship." The Syhaari's head drooped as he recalled that moment. "I think he believed I would perish there. *The Searcher* detached from the scoutship and set it adrift. And I waited to die."

"But you didn't," said Kirk. "I'm guessing Tormid left you there so the Breg'Hel would have someone to blame for what happened to their crew. But instead of a corpse, they got—"

"A prisoner," Kaleo broke in.

"They found me. They healed me. Then they *punished* me." All the fight seemed to go out of the older Syhaari, and he sank to his haunches. Uhura heard the deep sorrow in his words and felt a pang of empathy. "Another Breg'Hel vessel arrived, and when they boarded . . . they cried out, with a sound unlike anything I had ever heard before. A raw scream of pain for their loss. And I was at the center of their anger. I could not tell them I had no part in it. They reviewed their visuals . . . " He waved at the screen. "They did not differentiate between Tormid's actions and mine. His crimes were revealed to them, and I paid the price in his stead."

"And so you have been held here, on this ship, for years?" Arex studied Rumen carefully.

"Yes. I am moved back and forth from a sleeping cell to this chamber once each ship's day. At first, there would always be one or two of them here, waiting for me. Young ones and old ones. Some of them beat me. Some screamed at me in their language. I came to deduce that they were the family members of those who had died on the scout. They came to make me pay, and as I could manage no more than the most basic communications with them, I was forced to endure it. After a while, it stopped. But the ones on this ship, they still hate me." Rumen tapped his arm, where Uhura had noticed the crimson rings on the limbs of the Breg'Hel. "The coloration they have here? I think it has some kind of meaning, a signifier for a clan or a domestic unity."

"That would fit the evidence," said Xuur. "The Federation Diplomatic Corps are aware of many cultures with a clan-based society. Several of them share the consideration that an assault on one of their kindred is an attack on *all* of them."

"Hence their desire for bloody vengeance on the Syhaari people," said Kirk, grim-faced. "I've had a bad feeling about Tormid from the very moment I met him. Spock and Scotty both suggested that he was keeping something from us. But I never thought it could be something like this." He turned to Kaleo. "You see what this means, don't you? Those warp drive systems that Hoyga was so reticent to let us take a look at, they're not the product of some grand intuitive leap that Tormid made. They're based on stolen Breg'Hel technology."

"I want to deny every word of this," said Kaleo. "I want to say it is a lie, but I know Tormid and I know . . . I know it is true." She gave a shuddering sigh. "One soul's greed has doomed our species, Kirk. And I fear you and your crew will suffer along with us because of it."

———

Spock made his way up the deck levels of *The Light of Strength*, using the multiple handholds built into the walls to ascend to the command cupola at the bow. Like their buildings back on Syhaar Prime, the Syhaari ships had no ramps or stairs to move from deck to deck, but were served only by elevators or direct movement through open passageways in the floors and ceilings. A human might have found the climbing and swinging motions required to be tiring, but Spock's Vulcan constitution was hardy, and if required, he could have run a circuit of the craft without breaking a sweat. But still, it was not lost on him that Tormid had directed Spock to beam aboard on the ship's lowest level and then come to him via the longest way around. *An act of passive aggression,* Spock thought. *A small way in which Tormid wishes to remind me that he is in the superior position here.*

It was foolish illogic of a kind that he had encountered more than once, and Spock paid it no mind. If Tormid meant to begin this private meeting by placing the *Enterprise*'s first officer "off his game," as Doctor McCoy would have put it, then he had seriously misjudged Spock's character.

He emerged in the small, dome-like chamber to find Tormid poring over a portable screen upon which a tactical plot of the Sya system was displayed. The scientist-commander was carefully moving groups of icons back and forth across the panel's touch-sensitive surface, playing out battle scenarios against the inexorable approach of the leviathan.

"I hope your reason for interrupting me is a good one," Tormid said without looking up.

"I believe so. Thank you for agreeing to speak with me in person." Spock approached to a respectful distance and waited with his hands behind his back. From where he stood, he could pick out a lone glyph on the screen that signified the *Enterprise*. Tormid seemed to be ignoring it.

"Why are you still here?" he said tersely. "If you do not wish to retreat and lick your wounds, then why do you dither? Why not join us in the preparations for the battle?" Tormid looked up. "Or better still, summon more of your so superior ships to come and aid us in the monster's extermination."

"We will remain here to assist you," Spock replied.

"In a nonmilitary capacity!" Tormid countered. He tapped the bright green icon that designated the leviathan itself. "This freak of nature has already damaged your vessel, killed your captain and crewmates—"

"There is no evidence that the *Icarus* crew is dead," said Spock, but Tormid kept talking.

"—and you show no desire for justice?" He eyed the Vulcan. "Are all you offworlders the same? Have you moved so far from your homeworlds that you no longer care about the violation of sovereign territory?"

"On the contrary, Starfleet protects the integrity of its borders, and those of its allies, with the utmost vigilance," answered Spock.

Tormid rose to his feet. "I thought that was what we Syhaari were. Your *allies*, at least in some fashion. But now you refuse to stand side by side with us in this, our hour of need?" He gave a negative growl. "You are only feast-day friends, then. Here to eat with us, but turning away when we ask for a meal in kind."

"There is no incentive in a frontal assault against the intruder object. That is why I will not give the order to take part in your attack plan."

Tormid came closer, and his scent filled Spock's nostrils. "What are you made of, Vulcan? The humans, they seem to have a spirit like ours, but you? You are a cold thing, bereft of passion. A computing device that walks and talks!"

"I am governed by logic," Spock explained, his neutral expression never altering. "My species have learned to master the chaos of emotions. We operate on pure reason and objective truth. Vulcans do not allow themselves to be swayed by emotive extremes."

Tormid seemed to take that on board, scowling at the concept. "Kirk was your commander, and I would surmise he was also your friend, if that is something your kind allow yourselves to have." The Syhaari studied the Vulcan as if he were some artifact in a museum. "Yet you do not wish to punish those who harmed him?"

Some distant part of Spock, buried deep, *did* feel for his missing colleagues. But it would not, could never, be the thing that governed his actions. "Violence for the sake of vengeance solves nothing. Captain Kirk would be the first to agree with that statement, as would Lieutenants Uhura and Arex, Envoy Xuur . . . and, I imagine, so would Captain Kaleo."

At the mention of Kaleo's name, Tormid's expression became brittle. "She wants to be like your Federation so much, and I think it has diluted her views. Now she has paid the price." He gestured at the transparent dome and the gray expanse of space beyond. "The Syhaari have always struggled, Commander, challenging the odds that have been ranged against us. We learned to trust only grudgingly, to protect what is ours, to seize opportunity when we can. I think Kaleo has forgotten that."

"You speak freely of the Syhaari character," Spock replied. "But I wonder, sir, if you actually speak of your own."

Tormid gave him a dismissive snort. "They are the same." He turned and loped away. "My time is limited, offworlder. Full command of the Syhaari star force is now my responsibility, and that means dozens of rangers and explorers to be marshaled for the coming confrontation. The . . . leviathan, as you call it, is on a direct course to Gadmuur. I have a battle to prepare for, and unless you have something to contribute, go back to your starship."

"I reiterate: your plan of action is gravely flawed,"

Spock said bluntly. "The presence of the *Enterprise* as an additional combatant would not tip the tactical advantage in your direction." He took a step toward Tormid, the only outward sign of the frustration that colored Spock's thoughts. "Even with our help, your ships will not be enough to drive off the intruder. Your weapons cannot harm something of such mass."

"Each of my craft can become an antimatter bomb at a single word of command," said Tormid. "If we must hurl them like arrows, we will."

"That will only deplete your forces further. I implore you to not to commit to a military action at this time. It is my firm belief that the crew of the *Icarus* are still alive, and that they will do all they can to find another solution to this dilemma. I ask you to give them time."

Tormid showed his teeth. "Ah. I was wrong about you, Vulcan. You *do* feel something. It is *fear*. You are too afraid to accept the truth that already stares you in the face." He shook himself and grimaced. "Kirk is dead. They're all dead. And we will all suffer the same fate if we do not beat back this alien threat!" Tormid went to the dome. "Our conversation is over. You have nothing of value for me."

Spock was silent for a moment, considering Tormid's intractable response. He reached for his communicator, but before he flicked it open to summon *Enterprise* to beam him back, another question pressed at the Vulcan's thoughts. "I find myself asking what it is that *you* are afraid of, sir. What is it that so troubles you, that violent conflict is the more palatable alternative?"

"Get off my ship," Tormid growled, without looking back at him. "And stay out of our way."

———

There was no warning before the Breg'Hel came for them.

The iris hatch suddenly cranked open with a wet hiss, and a pair of the reptilians strode into the holding chamber, each one brandishing a metallic baton that telescoped into a short lance.

Kirk saw Rumen flinch at the sight of the weapons and shrink back into the shadowed corner where they had first found him. Despite herself, Kaleo bared her teeth, the echo of her comrade's actions making her angry. Kirk had to wonder what indignities the other Syhaari had suffered at the hands of his captors to make him react in such a manner.

On the other side of the open door, he glimpsed three more Breg'Hel, each of them wearing the same kind of belt-and-waistcoat outfits, each constantly in motion. They moved from foot to foot, shifting their weight as if they were nervous. *Perhaps so,* he thought. *They've never seen a human or a Rhaandarite or a Triexian before. They don't know what kind of threat we could represent.*

The nearest guard gestured with its lance and spoke. Uhura's universal translator immediately interpreted the words. "Who among you is the parent?"

Kirk exchanged glances with Xuur and his communications officer.

"Father-mother?" said the guard, trying again.

"I think he means *leader*, sir," Uhura offered. "The UT is still processing all the syntax."

Kirk nodded and stepped forward. "I am."

"Father-mother," the guard said again, this time more insistently.

"I am." Xuur moved to stand at Kirk's side and flashed him a sly wink.

"You will accompany us," said the other Breg'Hel. "There are questions."

Uhura placed the translator device in Kirk's hand. "Keep it running, Captain," she told him. "The more the UT can sample their language, the better our communications will get."

He nodded. "You're in charge until I return. Keep our people safe."

She gave a determined smile. "Will do, sir."

"Follow!" ordered the first guard, retracing its steps through the hatch. Kirk clipped the translator to his uniform and did as he was told, with Xuur a step behind him.

Back out in the corridor, the Breg'Hel guards closed the hatch and then formed a circle around them before moving off.

"It seemed the right thing to do," said the diplomat, heading off Kirk's question before he could voice it.

"I just don't want these beings getting the wrong idea about our relationship, Envoy."

"You flatter me," she allowed. "And to be honest, yourself a little into the bargain."

He raised an eyebrow at her tone. "Is that so?"

Xuur kept walking and didn't meet his gaze. "There are other things your FDC file says about you, James."

"And I'm sure they're all equally unbiased," he said dryly. For a moment, Kirk concentrated on placing one foot in front of another, calling on his low-*g* training to prevent himself from bouncing with each step. He quickly slipped into the rhythm of motion. The reduced gravity aboard the Breg'Hel ship could make someone raised in a Class-M standard environment become clumsy if they were not watchful. For her part, Xuur also adapted quickly, something that Kirk hadn't expected. He thought again about the diplomat, about how much of her he couldn't read. *Like it or not, we're working together now.*

"This vessel," she spoke quietly, jutting her chin at the curved corridor around them, "at first I believed it was carved out of an asteroid, but I was mistaken. The rocky material it is made of, it almost seems . . . sculpted."

"*Molded* might be a more accurate term," Kirk

allowed. "I think what we're looking at here is some sort of cast structure, fabricated from a solidified fluid medium."

She nodded. "Yes, I see." Xuur pointed as they walked beneath a vein of yellowish crystal that described a helical pattern around the walls. "And that material? Perhaps something injected into the structure as it forms?"

Kirk eyed the faint glow coming from deep inside the lines of mineral. "You could be right. It looks like dilithium, but without a tricorder there's no way to be sure."

"A ship made of stone and crystal," said Xuur. "Not quite grown like Tholian vessels, not quite repurposed from planetesimals, but some combination of the two. I wonder, what would we see if we could compare the atomic structure of this ship with the leviathan creature?"

He considered the question. "Interesting point. If we can make peace with these beings, perhaps we can come back with Mister Spock and a geology team."

"One step at a time," Xuur replied. She was about to say more, but fell silent as a pair of Breg'Hel crew members—dressed differently from their captors—scuttled past. Without breaking their pace, the two of them clambered up the curved walls and hesitated, their large eyes swiveling to watch the two captives pass beneath.

Where the aliens had climbed the walls, Kirk saw

there were more of the strange ivy-like plants that coated the walls of the holding chamber. But where the ones in the cell had been festooned with light-emitting buds, these plants had wide, oval leaf structures that reminded him of lily pads. *Maybe a component of their life support system*, he guessed, *a natural air scrubber*. Looking closer, he spotted fat beetles with iridescent green carapaces moving around in the foliage. Never taking its eyes off him, one of the watchful Breg'Hel reached out and snagged one of the bugs, popping it into its mouth with a crunch of chitin.

The corridor widened into a windowless spherical chamber where dozens of Breg'Hel hung from all angles, each of them splayed over carved protruding nubs of rock that ended in glassy discs, each aglow with symbols and shapes Kirk couldn't interpret; but he knew a command center when he saw one. Still, there was no central point that he could find, nothing that resembled a captain's chair like he had aboard the *Enterprise*. It was only when another pair of Breg'Hel skittered down toward them that Kirk realized he was looking at the ship's masters. The two of them differed from the rest of their crew by coloration, both with skin a shade of pale turquoise Kirk had not seen anywhere else. They were slightly taller too, with a whitening around the edges of their scales that became apparent as they approached.

Xuur pieced it together first. "They're older than the rest," she said. "The . . . parents?"

Is it possible? Kirk wondered, looking around the command center at the other, younger Breg'Hel. He knew that reptile life-forms could produce large clutches of eggs in a single fertility cycle. *Could this whole crew be the literal* family *of these two?*

The guards parted to allow the elders to examine Kirk and Xuur, and the captain saw another of their kind move up to accompany them—the yellow-skinned "secure-master" who had taken them into custody in the landing bay.

"Zud'Hoa," said Xuur with a bow, "to whom do we have the honor of addressing?"

The yellow Breg'Hel gave a shake of its head that seemed dismissive, and spoke in its halting, chirping cadence. "Father-Mother. These are the aliens that seek to interfere with the war plan. They are of the not-known."

The elder on the left, differing from its partner in the stark bottle-green coloration of its eyes, tilted its head and spoke. "I am Ret'Sed."

"I am Ead'Aea," said the other elder, whose eyes were a darker amber shade. Neither had any immediate visual signifiers to suggest gender.

"We co-command this vessel and the seeking of retribution." Ret'Sed looked them up and down. "How is it that we converse in each other's language?"

Slowly and carefully, so as not to alarm the aliens, Kirk unclipped the universal translator and showed it to them. "We have a technology that allows us to communicate. We might be able to share it with you, if you wish."

"The known do not possess this instrument." Ret'Sed's tongue flicked at the corner of its mouth, and then the alien looked Kirk in the eye. "You will identify yourself."

"James T. Kirk, captain of the *Starship Enterprise*. This is my colleague Envoy Xuur. We represent the United Federation of Planets, a galactic coalition of allied worlds, and we are here in the spirit of peace."

Xuur nodded. "Indeed. We are not the enemies of the Breg'Hel. We have no wish for violence between our peoples. We ask only that we may speak with you."

"There has been much violence already," Ead'Aea replied firmly. "At the hands of the known."

"The Syhaari?" said Kirk. "Yes, that may be so. But those were the acts of one individual. To blame millions for one person's mistake—"

Ret'Sed and Ead'Aea both reached for each other's hands and clasped fingers. "Blood-kin family and dynasty-children perish, that is a deed that cannot be undone," said Ret'Sed. "One crime is all crimes."

"One guilt is all guilt," added Ead'Aea. "One blame is all blame."

"Those who crewed the scout vessel, they were your kindred?" asked Xuur.

"A splinterhood," said Zud'Hoa, with a clatter of teeth. "Sister-cousins perished there. A grave injustice."

"Not only lives were taken," Ead'Aea went on. "Matter and substance. There was theft, not-known Xuur. Murder and theft."

Kirk thought about Rumen's explanation back in the holding chamber. He could only begin to gauge the scope of the Breg'Hel societal structure on this first meeting, but it seemed his assumptions and those of the Syhaari pilot had been close to the mark. The lizard-like aliens appeared to have a complex web of interrelationships and familial loyalty that Tormid had blindly ripped through with his fear and ambition.

"The known did this," intoned Ret'Sed. "Of that there is no doubt. You have seen the visual-witness. A threat to the greater brood exists here, and it must be expunged."

The alien is a danger to us. Kirk heard the echo of Tormid's words in the Breg'Hel commander's statement.

"Captain," Xuur whispered, nudging him with her elbow, "look there." He turned in the direction the envoy was indicating and saw a visual display on one of the larger control units. It was a long-range image of Gadmuur, the orbital shipyards and space platforms appearing as glittering motes of light around it.

He couldn't determine how far they were from the planet, but it was clear to the captain that the arrival of the *Icarus* had not slowed the Breg'Hel approach. He took a breath and raised his hands in what he hoped was a universal gesture of goodwill. "You see that we are not from this place, and you know that we had no part in what happened to your ship and your people."

"This is so." Ead'Aea blinked. "It is why you are being given audience. The question. Why are you here, not-known Kirk?"

"To *intercede*," he said, taking the opportunity. "Warfare is destructive, and it ultimately leads only to more bloodshed. We can make a promise to you, the Breg'Hel, on behalf of the Federation. Hold back your advance into Syhaari space and in return we will help you seek a different path to resolution."

Xuur nodded. "The Federation can take a neutral stance in this conflict. We can mediate between the Breg'Hel and the Syhaari. Your grievances will be heard. Together, we will find a way to provide you with restitution and justice. A way that does not require acts of war and greater murder."

The aliens fell silent, and for a moment Kirk was afraid they had misunderstood what he and the envoy were offering. Then Ead'Aea released Ret'Sed's hand and pointed a thick, fleshy finger at them. "You, the not-known of the Federation. We have no quarrel with your kindred. We will release your small-craft, you may go to your vessel and depart without punishment."

"What about Rumen and Kaleo, the Syhaari?" said Xuur.

"The known will remain our prisoners," grated Ret'Sed. "They are blamed."

"Your offer is rejected," said Ead'Aea. "An arbiter is not required. We will find justice in our own manner."

Kirk's lips thinned. "I can't stand by and let that happen," he told them. "I understand your pain, but you must see . . . those you have already attacked, and those you plan to attack . . ." He pointed toward the image of Gadmuur. "They are not the ones who hurt your kindred. You are striking at innocents."

"One crime is all crimes," spat Zud'Hoa. "This is truth."

Ead'Aea raised a hand, and the guards returned, moving back to surround Kirk and the envoy. "No more words. You were given a choice. You did not take it. You are now the known, Kirk and Xuur. You will suffer the same punishment as the deserving."

With a snap of metal on metal, the guards extended their lances and crowded in on them.

Ten

The distant light of the sun Sya fell upon the intruder as it closed in on the star's third planet. Those down on Gadmuur's arid surface, who turned their faces to the thin, cloudless sky and held their breaths, could see a ghostly sketch of the object as it approached. Passing inside the orbital path of Gadmuur's outer moon, the leviathan's presence began to stir the larger planet, its gravitation exerting a tidal force on the atmosphere. Storm cells formed spontaneously, hurricanes full of razor-edged dust sprouting across the plains. Almost all the workers on the industrial colony ran for the safety of their underground bunkers, and so it was that only a handful remained to see the distant flashes of fire that marked the battle raging above them.

The ships of the grand Syhaari flotilla waited until the last possible second before they committed themselves to the engagement. There had been a hope, a vain and wishful one, that the monolithic intruder might veer away when faced with a sky filled with warships. But the leviathan did not turn, its first act of defiance to bleed off velocity through the discharge of massive surges of electroplasma, preventing itself from taking a collision course into Gadmuur's gravity well. Such a meeting would have torn apart both the planet and the strange, monstrous life-form—but the leviathan was not here to martyr itself.

The word came from the command deck of *The Light of Strength*, and with the dedication born of desperation and hope in their hearts, the first flights of Syhaari rangers blazed a trail from their staging points and into weapons range with the alien object. Twenty ships, some of them veterans of exploration missions to the outer worlds of the Sya system, others having only been sealed up days ago and launched from their drydocks while their welds were still fresh. Each had a skeleton crew, a need forced on them by the nature of their battle plan, with every trained spacer recalled from other duties to join the fighting line. In the hours before the final order had come, the makeshift crews had drifted in the darkness, opening collective comm channels to one another so that they could share clan-hymns while they marked the time. The Syhaari kept up their spirits with the gruff singing as best they could, until the leviathan grew large on their scanner screens and the inexorable approach made them all fall silent.

Of the crews aboard the twenty ships in the first wave, there would be none that would sing again. The rangers came at the object in an angry swarm, releasing salvoes of fusion missiles that roared across the distance between attacker and target. Lines of bright light webbed the zone around the leviathan before the myriad warheads fell in tumbling, corkscrew paths through the object's outer atmospheric mantle. Ripples of chain reactions detonated over the leviathan's surface as it reacted to the aggression.

The plan had been to concentrate all the firepower of the first wave in one spot on the leviathan's crust, to be the equivalent of a thousand needles stabbing a giant in the same place. If they could *wound* this thing, if it were possible to make it *bleed*, then perhaps it would see the error of its ways and push back against the malevolent impulses that was driving it forward.

But that was not to be. The leviathan's ephemeral corposant sheath, glittering like captured lightning, flashed brightly as the fusion missiles struck. They detonated early, *far too* early, and clouds of fire bloomed in an ugly crimson smear across the object's southern hemisphere.

The leviathan seemed to shudder. Whatever consciousness it possessed, the Syhaari attack force had certainly succeeded in getting its attention. Torrents of amber flame grew out of electrostatic reactions in the stone flesh of the leviathan, and towers of lightning rose from the surface in dazzling profusion. Burning through the haze of nuclear smoke brought forth by the missile bombardment, the great pillars of energy became writhing serpents as they passed into the vacuum. Branching wildly, the storm of power engulfed the twenty rangers as their commanders tried in vain to alter course and gain distance. In panic, one junior captain, who had never before steered anything bigger than an aero-lifter, killed himself and his crew by flying into the fusion drive plume of a sister-ship. His self-inflicted ending came only a fraction of a second before his nineteen cohorts were speared by the leviathan's vicious counterattack.

Lines of lightning pierced the hulls of the rangers, opening them to the void, jumping from ship to ship in manic jolts. Reactor cores overloaded, unspent missiles cooked off in their launching tubes, and then the first wave was gone.

The second wave was only moments behind the leaders, all of these smaller and more maneuverable ships that had been hastily converted into gunboats bristling with retrofitted particle cannons. Their crews could do nothing but watch the deaths of their comrades in as much time as it had taken to draw a breath.

Ahead of them, the leviathan gathered up more power to meet their approach with the same terrible violence.

On the bridge of the *Enterprise*, the only sound Montgomery Scott could hear was the rough gasp that escaped his throat. His flesh crawled as a sudden, horrible chill washed over him. There on the main viewer, the mad fires cast out by the alien intruder were briefly dissipating to reveal the graveyard of dozens more Syhaari ships. *Nothing there*, he thought to himself, *only dust and debris.*

"Mother of Ages," whispered M'Ress, breaking the silence. "Could anyone have survived that?"

Scott looked across the bridge to where Ensign Haines was clinging to the science station, her knuckles white around the viewer hood. She met his gaze with a bleak shake of the head.

"The next group of Syhaari vessels is still closing with the object," said Sulu, finding his voice. Before him on the helm console, the prism-shaped alert light blinked a steady red beacon.

"How many of them in the next wave?" asked Scott.

Lieutenant Leslie answered the question. "Eight ships, sensors reading three life forms on board each. Damn, they're just flying right into the teeth of that monster." He turned back to look at Spock, who sat still as a statue in the command chair. "Sir, it's not a military operation, it's a suicide charge."

"A point I made to their commander myself," Spock said quietly.

"And what does he hope to do, sir?" Scott shook his head. "Keep feeding ships to the beast until it runs out of energy? I don't think the leviathan will choke."

"If they're trying to slow it down, they've already failed," said Sulu. "Those fusion detonations? It took the damage without flinching."

"With no distinct target in the form of a Breg'Hel craft, there are few other tactical approaches open to the Syhaari," noted Spock. "And I doubt those beings will reveal themselves until they are ready to."

Scott frowned. The *Enterprise* had lost all track of the ships that had taken the *Icarus* within seconds of them passing behind the leviathan's energetic penumbra. He knew as well as anyone that the Breg'Hel—even if they were somehow herding the great cosmozoan—were beyond anyone's reach for the moment.

"Second wave of Syhaari ships is twenty seconds from weapons range," Sulu noted. "They're still going in."

"We have to do something!" said Leslie. "Warn them off!"

"They are not unaware of the situation, Mister Leslie," Spock reminded him. "Those crews are following their orders."

"Syhaari ships now firing in salvo!" said Sulu.

Scott looked around to see the glittering beams of their weapon discharges shimmer brightly across the face of the leviathan, new blooms of exotic radiation flaring where the shots interacted with the object's strangely charged atmosphere. Almost immediately, the lightning-force that had retaliated against the first wave of ships began to re-form. The smaller, more agile ships of the second wave broke away and powered back toward the main body of the Syhaari reprisal fleet, but Scott knew in his heart of hearts that they would not be quick enough. "Commander, sir . . ." He gave Spock an imploring look. "Leslie's right. We can't just sit here and be spectators to a massacre!"

The Vulcan's stoic expression never changed; he simply nodded once. "Mister Sulu, adjust attitude to mark three decimal two and take us in at half impulse power. Mister Leslie, bring our deflectors up to maximum and divert all energy from weapons systems to enhance them."

The *Enterprise*'s helmsman and the navigator didn't need to be told twice. Suddenly the view on the main screen shifted as the ship left its station far outside the conflict zone and raced into the heart of the battle.

Kaleo listened intently as Kirk relayed the conversation he'd had with the Breg'Hel commanders, interrupting only once or twice to clarify a minor point. When he was finished, she let out a low, whistling sigh. "You should have accepted their offer, Kirk. These beings are correct about one thing—this matter is between us and them. There is no merit in risking your lives into the bargain."

Rumen spoke up from where he sat slumped against a rough-hewn wall. "Sister is right. If we have fallen into this war by the act of one of our kind, off-worlder blood should not be shed because of it."

"This isn't the first time my crew and I have been

caught in the middle of someone else's battle," Kirk told them. "We weathered it then, and we'll weather it now."

At his side, he saw Xuur give a shallow nod. "Yes, of course. The conflict between Eminiar and Vendikar."

"How did that end?" said Kaleo.

"Better than it started," Kirk replied, before Xuur was tempted to rake over the coals of that incident. "And the Federation always stands by its friends. Isn't that right, Envoy?"

The Rhaandarite woman nodded again. "We strive to do so."

Rumen gave a heavy sigh and took Kaleo's hand. "My friend and pupil. Glad as I am to see you, I wish now you had not come." He sniffed at her fur. "Too dangerous. You should not be out here in—"

"Be quiet, you old fool," she said gently. "That's no concern of yours."

Nearby, Lieutenant Arex folded his three arms in a complex knot of limbs and elbows. "Captain, analyzing what you said. It seems that the Breg'Hel have closed off all avenues of diplomatic approach. I fear that may only leave us with other, more . . . *kinetic* methods of persuasion."

Kirk didn't answer straightaway, but the fact was the Triexian was right. "They seem intractable," he went on. "We tried to seek common ground with them, but we came up empty."

"Maybe violence is ingrained in their culture," said Uhura ruefully. "We've seen that in other martial species, like the Klingons and the Romulans."

"No." Rumen said the word, then shivered, realizing they were all watching him.

"You have something to add?" Kirk prompted. "Please, go on. You've been aboard this ship for months, exposed to the Breg'Hel for all that time. Any insight you have could be vital."

Kaleo went to his side and stroked his shoulder. "Brother, listen to the human. If you know something, tell us."

Rumen fidgeted and then shook himself. "It is just . . . with all due respect to your sister officer, Kirk, and in spite of the evidence to the contrary, I do not believe the Breg'Hel are a warlike species. I would say they have been driven to this violence by something in their character. Because of their wounding at Tormid's hands."

Kirk listened carefully to Rumen's words. "You said before that the Breg'Hel are a network of blood relations and family ties; that they *keenly felt* the deaths of those killed on the scoutship."

Rumen's large, hairy head bobbed in an approximation of a nod. "It is almost as if it were a physical wound upon every one of them."

"What if it is?" said Uhura. "Or, something like it? When we lose someone we care for, we suffer emotional pain and trauma that can last for a lifetime.

What if the Breg'Hel connection is more empathic in nature?"

"That would explain some of their behavior," said Xuur. "If only we had a telepath with us. Captain Kirk, I think that the Breg'Hel might share a low-level psionic link with other members of their bloodline. When one dies, they all feel it. Quite literally."

Kirk nodded. "I've heard stories of human twins separated over great distances who felt a shock when their sibling was injured or perished. What you're suggesting is something on the same spectrum." He blew out a breath. "No wonder they want to strike back. 'One crime is all crimes,' that's what Ret'Sed told us. They felt those deaths on the scoutship, and the anger at that is what drives them now."

"It also explains why they didn't seem to grasp the concept of individual responsibility for those actions," added the diplomat. "The Breg'Hel see other species as they see themselves, a community that shares all accountability for deeds done."

"If that is so," Kaleo said quietly, "then how far will their punishment of my people progress? How many of us will they destroy before their need for revenge is sated?"

Kirk had no answer to that question. "We can't stay here and wait to find out. I'm inclined to follow Mister Arex's suggestion and take a more forceful tack."

"A prison break?" said Uhura.

"We've busted out of cells more than once, Lieutenant," Kirk replied, moving to the iris hatch to study its rigid surface. "And this is our first obstacle."

"I could rig one of our communicator batteries to overload," said the communications officer. "But it'll be messy and hard to direct the discharge. There's no way to know if it'll even dent that metal."

Xuur gave a heavy sigh, and she reached up to her forehead to remove the jeweled band she wore there. "I may have an alternative." The envoy turned the ornament over in her hands and revealed its inner surface. A matrix of tiny circuits and components glittered there. "This might be of use."

Kirk took it from her. "What am I looking at here, Veygaan? A recording device?"

"Much more than that, James," she said with a wan smile. "The band contains a visual processing system, sensing gear, a holographic projector. It provides me with valuable real-time information when I am in conversation with others."

He held it up in front of his face and blinked in surprise as a hitherto unnoticed beam projected a panel of virtual data directly into his right eye. Kirk aimed it at Kaleo and saw the device respond to the Syhaari's silhouette. "Are concealed lie detectors standard issue for FDC diplomats?"

"That is a simplistic description," said Xuur. "The band is an . . . enhancement I use in parallel with my own skills."

"And you record everything around you, every private word said, without the knowledge of others?" Kirk handed the device back to her, frowning. "I don't know how many regulations or statutes that violates. I'm guessing it's a lot."

Xuur's ever-demure mask slipped. "We can go back and forth over any recriminations later," she sniffed. "The fact is, the band has other functions that Lieutenant Uhura might be able to turn to a more offensive use." The envoy nodded toward the hatch.

"Let me see that thing," said the communications officer.

———

Scott met Spock's gaze across the *Enterprise*'s bridge. "Orders, sir? With no power to our phasers or photon torpedoes, we can't—"

"We have already seen there is no purpose to firing randomly at the leviathan," the Vulcan broke in. "And I will exhaust every possible nonviolent approach to this situation before I order aggressive action." He nodded toward the engineering console. "What is the status of our tractor beam emitters, engineer?"

"Fully operable, sir," Scott answered without hesitation.

"Your ancestors, the people of Scotland. Many of them were fishermen."

The statement came out of nowhere, and Scott was wrong-footed by it. "Um. Aye, sir, that they were."

"Let us hope their skills transferred to you. Man the emitters, Mister Scott, and prepare to cast a wide net."

"Oh. I see . . ." The engineer suddenly understood the first officer's plan, and a grin split his face. He raced back to his console and ran through the tractor beam power-up sequence in a fraction of the time it would normally have required.

Out beyond the main viewer, a bow wave of lighting shards rose from the surface of the leviathan, lashing at the sterns of the Syhaari ships. "Return fire incoming," said Sulu. "Fourth power energy field, the same frequency and radiant signature as what hit us before."

"Put us between the line of fire and the Syhaari ships," ordered Spock. "Lieutenant Leslie, extend our deflectors as far as you are able and screen those craft."

Sulu nodded to himself as he saw where the first officer was taking them. "I can angle the ship to put the maximum aspect in front of the smaller vessels. But we won't be able to stand up to a sustained bombardment, sir."

"Acknowledged, Mister Sulu. Fortunately, the data our sensors gathered from the leviathan's earlier attack on the *Enterprise* has enabled me to remodulate our shields to provide a greater degree of resistance."

Scott frowned. "How much greater?"

"Thirteen percent," said the Vulcan.

"That'll have to do," he replied.

"Viewer angle on the other ships," Spock ordered, and the screen flicked to an image of the fleeing Syhaari gunboats. "Lieutenant M'Ress, send a message to those vessels and warn them to brace for collision." Without waiting for the communications officer to respond, he looked back toward Scott. "Are we ready?"

The engineer drew a deep breath. "There's a lot of moving targets. I'm having to split the beam loci multiple times . . . but yes, sir, we're ready."

"Helm, compute escape course and stand by to execute." Spock leaned back in the captain's chair, as composed as if he were giving an order to set out on a cruise around the moons and back. "At your discretion, Mister Scott."

"Incoming fire!" cried Leslie, a split second before the upper reaches of the *Enterprise*'s shield barrier was slammed by the leviathan's lightning surge. The starship rang like a struck bell, and for a moment Scott felt the deck beneath his feet flex alarmingly as the structural integrity field lagged in compensating for the impact. A flood of crimson warning lights burst into being across his console as the ship made its pain known to him. Seconds passed, seeming to extend indefinitely, as the Starfleet vessel took the brunt of the barrage that was meant to destroy the second wave of Syhaari ships.

He heard the clatter and thud of debris banging off the hull of the starship as they moved through the area where the first wave had met its end. What was left of those ships and crews was now nothing but ashen remains strewn across the void.

On a tertiary screen, a string of green ready indicators blinked, and Scott's jaw set as he activated the *Enterprise*'s tractor beam emitters in sequence. It was a tricky job at the best of times, even without aiming from one moving platform at another—*no, scratch that, at* many *other moving targets*—not to mention the added computation he was doing on the fly regarding mass and relative velocity. Get it wrong, and the attractive gravimetric power of the tractor beam could induce shear forces that would rip the target apart or, worse, set up a feedback pulse that could tear the emitter right out of the *Enterprise*'s hull.

"Mister Scott?" prompted Spock.

"Aye, let's reel them in, then." He pressed the key that committed them to the action, and somewhere along the starship's keel, glittering tractor beams stabbed out across the dark and hooked the dozen smaller vessels.

It was a testament to Scott's skill that not one beam missed its target. The crews on the Syhaari craft, understanding what protection was being extended toward them, cut their engines and let the *Enterprise*'s transferred momentum gather them up. The engineer deftly shortened the gain of the multiple tractor beams and pulled the little gunships closer. He ignored the warnings threatening overloads from the emitters and pushed the systems well past their safety protocols. Even as the starship rocked beneath the leviathan's bombardment, Scott kept his hands on his controls, manipulating the tractors to keep the other vessels safe.

Fire blazed around the disc of *Enterprise*'s primary hull, for long moments bathing it in a hellish inferno—and then they were abruptly free of it, sweeping out of the far side of the attack corridor.

"Shields down to twenty-seven percent," called Leslie. "Some hull damage."

"Sickbay reports no casualties," added M'Ress.

Sulu called out from his station. "We're clear of the leviathan's fire."

Scott nodded to himself and executed an emergency shutdown of the overheating tractor beam projectors before they were ruined beyond all repair. He watched as the Syhaari gunships tumbled, the vessels that moments ago had been a heartbeat away from obliteration reigniting their engines and moving off.

Multiple, overlapping voices issued out of Lieutenant M'Ress's console. "Hails coming in from all the craft," she explained. "They're thanking us for intervening."

Spock nodded once. "Mister Sulu, bring us about and maintain separation from the leviathan."

M'Ress spoke again, the feline communications officer pressing a wireless receiver to her arched ear. "Another hail, *The Light of Strength*."

"Our friend Mister Tormid?" said Scott, rubbing a sheen of sweat from his forehead.

"No doubt," Spock agreed, and gestured to M'Ress to open the channel. "This is the *Enterprise.*"

Tormid let fly with a string of strident, angry grunts that the universal translator couldn't parse, although Scott knew the sound of curse-words when he heard them. *"What are you doing, offworlder? This is a military operation, you cannot simply interfere with it at a whim!"*

"I believe the correct response at this juncture would be to say 'You are welcome,'" Spock replied coolly. "And given the effect of your initial attack on the intruder, I would suggest you consider revising your operational plan. Immediately." He nodded to M'Ress, and she ended the communication.

"Commander . . ." Ensign Haines spoke up, her manner halting and fearful. Her gaze was fixed on the display through the science station monitor hood. "Long-range sensors are picking up a large number of new targets, becoming distinct as they move out from behind the leviathan's mass shadow."

"Vessels?" asked the first officer.

Haines gave a nod. "Aye, sir. The same craft we saw before, the ones that came out to meet the *Icarus.* But more this time, a lot more."

"On screen," he ordered.

Scott looked up at the viewer as it reframed a section of the leviathan's upper quadrant. Rising up out of the plasmatic haze of the living planetoid's atmosphere were dozens of dull, vaguely ovoid shapes propelled by jets of blue fire. To the engineer's eye, they looked liked mailed fists grasping clusters of glass daggers. "So the ones with their hands on the beast's leash have decided to show themselves, then. Can't tell if that bodes ill or not."

Sulu's next words answered that question for him. "Energy signature building inside the leviathan, sir. Twice the power levels we saw before. It's preparing to attack again."

"Do you feel that?" said Arex. He placed a hand on the stony wall of the holding chamber. "A tremor, somewhere else in the ship, an engine coming on line. I think we're moving under power again."

"Then we have no time to lose," said Kirk. "Ready?"

"I've tried to escape before," said Rumen, taking up a place in front of the glassy screen. "Several times. I never got far."

"You were alone then," Kaleo said, not unkindly. "This time, we'll take you home."

"I would like that." Rumen bowed his head and filled his lungs. "Step back, everyone." He balled his huge hands into fists and rolled his shoulders. Then, with an ear-splitting roar, the muscular Syhaari attacked the screen panel with his bare hands, smashing into it over and over, splintering the quartzlike material with each heavy blow.

Kirk winced as he saw the breaking glass draw blood from Rumen's hands, but the Syhaari did not stop. Fluid leaked out of the broken screen, and a sharp, acidic smell filled the air.

"I hear something," called Arex, who crouched low by the far side of the hatch. "Yes, movement."

"Be ready," Kirk told Uhura. "We get only one shot at this."

"Aye, Captain." The communications officer held up Xuur's headband, the central ornamental jewel aimed at the doorway. A mess of hair-fine optical cables connected it to a gutted communicator, and Uhura's finger hovered over the device's transmit key.

With a low thud of magnetic bolts, the iris hatch unlocked and the curved metal petals retracted away into the walls. Revealed behind it were the forms of four Breg'Hel guards, each with their batons drawn and ready. In the perpetual gloom of the alien ship, their scaled bodies were wraithlike shadows.

"Now!" shouted the captain, and he turned away, covering his eyes.

Uhura stabbed the button and activated their makeshift weapon; the artificial gemstone in Xuur's headband concealed an imaging module, but the component could also be forced to emit a frequency of light if correctly modified. A sudden flurry of brilliant white flashes strobed inside the dimly lit holding chamber, and the Breg'Hel guards with their large, unprotected eyes were blinded. The aliens squealed in pain and fell back—but not before Kirk, Arex, and Kaleo were upon them.

Kirk's fist connected with the scaly jaw of one guard, and the Breg'Hel staggered backward. He struck again, and the alien's thick pink tongue flapped out of its mouth as it went down, out cold. Kaleo, reacting with great speed, disarmed another Breg'Hel and used the stunner in the tip of its baton to dispatch it. For his part, Lieutenant Arex took on the other two guards, landing multiple blows at once by using the low gravity to pirouette on his central leg. They quickly fell, and Kirk found himself nodding in approval.

"Impressive moves, Mister Arex," he noted.

The Triexian gathered up a pair of fallen batons. "Learned in my youth, when I danced. I would offer to teach you, sir, but you lack the correct number of limbs."

Kaleo went to the door and beckoned the others into the corridor. "Quickly! We must not tarry."

Uhura stepped through and took a baton from Arex, with Xuur and Rumen following close behind her. The envoy was helping the Syhaari walk, and she had torn off a length of her sleeve to make into rudimentary bandages for the cuts on his hands. "What about them?" she asked, nodding toward the guards.

"We'll let them sleep it off," Kirk replied, gathering up the Breg'Hel he had knocked out and shoving it back through the open hatch. Arex helped him with the others, and when all the guards were inside, Kaleo found the controls that sealed the door from the outside.

"You escaped before?" Uhura asked Rumen. "How fast are they at responding to something like that?"

"Fast," said the Syhaari. "Groups of guards patrol all areas of the ship. They'll know we have attacked their people."

"That empathic response again," agreed Kirk. He glanced around; a number of corridors branched off from the area where they were standing. "Arex. Do you remember the way back to the landing bay where they brought the *Icarus* aboard?"

"It's ingrained in my memory, sir," he said, tapping his bulbous brow.

"Then it'll be up to you to take the lead. This isn't going to be easy, you'll have to get the shuttle out and away, damaged or not . . ."

"Have you forgotten there is probably a battle raging out there?" said Xuur.

"We'll make it," insisted Uhura.

Kirk nodded. "Contact me when you're clear of the ship."

His officers froze. "You're not coming with us?" said Rumen

"I'm going back to the command center," he told them. "I'll get in the way, distract them, surrender myself to the Breg'Hel if it comes to that. Maybe even try another shot at talking them out of this madness."

"Captain, you can't . . ." Uhura took a step toward him, but he waved her off.

"The lieutenant is right!" Xuur's eyes widened. "What's to stop them killing you?"

"We don't have time to argue!" Kirk snarled. "You have your orders, carry them out!" He pointed a finger at Xuur. "And before you tell me you don't have to obey, Envoy, I'll remind you to review your Starfleet regulations. In a situation like this, the captain's word is *final*."

"It is," said Kaleo, handing off Rumen to Arex. "Which is why *I* am coming with you."

"Sister, no!" said the other Syhaari, placing a hand on her chest. "You cannot, not while you—"

She silenced him with a gruff snort, brushing off his hand. "The decision is made, Rumen! Kirk returns to face these creatures and one of us should go with him." Kaleo met Kirk's gaze with a defiant glint in her eye. "Anything else would be in defiance of a captain's orders."

"So be it," said Kirk, but the words had hardly been spoken before he heard the clatter and rustle of movement somewhere farther down one of the stone corridors. "Uhura. The *Icarus* is under your command now. Get her home. Tell Spock everything."

She gave a nod. "I'll see you again, sir, soon."

"I hope so, Nyota. I hope so." He watched the others move off, and then turned back to Kaleo, testing the weight of the stunner baton in his hand.

"The odds are stacked against us once again," said the Syhaari. "It's almost starting to feel like that is the way of things."

He eyed her. "You have a tendency to put yourself in harm's way, Captain Kaleo. Why is that?"

Her round face split in a toothy smile. "Look in a mirror, Captain Kirk, and ask that question of yourself." She gestured with her baton as the sounds of Breg'Hel reinforcements grew nearer. "They'll be here in moments. Which way to the command center?"

Kirk beckoned her. "Follow me."

Eleven

A killing radiance exploded from the malignant haze surrounding the leviathan as it rolled through the void, pushing into the defense lines over the planet Gadmuur.

With an actinic flare of power, the colossal creature spat a discharge of arcing electrical energy into the largest of the Syhaari orbital shipyards. A curved web of metal gantries, cables, and ovoid command modules, the space platform was designed to service dozens of spacecraft at once, but now—*mercifully*—it was empty, evacuated in a panic only hours earlier.

None of that mattered to the alien intruder intent only on mass destruction. The leviathan's lightning surge flashed over the orbital station's open structure, leaping and sliding down the length of it, leaving devastation in its wake. Control pods blew apart, vomiting their contents into the vacuum, jets of gas and fluids leaving clouds of glittering vapor as they expanded outward. Support frames designed to hold rangers and explorers collapsed in on themselves, twisting in the grip of warring magnetic fields, ripping away and tumbling into Gadmuur's gravity well. The platform began to deform and come apart, shedding plasma fire, fragmenting until the elegant basket-weave shape of its original form was a mess of colliding girders, flash-frozen chemicals, and second-order detonations. Knocked out of its orbit by the attack, the ragged slick of debris that remained started its final passage around the third planet.

Wreathed in fire, the leviathan shimmered behind the luminous sheath of its own energies, and trailing behind it came the ships of the Breg'Hel. Fresh jags of power rippled out from the core of the living planetoid, licking at the wreckage-choked sky all around it.

"The orbital station was empty," Ensign Haines reported, in a dead voice. "But that's barely a kindness. When a few thousand tons of platform on terminal trajectory cuts through Gadmuur's atmosphere, there'll be nothing to stop it laying waste to hundreds of kilometers of the surface along the descent line."

Spock remained expressionless, watching the death throes of the shipyard. Perhaps, with two or three more ships like the *Enterprise*, perhaps if they were not in the midst of an invasion, it might have been possible to get ahead of the mass of the obliterated platform and do something to nudge it into a different orbital path. He made a quick calculation; no, even beaming photon torpedoes into the wreckage to try and break it up would make the matter worse, resulting in damage scattered over an even wider area. He hoped that the colonists down on Gadmuur would be able to clear the path beneath the falling debris—but for now their fate was of secondary consideration to him. His first duty was, as always, to the *Enterprise* and his orders.

"That target was an illogical choice," he said aloud, glancing across at Lieutenant Sulu. "There was no tactical value in destroying it while other defender vessels are still active nearby."

Sulu confirmed that with a nod. "Aye, sir. Three formations of Syhaari rangers are in close proximity to the leviathan, but it ignored them all to go after the station."

"It can't be attracted by size or by the highest energy output," reasoned Scott. "If that were so, it'd be chasing *us*."

"Target is moving again!" called Lieutenant Leslie. "Homing in on one of the ranger formations. They're burning hard for high orbit, trying to make a break for it."

"Distance?" asked Scott, but Spock knew the damning answer before Leslie responded.

"Out of our range, sir."

After intervening in the disastrous first attack, the *Enterprise* had extended away from the melee in space to repair the shields and stay beyond the reach of the intruder's deadly firepower—but the starship was still close enough to witness every moment of the leviathan's brutal assault.

"It's too late for them," Sulu said bleakly. As he spoke, pinpricks of fire blossomed on the main view-screen as the planetoid unleashed a monumental, frenzied storm of overkill on the smaller ships. The flight of Syhaari vessels was gone in an instant, leaving only radioactive dust behind.

Each attack that came from the leviathan seemed more wild than the last. Where at first its behavior had exhibited some manner of direction behind it, it was becoming increasingly clear to Spock that the vast extrasolar life-form's ferocity was slipping out of control. What happened next all but confirmed the grim hypothesis that he was already forming.

"Look there!" called Scott, pointing at the viewer. "D'you see it, Commander?"

Spock nodded. He could pick out a single alien vessel, one of the asymmetrical craft belonging to the Breg'Hel. The engineer had caught sight of it as it moved out of formation in the leviathan's wake, and now it was clear to see, light flashing off the crystalline elements of the hull.

"Scanning," said Haines. "I'm detecting irregular fusion pulses from the craft. Perhaps a drive system malfunction, sir . . ."

"Until now, those craft have not ventured beyond a zone of magnetic interference emanating from the poles of the leviathan," noted Spock. "This is an unusual event." He could see that the other Breg'Hel craft were scrupulously maintaining their own positions well within the magnetic zone; it could only be a blind spot that the massive cosmozoan's consciousness somehow did not register.

"It's turning." Scott studied a tactical plot on a secondary monitor. "Or at least, it's trying to."

"Reading a localized power surge," said Sulu. "The leviathan . . . I think it senses the Breg'Hel ship."

With what could only have been a very deliberate, directed act, the planetoid flicked a spear of lightning out from its surface and bifurcated the errant Breg'Hel vessel. Stony matter and shards of energized crystal were scattered, the craft obliterated as quickly and as violently as the Syhaari ranger ships had been only moments earlier.

Scott let out a breath. "They're driving that thing somehow, running it angry like a mad bull," he said. "And that's what happens if you get caught on the horns. The beast doesn't see any difference between friend or foe."

"That ship, it fell out of position and paid the price," added Sulu. "Letting that creature run wild, it's madness!"

"If they are driving it, as you say, Mister Scott, then they must be using some instrumentality to do so." Spock rose from the command chair and turned to face Lieutenant M'Ress at communications. Before the *Icarus* had departed on its ill-fated diplomatic mission, Spock had made sure the Caitian had been fully briefed by Lieutenant Uhura—specifically on her attempts to isolate any signals passing directly between the leviathan and the Breg'Hel. "What have you found?" he asked M'Ress.

Her ears swiveled and wilted slightly, the Caitian equivalent of a frown. "I've been running signal traffic analysis since the first approach, sir," she told him. "There's certainly something there. Trace pulses, in the same ranges as that declaration message that Uhura decoded. But I can't isolate them. There's just too much additional noise."

"Define 'noise,'" said the science officer.

M'Ress's paw twitched in agitation. "Commander, the leviathan itself is emitting a constant stream of incoherent transmissions on tertiary subspace wavebands. It . . ." She halted, trying to frame her words. "Sir, it's as if the creature is constantly *howling*."

Spock considered her words. If the leviathan was enraged, if it was in pain, such behavior would make sense. "Let me hear it."

"Aye, sir." Warily, M'Ress touched a control and suddenly the *Enterprise*'s bridge was filled with a peculiar, phantasmal moan. The tone conjured up recollections of waves striking a stone beach, of ghostly echoes through caverns and wind across wastelands. To Vulcan ears it was a uniquely mournful, yet coldly enraged sound.

Spock remembered another line of the Tennyson poem from which Captain Kirk had drawn his name for the cosmozoan. "'In roaring he shall rise and on the surface die.'"

"Sir?" said M'Ress, unaware of the reference.

"It is unimportant," said Spock. "I have heard enough."

"Like the voice of a revenant," muttered Scott as M'Ress switched off the audio link. "What have they let loose here, sir?"

Spock's eyes narrowed. "I fear it is a force they cannot control, Mister Scott."

———————

"Are you certain this is the best course of action?" said Kaleo, nervously glancing down the rough-hewn corridor. She gestured at the sealed hatch blocking their path. "If we proceed, we enter a nest of *yoleh*."

"I assume that's not a good thing," Kirk replied, adjusting the power setting on the baton in his hand.

"*Yoleh*," she repeated, making a small shape with her fingers. "Fat, stinging insects that attack in swarms when threatened. You have something like that on your human worlds?"

"I understand the analogy." He nodded. "But we're running out of options. Sooner or later, the Breg'Hel will recapture us. We have to make a statement now, while we still can." He paused. "Kaleo, do you trust me?"

Her head bobbed. "Yes, James, I do. Even if you are

a peculiar-looking alien and bald of face, I trust you. I owe you that."

Kirk smiled. "I told you before, you don't owe me anything. But if you offer me your trust, I'll promise you won't regret it."

She eyed him. "You are persuasive. I see why the Rhaandarite is attracted to you."

"What?" His smile fell away. "I think you're mistaken."

"And I think you're denying something you already know." Before he could answer, she waved a long-fingered hand at the hatch. "Go on. Open it, before I change my mind."

"Cover your eyes." Kirk looked away and jabbed the tip of his baton into a control pad sculpted out of the carved wall. Sparks flew and suddenly the hatch chugged open, the metallic petals of the iris clanking as they retracted.

Beyond was the command core of the ship, the dim space lit by glowing screens and bulbous bioluminescent plants. The Breg'Hel crew were caught by surprise, unprepared for two aliens to suddenly storm into the heart of their vessel, in the middle of a tactical engagement.

Kirk saw the yellow-skinned security officer Zud'Hoa react to the intrusion, drawing a brace of telescoping batons and launching forward. The Breg'Hel sprang into a defensive stance between the two intruders and the elders Kirk had spoken to before.

Kirk called to them before things got out of control, letting the universal translator shift his words into their speech. "Ret'Sed! Ead'Aea! This has gone on too long. The aggression must end!"

Zud'Hoa made a growling sound in the depths of its throat. "You speak of aggression, but we all feel the blows you struck, now-known! You are no better than that-kind!" The Breg'Hel aimed a baton at Kaleo. "Violent barbarians. You must be punished."

"You gave us no choice," said Kirk. "I regret what I did . . . but I was not willing to let my people languish in a cell while you attack the Syhaari."

Another of the command crew, until now frozen in silence at one of the tubular console displays, abruptly spoke up. "There is disorder in the reception bay! The small-craft of the now-known is attempting to depart, despite the damage it suffered."

Kaleo menaced the console operator with her stolen baton. "Step away from those controls," she ordered. "You will let them leave."

"Do as the alien says," said Ret'Sed, after a moment.

"I will release the hatch." The operator tapped out a code string across the touch-sensitive screens, then backed off, skittering away up a curved incline.

Kaleo chanced a look at the oval screens and gave a disgusted grunt. "These readouts mean nothing to me . . ." She paused, thinking, then raised the baton. "If I destroy the panel, they won't be able to renege—"

"No!" said Ead'Aea, before Kaleo could act. "Cease, cease, you animal! There is great delicacy in these mechanisms, and unity between them! You wound the ship if you break them!"

"Is that so?" Kirk let his weapon hang, and with his free hand he removed the communicator on his belt, flicking it open. "*Icarus,* this is the captain. Uhura, do you hear me?"

The reply came quickly, but it was heavy with distortion. "*Reading . . . sir. We are away . . . navigation is difficult . . . no sign of pursuit.*" A rattle of static briefly blanked out Uhura's words. "*Sir, what about you and—*"

"Get to safety, Lieutenant," he ordered, cutting her off. "Kirk out."

"We are allowing the small-craft to exit the conflict zone," grumbled Ret'Sed. "Now you surrender to us."

Kirk shook his head. "I don't think we will." He pointed at the vacant console. "Kaleo, if anyone makes a move against us, destroy that panel." She nodded, taking up a ready stance.

"You are truly low," spat Zud'Hoa. "That could cause great harm to all of us, even you!"

"We are *desperate*!" Kaleo said angrily. "You have made us so, by turning your star-blighted monster on our worlds!"

"That is only what you have earned," said Ead'Aea. "*You* did the first harm. *Your* kind."

"And how much harm is it going to take?" said

Kirk, pitching his voice at a steady level. "Tell me. You are the co-commanders, you are in charge here. How many of the Syhaari must you see dead in order to sate your need for revenge?"

"It is not revenge, it is balance." Ret'Sed's eyes flicked back and forth. "Punishment is done, and enough that this known-kind will never venture beyond their cloud-home again."

"They want to terrify us into hiding on our worlds," said Kaleo. She bared her teeth. "I have news for you, alien. The stars do not belong solely to you!"

"You are the aliens!" Zud'Hoa barked, taking a menacing step forward. "Your kind, not us!"

Kirk's lip curled. "That's not how it is at all," he told them. "*Every one of us is an alien out here.* We are not born in the void. That's the one thing that we all have in common, don't you see? And we have only two choices before us, no matter if we're Breg'Hel, Syhaari, or human. We can share the stars in peace, or we can fight over them in violence. I come from a coalition that wants the former, not the latter."

Ead'Aea glared at him. "And yet your Federation allies with murderers."

"I saw the evidence," Kirk allowed. "Yes, I admit it is damning. Tormid—the one who attacked your people on the scoutship—he did something terrible, driven by fear and weakness. He must answer for his actions, none of us disagree on that. But he was just *one* being. This indiscriminate killing in the name of his misdeed . . ." Kirk shook his head, searching for the right words. "How is it right? How many must die? Haven't you done enough?"

Kaleo opened her mouth to speak, and something like a sob escaped her. She stiffened, trying again. "Are our lives worth so little in your eyes? Please, I beg of you. *Stop this.* Whatever you are doing to control that planetoid, turn it away. End it."

"The punishment," Zud'Hoa began, faltering. The fire that had burned in the Breg'Hel's words faded in the face of Kaleo's plea. "It must be carried out in full. That is our way."

"This is war you are waging, not a quest for justice," Kirk told them. "It went beyond any fair definition of reprimand the moment you unleashed that beast on the Syhaari." He looked around, taking in all of the Breg'Hel. "And you have to know, if you make such warfare without consideration, if you leave a trail of destruction across space, you will draw the same fate upon yourselves."

"Is that a threat, now-known?" Ret'Sed glared at him, baring needle-sharp teeth.

"It's a warning," Kirk countered. "Out here, habitable worlds are few and far between. But you light fires in the dark, and you'll draw the attention of others. There are more intelligent species in this region than you realize. As we speak, survey ships from the Klingon Empire are scouting the edges of this sector, vessels crewed by a warrior culture who live only for conquest. They would look upon the Breg'Hel and Syhaari and destroy you both out of hand rather than risk tolerating any threat you might represent." He sighed and felt like a great weight was settling upon him. "Violence only begets violence. We have to break the cycle." Kirk threw up his hands, imploring them. "Tell us! What do we have to do to stop this?"

When Ret'Sed spoke again, it was with a sorrow that Kirk had not heard before from the reptilians. "Our ninth-born children were crew on the scoutship that met the known. Broodlings grown, splintered off on a daughter-vessel. They were at the start of their own family-dynasty. Then killed. All their potential lost forever."

Kirk broke the silence that fell in the wake of the words. "I am sorry for your loss."

"Can you restore life to them, Human-Kirk?" Ead'Aea said quietly. "Give breath again to those we carried in our wombs, whose eggs we warmed? What can you give in return to staunch the ever-pain?"

There was a clatter of metal on stone, and Kaleo let her baton drop. She pulled at the fastener on her uniform and let it fall open, revealing her bare torso beneath. "I will balance the loss," she said, her voice thick with emotion. "In my people's stead. I will trade pain for pain. Life for life." She placed a long-fingered hand on her belly.

Kirk's blood ran cold as he realized what Kaleo was offering. "No, wait—"

"A child," said the Syhaari commander. "My life and that of my unborn child, in payment."

———

"Mister Spock," Sulu spoke up, drawing the first officer's attention, "the remaining Syhaari forces are regrouping into a spearhead formation. Extrapolating their heading, I think they're intending to make a direct run at the Breg'Hel flotilla."

"They'll never get close enough to take a shot," said Leslie. "There's a mad moon between them."

Standing beside the empty command chair, Spock folded his arms. "Lieutenant M'Ress, contact Tormid and warn him once again of the folly of any direct attack."

"All Syhaari ships are ignoring our hails, sir," she replied.

"As if that's a surprise," Scott said dryly.

"They're moving in," added Sulu.

Spock made a decision, not pausing to wonder what half of him—human or Vulcan—might have motivated it. "Bring us closer, Lieutenant, three-quarters impulse power. Maintain minimum target aspect toward the intruder."

Sulu's hands traced over the helm panel, and the *Enterprise* shifted up to speed, pushing away from its holding position and curving back in toward the conflict zone at high thrust. At his side, Leslie was already bringing the deflectors back up to full power.

The navigator hesitated with his hands over the prefire controls for the starship's offensive subsystems.

Spock said nothing, only gave Leslie the slightest shake of the head. He noted the human's momentary pause—the smallest iota of disagreement—but then the young lieutenant nodded.

"Tormid's ship is at the tip of the formation," said Scott. "Leading from the front this time, it seems."

"If he hopes such an act will make a statement, it may well be his last," noted Spock.

"They're going for it!" said Sulu.

On the main viewer, the Syhaari defensive force came at the leviathan in a wall, dozens of silver darts moving at maximum velocity in an attempt to make a high-speed pass around the rogue planetoid and target the Breg'Hel. It was a bold maneuver, but a flawed one, and even as the ships committed to the act, Spock saw the firestorms being born in the depths of the leviathan's atmosphere.

As the Enterprise drew closer to the leading edge of the defender fleet, there was a moment when it seemed as if the blunt Syhaari tactic might actually work. But then the shroud around the cosmozoan erupted with rods of amber fire that blazed out in every direction.

Some of the Syhaari commanders, those either possessed of foolish courage or dogged relentlessness, carried on regardless. Many of their ships were caught and immolated. Others, perhaps not the veterans, these captains the less space-hardened of their pilot corps, lost their desire to cross the line of destruction and veered off, stressing their craft almost to the breaking point. A few were too slow, fires burning the hulls of the ships open as they skimmed the nimbus of lightning fields.

It quickly became a rout. Command and control among the Syhaari ships fragmented before the unchained rage of the leviathan. The living planet spat blast after blast into the space around it, beating at vessels that were already torn open long after they were no longer a threat.

Spock caught sight of *The Light of Strength* as the craft threaded through the blinding forest of lightning towers. It was already firing missile barrages ahead of it into the magnetic zone, in the vain hope that a random shot might make it the distance to strike at one of the Breg'Hel craft.

Then a sword blade made of yellow sun fire carved up out of the leviathan's exosphere and sliced the command ship in two. The aft section, where the warp core and main engines were mounted, detonated into a storm of debris almost immediately, the matter-antimatter reactor consuming itself in a fraction of a second. The shockwave slammed into the remains of *The Light of Strength* and sent it tumbling away. Spock grabbed the red rail around the lower section of the bridge as the same blast wave buffeted the *Enterprise* a second later.

"Sir, we get any closer and we'll be hit too!" said Sulu.

"I am aware, Lieutenant," Spock replied.

"Commander!" Scott called out to him. "I can save some of these people, if you give me shields and transporters—but you've got to do it now!"

Spock weighed the decision in less than a heartbeat; again there was something of him that wondered where the choice was coming from. After all, a Vulcan captain aboard a Vulcan starship would never be where he was now, with the vessel under his command willfully going into danger for a people who did not want their help. A Vulcan captain aboard a Vulcan starship might simply have stood by and watched the leviathan wreak its havoc.

"Proceed," Spock commanded. "Mister Sulu, on Mister Scott's word, reverse course and get us out of the danger zone."

"The *Light* is coming apart," said Haines. "Losing crew life signs."

"We'll do something about that," Scott replied, and he dropped the deflectors, for one terrible moment rendering the *Enterprise* totally vulnerable. "All transporters locked in sequence and—*energizing*!"

On the viewscreen, what was left of the Syhaari command ship came apart and vanished into the cloud mass surrounding the leviathan.

———

I'm a fool, Kirk told himself. *I let her come with us, and I never once stopped to consider how much Kaleo had at stake.* Suddenly, half-finished comments and unspoken exchanges between Kaleo and Rumen clicked into sudden clarity. He reached out to the Syhaari. "Why didn't you tell me you were pregnant?"

"Is it your concern?" Kaleo challenged him. "I think not." She gave him something like a smile. "I've learned a little of your human ways. You would have insisted I remain on Syhaar Prime, out of reach of any potential harm. It is not how my people do things, Kirk. Parenthood does not preclude me from my duties."

"It's one thing to risk yourself, but an unborn child . . ." He trailed off as several of the Breg'Hel closed in around them. But the manner of the aliens was not hostile—they seemed *fascinated.*

"If we did not accept risk," Kaleo replied, "my race would still be living in the trees. You reminded me of that, my friend."

One of the Breg'Hel co-commanders dared to come forward, reaching out a thick-fingered hand, pointing. "The unhatched are the most precious resource," said Ead'Aea. "Worth more than the purest star-crystals, the densest of metals. You offer that?"

Fearlessly, Kaleo reached out and took Ead'Aea by the wrist. She pulled the Breg'Hel close and placed its hand on her belly. "The life of my life is here. If we are the cost of stopping your advance, I will pay the price. Stop this, let the human go. Take my . . . take *our* blood in kind."

Kirk said nothing, knowing it would be up to Kaleo's bravery to carry the day. From the corner of his eye, he noticed one of the other Breg'Hel bridge crew muttering intently into what had to be a communicator device with a field of flashing indicators before it. *Something's wrong*, he guessed, but the co-commanders didn't appear to notice.

"Is that enough?" Kaleo was saying.

Ead'Aea drew its hand away and looked questioningly at its partner. "In truth," began Ret'Sed, "we never considered your kind capable of such a thing. The known are . . ." It paused, rephrasing its words. "The Syhaari were thought to be bestial and heartless."

"I've been traveling through deep space for many years," Kirk offered. "I've met many new life-forms, some like me and some not." He nodded toward Kaleo. "And what I've realized is that the capacity for selflessness is in all of us. Just as we are all capable of anger and fear and hatred." He held out his hands, in the universal gesture that said *I have no weapon, I conceal nothing from you.* "All we need to do is decide now that we will try to make a peace, try to repair the damage done."

Ret'Sed and Ead'Aea exchanged a long, unreadable look. *Was that sorrow there?* he wondered, wishing for a moment that Xuur was with him to interpret the alien response.

Finally, Ead'Aea stepped back and spoke. "Cease," it said. "Ship-speak to all. Cease the advance and draw back the control. We have done enough. Perhaps too much."

Ret'Sed gestured at Kaleo and Kirk. "No more lives will be taken. The Syhaari have known our pain. This mother-parent makes that clear to us."

Kirk held his breath, afraid that he had misread the situation in some way, and that the offer of a ceasefire would turn out to be something else. Then Kaleo was at his side, grasping his hands with her long, fur-covered fingers. "We did it, James," she said. "The two of us, we made them listen."

A grin split his lips and he nodded at her. "The two of *you*," he corrected gently. "I just did what I could—"

A low cry of distress from one of the other Breg'Hel cut through his reply, and Kirk's head jerked up, finding the same operator he had seen moments before. The alien's control panel was now a riot of strobing glyphs and twitching displays that exhibited complex waveforms. The captain was immediately reminded of subspace radio patterns, but they were unlike anything he had ever seen before.

"I gave the command to cease," Ead'Aea barked. "Why have we not been obeyed?"

"Show visualization," said Ret'Sed, arms raised to the air.

Kirk blinked in surprise as a shimmering band of dark color appeared out of nowhere, suspended in the air. A thick ring of jumping, flickering dots formed into a mosaic of distinct images displayed in a 360-degree arc. "A holographic viewscreen," he said aloud. "It must be feeding directly from the exterior of this vessel."

"Look there. The rest of their flotilla." Kaleo pointed at a cluster of unfinished shapes in one sector of the wraparound display, rock-and-glass forms that resembled the ships the *Icarus* had met in deep space.

He nodded, finding the silhouettes of a dozen dart-shaped Syhaari rangers. Some distance beyond them, he picked out the distinctive ice-white hulls of the *Enterprise* and the wounded shuttle *Icarus*. He released a sigh of relief to see the vessels still intact, still safe.

The possibility that there might be an end to this rose in him. But that certainty vanished in the next second.

A dark form, broad enough to eclipse a full third of the holographic screen, came into sight. Kirk saw shards of lightning crossing its nightside surface, in the shadows where the brightness of the star Sya did not fall. The leviathan was impossibly close, and the strange depths of the hologram made him feel as if he could reach into the image and let his hand sink into the cloudy mantle surrounding the planetoid.

He had faced phenomena of great scale before—remembering the neutronium-hulled "doomsday machine" that had obliterated one of the *Enterprise*'s sister ships, a black sun, a gargantuan amoeba, even the hand of a self-proclaimed god—but none of them had radiated the same sense of unchained fury that this living world gave off. On some primal, animalistic level, Kirk felt profoundly threatened by the monstrous being. He was all too aware that it could destroy him without ever taking notice of his existence. It robbed him of his breath to be suddenly faced with so stark a sense of overwhelming menace.

Ead'Aea was still berating one of the command crew. "Respond! Commit to the order and make it respond!"

The operator's head sank and membranous lids flicked over its eyes. "Father-Mother, I try, but the call goes unheeded. It refuses to respond to me!"

"Again! Again!" snarled Ead'Aea.

Kirk approached, trying to see more of the control panel. "Your leviathan . . . you restrain it with this system?"

Ead'Aea glared at him, then looked away to Ret'Sed. "The leash slips."

Ret'Sed stiffened. "We have lost one craft already. We cannot afford to lose more, not if we mean to disengage."

"The call is refused," reported the operator. "I hear nothing but rage in return."

"Oh no," whispered Kaleo, drawing Kirk's attention away from the Breg'Hel's ominous declaration.

The scatterings of amber-gold lightning weaving beneath the clouds of the leviathan were no longer moving in random shoals. As Kirk watched, he saw the same fiery collisions that he had witnessed via long-range sensors, but now so close they dazzled him. Breg'Hel crew members wailed in pain and covered their bulbous eyes as bright yellow fire filled the holograph screen—and then the planetoid ejected its wrath into the darkness.

Lashing out in all directions, spears of lightning blazed away at every angle, heedless of whatever target they found. With the *Icarus* now recovered, *Enterprise* was far enough away to bank into a swift evasive turn, but once again a swath of Syhaari starcraft were ripped open by the angry power of the leviathan.

They did not perish alone; the living planet's rage was shared equally with the vessels at the leading edges of the Breg'Hel flotilla. Kirk saw the rough-hewn, rock-hulled vessels blown apart by incredible electrostatic stresses, one after another blasted into dust. All around him, the gecko-like aliens cried in a chorus of shared empathic agony—but that was cut short when a pulse of fire lashed out at the command ship and hit it hard.

Kirk's footing was gone in an instant, and he found himself slammed up against the curved ceiling before being unceremoniously hurled back down again. He landed badly, spitting blood, managing to scramble into a crouch. Nearby, Kaleo tried to stagger to her feet, and he went to the Syhaari captain's aid. Smoke that stank of burning vegetation and singed hair made him choke. There was a dull buzzing in the air that seemed to come from the walls themselves, and he could sense the push-pull in his gut as the Breg'Hel ship's internal gravity generators cut in and out.

"That . . . that wasn't even a direct hit," managed Kaleo. "It's turned on them, Kirk. Their monster has broken its chains and gone mad."

He said nothing, pressing forward, back toward the center of the command area. They came across the operator who had spoken before, the skinny, white-and-red Breg'Hel unconscious, thin streamers of blood issuing from its nostril pits as Ead'Aea tried in vain to wake it.

Ret'Sed grasped the console as if it were the only thing holding it in place and peered bleakly into the stuttering band of the holograph. "We should never have come here," rasped the alien. "I swore it was a mistake, but none listened. Blood burned too strongly. Now we will all pay for that."

"Can't you get that thing back under control?" Kirk demanded, finding his voice.

"We are no longer the masters, known," Ret'Sed shot back. "It obeys only the fury we kindled within it."

The image on the viewer twisted as the ship rolled in an uncontrolled tumble, but Kirk could still see clearly enough as the leviathan lashed out at Syhaari and Breg'Hel alike, laying waste to anything that passed within the sphere of its notice. Forcing its way through a tide of rubble and wreckage, it began to pick up speed, riding waves of compressed gravity out of its orbit around Gadmuur. Kirk saw a ripple of distortion as the object warped space like a stardrive.

Kaleo saw it too. "Where is it going?"

Ret'Sed's gaze dropped back to the console. "It has tired of this place. Moving now, yes. Toward the second world."

"Syhaar Prime," said Kirk, a dark understanding coming to him. "This isn't over yet."

Twelve

Spock heard the door chime echo inside Captain Kirk's quarters and then the sound of his commander's voice. "Come in."

The first officer entered, his report marshaled and ready to relay, but Kirk held up a hand before he could speak.

"This'll just take a moment," said the captain, in the middle of shrugging on a fresh uniform. He fastened the green wraparound tunic at his waist and returned to what he had been doing when Spock had arrived. "Computer, resume log recording."

"Working," replied the device.

"Following our confrontation with the Breg'Hel co-commanders, they agreed to a ceasefire. Kaleo was able to convince them to let us beam back to the *Enterprise,* and we are now in pursuit of the planetoid life-form, but the damage to our warp engines means we can only maintain a low velocity. Mister Scott's latest estimate puts us approximately fifteen minutes behind the target." Kirk shot a look toward Spock, a question in his expression, and the Vulcan gave a curt nod of agreement. He had double-checked the engineer's calculations himself, and the time delay was correct.

Kirk went on. "We've transmitted a warning to Syhaar Prime, but with the majority of the Syhaari defense force having been engaged at Gadmuur, there are precious few combat-capable vessels in orbit around the second planet. Frankly, even if there were, it wouldn't be enough to stop the leviathan or to evacuate the major population centers." The captain leaned forward on his desk, looking into the middle distance. "Many craft, both Syhaari and Breg'Hel, were lost at Gadmuur, but for now we have something approaching a ceasefire. The remnants of their forces are following in close formation with us, and the truce seems to be holding. Envoy Xuur is in the process of assembling an emergency summit meeting aboard the *Enterprise*, which I have offered up to both sides as a neutral location." He paused, frowning. "Time is against us, but it is my hope that together we may be able to navigate through the mire of this conflict and find a way to halt any further loss of life. End recording and transmit to Starfleet Command."

"*Log complete,*" reported the computer.

Kirk let out a breath and sat heavily. His fatigue was clear, and it was a rare moment that Spock's captain would have showed it so openly, but there were only the two of them in the room.

"Any change in the status of the leviathan?" said Kirk.

Spock shook his head. "Negative. The object's heading remains constant. At this time, sensors indicate that its internal power is almost completely channeled into propulsion and maintaining structural integrity. Any potential for offensive response is, for the moment, greatly lessened."

"That's something," said Kirk. "At least it can't hurl more of those lightning bolts at us."

"Not at this range," Spock noted. "However, if we move into close proximity, it will react."

The captain accepted that with a curt nod. "How are Uhura and Arex?"

"Doctor McCoy has released them from sickbay. While the *Icarus* may be out of service for some time, it served well beyond its abilities bringing them to safety."

"I've put commendations for both of them in the log," said Kirk. "I'm sure the envoy brushed off any concerns Bones had in a heartbeat, but what about the Syhaari pilot we rescued?"

"Mister Rumen has been treated for malnutrition and a minor viral infection, but his condition is good. Kaleo's species is a robust one."

"I'm pleased to hear that." He paused. "What about Kaleo?"

Spock raised an eyebrow. "When the doctor suggested she relocate to the infirmary because of her physical condition, she refused in no uncertain terms. There was an implied threat of violence."

"I don't doubt it. We're caught between two very passionate, very emotive races here, Spock. Tempers are running high on all sides."

"So I have observed. I will endeavor to make allowances."

Despite the seriousness of the moment, Kirk gave a dry chuckle. "Your forbearance is appreciated as always, Commander."

Spock continued his report. "The representatives from the Breg'Hel have been beamed aboard and are waiting on the hangar deck."

Kirk's manner cooled. "What about Tormid and the other Syhaari?"

"Tormid was fortunate enough to survive the destruction of *The Light of Strength*, along with Hoyga and representative Gatag, who were also aboard. Mister Scott's timely use of the transporters managed to save the lives of several of that vessel's crew. Tormid and the others are currently in visitors quarters. I took the liberty of posting a security detail." Spock paused, considering his next words. "Sir, having heard Lieutenant Uhura's preliminary report about your encounters aboard the Breg'Hel command ship, I find it difficult to conceive of a situation in which our current predicament will become *less* volatile rather than more so."

The captain stood up again, pushing away his

weariness. "Our primary concern is stopping the leviathan's rampage," he said. "But to do that, we'll need a unity of purpose between everyone here. And we're not going to get that without starting from a place of truth."

"I do not believe Tormid will agree."

Kirk's eyes narrowed. "No doubt."

Spock's prediction was, as ever, quite correct. It took less than five minutes for the meeting to devolve into a shouting match.

The *Enterprise*'s hangar deck had been temporarily repurposed as a gathering area, and the sounds of angry voices—the barking snarls of the Syhaari and the wet growls of the Breg'Hel—echoed off the metal walls. On one side stood the reptilians, the co-commanders Ret'Sed and Ead'Aea surrounded by a cohort of green-skinned guards led by Zud'Hoa; on the other, the simianoids clustered together and glared at the invaders, with Tormid the most vocal. The only one of their kind that stood apart was Kaleo, who had very deliberately chosen to place herself with Xuur, ch'Sellor, and the rest of the Federation party.

The envoy glanced at Kirk and Spock. "Do you have security standing by?"

Kirk gave her a nod. "If it comes to it." He had to raise his voice to be heard over Tormid's thunderous yelling.

"This is nothing but a web of lies!" spat the Syhaari scientist, angrily waving his arms. "These alien horrors invade our space with their monstrous colossus and then dare to blame us for it?"

"Not *us*," Kaleo broke in. "*You*."

Tormid rounded on her. "You understand nothing, Kaleo! You've spent too long with these offworlders, you're starting to sympathize with aliens over your own species! How can you take the word of these creatures over the proof from a fellow Syhaari?"

"The accusation is a proven truth," chattered Ead'Aea, and there was a deep hatred in its voice. "You are a coward, a thief, and a child-killer! And while the known Kaleo has proven to us there is honor in your kind, you are clearly empty of it!"

"Do you hear the creature decry me?" Tormid spun to address the rest of his party. Hoyga and Gatag nodded at his words, but the others—among them Kaleo's first mate Zond and several others from the Learned Assembly of elders—shifted nervously, uncertain how to react. "They justify mass murder by saying it is justice? And then pretend they cannot control their living weapon?" Tormid bared his teeth. "If these Federation fools were not standing in my way, I would end you for your insult!"

Tormid's firebrand oratory seemed to rally many of his fellow survivors, and for a moment the balance of the meeting seemed to tip away. Kirk felt it in the air, the tension crackling around him, and he was glad that Xuur had agreed, at his insistence, that everyone at the meeting be searched for weapons before it began. If they did not keep control of this, the conference would soon degenerate beyond any hope of an accord.

"We are not here to apportion blame!" said Xuur, but her words were being drowned out.

Kirk put a hand on her shoulder. "With all due respect, Envoy, I don't think your method is going to work." Before she could object, the captain took a deep breath and cut loose with the sharp, hard snarl that had given pause to errant junior officers, bellicose admirals, and many of the *Enterprise*'s adversaries over the years. "There is guilt on both sides of this room!" he bellowed. "No one has the right to claim they have done nothing wrong!"

His words had the desired effect, cutting through the tirade, bringing a moment of silence in their wake. Before the momentum could fade, he rocked off his heels and strode forward, turning toward the Breg'Hel party.

"You say you were attacked first," Kirk challenged Ret'Sed, seeing Zud'Hoa bristle at his tone. "You demand reparation. Your military response was far beyond rational proportion! Your anger drove you!"

"This is so," agreed the co-commander, biting out each word.

"You reacted harshly because your family died. Because your ship was ransacked."

"This is so," repeated Ret'Sed; the alien seemed grim, sad, and furious all at once.

Kirk rounded on Tormid. "And *you*, sir. You deny that version of events. You say you have never seen these beings before, that their claims are baseless."

"Of course!" The Syhaari scientist hesitated, then drew himself up to his full height, a head taller than the captain. "I agreed to this meeting only because your crew intervened to rescue mine, Kirk. That does not give you the right to interrogate me!"

"This is neither an interrogation nor a trial," Kirk shot back. "This is a statement of *facts*." He held out his hand to Spock. "Tricorder."

The Vulcan handed him the device, and he flipped up the display. Trains of data streamed over the small screen.

"What is that?" said Gatag, craning his neck to peer at the tricorder.

"Fact," said the captain, knowing that what he said next would either end an interstellar conflict—or inflame it. "In the past few hours, my chief engineer has conducted a series of high-intensity, deep-pattern sensor sweeps of several Syhaari starships on my direct orders."

Hoyga growled with annoyance. "How dare you invade our privacy, human!" She jabbed a finger at Xuur and ch'Sellor. "We were promised this would not be done!"

"Yes, I agree that it is a violation. But I'm afraid that Starfleet Command's operational protocols during military operations supersede any diplomatic guidelines," Xuur said mildly. "Please rest assured that a complaint about Captain Kirk's behavior will be placed in his file with the Federation Diplomatic Corps."

Along with all the others already there, Kirk thought to himself, pressing on. "It seems there's a good reason why you didn't want my first officer taking too close a look at your new engine designs." He nodded toward the Vulcan.

Spock picked up the thread of the conversation. "The more recent Syhaari designs for space drives capable of warp factor three and higher, allegedly originated by Mister Tormid, are almost identical to the bilobed forced-matrix structure of Breg'Hel warp engines. Given that first-generation Syhaari warp drives follow a single-stream design philosophy, the likelihood of developing so radical a departure in a short period with no outside stimulus is . . . unlikely."

Tormid bared his teeth in a snarl, but he did not speak. Kirk continued. "That so-called revelation you claimed you had. It seems to be little more than knowledge gained by reverse-engineering stolen data. How do you explain that?" He advanced on the Syhaari scientist. "I put it to you, sir, that you *have* encountered the Breg'Hel before, you acted without thought to the consequences, put the lives of thousands of your own people at risk, and then *lied* about it. All in the name of your own advancement."

"You have shamed us," said Kaleo in a low voice.

"Th-these are grave accusations indeed!" spluttered Gatag, his hands knitting together. "Tormid! How do you answer the human's words?"

Tormid rounded on the elder, his eyes flashing. "How do I answer?" he spat. "You ask me that? After the prosperity I have brought to our people?" Gatag reeled back, unprepared for the force of his ire. "These *aliens*," he snarled venomously, extending a long arm to point at Kirk and the others, "these offworlders are the ones who must explain themselves." Tormid rolled his head on his thick neck and crossed the hangar deck until he was almost nose to nose with Kirk. "This is conspiracy, yes! This so-called benevolent Federation is playing the Syhaari Gathering as dupes. They come to us in the guise of friends with talk of advanced technology and membership in some vast galactic union, but what do we really know of them? Then these lizard-skinned murderers appear and unleash a beast of war on our worlds." He pointed at Ret'Sed and the simmering Breg'Hel party. "And now I am the guilty one? This is a *ploy*! A scheme designed to make us doubt ourselves! They are in collusion, one playing the role of friend and the other of an enemy, but working in harmony when our backs are turned!" He prodded Kirk in the chest. "You have come to take our worlds, is that it? Make us grateful to you, suborn us all just as you have done with Kaleo." Tormid turned his head and spat, then drew in another breath. "She may have been weak enough to believe your deception, but we are Syhaari, we will never—"

I've had enough of this. Kirk reached down and pulled out his communicator, flipping it open to speak into the audio pickup. "Bones, bring him in."

Across the hangar deck a door hissed open and McCoy stepped through, followed by a tall, rangy figure that could only have been another Syhaari. The new arrival's head was bowed, and he walked with some difficulty, leaning on the doctor to make his way.

"Who is this?" said Gatag, momentarily distracted from Tormid's outburst.

As close as he was to the scientist, it was only Kirk who noticed Tormid tense, and the faint gasp of surprise as he recognized his former pilot.

"I am Rumen," said the other Syhaari. "Former crew of *The Searcher Unbound*."

"Impossible," gasped Zond, his gaze flicking back and forth between Rumen and Hoyga. "You reported that he was killed on the mission, in the accident that claimed the rest of the *Searcher*'s crew . . ."

"How can this be? Tormid and Hoyga were the only ones to return," Gatag insisted. "The bodies of the others . . ."

Kaleo shook herself. "Rumen's corpse was lost, do you not recall? At least, that was what Tormid told the

Assembly. Only traces of Rumen's genetic material remained on the ship."

Rumen stopped, his stance making it clear he was in pain but refusing to back away. "He left me behind, left me for dead," said the pilot, not in anger as Kirk had expected of him, but with bone-weary sorrow. "My bio-data was recorded in the *Searcher*'s memory banks. For someone of Tormid's intellect, it would not have been difficult to use the ship's fabricators to create organic matter with the same gene code."

Kirk remembered the peculiar meat dish he had been given at the greeting feast on Syhaar Prime, patterned after his own genetic data. It all clicked into place. Tormid had used the same technology to explain away Rumen's absence.

"That one bore your punishment," hissed Ead'Aea, shifting from foot to foot. "But now your crimes are revealed to all, known-killer Tormid. We have images of your callous acts. We will show them."

And at that, Tormid found his voice again. "This is trickery," he insisted, a momentary tremor in his voice soon left behind by a rising snarl of fury. Anger was all he had now that his mendacity was clear. He glared at Hoyga, as if warning her not to dare to speak against him, and the Syhaari engineer visibly recoiled. "That person is not Rumen, it must be . . . it *is* some fake! These are aliens, the depths of their abilities are barely known to us!"

Kirk caught the sense of disbelief rising in Gatag and the other Syhaari survivors.

The elder's doubt faded as he spoke. "Tormid, enough of this. You must answer now. Is it true?"

"I left Rumen behind because . . . he betrayed us!" Tormid shouted, discarding one lie for another. "These creatures, I . . . I protected you from them, you fools!" He backed off a step, searching the faces of his kinsmen for some measure of support, but finding only confusion. "Do you understand?" Tormid became more desperate by the second as Kirk watched his scaffold of deceit fall apart around him. "I gave us the keys to the stars!"

"You took us into fire and destruction," said Kaleo. "And for what? Only your glory, not for the children of Sya."

Tormid's strangled expression shifted, becoming ugly and full of hatred. "You ignorant, ungrateful whelps!" He flicked back his arm, and too late the captain realized that security's search of those attending the meeting had not been thorough enough.

A metallic strip of material, that until this moment had simply seemed to be some sort of decoration on Tormid's sleeve, now slid down his forearm and into his grip, stiffening into a blunt-tipped blade as it went. Kirk had seen memory-metals before, but never one like this, morphing into a short sword before his eyes.

Tormid swung it wide in front of him, and Kirk ducked, feeling the rush of air over his face as it slashed at nothing. A breath closer, and it would have cut him open from brow to mouth. "I will not submit to these lies, alien! I will not—"

Then as suddenly as the attack had begun, it ceased. Tormid's body went rigid and he became as stiff as his trick weapon, his gaze turning glassy.

"That will be quite enough," said Spock, his right hand clamped firmly over a series of pressure points at the nape of Tormid's bare neck. All energy fled from the Syhaari, and he sank to the deck, eyes fluttering closed.

Kirk brushed absently at a speck of lint on his tunic and beckoned the red-shirted security guards who had burst in at the first sign of trouble. "Put our guest here in the brig."

"No!" cried Ead'Aea. "Inadequate! The crime is spoken and known. Even this one's kindred see it now. Give him to us. Blood cost and punishment will be taken."

"Blood cost," echoed Zud'Hoa, hands flexing to reveal short, dark talons beneath their flesh. "Punishment."

Xuur stepped forward to stand directly between the Breg'Hel and the Syhaari. "We will not allow that. No blood will be shed in this place. Captain Kirk granted the *Enterprise* for this meeting in the spirit of peace."

Kirk nodded. "It's up to both of your people to decide what to do with Tormid. He should have a fair trial, in public, so that what he did wrong is made clear to everyone. But until that happens, he stays in Federation custody. "

"Agreed," grated Ret'Sed. "What say you, Syhaari?"

Gatag hesitated, then bowed slightly. "Agreed, Breg'Hel. If we are to end the cycle of destruction and anger between us, we must begin with this."

"It is agreeable to hear that declaration," said Spock as his captain gestured for him to carry on. "But I am afraid a more immediate problem faces all of us, one that must be resolved."

"The leviathan," said Kirk, glancing at the Breg'Hel. "Your weapon."

"The creature was commanded by our aura-techs through a nexus of inductors," said Ead'Aea. "We drew it from a herd grazing the gas streams surrounding the outer nimbus of the home-nebula." The Breg'Hel paused, blinking. "It was not a deed done lightly. In light of the gravest possible threat from outsiders, we believed we had no choice. Punishment to be done."

"All future threat to be neutralized," added Zud'Hoa. "So in high aggression we came to attack."

"You succeeded," Kaleo said bitterly. "Too well. How do we stop its rampage?"

"Unknown," replied Ret'Sed. "We have never taken an act to these lengths before. The compulsion we transmitted, the incitement. When deactivated, docility should have returned. It did not."

Spock nodded. "I have a hypothesis. I suggest that the continued application of your compulsion effect has pushed the planetoid life-form beyond the point of rationality."

At his side, McCoy's expression darkened. "They drove it mad?" The doctor shot an acid look at the reptilians. "A peaceful creature goaded into rage and violence. What the hell did you think would happen?"

"Bones," said Kirk with a shake of the head, "not the time."

It was a rare moment that Spock found his thoughts in line with McCoy's, but in this they shared a similar disgust—although the Vulcan kept his feelings to himself. "Given the leviathan's recent behavior patterns, I predict that it will continue to attack all high-mass targets within range of its sensorium."

"Our homeworld . . ." muttered Zond.

"To begin with," continued Spock. "Then the inner planet Neliin and, finally, it will likely be drawn toward the star Sya itself."

"Wouldn't that destroy it?" said Kirk.

"Indeed. The subspace waves being broadcast from the life-form suggest it is in pain as much as it is enraged. Eventually, it will seek a respite from that agony. Through its own death, in a final suicidal impulse."

Ret'Sed nodded. "This is so. The creatures plunge

into the hearts of protostars when they reach the end of their life spans, in a great dying."

"But that thing out there *isn't* at the end of its life!" insisted McCoy. "It's not fading away, it's gorged itself on displaced matter and energy. And if Spock's right, it'll keep on doing so until it chokes on it!"

The captain's jaw set as he guessed what dark possibilities lay at the end of the logical progression that Spock had already determined. "If the leviathan interacts with a star's energy, what will be the result?"

"A critical mass of subspace fields. The most probable outcome would be an explosive interaction of cosmic forces, enough to obliterate the life-form and resonate into several tertiary spatial domains."

McCoy scowled. "Less technical, Spock."

He took a breath. "The star Sya would undergo immediate collapse into a forced supernova. All planets in this system would be annihilated, and the resulting gamma-ray pulse would not only penetrate the Veil, but affect local space out to a radius of several light-years. Including the territory of the Breg'Hel."

Envoy Xuur's hand went to her mouth in shock, and nearby Zud'Hoa made a weak, fluting sound in its throat. "We . . . have destroyed ourselves," it whispered.

"Not yet." Kirk gave his first officer a grim nod of agreement, and then turned to face the assembled group. Terse, half-muttered words were already being exchanged among the Syhaari, and Spock's acute Vulcan hearing caught the sense of Tormid's anti-alien anger being rekindled, even though the scientist was no longer present on the hangar deck. Kirk and Xuur seemed to sense it too. The moment was balancing on a knife-edge.

It was the envoy who went straight to the heart of it. "This is not a time for blame," she said firmly. "Even though that need is heavy in the hearts of both sides. That is something for tomorrow. The question that must be answered *now* is this: Can you put aside your need for reprisal and move forward together against this threat?"

"We will help you," said Kirk. "My ship, my crew, every last iota of knowledge the Federation has at its fingertips. If we pool our resources, we can find a solution, but you must decide *now*."

In silence, Ret'Sed and Ead'Aea bowed to the Syhaari, joined a moment later by Zud'Hoa and the others in their party. Slowly, Gatag and his people mirrored their action.

Time passed as the *Enterprise* continued its pursuit of the leviathan, and from Kirk's perspective it seemed to move with that strange flexibility that only a crisis could bring. Minutes could drag on forever, hours could flash by in what felt like seconds, and inexorably, they were getting closer and closer to Syhaar Prime and the potential devastation of a world and its people.

Looking to clear his head, the captain found himself on the observation deck above the hangar deck, lost in the view of the void beyond the hull. The strange slate-colored sky within the Veil still unsettled him, used as he was to seeing only blackness and stars though the viewports.

"James?"

He looked toward the voice and saw Kaleo standing in the hexagonal entranceway. She cocked her head, watching him intently. "Is something wrong?" he asked.

She took that as an invitation and came closer. "If by that you mean, is something *more* wrong? Then, no. In fact, the discussions with the Breg'Hel are quite civilized. Your envoy and her aide have seen to that."

"Xuur has her talents, that's for certain." He forced a smile, but couldn't hold it.

Kaleo saw that and paused, becoming formal again. "I am sorry, Captain. I am disturbing you. I know full well how hard it is to find a quiet moment with your thoughts." She turned to go. "We shall speak later."

"No." He held out a hand. "I think I could use another perspective. And I don't want you going back down there to tell Xuur you found me brooding."

"I would never say such a thing."

Kirk beckoned her toward the exterior windows. "Come here. Take a look." He pointed at something. "You see it? We're just on the edge of visual range."

The Syhaari peered out. "That shimmer, in the distance? Is that the creature?"

He nodded. "The leviathan . . . or more accurately, the gravity distortion effect around it lensing local starlight. We're closing in on it, but I don't know if we'll be able to catch it . . ."

"Yes," she said quietly, before he went on. "It is quite remarkable. That such a creature could exist, that it could travel through space like a starship."

"I've seen a lot of very unusual things, and this ranks up there with them," he agreed. "Spock tells me that the leviathan is a silicon-based life-form, possibly with primitive instinctual intellect. Its physical structure is heavy with dilithium deposits in the outer crust, and that's what allows it to distort space-time to produce motion, through some kind of controlled energetic release."

"A naturally occurring warp drive in a life-form that moves through space as birds move through air or fish through the water." She made no attempt to hide her wonderment. "Incredible. We could learn so much from it."

Kirk studied his fellow captain. "Yes, we could."

Kaleo gave a low grunt. "You're surprised to hear me say that. After all the destruction that creature has wrought on my people, you think I would only want to see it ended."

"I'm not surprised," he admitted. "I'm pleased. Someone like Tormid would never be able to see what you see when you look out there. That's how I knew when I first met you, Kaleo, that we shared a kindred spirit."

"We are both explorers at heart," she agreed. Then a shadow passed over her face. "But fate has pushed us into a different role today."

He nodded, feeling the edges of a bleak mood threatening to crowd in on him. "We may have to kill it, Kaleo. A being that has no control over its actions. A victim in this as much as anyone else. But it's one life against countless millions."

"It is not a matter of numbers," she said softly. "Who knows that horrible equation better than us, James? We are captains, and with command comes the implicit truth that we must balance lives against lives, with each order we give." Kaleo looked away, staring at the deck. "I have done so in the past, and I carry the scar that does not heal. I do not need to ask you if you have done the same, I know you have. I have seen it in your eyes."

"It can be very lonely in that chair," he admitted.

"Just so." They stood in companionable silence for a while, before Kaleo stretched her arms and spoke again. "Would you accept advice from me?"

"I could use some," said Kirk.

She went to the ports on the far side of the gallery, the inner portals that looked down on the hangar deck. "When the *Enterprise* answered *The Explorer Beyond*'s distress call years ago, you changed many things about my world when you came to our aid. Not just that you opened our eyes to the reality of a larger universe and the presence of other intelligent beings in it. You showed us where we could go. You gave me a glimpse of what we could one day achieve." Kaleo paused, and past her Kirk saw the Syhaari and Breg'Hel parties mingling with Spock, Xuur, and ch'Sellor as they worked together. "But the most important thing was *that*." She tapped on the window, indicating the group below. "The object lesson. That in unity, we can do great things. I believed it then. I believe it now." She met his gaze. "And so do you. Don't lose sight of that."

He nodded. "Good speech."

"I observed you closely and took notes."

Kirk felt a grin pull at his lips. "I may not be the best example to follow. Just ask Xuur."

Kaleo chuckled. "One day, I will let you read my personnel file. Then we shall compare who of us is the least obedient of commanders."

The two-note tone of a synthetic bosun's whistle sounded, and Kirk heard McCoy's voice issue out of an intercom grille on the wall. "*Sickbay to Captain Kirk. Respond, please.*"

He tapped the activation stud on the wall communicator. "Kirk here. What is it, Bones?"

"*Jim,*" McCoy began, "*I think I might have something that could help with the leviathan. Lieutenant Uhura came to me with a suggestion, and I think we can make it work . . . but it's a little out there.*"

"Right now, no idea is a bad one," Kirk told him. "Tell me what you have."

"It'll be easier to show you rather then tell you. Get down here as quick as you can . . . and bring Ret'Sed. As much as I hate what they've done, I need a Breg'Hel eye on this."

Kaleo frowned. "With all due respect, Doctor, we are preparing for a battle, not a medical emergency."

"I don't see it that way," McCoy countered. "From where I stand, we've got a sick patient that needs treatment. It just happens that the patient is the size of a moon."

Thirteen

Kirk entered sickbay and found McCoy and Uhura crowded around a screen. Kaleo and Ret'Sed followed him in; neither had spoken on the way down to the sickbay.

The Breg'Hel's manner was glum, and it had not questioned why the *Enterprise*'s captain had requested its presence. But now the lizard-like alien became more animated, peering wide-eyed at the biomedical scanners and racks of working samples around the doctor's work area. "You are the healer-parent for this entire craft?"

"I'm chief medical officer, if that's what you mean," McCoy replied. "And one of many healers. A parent, not so much. Although I have been known to dispense fatherly advice from time to time."

"The crews of Breg'Hel ships are a single extended family," Uhura noted. "Their doctor is probably a cousin or grandchild of the commanders."

"Like the old Boomer transports from Earth back in the day, I suppose," said the doctor. "I can see why that would make you take something so personally."

"Bones," prompted Kirk, folding his arms. "You said you'd both come up with something for us?"

"A theory," he replied. "I'll warn you now, it's a stretch, Jim. But after seeing Uhura's data, I couldn't stand by and say nothing." McCoy turned the screen before him to face the group, loading a data card into a nearby media slot. "I'll be honest, I felt like a damned spare wheel ever since that creature showed up. Just waiting for the next attack, the next casualty, instead of doing what we were supposed to be here for . . ." He paused, cutting off his own train of thought. "Not relevant. So here's the thing." With a flick of a switch, the screen lit up and Kirk saw a cutaway anatomy diagram of a familiar dome-shaped life-form. "*Janus hominidae*, our friend the Horta."

Ret'Sed gave a slow nod. "I recognize the similarities."

"We've been looking at that planetoid out there and thinking of it like some kind of natural disaster," said Uhura. "Thinking about how to react to it instead of being proactive. But then I remembered what happened on Janus VI with the Horta."

McCoy tapped the screen with a stylus. "The Horta is the same kind of creature as the leviathan. And we . . . *I* . . . cured her of an injury. If we start looking at the leviathan like it is a sick animal instead of a force of nature, then the question becomes—"

"How do we heal it?" said Kaleo.

"Exactly." McCoy nodded and switched images.

The new display was a tactical scan of the rogue planetoid. "Uhura said that she and Spock detected multiple layers of subspace energy radiating throughout the structure of the leviathan, right?"

"That's correct," said the communications officer. "It can generate a number of different frequencies by resonating elements of its internal structure. The power to do so comes from vast biochemical battery glands as big as inland seas."

McCoy's tone grew stronger as he warmed to his subject. "If this creature has some form of intelligence, it isn't collected inside a chunk of gray matter as it is for carbon-based life like us." He tapped the side of his head with a finger. "It's got to be distributed. There are complex lattices of mineral crystal inside the leviathan, similar to the duotronic circuits in a computer. And I'm willing to bet that the energy moving around in there is the same as the electrochemical impulses that make us bags of bone and meat walk and talk."

Kirk considered his friend's words. "You mean its body is also its brain? No wonder it reacted so harshly against any perceived threat." He paused, thinking it through. "Say your theory is right, Bones. How does that help us?"

"We're talking about erratic brainwave patterns driving violent behavior here, Jim, no different from the kind of thing Federation medicine treats at the Tantalus colony and Elba II. Only the scale is different."

"We believe it might be possible to create a counter-wave pattern that could reverse the effects of the leviathan's madness." A weary smile crossed Uhura's face. "Call it music to soothe the savage beast."

"Your hypothesis fails at this stage," said Ret'Sed. "The outer mantle of the creature is too dense for the transmission of such a spatial frequency. It would never be able to penetrate the interior."

"You're not thinking like a doctor, sir," replied McCoy. "We don't heal from without, we heal from *within*."

Kirk released a breath, his eyes narrowing. "You're actually proposing we send a ship *inside* the leviathan? And you do understand that the amount of power that would be required would need a matter-antimatter core to supply it?"

"I know, Jim. I'm not going to sugarcoat it. Uhura ran the numbers. We'd have to use the *Enterprise*."

"No." Ret'Sed twitched as it replied. "One craft would not be enough. To be certain of a full propagation of a counter-wave, more are required. Two, four more, to be assured of success."

"We could launch shuttles under remote control," said Uhura.

Kirk shook his head. "Not enough power. It has to be a starship."

McCoy gestured at Kaleo and Ret'Sed. "You people have a few of those with you, right? I mean, we've been saying all along this is a team effort."

"It could be done," said the Breg'Hel, after a moment. "Risk is high. But there are large fissures on the surface of the creature's dermal layer that give access to voids within its core. We venture into them to gather the raw matter to build our starcraft, but never too deeply."

Kaleo had hardly spoken since they arrived in sickbay, and now Kirk turned to study her. The conflict he had seen in her eyes before was there again. "You have something to add?"

The Syhaari folded her long arms around herself. "Your officers' plan tenders a kind of hope," she began.

"I'm sensing a *but* coming up," said Uhura.

"It is not without grave danger," Kaleo went on. "And I must tell you that Gatag has been in communication with the Assembly on Syhaar Prime. There has been talk of concentrating on a terminal option."

Ret'Sed shrugged. "My people also speak of such an act. Suggested implementation, several vessels with drive cores set to achieve overload criticality sent into the mantle of the creature. Detonations of a high order may wound it gravely enough to cause death-cessation."

"*May*?" snarled McCoy. "And what if you *don't* kill it? A wild animal is bad enough, but one that is crazed *and* wounded?" He shook his head, sickened by the idea.

Kirk didn't answer the doctor's words, but there was nothing in Ret'Sed's declaration that he too had not already considered. The situation had become so grave that even the unthinkable had to be entertained.

"Lieutenant, Doctor, draw up a plan of action," he ordered after a moment. "I'm going to make an attempt to end this crisis with no further bloodshed."

———

Ranged against the curtain of distant gas and dust, the planet Syhaar Prime eclipsed its parent star as it became distinct ahead of the ragged survivor fleet. The Syhaari homeworld was a black orb, featureless and silent, haloed by flickers of sunshine. Rising before the planet, moving closer with each passing second, the leviathan was its dark, hellish twin.

Wreathed in the same deep shadows, the rogue glowed with a malevolent inner light that spilled from the fissures across its surface. A faint, narrow comet tail of dispersed energy coiled away from the living planetoid, shimmering and ephemeral—the byproduct of the peculiar natural warping effect that allowed the creature to skip across the surface of normal space at light velocity.

Beyond it, the distance between them shrinking, the Enterprise led the flotilla of damaged ships and desperate crews. Luck and time had been on their side. They would intercept the leviathan before it reached orbit of Syhaar Prime, but now their strategy was heavy with risk. Succeed or fail, divert or destroy, it would all be decided within the next few hours.

Scott looked up from the display on the bridge engineering station and found Captain Kirk. "Sir, engines are now beyond the red line, power at one hundred and ten percent. We can hold there for the next few minutes, but after that I'll have to dial them back. Otherwise, we risk a catastrophic blowout."

"Noted," said Kirk. He glanced at the Syhaari commander Kaleo, who stood at his side, then to his chief engineer. "Use your discretion, Scotty, but don't let that thing get away from us. We'll only get one shot at this."

He nodded. "Aye, sir, that we will." On first hearing of the scheme hatched by Doctor McCoy and Lieutenant Uhura, Scott's reaction had been—predictably—one of shock. The *Enterprise* was no stranger to extreme and unusual environments, from the depths of a gas giant's atmosphere to the event horizon of a black hole, but as far as the engineer could recall, this was the first time someone had ever attempted to fly a starship *inside* a planet.

But every argument he had against the idea, no matter how logical, no matter how factually accurate, paled against the reality that billions of living beings would perish unless the leviathan could be stopped in its tracks. And so, Montgomery Scott did what he always did whenever he was presented with a nigh-impossible engineering challenge. He put aside his gut reaction and concentrated on the contest of the thing, as if he were squaring up to the laws of physics to answer the dare they had put in front of him. *The rules say this can't be done*, he thought to himself, *so let's find a way to do it.*

Scott set to work programming the complex vectors that would be required by the *Enterprise*'s structural integrity field generators to compensate for the shifting gravity fields as they first approached, then ventured into, the leviathan's inner structure. As he did so, from the corner of his eye, he saw the captain straighten in his chair and call out to Lieutenant M'Ress. "It's time. Put them on the screen."

The main viewscreen switched to a partitioned display of four separate images. Each one was being relayed from the bridge of another starship—two of them Breg'Hel vessels, the others the least-damaged pair of Syhaari rangers.

"Enterprise, *Rumen reporting*," said the gravel-voiced simianoid. "The Moon's Rise *is ready to proceed.*" Scott had heard that the former pilot had insisted on taking command of one of the craft for this operation, refusing point blank to remain with Gatag and the rest of the elders on one of the other ships trailing behind them.

"*Zond here*," called the Syhaari aboard the sister vessel. "The Day Ahead *signals ready.*"

"You make us proud," said Kaleo, making a ritual

gesture to her second in command and her former teacher. "Have you modified your deflector arrays according to Commander Spock's specifications?"

"*Confirmed,*" said Zond. "*We'll deploy once we reach optimal position to relay the counter-wave.*" For his part, Rumen simply bobbed his head.

Kirk addressed the other two beings on the screen; the spindly, scaled Breg'Hel both seemed twitchy and nervous. "Ead'Aea, Ret'Sed, what is your status?"

"*Ready,*" they chorused. "*Retro-reflectors have been configured to the correct signal potentiality,*" Ead'Aea went on. "*I will say this now: I do not share my partner-mate's conviction that this will work. But blood bonds and love-trust supersede logic in this desperate hour. We will follow you,* Enterprise. *Lead the way.*"

Kirk gave a nod. "Last chance to stay behind," the captain told Kaleo. "Gatag and the others don't believe we can do this either. If they're right, they'll need someone to look to in the aftermath."

"Gatag is afraid, and he has every right to be," Kaleo replied evenly. "But we are committed to this course of action." She turned toward the science station, where Spock and Uhura were still working on refining the counter-wave profile. "We are in this together."

The captain didn't reply. Instead, he leaned forward in the command chair and called out to Sulu and Arex at their stations. "Gentlemen, Scotty has given us the means, so let's not waste a second more. Set a heading for the heart of the leviathan, and take us in."

"On our way," confirmed Sulu. The image on the screen returned to the dark shadow play of an eclipsed world and the great cosmozoan.

Scott felt his gut tighten, but he buried the sensation before it could take hold. It went against every fiber of his being as a spacer to see a planetary surface rising to fill the viewscreen, yet the engineer didn't look away.

Spock plucked a data card from his terminal and stepped down from his station. "Captain, with your permission, the lieutenant and I will head down to the deflector control room."

"We'll be able to directly modulate the counter-wave from there," noted Uhura. "The difference in reaction time could prove critical."

"Go," said Kirk. "Give the word when you're ready to broadcast the signal through the main deflector dish. We'll channel full power to you on the mark."

"I just hope it'll be enough," said Uhura.

"It will work," Spock told her, as matter-of-fact as ever. "Your insight may well prove to be the solution that has eluded us."

"Just make sure your lullaby is a good one," Kirk told them, turning back. "Steady as she goes, Mister Sulu—"

In the next second, the *Enterprise* passed through

a region of gravimetric shear, and suddenly the hull groaned as metal distorted and flexed.

McCoy felt the tremor come up through his boots, and he braced for it with the experience born of hundreds of similar moments. But Envoy Xuur wasn't quite as nimble as she looked, and the Rhaandarite ambassador almost lost her balance before the doctor's arm shot out to grab her elbow. "Easy up, now," he told her as the lights in the corridor flickered. "It sounds like Jim has put us on our path."

"It would seem so," she said, covering with a flash of annoyance. "A warning might have been appreciated." Xuur continued swiftly on toward the brig, and the doctor strode to keep up with her.

"You chose to stay on board this ship," McCoy said, making the words a mild admonishment. "Why didn't you go with ch'Sellor?"

"I *ordered* my aide off the *Enterprise*," she corrected. "In point of fact, he was quite upset about it. He's very protective of me." Before McCoy could pick up on what that might have meant, Xuur went on. "If we all die in there, someone needs to be able to contact the Federation and tell them what took place."

"Put us all in for posthumous commendations, you mean?"

Her lips thinned. "Despite what you may think of me personally, Doctor McCoy, I didn't join the diplomatic corps for the accolades. But if I am going to earn them, I'd like it not to be because I perished in the line of duty."

"Guess I can't argue with that."

They walked toward the brig, and a second tremor echoed through the deck, once again dimming the lights as power levels fluctuated to compensate. Xuur was ready for it this time and didn't lose a step. "You don't have a lot of time for people like me, do you?" She eyed him.

"Normally I'd deflect that," McCoy admitted, "but as we're going into harm's way, heck, I'll be honest with you. *No.* I don't have time for people who think one thing and say another, and do it as their calling."

"I lie for a living, is that what you think?"

"I call it like I see it," he said with a shrug. "I can't think of a single time the FDC has put someone on board this ship that it hasn't become a problem. Right now is no exception."

"Has it occurred to you that maybe the *Enterprise* crew is the problem, not the other way around? Your captain's ability to play fast and loose with the Prime Directive is the stuff of legend where I come from. And not in a good way."

McCoy scowled and fiddled with the tricorder hanging at his hip. "I'll tell you this. What you think is a set of absolute rules that can be written down and adhered to in every single circumstance is nothing of the sort. General Order One is a guideline. It's up to the people at the sharp end of the spear to interpret it according to the situation they're in. Second-guessing someone from the comfort of a nice office half a galaxy away never works."

"But I'm not half a galaxy away, Doctor," she replied. "I'm right here, with all of you, in harm's way."

"Good," he told her, "maybe you'll learn something."

Xuur's eyes narrowed, but she let the barbed comment pass. They reached the brig, and the security guard on duty stood aside to allow them access to the single occupant of the cells

Tormid sat on a narrow bunk behind the invisible energy barrier that barred any attempt at escape. His long arms were folded over his shoulders, and his dark, deep-set eyes burned with a steady fury.

"He say anything, Ensign Lopez?" McCoy asked.

Lopez grimaced. "Nothing I'd want to repeat, sir."

When Tormid saw the envoy, he cocked his head and curled his lip in disgust. "You have no right to hold me in this place," he spat at her. "I am a citizen of the Syhaari Gathering, and your Federation has no jurisdiction over my liberty!"

"Not so. Your government has agreed to your temporary confinement," Xuur told him.

"You're considered a threat to the safety of this vessel and the instigator of an interstellar war," McCoy said flatly. "You're not exactly on firm ground when it comes to throwing your weight around."

The Syhaari shot to his feet and snarled something venomous in his own language. "Hairless simpletons, all of you. You set one of your freakish alien kind on me, attacked me!"

"Because you drew a sword!" McCoy snapped back.

"That was a ceremonial blade," Tormid snorted, dismissing his rejoinder as if it were meaningless. "I would not expect you to understand. If I am to be accused of crimes, I will hear it only from my own species! I refuse to listen to your words."

"We're not giving you a choice," said McCoy. "In fact, if I were you, I'd start telling the truth about what you did on the *Searcher*. Before you dig yourself in any deeper."

Tormid turned a glare on him that was hot enough to sear the paint off the bulkhead. "What do you know of truth? Everything I have done was for the good of my species, offworlder. I made them stronger. I gave them *focus*."

"You brought war and destruction down on their heads," McCoy countered. "Good job."

Xuur straightened, intervening before the argument could build. "Mister Tormid, the doctor is here to take a tricorder scan of you for our official records." McCoy plucked a handheld sensor from a compartment on the device and set it to read the Syhaari through the force field. "For matters of legality and full transparency," the envoy continued. "Rest assured, you shall face criminal charges from the Gathering and the Breg'Hel. As the ranking civilian representative of the United Federation of Planets, who have offered their help in mediating this issue, I'm here to extend you a formal offer of legal counsel."

Tormid barked with bitter laughter. "Imbeciles! I won't live long enough to see the inside of a trial-hall, and neither will you!" He pointed at Lopez. "I heard this one speaking to another. Is it true that your idiot of a captain is actually trying to penetrate the interior of that monstrosity out there?"

"We're going to undo the damage you've done," McCoy told him.

"*I* did not drive a colossus into a killing rage," he retorted. "*I* did not set that thing on a blind rampage across the stars; that deed lies at the feet of those scale-faced creatures you mean to make peace with!"

Xuur ignored his reply. "The leviathan must be calmed. We are all working together toward that end."

Tormid spat on the deck. "Absurd!"

"I have every confidence in Captain Kirk," said Xuur, so smoothly that McCoy almost believed her.

"Then we are all dead," Tormid snarled, and he came up to the threshold, setting the force field buzzing. "And Kirk has murdered us!"

Enterprise fell toward the surface of the leviathan like a diving hawk, integrity fields and deflectors humming from the friction as the ship plunged into the planetoid's turbulent gravity well. Flanking it, the four Breg'Hel and Syhaari ships fought their own battles against the crackling mass of corposant, amber jags of lightning flickering through the clouds that surrounded the massive creature.

Built for the rigors of space, the *Enterprise*'s hull moaned as it was stressed in ways it was not designed to experience. Tension pulled at the roots of the engine pylons, at the neck of the vessel, and at the leading edges of the primary hull, where the saucer bit into the chaotic shroud of storms. One small error of judgment at the helm, or a navigation plot a degree off true, and the starship would dash itself against the rocky mantle of the living planetoid in a blaze of a warp explosion. But the ship was beneath the steady hands of two of Starfleet's finest, and even with the maelstrom raging around the vessel, Sulu and Arex threaded the needle.

———

The captain felt his breath catch in his throat. His hands gripped the arms of his command chair, and by sheer force of will, he pushed forward his belief, his certainty, that his crew would make it through. Outwardly, he maintained an air of calm focus, but to say that James T. Kirk was without fear in that moment would have been a lie. Only a fool could have looked the leviathan in the eye and not felt afraid; he knew that his bridge crew all shared the same emotions.

They were determined, they were ready, and most of all, they were courageous.

Bravery in the face of danger, at the edge of the unknown—this was not the absence of fear but the control and mastery of it. Kirk allowed himself a wry smile, reflecting on how Spock would have considered such a statement to be eminently logical. He glanced around the bridge and saw that courage everywhere he looked.

"I have the rift on my scope," Sulu said tightly. "Eight degrees off the port quarter."

"Compensating," said Arex, all three of his hands flying back and forth over the switches on his panel. "Twenty-one seconds to closure."

"The other ships are still with us," said Kaleo, who held tight to the bridge rail at Kirk's shoulder. "Not far now."

He gave a curt nod and spoke into the intercom at his side. "All decks, this is the captain. Red alert. Be ready for anything."

———————

The leviathan reacted to the intrusion. Yellow fire spun and danced around the invader ships. The sky twitched, as the flesh of a humanoid might reflexively respond to the presence of an insect crawling across it. The deadly lightning sought out the irritants, questing blindly for something to strike.

Enterprise burst through the lower strata of the

cloud mass, and before it lay a vast, serrated plain, the stone "skin" of the moon-sized life-form, lit by charged particles leaking from veins of raw dilithium. Massive fissures in the surface bled towers of gas and volcanic smoke, glowing with radiation through thin, toxic air laced with rains of ash-fall.

The largest of the rifts, a yawning chasm ringed with a dense forest of poisonous crystalline growths, grew larger as the starships spiraled in toward it. They had passed beyond the point of no return now, and to attempt to reverse their heading would be suicidal. Sensor sweeps were probing ahead into the hellish fires, and the *Enterprise* plunged in, meeting a web of shimmering discharges thrown up into its path. Unable to alter course, the Starfleet vessel took the full force of the electroplasma surge, and the threads of brilliant energy washed back over the hull from bow to stern.

Then it entered the churning inferno, vanishing within the leviathan and lost to those outside, who watched in silent terror.

———

The violent aftershock of the energy strike sent tendrils of power through the points where the *Enterprise*'s ephemeral deflector shields were at their weakest. Streamers of current sought points of least resistance, burning through vent grids or sensor vanes on the outer hull, then raced down along lines of conduit, blasting packets of duotronic components into melted slag. Localized power outages occurred all across the ship as systems overloaded and breakers tripped. Up on the bridge, Lieutenant Commander Scott threw himself into a frantic race to reroute power before some blackout claimed a vital system and sent the whole ship into oblivion.

It was impossible to predict that one of the minor circuits ripped apart by the energy surge was a power regulator matrix in a Jefferies tube directly above the *Enterprise*'s brig.

With a sound like a mechanized saw slicing through the trunk of a tree, the regulator blew apart with enough force to tear open a section of the overhead. Xuur cried out in shock as a heavy panel crashed down on Ensign Lopez, flattening the luckless security guard before he could react. All power in the corridor faded in the same instant—lights momentarily dimmed to nothing, and the force field keeping Tormid a prisoner was suddenly absent.

McCoy rushed to the injured security officer, his boot clipping Lopez's phaser where it had fallen from the man's nerveless fingers. As emergency batteries kicked in, flooding the compartment with a pale light, the doctor stopped short. He didn't need a tricorder to tell him that the ensign was already gone. The horrible twist in Lopez's neck and the glassy stare in his eyes were more than enough evidence.

Then in the next second, something fast slammed into McCoy and knocked him to the deck. A muscular form, all legs and arms and flashes of fur, had burst from the cell the moment the power faded, shoving Xuur aside as it went.

Tormid gave an angry howl and struck the doctor again as he tried to get up. Then, as McCoy reeled, the Syhaari scientist scooped up the fallen phaser with one long-fingered hand and turned it on him. There was a flash of radiance that lit up the darkened corridor, a shriek of beam fire, and McCoy was struck point-blank in the chest. The doctor sagged back against the wall and crumpled into a heap. This time, he did not rise.

The escaped prisoner came around to aim the weapon at Xuur. "Well," he began, panting with exertion. "Opportunity presents itself. But then, I've always had a talent for exploiting chance events. It is a function of a superior intellect."

"There was no need to shoot McCoy!" cried the envoy as another deep bass rumble shuddered through the deck. "He was no threat to you!"

Tormid shrugged. "A disagreeable sort." He nudged the unconscious doctor with his bare foot, his prehensile toes poking at McCoy's body. "Still alive. Not what I wanted." He examined the phaser more closely, running his fingers over the weapon's controls.

"Is this what you did when you met the Breg'Hel for the first time?" Xuur demanded. "They came to offer your ship assistance, and for their kindness you killed them!"

"You understand nothing, offworlder." Tormid

aimed the gun at Xuur, baring his teeth as she shrank back.

"If you shoot—"

"That will only happen if you disobey," he told her. "You are going to help me."

"No."

Tormid studied the weapon's force-setting dial. "I do not understand the symbols on this firearm, but I imagine I could find the most lethal potentiality with some trial and error." He let the phaser drop to aim at McCoy. "I will end his life. And then yours, if you defy me." He paused, letting the threat hang in the air. "Do you think I am incapable of that?"

Xuur remembered the images she had seen projected on the wall of Rumen's cell back on the Breg'Hel command ship, the recordings of Tormid cold-bloodedly dispatching the crew of the alien scout vessel. Had she still been wearing her headband, the device could have told her what the Syhaari's biometric readings said about his frame of mind, but she didn't need that to be sure. "No," she repeated. "I know exactly what kind of being you are."

"Good. That will make things simple." He gestured with the weapon as the *Enterprise* trembled again. "Tell me how Kirk's crew intend to stop the creature. Tell me how and where it will be done, and at the end of this I may still let you go home to your precious Federation."

Fourteen

The *Enterprise* and its flotilla emerged into what the philosophers and poets of old Earth would have considered a hellscape.

A cavernous void large enough to engulf a city extended away around them. Jagged peaks rose and fell on all sides, mountain ranges of stalactites and stalagmites retreating into the gloom. Sickly crimson-hued illumination spilled out of pits packed with magma-like slurry, and stark flashes of the now-familiar amber lightning coursed down veins of glistening crystal threaded through the scene. A haze of chemical mist swirled, and large, seemingly random torrents of energy darted back and forth across the open chasm, each one leaving an aftershock of charged particles radiating out to buffet the five intruder vessels.

Sparks flared off the shields as the ships pressed on, hazarding deeper into the very bones of the leviathan. For every craft and crew, this was a place so alien that none had dared venture there before.

All around them, the gigantic cosmozoan stirred, sensing the intrusion.

———

Kaleo whispered something under her breath, and Kirk tore his stare from the dramatic sight on the main viewscreen. "Are you all right?"

She held tightly to the back of his chair. "By all the light of Sya, *no*. That . . ." Kaleo swallowed hard. "It is incredible. And terrifying in equal measure." The alien captain gathered herself and met his gaze. "You think that too, I see it in your eyes. Strange how that heartens me."

"It surprises you that I'm awed by that out there?" Kirk frowned. "Why?"

"I wondered, in all your explorations, if the unknown had become ordinary to you. I see now that is not so, and I am pleased. It makes me want to live through this all the more, so that I might see what you have seen." She looked away. "I am distracting myself with foolish thoughts."

He shook his head. "If I've learned anything, it's that the moment you think the universe has shown you all the strange, wondrous, humbling sights it hides, it proves you wrong with something more." Kirk gestured at the screen. "Case in point."

"Captain?" Ensign Haines called out from the science station. "We're getting good sensor returns from our photic sonar array. I'm feeding that data directly to the Syhaari and Breg'Hel ships. But I'm also registering coherent peaks of delta radiation in the rock structure, similar to what we saw before when we first encountered the object."

"It knows we're here," said Sulu. "It's reacting."

"Sir, I've lost visual communications," M'Ress broke in. "But still maintaining contact with the other craft. They're reporting a gradual intensification of background radiation around them."

Scotty looked up from his console. "Aye, we're getting that too. But our shields are tougher, so the needle isn't moving just yet."

"We need to work fast," said Kirk. "M'Ress, Haines—make sure the other commanders know where to go and tell them to get under way." He leaned forward in his chair and tapped the intercom button. "Bridge to deflector control."

"Spock here."

"It's time, Commander. Start the counter-wave broadcast."

"Acknowledged," replied the Vulcan. *"Activation in five seconds from my mark."*

The intercom clicked off and Kirk sat back, trying without success to dispel the tension in his muscles. "Now we wait."

"If it does not work?" Kaleo asked the question without looking at him.

Kirk caught Lieutenant Arex's eye, and the navigator gave his captain a solemn nod. A single key on Arex's fire control panel had been preset to launch a full salvo of photon torpedoes, each armed with a maximum-yield antimatter warhead. If this endeavor went awry, then the brute force approach would be the only solution open to them.

We'll have to slay the kraken, Kirk thought to himself, *or die trying.*

———————

Set above and behind the large copper-colored dish on the *Enterprise*'s secondary hull, the ship's deflector control room was a tall, narrow compartment that extended up and down through several decks. At the lowest level, a hex-grid barrier formed a partition over a live energy conduit running directly off the ship's mains, casting a warm glow off the bulkheads. The conduit connected to the complex dual mechanisms that made the dish function not only as the starship's main sensor array, but also as the primary projector matrix for its shields. In normal circumstances, deflector control was usually unmanned, with operational command slaved directly to consoles on the bridge— but for this mission, every last nanosecond was critical, therefore Spock and Uhura had taken direct control to ensure no errors could creep into the process. At the highest level of the compartment, the two officers stood at twinned consoles, each watching the moment-by-moment data stream coming from the dish.

"Ready," said the Vulcan, the clock in his mind reaching zero. "Activate."

Uhura tapped out a sequence of commands.

"Counter-wave profile is loaded. Deflector dish warm-up complete. Broadcast initiating . . . *now*."

Immediately, a peculiar atonal sound rushed from hidden speakers in the panel. It was a strange amalgam, part of it like the susurrus of water along a riverbed, part a fragment reminiscent of choral plainsong, another similar to the endless ambient moan of background radiation in deep space.

"No reaction," noted Spock.

"The Breg'Hel ships are not at their intercept points yet," said Uhura. "We're not getting an even signal distribution."

Spock nodded. "It seems Ret'Sed was correct. This will require a united effort to achieve a positive result—" He broke off, raising an eyebrow and glancing away.

"Sir? Is something wrong?"

The Vulcan returned to his work. "Nothing of consequence." He adjusted a dial. "Narrow the gain, Lieutenant. We will need to compensate as the Breg'Hel ships bring their relay antennae on line."

———

On the midlevel maintenance walkway immediately beneath the control area, Tormid pressed the emitter head of the phaser into Xuur's ribs and glowered at her. They had managed to enter the deflector control room and escape the notice of the Starfleet officers, but the envoy's constant fidgeting had caused a deck plate to creak, and for a long moment Tormid believed that the Vulcan had become aware of their presence.

But now, as the atonal song grew loud enough to mask any sounds of movement, he gave Xuur a shove and pointed the weapon at an interdeck ladder, aiming upward. He had already made his intentions clear to the offworlder female. If she attempted to interfere with his plans, she would pay the price.

Tormid had forced the whole scheme out of her, piece by piece, as they made their way from the brig to deflector control. At the height of alert status, the corridors of the starship were almost empty of crew, each of them at their assigned battle stations—and so hostage and captor were able to move swiftly and with little hindrance.

Xuur's explanation turned wheels in Tormid's mind, and his sharp but supremely self-serving intellect quickly constructed a way to turn the Starfleet plan to his advantage. First, he would need to remove all impediments to his success.

"Ret'Sed's ship is signaling it is in place and is deploying the relay." He heard the dark-skinned human female give the report, pitching her voice to be heard over the sound of the broadcast.

"Acknowledged," said the other alien, without looking up.

Tormid gave Xuur a shove to remind her of his orders, and reluctantly the envoy mounted the ladder, climbing quickly to the upper level.

Too quickly. All at once, Tormid realized he had underestimated the female's persona. After she surrendered to him outside the brig, her body language had been that of a defeated foe, her face downcast, eyes unwilling to meet his. In his arrogance, he had assumed her will to be cowed, but now he saw that had never been true. Xuur had been biding her time, waiting for the right moment to turn on him. She spun on the ladder and planted a savage downward kick in his face that almost knocked him off his footing. Then she threw herself up on to the control deck and cried out a warning.

"Commander Spock, look out! Tormid has—"

The offworlder had underestimated him, however. Like all Syhaari, long of limb and nimble by their nature, the scientist did not need the restriction of the ladder to move up from deck to deck. Instead, he rocked from one support to another, crossing the distance in a fraction of a second, swinging wide and high on one arm. At the end of the other, he gripped the phaser, and he used it to shoot Xuur in the back. She went down two steps from the ladder, all potency abruptly gone from her form.

Tormid completed a swing that deposited him squarely on the deck, directly between the two offworlders. "You will join her if you move without my permission."

"How did you escape the brig?" said the Vulcan, his face infuriatingly devoid of any emotional cues.

"I exploited an opportunity," he replied.

"That power drain, when we passed through the mantle?" wondered the female. Then her expression hardened. Unlike the male, her anger at Tormid was very easy to see. "I'm going to help her," she said, nodding toward the envoy's fallen form.

"Was I unclear?" Tormid aimed the weapon at the lieutenant. "Move and I shoot. Envoy Xuur did not seem to understand that simple command. And see what happened to her."

"What do you hope to accomplish here?" Spock maintained a steady gaze upon him. "If you interfere with this operation, it will mean our destruction and ultimately that of your world."

Tormid showed his teeth in a wide, feral smile. "A question for you, alien. Scientist to scientist." He waved at the consoles and the streams of data from the growing counter-wave. "Have you considered the outcome of adjusting the potentiality of your soporific broadcast *upward*, into the more volatile frequency ranges? If one were to, say, remove all safety interlocks regulating the power of the signal?"

"Such an action would be unproductive," Spock replied.

"I disagree!"

The female shook her head. "What you're talking about would only duplicate what the Breg'Hel did at the start . . . it would agitate the leviathan even more!"

"Your thinking is limited," Tormid sniffed, annoyed that the offworlder could not see his intention. But a flicker of understanding in the Vulcan's eyes told him that the *Enterprise*'s science officer did see the line of his reasoning.

"The neurocrystalline structure of the creature's brain resonates on a specific subspace frequency. I suspect what Tormid is suggesting is nothing less than broadcasting an overpowering signal on exactly that rate. A signal powerful enough not to simply enrage the leviathan . . . but to destroy its neural structure."

"That . . ." The woman's expression shifted to one of pure shock. "The power output to do that would blow out the deflector dish, not to mention overloading the systems of the relay ships! You'd destroy the Breg'Hel ships and your own as well!"

"A few more deaths." Tormid shrugged. "Unavoidable. But I have faith that the steadfast Captain Kirk and his crew will be able to escape with the *Enterprise* more or less intact." As he spoke, he was already planning his way off the Starfleet vessel and his explanation to the Assembly. Who would be believed, the offworlders who had brought chaos in their wake, or the embattled but heroic explorer? In the confusion, it would be easy to rally his supporters and decry every alien as an invader. Without their monster, the Breg'Hel would be vulnerable, and Tormid did not believe for one moment that this irresolute Federation— with all their self-defeating rules and high-handed morals—would dare to risk firing on Syhaari ships.

Yes, he told himself, *I can still emerge from this as a victor.*

"We will not assist you in any way," the male said flatly.

A chime sounded from one of the panels. "Incoming message from Ead'Aea," said the female. "Reporting that the second Breg'Hel ship is in position and deploying their relay."

"If Lieutenant Uhura does not respond to the Breg'Hel immediately, they will become suspicious," said the other offworlder. "You must allow her to do so."

"No," Tormid said with an airy shrug. "I have been observing your kind since we first met, and I know you believe you are more intelligent than my species. You will attempt some sort of subterfuge."

Uhura scowled at him. "We've never once said or done anything that proves we look down on the Syhaari! The Federation has treated you like equals from the start!"

"Debatable," snapped Tormid, "at best."

"Not so," Spock offered. "But it is an understandable emotional reaction from a being suffering from an acute sense of inferiority. Your outward persona would appear to fit within that type, sir. It is easier for you to justify your own actions to yourself if you can characterize us as your antagonists."

It was the wrong thing to say to Tormid, and he bared his teeth in a snarl. "I have no need to justify anything I have done!" He jerked the phaser. "Step away from the controls. I am perfectly willing to silence both of you if my patience is tested!"

Reluctantly, Spock raised his hands from the controls in front of him. "Do as he says, Lieutenant," he ordered.

———

"Zond's and Rumen's rangers are locked in and broadcasting the counter-wave," purred M'Ress.

Kirk nodded. "What's the status of the Breg'Hel ships?"

"Ret'Sed's craft is in position," reported Haines. "Still awaiting the go signal from the other vessel, sir."

Kaleo sniffed warily. "This is taking too long."

"Captain"—Scotty shot him a worried look—"if we don't have a symmetrical transmission coming from the flotilla, it'll disrupt the whole counter-wave. It's all or nothing here."

"Understood," Kirk replied. "Ensign Haines, what's the problem?"

The young woman frowned at the readout on her display. "I'm not sure, sir. Ead'Aea's technicians have deployed their relay antenna, the signal from the *Enterprise* should be synchronized with them . . . but it's not."

"Aye, the lassie has it right," Scott confirmed. "The problem is at our end of things, not theirs."

A sudden flash of yellow fire blazed over the viewscreen as an energy discharge cut across the cavern. "The leviathan's agitation is turning inward," said

Kaleo. "It's trying to dislodge us, pick us out as if we were ticks beneath its fur."

Kirk leaned forward, reaching to tap the intercom button. "Bridge to deflector control, do you read?"

After a moment, M'Ress tapped the remote receiver in her ear. "No answer down there, Captain."

"Spock!" called Kirk. "Uhura! Respond—"

The sharp hiss of the turbolift doors cut him off before he could finish his sentence, and from the corner of his eye, the captain glimpsed a pale figure in a blue uniform tunic stagger out, on the verge of falling to the deck.

———

Uhura obeyed the first officer's command, allowing her dislike of the order to show plainly on her face. "This won't end well for anyone," she told Tormid. "You most of all."

"I am willing to take the chance," growled the Syhaari. "I have *always* been willing to risk my life for the sake of my species. A pity that so few have been able to understand that." He moved to Spock's console and flicked his gaze over the display. "Yes. I see how this works. Clever. And simple enough for me to co-opt for a different outcome."

"You are highly intelligent," Spock allowed, moving slowly and carefully, but never beyond arm's reach. "That is clear. However, I question if your morality is as sophisticated as your intellect."

"Your morals are as alien as you are, offworlder," Tormid said dismissively, making a few experimental taps on the controls.

Uhura refused to allow that to pass unremarked. "That's not true," she argued. "I've met enough of your people to know that the Syhaari are not a cruel race. Captain Kaleo, Rumen, Zond, and Duchad. I'm a good judge of character, and each of them seemed like decent people to me."

"How kind of you to grace us with your praise!" Tormid snorted with derision. "And fitting that you pick those with the clearest lack of will to give it to!"

"What you consider a deficiency of resolve, we see as compassion," Spock replied. "And compassion is a core tenet upon which the United Federation of Planets was founded. You will forgive me, sir, if I say I hope that *you* are the exception to commonality of your species, and not Kaleo and the others."

"The Syhaari respect strength," said Tormid. "And while some of them may have mistaken your technological prowess to be that, it is clear to me now that your Federation is lacking. You have power, but you balk at employing it." He weighed the stolen phaser in his hand. "This device alone has the power of ten of our beam guns . . . and this starship?" The scientist pointed at the walls. "On its own, you could have brought us to our knees with it. But instead you came with diplomats and you *talked.*" He directed a sneer toward Xuur's fallen form.

"Bridge to deflector control, do you read?"

Captain Kirk's voice blared from a speaker on the panel, and it caught Tormid by surprise. He spun, almost as if he expected to see the *Enterprise*'s commanding officer there in the room with them.

Tormid's moment of confusion was exactly what Spock had been waiting for. Uhura saw the Vulcan rock off his heels, instantly moving from stillness to action. He shot toward the Syhaari and grabbed his arms, forcing the phaser up and away; but Tormid was prepared for the attack, having learned the hard way about turning his back on a Vulcan down on the hangar deck. They struggled for a moment, Spock's innate strength matched evenly against the dense, ropey musculature of the simianoid.

Uhura hesitated for a fraction of a second. Part of her was compelled to rush to Envoy Xuur's side and make certain the woman was still breathing—a heavy stun blast could still be very dangerous—but another, more logical part of her knew that unless the alarm was raised, Xuur's life would be forfeit along with that of everyone else.

"Spock! Uhura! Respond—" A second shout from the intercom, abruptly cut short, spurred her to action. The lieutenant dove toward the sound of the voice, reaching for the emergency alert button.

As she got to the console, Uhura heard a violent grunt of effort and a crash of noise. Tormid had turned a foot in against Spock's leg to throw him off balance. Like all his species, the Syhaari's lower limbs ended in something more like hands than feet, and thick finger-like toes gripped and pulled, robbing the Vulcan of stability.

Uhura turned to see Spock desperately scrambling back up from where he had fallen, but Tormid was already spinning about, turning to aim the phaser across the compartment at *her*. Time seemed to thicken and slow, and everything in the moment became unnaturally sharp. Tormid's snarling face, the alert button just beyond her reach, the strange artificial chorus of the counter-wave signal.

She braced herself for the energy bolt that she knew was coming, wondering if she would ever wake again after the stun blast took her down.

There was a blue blur of motion, a shriek of a phaser discharge—and suddenly Uhura was watching Spock collapse, first to his knees, then down into a heap, his eyes rolling back to show the whites. *He took the shot meant for me.*

The first officer had thrown himself in front of Tormid, absorbing the blast point blank, and for his bravery he now lay silent and unmoving next to Xuur. Heedless of what might happen next, Uhura went to his side. Like the envoy, Spock was still alive, but his breathing was shallow, and his body still trembled from the shock that had gone through it.

She felt a hard prod at her back and looked up with barely contained fury in her eyes. Tormid stood tall over her, the phaser aimed at her head. "Get up, and do not test me again. A hostage will be useful . . . but only to a point." He jerked the muzzle of the weapon away from his two fallen victims. "Move. *Now.*"

"Spock was right about you," she said, slowly rising to her feet, her hands raised. "But you can't see it. You'll never accept the chance you might be wrong. That's why you killed the Breg'Hel, that's why you're doing this."

"You know nothing," Tormid growled, and with one hand he gripped the power control sliders on the console, slowly easing the energy dials forward.

The tones of the strange chorus shifted, growing rough and strident. The sound hurt Uhura's ears, and she winced as it became louder with each passing moment.

"*Jim!*" gasped McCoy. "I . . . couldn't stop him. Had to warn . . ." Ashen and shaky, the doctor tumbled forward as his legs gave out.

Kaleo moved across the bridge in a blur of motion and caught McCoy as he fell from the turbolift, grabbing him before he could collapse. "I have you," she said. "It's all right."

Kirk vaulted from his chair. "Bones! What happened?"

McCoy waved the question away. "Forget me. Xuur . . . he must have her."

A sudden chill passed through the captain's veins;

there could be only one person his old friend was referring to. "Tormid."

"Got out of the cell . . . power failed." McCoy struggled to explain. "Ensign Lopez was down, tried to . . ."
He sucked in a ragged breath. "Tormid knocked me
down, hit me with a heavy stun. He's loose, Jim. Had
to get here . . . warn you."

"If Tormid is armed and he has a hostage . . ."
Kaleo's words trailed off.

Kirk looked back at the silent intercom panel. "I
know where he is."

M'Ress grabbed an emergency medical pack from
beneath her panel and guided McCoy to her chair. Too
weak to complain, he let her fill a hypospray and inject
him with a counteractive. "He'll be all right, sir," said
the Caitian.

The ship trembled again as another energy surge
shocked through the space around it, then a sharp
tone sounded from the science station.

Haines spoke up. "Contact from the second
Breg'Hel ship. They're confirming they received the go
signal from the *Enterprise*. Counter-wave is now being
transmitted from all flotilla vessels."

"Captain, something isn't right." Scott shook his
head as he studied the wave forms on the screen before him. "The subspace frequency being broadcast,
it's all wrong. The power output is varying toward
the upper bands when it should be dropping into the
lower range . . ."

"If Tormid is doing this, then I dread to consider what he means to accomplish," said Kaleo. "He must be stopped."

"Can't just cut the transmission," Kirk muttered, thinking aloud. "No time. I've got to get down there, get it back on track . . ." He turned, beckoning his chief engineer. "Scotty! You can handle things up here without me for a while. Take the conn."

The other officer nodded at the order. "Aye, sir." Scott strode across the bridge to the command chair.

Kirk put a hand on his chief engineer's arm and spoke quietly, adding, "You know what to do." It wasn't a question, but an affirmation. Scott, better than anyone on the bridge, knew that if the worst came to pass, the *Enterprise* might need to be sacrificed.

"Aye, sir," repeated the engineer in a low voice. "I'll do what has to be done."

Kirk nodded and dashed into the turbolift. As he twisted the activator control, Kaleo nimbly slipped in between the closing doors to join him. This time, he didn't question her reasons for coming along, only nodded. Each of them understood the stakes at hand only too well.

"Deflector control," he ordered, and the lift accelerated away.

———

With each new pulse from the *Enterprise*'s deflector dish, the soothing murmur of the counter-wave mutated, growing ever more jagged and brutal as it went on. Each pulsation echoed across the void inside the leviathan before being scooped up and rebroadcast by the smaller Syhaari and Breg'Hel starships. Their crews were starting to notice that something was amiss as the signal hit them with the force of a storm surge beating at a shoreline, worsening as it went— but none of them dared to close down their relays, all knowing what greater prize was at stake. Zond and Rumen, Ret'Sed and Ead'Aea, they and their crews had ceded their control to the Starfleet vessel, and by the time they realized what was wrong, it would be too late.

Uhura saw that dark end unfolding in her mind's eye as she watched the wave form display shifting from calm and steady geometric patterns toward a frenzied mess of energetic spikes. The deck shifted under her feet as the *Enterprise* rocked in the wake of more furious discharges from the leviathan.

Somewhere out there in the cavern walls, the stony flesh of the living planetoid was resonating with a terrible vibration that shook and cracked the rock-skin. Uhura could almost sense the agony resonating through the titanic cosmozoan, and she remembered the sound of its subspace howls captured by Lieutenant M'Ress.

"You're going to kill it," she gasped.

"That is my intention," Tormid replied. "Was I unclear?" He continued to push the power output con-

trols toward the redline. "Soon your captain will have
no choice but to abandon this idiotic act and flee."
The Syhaari waved toward the walkway leading to the
lower levels of the compartment. "I have already sev-
ered the control linkages down there that allow your
bridge to take remote command of this system. They
will not be able to stop me."

"You thought of everything," Uhura admitted,
moving slowly along the nearest panel. "And when
you've murdered this creature, what then?"

"The extermination of a predator is not murder,"
he replied. "It is required."

Reaching by touch alone, never taking her eyes off
the Syhaari, Uhura's slender fingers slipped over the
face of an intercom module, and she tapped the activation stud. "And will you turn on me next? How much
more blood are you going to shed?"

———————

"Wait!" Kirk skidded to a halt in the corridor and held
up a hand. "Listen!"

Kaleo stopped in an instant and stood there panting. They had both sprinted from the turbolift, but
suddenly the *Enterprise*'s captain was cocking his
head, waiting for something.

"*I told you, you have value to me,*" said a rough
voice from a nearby intraship panel, echoing slightly.

Kaleo blinked. "That's Tormid. What is he doing?"

Kirk waved her to silence as he went to the panel.

"I will take one of those shuttle vessels of yours," the scientist went on. *"You come with me. As insurance against any more foolishness on Kirk's part."*

"How are we hearing that?" Kaleo looked around the plain corridor, spotting the sealed door to the deflector control room up ahead.

"The captain is a lot of things, but a fool isn't one of them." Uhura's voice, louder and clearer than Tormid's, issued out. *"He'll stop you."*

"My communications officer," said Kirk, in a low voice. "She's very resourceful. She must have opened the intercom. We're listening to everything going on in that room."

As if she anticipated the next question on both their minds, Uhura went on. *"You could have allowed Envoy Xuur and Commander Spock to leave. You didn't have to shoot them. They both need medical attention."*

Kirk reached behind him and pulled a device from the small of his back. Kaleo recognized it as a smaller version of the beam pistols carried by the Starfleet crew. "What do you intend to do?" she asked.

A long, turbulent shudder ran along the length of the corridor, and alarmingly, Kaleo thought she saw the bulkheads of the vessel shift and flex. The bombardments of wild energy striking the *Enterprise*'s shields were worsening.

"Act fast," Kirk replied, and moved carefully toward the deflector control room door.

"What exactly are you doing at that command

console?" Uhura's question floated through the air, her tone becoming a challenge. *"Do you even know what those controls are for?"*

Kirk nodded to himself. "She's telling us where he's standing." He moved to one side of the door, out of range of the autosensor that would open it on approach, directing Kaleo to do the same. He checked his weapon again. "If we weren't swimming in subspace radiation, we could just beam them all out of there, let Scotty sort out the patterns in the buffer."

Kaleo's fur stiffened as a dark truth occurred to her. "Tormid will never surrender. He may force you to—"

"What are you doing? Get away from there!" Tormid's voice was suddenly loud and harsh. *"I warned you not to test me!"*

———

The Syhaari took two long-legged steps toward Uhura and saw the blinking activation light atop the intercom panel. He glanced back at where he had been standing and scowled. "Clever. But your warning counts for nothing." Tormid balled his fist and smashed the intercom with a single heavy blow. "You will pay for that," he shouted, snarling over the constant atonal howl of the corrupted counter-wave broadcast.

Uhura spun away as he grabbed at her, planting a chopping karate blow in Tormid's chest that landed poorly, sliding off his ribs. She had only a vague idea of how Syhaari physiology worked and no clue where vulnerable nerve points might be beneath his furry epidermis. On instinct, she went for the soft tissues of his throat, ducking and striking again. A half-spent breath exploded from his chest in a spit of pain, and the lieutenant knew she had hurt him—but the alien had at least twice her body mass in his rangy, muscular form and stamina to match.

Tormid clubbed her with the flat of his free hand and she staggered back, pain sparking in her skull. From the corner of her eye, she caught sight of the control room door hissing open on the far side of the compartment. Uhura reeled against the safety rail ringing the access shaft and shook off the blow.

"Drop the phaser!" called the captain, coming in at a pace with Kaleo on his heels.

Tormid's lengthy arm snaked around Uhura's throat before she could react, and the Syhaari pulled her into an uncomfortable embrace. He jammed the phaser into her cheek.

"No," said Tormid. "I imagine the female will die if I fire into her skull, even if the weapon is on a stun setting. You, Kirk, drop *your* weapon."

"This is over!" yelled Kaleo, stalking around the edge of the access shaft. "Can you not see that, Tormid? How much more must you destroy before you understand?"

"Be silent!" he roared. "You are tainted by these aliens, you weakling! I always said you were irresolute, but you have proven it by putting your allegiance with these hairless maggots! You are a traitor to Sya! You do not have the courage to do what must be done!" His finger tightened on the phaser's trigger.

"*Stop!*" cried Kirk. "All right! You win!" He opened his hand and let the small palm phaser fall to the deck. "Let my officer go! Let her and Kaleo take Spock and Xuur, let them leave. *I* will be your hostage, Tormid!" He sagged, as if his will to fight had fled from him. "I'll do whatever you want. As long as you don't hurt any more of my crew."

For a long second, Uhura thought that Tormid would shoot her anyway, just out of sheer spite. But then he placed a hand between her shoulder blades and gave her a vicious shove. "Get out," he snarled, waving toward the fallen. "And take that refuse with you."

Uhura glanced at her commanding officer, and he gave her a wan nod in return. She knelt, hauling the Rhaandarite envoy to her feet, and with difficulty, she shuffled to the door. It opened to reveal two security guards, with weapons drawn and ready.

"No!" Kirk held up his hands before they could advance. "Matsuo, Garner, stand down. No one is to open fire, is that clear? That's an order."

Kaleo, easily bearing Spock's weight in her ropey limbs, moved to the door and handed off the unconscious first officer to one of the guards, then she stepped back and raised her hands as well. "I'm not leaving, Captain. If you stay, I stay."

"You're making a habit of that," he noted.

"I accept this trade," said Tormid. "It means that one of you is now expendable."

Uhura saw the Syhaari shifting his aim back and forth between the two of them, considering which he was going to shoot. The door whispered shut and suddenly she was in the corridor, amid a refrain of groaning hull metal and warning sirens.

"What do we do, Lieutenant?" said Matsuo, kneading the grip of her phaser.

Uhura straightened, knowing that she had to take command of the situation. "Get a medical kit," she ordered. "We have injured here."

Matsuo dashed away to a nearby emergency supply locker, and Uhura found the other security guard staring at the closed door. "But what about Captain Kirk?"

"He knows what he's doing," she told Garner.

I hope, Uhura added silently.

Fifteen

The leviathan crossed the edge of the atmospheric interface in a brilliant crimson flash, cutting a great wake through the sky of Syhaar Prime that could be seen across the planet's northern hemisphere.

Fire rained down on the surface as the titanic creature willingly seared itself against the friction, and in its passing towering energy spikes ripped open clouds and sent streamers of electrostatic discharge in every direction. Unprotected systems, overwhelmed by the ambient energy, burned out. Lights across hundreds of settlements and outer domains darkened as power was lost.

For the frightened Syhaari in the cities and the forests, there was little they could do but look upward and see the great blood-colored orb passing overhead. Like the baleful eye of some mythic giant, it stared down on them, an omen of a terrible fate.

For those in space, following the planetoid as closely as they dared, the horror was every bit as real. For the observers—the Andorian diplomat ch'Sellor, the elder Gatag, and the engineer Hoyga among them—the terrible consequence of the leviathan's mad fury unfolded before their eyes. The sudden gravitational effect of the living planetoid's near passage was sending out earthquake shocks and stirring freak tidal activity, and already sensors were detecting the start of state-changes in Syhaar Prime's upper atmosphere as uncontrolled torrents of subspace radiation tore through ozone layers and polluted the night sky. Like a predator raking its claws across a prey animal's flesh, even a passing encounter with the leviathan would cause catastrophic damage. The planet would bleed out and perish unless the beast's rampage could be stopped.

But with no way to contact the brave souls who had dared the attempt to silence the storm of rage, they could do nothing but watch and wait for the end.

Tormid fired a blast of light into the security pad near the door and sparks gushed from the magnetic locking mechanism. "It pleases me you are here," he said, sneering. "It is fitting that you see the failure of your ideals at close hand." He took a step toward Kirk. "How does it feel, human? To know that the lofty principles you espouse mean nothing now? That perfect Federation you tried to subsume us into, it is a shared delusion, a product of naïve dreamers."

Kirk kept his hands raised. "You don't know us at all," he said firmly. "I'm sorry to say I've met your kind before, and each time I hope it will be the last. But here you are again. Believing you are enlightened. Blinded by your arrogance."

"*Which* of us is the arrogant one?" Tormid asked, shooting a venomous glare at Kaleo. "I, who want only to see my people prosper? Or you, Captain Kirk, coming to the Syhaari Gathering with your high-handed intent, deigning to grace us primitives with the gift of your attentions?" Before Kirk could respond, he went on. "Did it ever occur to you that some of us do not want your help?" Tormid pointed at Kaleo. "She and others like her, they were the ones who summoned you. Greedy for your favor after being dazzled by your grand starship."

"But not you?" said Kirk, sensing a way to attack the scientist's ego at its most vulnerable point. "You wanted us to come here just to see what you could get from us, am I right? You think us weak because we showed Kaleo's crew compassion, and you wanted to see just how much advantage you could take!"

"If you give away power, you do not deserve it," sniffed Tormid. "Knowledge must be ripped from the universe by force, it is never given without price! I have always taken what was needed when the opportunity arises."

Kaleo made a sound halfway between a snarl and a sob. "From the bodies of the dead?"

"The Breg'Hel are invaders!" he thundered back at her. "Destroyers!"

"Only because you gave them no other choice!" Kirk came forward before Tormid could turn the phaser on the other Syhaari. "You act like you're an intelligent being, but you're shortsighted and ignorant. You never once considered the consequences of your actions! All this, every life lost and ship destroyed"—he aimed a finger at Tormid's chest—"it's on you."

"The Breg'Hel did terrible things," said Kaleo, "but they did them out of fear, fear of *us*. And fear is why you killed them in the first place."

"You didn't wait to talk with them, you didn't even try to make a peaceful first contact." Kirk met Tormid's seething gaze. "You let your fear rule you, and everything you've done since then has been in denial of that truth."

"I am not afraid," Tormid growled, aiming the phaser. "Not of *you*."

"*Liar*!" Kirk shouted the word back at him. He sensed Tormid's anger was about to break its banks, and he kept pushing. "You're afraid of change. Afraid of faces that you don't recognize, voices you've never heard before! You live inside the Veil, in a tiny bubble of space, and you think that is the whole universe, that you're somehow master of it all. But you're afraid of the galaxy out there and everything in it. You lack the insight to see that all of us are striving for the same things, that we have more in common than we do in disparity!"

"The human is right," said Kaleo, a look of pity in

her eyes. "You call yourself a scientist and an explorer, but you're neither. In every way, you . . . are a *small* mind."

"You dare!" Tormid's self-control broke, and he whirled, bringing the weapon to bear on Kaleo; but as he squeezed the trigger pad, Kirk was launching himself at the Syhaari, slamming into him with enough force to knock his aim off target. A blue streak of coherent particles struck a panel near Kaleo's head, blowing it open.

She ducked and scrambled away, hesitating for a split second as Kirk followed through on the attack. The *Enterprise*'s captain grabbed at Tormid's gun arm with one hand, and found purchase in a fistful of fur with the other. "Kaleo, go!" he shouted. "Revert the transmission, before—"

Tormid let out a savage roar and punched him hard in the sternum. Kirk felt something crack and a sharp, stabbing pain, but he pushed on. Slamming the Syhaari's arm against the safety rail around the access shaft over and over again, he fought to keep up the pressure on his opponent and not falter.

Dimly, he was aware of Kaleo racing to the main deflector control console. *Got to give her time*, he told himself, and with another surge of effort he smashed Tormid's wrist against the rail. The Syhaari bit out a cry of pain and his long fingers jerked open in a spasm. The phaser fell and clattered over the edge of the shaft.

But the victory was short-lived. Tormid's free hand came up again, this time in a wide, open-fingered blow that swallowed up Kirk's face in a suffocating grasp. The two of them spun about, reversing position, and the captain was flattened against the safety rail, the angular metal of it digging into his spine.

The thick flesh of Tormid's heavy palm cut off any attempt Kirk made to draw a breath, and he felt himself losing ground, his boots skidding on the deck. Blindly, Kirk brought his hands together and threw them forward again in a double-fisted punch that found a soft, fleshy patch near where a human would have a solar plexus. Landing a blow there seemed to have a similar effect, and Tormid wheezed, releasing his grip on Kirk's face but not the pressure on the captain's torso.

Kirk tried to struggle free, catching sight of Kaleo bent over the command panel. He could see her drawing down the overloaded power controls and hear the falling cadence of the counter-wave as it shifted away from its screaming, destructive pitch and back toward more moderated tones.

Tormid saw it too, and writhed, caught between his intention to end Kirk's life and his plans for killing the leviathan. "Stop!" he spat. "Do not interfere!"

"Too late," Kirk managed, through a gasp. "You've failed!"

"Not yet," growled Tormid, and he put his full weight into the fight.

Kirk felt the air leave his lungs as Tormid crushed him against the rail. Fire burned across his chest and his balance disintegrated. He slipped, his body going over the edge, his arm flailing into the open space of the access shaft. A steady pulse of glowing light—the mains feed to the sensor dish—illuminated the ducting beneath, but the color was fading from everything around him. Grayness gathered at the corners of Kirk's vision.

A jolt of fear shocked through him: *Of all the places to die, I never expected it would be somewhere like this.*

Inexorably, Tormid was pushing him toward a terminal fall. Stronger than a mere human like Kirk, all the powerfully built Syhaari had to do was keep up the pressure, and in a moment gravity would finish the job for him.

Gravity.

Less than a thought, more an instinct, a defiant impulse drew on some deeper reserve of Kirk's strength. He used it all to propel himself forward for one brief moment, knowing that doing so would shift his weight and make his fall a certainty—but in that motion, he grabbed at handfuls of Tormid's tunic and pulled hard.

Knocked off balance by the sudden action, the Syhaari lost his grip and came with Kirk over the edge of the safety rail. There was nothing to stop them plummeting three decks down into the pulsing power feed. Gravity took hold and both opponents vanished into the shaft.

Kirk thought he heard Kaleo cry out his name. Then he was tumbling through the air, tangled with Tormid's spindly limbs as they cracked against the walls and spun away.

He twisted as they plummeted, drawing on experience from a youthful, reckless dalliance with orbital skydiving to remember how to manage the fall. Kirk's outstretched hands smacked a protruding support frame, and by reflex his fingers contracted. It took his weight, and it was all he could do not to fall away again when the pain of the hard contact sparked through him from the site of his broken ribs.

Below, Kirk heard rather than saw the crash of breaking metal as Tormid's unarrested plunge ended with him smashing through the hex-grid safety grille. There was a deep, resonating buzz as living matter connected with the power train—and then nothing.

———

Great tectonic shifts quivered over the surface of the leviathan, and across the frequencies of subspace, the living planetoid howled in pain. Its primitive animal mind, unable to process what had happened to it, struggled to do anything other than scream at the void and attack everything around it.

It had been driven by the cries broadcast from the stone-metal-fragments that trailed about it, first forced from its feeding grounds in panic and then harried across the empty wastes of interstellar space where nourishment was scarce. And just as it encountered a dust cloud that might sustain it, the screaming clarion that compelled it drove the leviathan to fury, making it lash out.

Again and again, the anger-pain had come, until at last a kind of berserk madness had taken hold. All meek and passive thought-action crumbled and left only fury behind. It became an inferno that fueled itself. Destruction and violence were all that it craved— its *own* destruction most of all. Perhaps only then, the agony would cease.

Amber fire collected in massive auroras about the planetoid's equator, building and building into a store of energetic potential. Unleashed in a barrage of lightning strikes, it would be able to rip open the surface of the planet below, punish it for the strangle-grip of its gravity, strike back at the creators of the pain, at everything.

The pain—

Something was changing. Deep inside itself, in the caverns where rock and crystal and electrochemical masses made the leviathan live, a song was being sung.

And in that moment, the rage held.

———

Every effort was like a knife through his chest, and Kirk tasted blood in his mouth. But it was impossible to stop, beyond him to halt for even a moment to try to catch his breath. To do so would be to risk losing his grip and falling, and now it was only dogged forward momentum that carried the captain on. Hand over hand, he climbed back up the shaft, through the smoke sizzling from the damaged power feed, fighting down every racking cough in case the next one made him black out.

After what seemed like an eternity, his hand slapped on the deck, and Kirk hauled himself onto the deflector control room's upper deck.

Kaleo was still at the console, desperately fighting it as streamers of red warning strobes lit up the command panel. She caught sight of him, at once alarmed and relieved by his ragged appearance. "James! Where is Tormid?"

Kirk didn't answer, instead using all his available strength to rise to his feet. "Stay there," he told her, moving to the secondary console. "We need to work together to . . . to make it safe." Immediately, Kirk saw that the complex interwoven frequencies of the counter-wave were dropping out of unity, fraying like threads pulled from a worn tapestry.

Uhura would be able to fix this in a nanosecond, he thought to himself. *But I don't have the time to get her back in here.* "Follow my lead," he called out, panting through his pain. "Moderate the power levels, just as before. I'll compensate from this station."

"It's not working," said Kaleo.

"It *will*," he insisted. "Trust me." He took another breath, wincing at the sharp stabbing aches down his chest, and worked the panel, slowly bringing the disrupted signal pattern back into true. He heard Kaleo grunt as she ghosted his actions, and moment by agonizing moment, they began to recapture the vital synchronization.

The sound of the counter-wave pulses, until now a cacophony of noise that beat at his senses, slowly transformed into something more akin to a melody. Kirk suppressed a smile. Was it coincidence that Spock and Uhura's shared creation of the signal had a harmonious component, given both of his officers' musical skills? He made a mental note to ask the Vulcan about that if—no, *when*—they had pulled back from the brink of destruction.

"*Deflector control!*" called a familiar voice, filtering up from another intercom panel on the console in front of him. "*Scott here! Captain Kirk, do you read me? What is your status?*"

Kirk dared to shoot a look over his shoulder and saw a patch of glowing cherry-red on the jammed door. His people were outside, cutting their way back into the compartment with phasers. He tapped the intercom's reply key. "Scotty, some assistance would be appreciated!"

"*Aye sir,*" Scott said, the worry in his tone immediately switching to a more businesslike manner. "*I'm tying in Lieutenant M'Ress and giving you a boost of auxiliary power.*" The engineer paused. "*I was afraid we'd lost you in there, sir. There was an interruption of the mains feed to the deflector dish, and—*"

"I'll explain later," Kirk spoke over him. "For now, pass the order to all ships in the mission group. Come about and head for the rift. We're getting out of here."

"Aye, aye, Captain."

Kaleo gave him a sharp look. "We are leaving? But the signal . . ."

Kirk blew out a weary breath. "We've done as much as we can. Now we're at the mercy of the beast."

The sky burned gold.

Streams of star fire, gathered in from cross-dimensional subspace domains and now made livid and visible, crackled around the edges of the leviathan. Talons, formed from energy that could barely exist in normal space, sparked and flared, and for the people on the night side of Syhaar Prime, it was as if the apocalypse had halted to consider its final act before laying waste to their world.

And then the fires *shifted*.

The wild lightning storm clinging to the curvature of the rogue planetoid did not reach out, but instead it collapsed inward. The conjured power fed back into the serried veins of raw dilithium crystal and made them glow with amber radiosity. Slowly at first, then with increasing degrees of speed, the leviathan began to turn about, rotating counter to the spin of the planet below it—then on a buffer of compacted gravitons, the massive intruder pushed itself away from close orbit of the Syhaari homeworld. Moving through currents of force in a manner that no conventional starship could achieve, the gargantuan cosmozoan departed. It left behind the destruction in its wake and the horror of the monstrous howls it broadcast across the vacuum.

Silent now, its strange mind-process aimed within, the leviathan listened to the soft resonance of the alien song that echoed inside its core.

Lulled into quiescence, the creature's monumental fury dissipated, and its every violent impulse faded into dim memory. Docile once more, as it was meant to be, the leviathan scarcely reacted to the passage of the alien objects—the metal-stone of the tiny life-craft—as they passed back through the rifts in its rocky mantle and powered away into open space.

Faint, celestial hunger stirred in the alien's thoughts, the need to heal and to replenish itself. On solar winds it tasted the scent of rich cosmic dust and spent stellar gas, and angling from the heat of the far-away star, the leviathan began a slow migration toward the distant gray wall of the Veil.

On Syhaar Prime, a dawn came that none who lived there had expected to see.

———

The Learned Assembly offered the use of an island in the middle of an equatorial inland sea as the site for what their media were calling "the reconciliation." An area of great natural beauty, but lacking in the giant super-trees that dominated much of the planet, it had been chosen as somewhere that the Breg'Hel would not feel overwhelmed by the landscape. The gecko-like aliens, used to life on board their ships and the desolate, arid moons of their birth, were awed by the panoply of green that grew from the rich soil, even here in the warmest of Syhaar Prime's climate zones.

Kirk and the landing party from the *Enterprise* watched the aliens climb gingerly from their dropship, each of them exiting the unusual craft with long, careful steps.

"Is it me, or are some of them shivering?" asked McCoy quietly.

"The ambient temperature here is cold by their standards," Spock noted. "As a Vulcan, I share some of their feelings. I prefer the warmth and the crisp air of a desert."

"Warm enough for me," muttered ch'Sellor, under his breath. The taciturn Andorian envoy was sweating, even in his light robes.

"Diplomacy is all about the act of compromise," Xuur told her aide. "That's the watchword for today over all others." She shot Kirk a sideways look. "Don't you agree, Captain?"

"It would seem so," Kirk replied. "At least we're meeting here and not where Ret'Sed wanted to." The Breg'Hel had actually suggested that this historic summit take place on the surface of the leviathan in a temporary environment bubble, as a gesture emblematic of conflict's end—but the envoy had gently persuaded them that a different location would be less problematic.

Still, there remained a symbolism here. The clean, blossom-scented air that Kirk had tasted on their first arrival was tainted now, even in this region, by a faint odor of smoke and dust. While the damage wrought by the leviathan's passing had not been as severe as that on planet Gadmuur or the ill-fated ice world Hokaar, the Syhaari world had suffered. He had no doubt that the natives wanted to impress that on the beings who had invaded their star system on a mission of blind revenge.

Kirk studied Xuur and his fellow officers for a moment. They had endured conflicts of their own. Each of them had come through the events of recent days the hard way, injured in the line of duty to a greater or lesser extent—but none of them allowed that to be visible today. For his part, the *Enterprise*'s captain was moving a little stiffly thanks to a medical patch on his still-healing ribs, but he tried not to show it.

He looked away and gave what he hoped was a friendly nod toward the small flock of remote media drones floating above the group. The airborne cameras drifted back and forth between the Federation party and the Breg'Hel, dithering over the aliens.

Ret'Sed and Ead'Aea stared back at the robots with undisguised interest, although their companion Zud'Hoa seemed ill at ease with the machines. Even the concept of an artificial mechanism with some degree of intelligence was new to the Breg'Hel, who saw everything in terms of living creatures.

"Captain, the Syhaari are here," said Lieutenant Uhura. She pointed to an open-topped air-skimmer as it appeared over the low tree line. The craft made a lazy turn and put down across from the Breg'Hel craft. Kirk saw Kaleo at the controls, steering it from a column like the helm of an ancient sailing ship.

Gatag and several other members of the Learned Assembly disembarked, followed by Kaleo and her colleagues Rumen and Zond. The three of them glanced in Kirk's direction and gave shallow bows.

"Did anyone say what became of Tormid's engineer?" said Uhura. "What was her name? Hoyga?"

"In custody, Lieutenant," said Spock. "The evidence Rumen and the Breg'Hel presented regarding Tormid's duplicity was very clear. Hoyga's involvement in maintaining his duplicity is undeniable."

"It is my understanding that they will strip her of rank and status," added Xuur. "Exile is the usual sentence. Hoyga will be sent to a penal center on Gadmuur to assist with the rebuilding there."

"She lied to protect Tormid . . ." McCoy considered that for a moment. "I imagine by the time she realized it was too late, there was no way out." He shook his head. "Greed and lies. Wherever you go in the universe, that's a path to sorrow."

"Admittedly, there was a certain pitiless logic to

some of Tormid's actions," said Spock. Before McCoy could rise to the bait, he went on. "However, logic without morality is another guise for cruelty. I suspect Tormid's sense of superiority favored the latter."

"A pity he's not here to answer for his crimes," said Kirk, watching the Breg'Hel and Syhaari exchange ritual gestures of respect. "He died believing he was right. He would have taken everyone down with him before he admitted he was wrong. And now its up to the rest of us to repair the damage he's done."

As if in echo of Kirk's words, Gatag opened his hands and spoke for the first time. "The motivation behind your invasion is now clear to us all," said the elder as he addressed the Breg'Hel. "One of our kind, acting on his own corrupted intentions, caused grave injury to your people and stole important materials from one of your vessels. The Syhaari Gathering regrets that a citizen of our worlds did such a thing, and by the light of our star and on the soil of our home, we swear to you that Tormid's deeds were never condoned by us."

"If he were alive, we would offer his punishment to you, but he perished aboard the *Starship Enterprise*." Kaleo stepped forward to offer Zud'Hoa a data device. "That is a scan of his remains. There was . . . little left."

The Breg'Hel warrior examined the scan record. "The known have technology that duplicates flesh-life. How can we be sure you have not done this now and the criminal-killer is not in hiding?"

"You're on, Envoy," said Kirk quietly.

Xuur gave a nod and stepped forward. "If I may speak? From the start, the United Federation of Planets has made itself available as a neutral arbiter in this situation. We will continue in that capacity, if both sides wish it."

"Agreed," said Ead'Aea. "The humanoids have earned our trust."

"The Learned Assembly agrees also," said Gatag.

Xuur bowed slightly and beckoned to McCoy. "Doctor? You have viewed that data. Will you affirm for all parties here that it is authentic and that Tormid is dead?"

"I saw the remains," McCoy said, grim-faced. "No one comes back from direct contact with a high-energy plasma stream."

"In death, the criminal escapes prosecution and responsibility," said Ret'Sed. "Perhaps it is a fitting fate. But there is great regret from our clans in the wake of this. We misunderstood the Syhaari. We believed you to be as we, that an act of one is an act that all are responsible for." The alien was silent for a moment. "We were blinded by rage and grief for the death-deed against our progeny. We went too far."

"A forgiving is sought by all," added Ead'Aea. "But the Breg'Hel will understand if the Syhaari cannot reach that state."

"Was that . . . an apology?" said McCoy quietly.

"The better question," Kirk replied, "is *will it be enough*?"

Gatag and the other elders did not answer straight-away, instead beckoning Zond forward. Like Kaleo, he too offered Zud'Hoa a data tablet. "In the spirit of contrition, we give the Breg'Hel this." He handed over the device. "That contains all the data in Tormid's personal storage stacks, every page of information he gleaned from what was stolen from your scoutship. Every purloined engine design, every last fragment. We will erase everything that he claimed to have created."

"That data is tainted by blood and deceit," added Rumen. "To keep it and know the truth of its origins would shame us."

To Kirk's surprise, Ead'Aea stepped forward and reached out to touch Rumen's face. The action was halting, gentle. "We have hurt you, and yet you do this?"

Rumen spread his broad hands. "It is right. And I know our friends from the Federation would agree. You said it yourselves, forgiveness is the only way forward, yes?"

"We'll do what we can to support whatever choices you make," Xuur agreed.

At his side, Kirk sensed his first officer shift slightly. "Spock, you have something to say?"

"A suggestion . . ." began the Vulcan. "I would respectfully note that a better course of action would be to find a solution other than the retardation of your society's advancement."

Xuur gave him a sharp look. "Tread carefully, Commander. You're skirting the edges of the Prime Directive here." The envoy's gaze met Kirk's. "He seems to have picked up your bad habits, Captain."

"I've learned to always listen when my first officer speaks," Kirk countered. "Carry on, Mister Spock."

Spock came forward, continuing. "I would propose that this moment of resolution be used as the foundation for something greater. Not just a ceasefire and the assuaging of blame, but also the opening of a path toward interstellar collaboration."

Kirk nodded, picking up the thread. "A sharing of technology and knowledge between the Breg'Hel and the Syhaari could benefit both species. And the Federation will be glad to assist."

A slow smile grew on Xuur's face. "A bold but worthy proposal. I concur. It can be done, if both parties are willing. And if one day in the future your worlds wish to join, the Federation would welcome you in the spirit of peace and friendship."

The Syhaari and Breg'Hel parties both said nothing, warily sizing up the other. At last, it was Gatag who broke the silence. "We would be open to this. What say you . . . visitors?"

Ead'Aea and Ret'Sed touched hands and whispered something in a gesture that seemed oddly human. Ret'Sed's head bobbed and Ead'Aea spoke up. "Agreement. Distrust and falsehood were the spurs that almost made us destroy one another. We must sweep them away and, in the new knowing that follows, see only truth." Ead'Aea took the data tablet from Zud'Hoa and deftly broke it in two. "We will begin again, as if this day were the first and we met as cautious friends."

A sense of relief washed over Kirk, and he caught Kaleo's eye again. The Syhaari captain bowed to him and put her fingers together in a gesture of thanks.

As the two groups came together to truly mingle for the first time, Kirk found Xuur standing at his side. She smiled at Spock. "Commander, you have a gift for mediation that, I admit, I never expected to see in a Starfleet officer. But then, given who your father is, I suppose I should not be surprised."

"I believe Sarek would disagree," replied Spock.

"Possibly," she admitted. "But if you ever get tired of working on the bridge of a starship, you might want to consider a career with the diplomatic corps." The Vulcan raised an eyebrow at that, but Xuur was already focusing her attention on Kirk. "Captain, you and your crew continue to amaze me."

"The feeling is mutual," he replied, earning a grin in return.

"I had considered that a ceasefire might be all we would come away with here today, but you . . . you pushed a little more, you took a risk." She shook her head, almost as if she couldn't believe it.

"It's what we do," said Kirk. "And in this case, it paid off."

"Indeed." Xuur drew herself up, becoming more formal. "And in light of that, My aide and I will be taking our leave of the *Enterprise* for the foreseeable future. Please see that all our baggage is transported down to the planet before you depart, along with whatever support equipment we will need."

"You're staying behind?" said Uhura.

"It would seem so," ch'Sellor muttered.

Xuur glanced at the communications officer. "We can't help these people from light-years away, Lieutenant," she went on, "as Doctor McCoy reminded me. Now that the danger has passed, the *Enterprise* has an ongoing mission to attend to. Ch'Sellor and I will remain here and act as Federation ambassadors-in-situ to the Breg'Hel and Syhaari. Diplomatic pathfinders, if you will."

"That's a very *take-charge* thing to do. I imagine that will look very good on your record," McCoy said, his lip curling.

"No doubt, Doctor," Xuur replied. "Our original mission here was to open relations with the Syhaari. It has not changed . . . only grown to encompass the Breg'Hel as well."

"You'll have your work cut out for you. But then, I think that you like a challenge," Kirk told her. "Spock, contact the ship, have Scotty make the arrangements."

As the Vulcan and the rest of the landing party moved away, making ready to beam up, Xuur came closer and spoke so only the captain could hear her words. "I am genuinely sorry that we did not get to spend more time in each other's company, James. I find you intriguing."

"Flattery will get you everywhere," Kirk deadpanned. He had to admit, Xuur represented the kind of challenge that *he* liked, even if she was FDC. "I'll make sure you have a long-range subspace radio with boost capacity. If you need help, call."

"I was just about to say the same thing to you." Her eyes flashed. "And don't worry. The report I will submit to the advisory board about you will be quite complimentary."

A dozen replies formed and faded in Kirk's thoughts, but in the end he just gave a brisk nod. "Good luck, Veygaan," he said as Spock threw him a nod. "I hope you find that place in the history books."

"I'll save you a page," said the envoy as the tingle of a transporter beam brushed over his skin.

Sixteen

Lieutenant Arex stood by the array of windows along the long wall of the recreation room and peered out into space. At a hundred kilometers off the *Enterprise*'s port side, the sleek aerodyne shape of *The Friendship Discovered* glistened in the faint light of the star Sya, and the navigator noted with professional admiration how the alien ship was maintaining an excellent separation.

Dwarfing both ships, cruising slowly beyond them both at a speed just below one-quarter impulse power, the great sphere of the leviathan moved with stately ease. A glow that reminded Arex of a winter sunset on Triex marbled the surface of the living planetoid, the honey-gold ember color brightening and fading over and over in a steady heartbeat pulse. Looking at it now, it was hard to imagine the massive creature had ever been the harbinger of destruction that loomed large over Syhaar Prime and Gadmuur, or that those worlds—and that this ship and Arex too—had come so very near to obliteration because of it. It seemed like that had happened a lifetime ago, even though it had only been a few days since the reconciliation meeting.

The leviathan was passive and quiet now, cruising through the inner range of the Great Veil, consuming quantities of stellar dust, ice, and free gases from the thick Oort cloud to replenish itself as it went. Commander Spock had reported that his attempts at another telepathic probe had sensed only docile intent from the creature and determined that now that it was nourished anew, the leviathan would depart the Sya system and migrate back to its place of origin in the protostar nursery. Arex had helped the science officer to supervise the launch of a series of noninvasive Class-2 probes that would move with the creature over the next few months and transmit telemetry about its life cycle back to Starfleet. No doubt there would be dozens of Federation exobiologists eager to learn more about it.

Arex sighed as he considered this, placing his right and central hands on the cool transparent aluminum of the viewport, while his third rubbed at his hairless head.

"Penny for your thoughts, Lieutenant?" said a voice behind him.

He saw Sulu's reflection in the port as the helmsman approached, and Arex's brow furrowed. "I am afraid I do not understand your vernacular. You are offering to pay me a fee for my knowledge?"

Sulu smiled, joining him at his vantage. "It's a

human idiom. I meant, what's on your mind? You seem distracted."

"That would be a correct assumption," Arex replied, and he inclined his head toward a nearby table. Abandoned there was a writing stylus and a data padd with no more than a few words sketched upon its surface. "I have been attempting to collate my thoughts about the last few days into a coherent structure, for a subspace message I intend to transmit to our mutual friend Pavel Chekov. But it does not come easily."

Sulu gave him an odd look. "You and Pavel are pen pals?"

Arex nodded. "That idiom I *am* familiar with. Yes, we correspond, we have done so since we became friends at the Academy. He left me a welcome note when I came aboard *Enterprise*. I feel it only right I reply to him, now that I have completed my first mission in what was his post."

"What's the problem?"

"You have been aboard this ship since the start of her five-year mission," Arex told him. "Respectfully, I would say you may be *used* to it."

"What do you mean?" said Sulu.

Arex sighed again. "When Pavel would send me a message discussing his most recent experiences aboard this ship, I must confess that I thought his descriptions to be somewhat embellished by the enthusiasm of youth. The stories of your encounters with the new and unknown were quite uncommon."

"You are not wrong," Sulu agreed with a chuckle.

"But now, after crossing paths with that . . ." Arex pointed out at the leviathan. "If anything, I wonder if Pavel's descriptions might have been *understated*."

"We have had more than our fair share of the amazing, some might say," allowed the helmsman. "It can be overwhelming, especially if you've been planet-side or on starbase duty for a long time." Sulu studied the gigantic alien life-form. "We're at the frontier, not just in terms of maps, but also figuratively." He grinned. "It's a challenge, isn't it?"

"You are not wrong," Arex repeated. "Is this truly how every assignment plays out aboard the *Enterprise*?"

"Oh no," said Sulu, his tone turning wry as he wandered away. "Most missions aren't as easy as this one."

———

Kirk leaned forward in his command chair, never taking his eyes off the object on the bridge's main viewscreen. The silent, majestic leviathan turned slowly as it moved through the haze of the gray dust clouds. "'And far away into the sickly light,'" he said to himself, "'from many a wondrous and secret cell . . .'"

"'The kraken sleepeth,'" said Kaleo as she stepped down from conferring with Spock at the science station. "Your first officer told me of your poet Tennyson and his work. I see now why those words came to your memory when we encountered the giant for the first time."

"Indeed." He called out an order to the crewman before him. "Helm, steady as she goes."

"Steady, aye, sir," replied Lieutenant Leslie.

"Leviathan's solar departure course is stable and unchanged." At Leslie's side, Ron Erikson pored over his navigation plots. The junior officer had insisted on being allowed to return to duty, and after a grudging dismissal by Doctor McCoy, he was back at his station. "Internal energy levels remain constant. It's humming like a bumblebee, Captain."

"Good to know." Kirk gave a nod. "We've seen more than enough of its sting for one lifetime." He glanced back at Kaleo. "Do you have what you need?"

She nodded back at him, her attempt at the human mannerism slightly halting. "Yes. Mister Spock has completed a full transmission of all data from his sensor readings of the leviathan to the *Friendship*, along with Lieutenant Uhura's subspace scans. It will take us years just to begin to understand that creature, but it will be worth the effort." She paused, thinking. "It's important we comprehend its nature. In time, that will help to heal the wounds it left behind."

"Agreed. I hope the alliance with the Breg'Hel will hold."

Kaleo frowned. "We will make it work. My species have always relished trials of strength and character. And perhaps it is long past the time that we ceased showy displays of prowess and concentrated on a more direct path." Her hand drifted toward her belly. "I want that for my daughter."

"Daughter?" Kirk repeated. "I didn't know you knew—"

"She'll grow up strong," said Kaleo. "We'll give her the precious gift we preserved here . . . a new future. And perhaps I'll take a lesson from the Breg'Hel and make my crew her extended family."

"Families on board starships? Maybe there's something to that." The *Enterprise*'s captain considered the possibility. "It won't be easy for you. But we'll do what we can to help you find your way."

She placed her hand on his forearm. "Thank you, Captain. You have proven yourself a strong ally and a good friend. That there are those like you and your kind out here"—the Syhaari gestured toward the viewscreen and the stars beyond—"it gives me hope."

"You took the words right out of my mouth. We're out here because of people like the Syhaari and the Breg'Hel, because of amazing things like the leviathan. If we can find new knowledge and new friends along the way, all the better." He smiled and stood up. "Captain Kaleo, it has been our honor and my privilege to sail with you."

The other captain bowed. "My ship calls," she said. "And I've been too long from my own bridge, but I'll return there having learned something from your Federation, I think, and with more than just this data." Kaleo held up a data storage cube and cast around.

"*Enterprise* has inspired me. I hope one day I can command a ship like this and range as far as you have."

"You will," he told her, and he meant every word. "The universe is vast and full of wonders, just waiting for an explorer."

She stepped past him toward the turbolift, bowing once more as she went. "We'll see you out there, Kirk. You can count on that."

The doors hissed open, and McCoy stepped out as Kaleo entered, the two of them exchanging a nod of farewell.

The doctor crossed to Kirk as Spock joined them. "So, we're back on an even keel," McCoy said. "Last injured man cleared sickbay five minutes ago. I'm hoping, Captain, sir, that I can keep the beds empty for a little while before you decide to put us in harm's way again."

"Trouble finds us, Bones, not the other way around." Kirk looked to his first officer for support. "Don't you agree, Spock?"

The first officer seemed to weigh the question, as if considering it with mathematical precision. "Statistically, Captain, this vessel *does* encounter a higher-than-average incidence of hazardous scenarios."

"Reason?"

Spock paused. "It would require further study to give a definitive answer."

McCoy snorted. "Meaning, Spock doesn't want to say our captain likes taking risks."

Kirk shook his head. "I'll never put this ship and this crew in a situation they can't handle. Our people know their jobs. They know why we're out here." He nodded toward the screen. "Because of things like that."

McCoy nodded. "I admit, it is a sight to see."

"Our ongoing mission opens up into unexplored space beyond this sector," Spock noted. "I imagine we will see more 'sights' that will challenge us as we proceed."

"Then let's not waste any time." The captain settled back into his chair and looked out across the bridge as the last remnants of the Veil parted and the infinity of the starscape filled the screen.

"Set a new course," said Kirk, "and take us there."

Acknowledgments

My thanks to Lou Scheimer and Hal Sutherland, Franz Joseph, Larry Nemecek, Michael Okuda, Denise Okuda, Debbie Mirek, Eileen Palestine, and Geoffrey Mandel for their works of reference and of fiction; Alec Peters and the *Axanar* crew for flying the flag; and forever with much love to Mandy Mills.

About the Author

James Swallow, a *New York Times* bestselling author and BAFTA nominee, is proud to be the only British writer to have worked on a *Star Trek* television series, creating the original story concepts for the *Star Trek: Voyager* episodes "One" and "Memorial." His other *Star Trek* writing includes the novels *Sight Unseen, The Poisoned Chalice, Cast No Shadow, Synthesis,* and the Scribe Award winner *Day of the Vipers*; the novellas *The Stuff of Dreams* and *Myriad Universes: Seeds of Dissent*; the short stories "The Slow Knife," "The Black Flag," "Ordinary Days," and "Closure" for the anthologies *Seven Deadly Sins, Shards and Shadows, The Sky's the Limit,* and *Distant Shores*; scripting the videogame *Star Trek: Invasion*; and over four hundred articles in thirteen different *Star Trek* magazines around the world.

As well as the nonfiction book *Dark Eye: The Films of David Fincher*, James also wrote the *Sundowners* series of original steampunk westerns; *Jade Dragon; The Butterfly Effect*; and novels in the worlds of *24* (*Deadline*), *Doctor Who* (*Peacemaker*), *Warhammer 40,000*

(*Fear to Tread, Hammer & Anvil, Nemesis, Black Tide, Red Fury, The Flight of the Eisenstein, Faith & Fire, Deus Encarmine,* and *Deus Sanguinius*), *Stargate* (*Halcyon, Relativity, Nightfall,* and *Air*), and *2000 AD* (*Eclipse, Whiteout,* and *Blood Relative*). His other credits feature scripts for videogames and audio dramas, including *Deus Ex: Human Revolution, Disney Infinity 3.0, Fable: The Journey, Battlestar Galactica, Blake's 7,* and *Space 1889.*

James Swallow lives in London and is currently at work on his next book.